PICKING UP THE BRASS

by

Eddy Nugent

WRITERSWORLD
United Kingdom . Spain . The Netherlands

Picking up the Brass

by

Eddy Nugent

ISBN 1-904181-92-9

WRITERSWORLD
9 Manor Court
Enstone
Oxfordshire
OX7 4LU
England
www.writersworld.co.uk

Printed and bound by CPI Antony Rowe, Eastbourne

Chapter 1

Every man an Emperor

Despite pondering it at length, I'm still at a loss as to why I actually joined the Army. Nobody I knew was in the Army; nobody I knew wanted to join the Army. Attitudes towards the Forces amongst my schoolmates ranged from mild apathy to outright hostility. I attended one of the biggest Catholic, all-boys schools in Manchester. Lots of the lads were of Irish parentage and had been brought up on stories of horrors, visited upon their ancestors by the evil, British Imperial Forces. Personally, I found myself in the apathetic camp. I didn't think about it much really. The only contact I had with people from the Armed Forces was when they had a recruitment wagon set up at the local fair in Platt Fields Park. This always consisted of the same scenario. A four-tonne lorry, covered with a camouflage net, would be parked up on the grass, and kids would be swarming over it like smelly locusts. A disgruntled Regular Army corporal would be there trying to keep them all from destroying his prize possession. Even to my untrained, 15-year-old eye, it was obvious that to be doing this particular gig, you would have to be the soldier that had been in the most shit that week. When he wasn't clawing eight-year-old boys from under the bonnet of the wagon, he was having to answer stupid questions from their older brothers.

"So what's it like then, Mister? Have you ever killed anyone?"

"No."

"Do you have to fire a gun?"

"Yes, it's the Army. One of the things you get given is a gun."

"Do you get to do karate?"

"No."

"Can you fly a helicopter?"

"No!"

All of his answers would be delivered with the same deadpan expression and monotone voice. That tiny throbbing vein, just above his left ear, was the only indication that this guy was close to losing his rag. Sooner or later, their parents would come along to clear them off the truck, and the corporal would think he was saved, only to have the dad saunter up, stand next to him, rock back and forth on his heels, and say: "So… you're in the Army, then?"

"Yes."

"I used to be in the Army, you know?"

"Yeah?" (The corporal would be frantically conducting an internal dialogue, advising himself to say nothing that would encourage this guy to regurgitate his entire National Service experience.)

"Yeah, 'course it was a few years ago. Summer of '56, to be precise."

"GET OFF THAT TRUCK YOU LITTLE FUCKERS!"

As a recruitment technique, it was fundamentally flawed, but it was preferable to hearing another story about blanco and bromide.

They came to the school once as well. It was quite an interesting talk, full of loud bangs and promises of excitement. This time it was a fat old sergeant, who was quite enthusiastic about the whole thing. He came a cropper when it came to the question and answer session, though. After the usual helicopter and karate enquiries, our English teacher, Mr Brooks, tore him a new arsehole. A bit of a bearded campaigner, straight from Central Casting, Brooksy proceeded to ask this guy probing, and extensively-researched questions about the British presence in Northern Ireland. It was like shooting fish in a barrel. Other than calling him a hippie a couple of times, the sergeant gave Mr Brooks the floor, enabling him to demonstrate to us all, his ability to ask probing, and extensively researched, questions! My only clear memory of the debate is that it made us late for metalwork.

So, as you can see, the Ministry of Defence had done no effective groundwork to get me to embrace its cause.

The first time I gave it a bit more thought was after seeing a documentary series called 'The Paras'. The episode that had a profound effect on me featured the recruits getting beasted for what seemed like the entire programme. The instructor was bellowing at them throughout and they all looked like they were just about to die from exhaustion. But through all this, I couldn't help thinking that it did look like a bit of a laugh. There was no logical connection between these two things, but there it was.

Providentially, or not, I went into Manchester City Centre the weekend after. It was a regular excursion. Three or four of us would go into town, with little or no money, and hang about the Arndale Centre for most of the day. The ulterior motive was to chat up girls, but I was completely crap at it, and avoided all female confrontation like the plague. Jimmy Connolly, who was at my level of romantic handicap, and I would shoot off and find something else to do, at the first opportunity. Usually, we'd go into Dixons. They always had the latest video games on display and you could get five minutes playing on them, until an acne-riddled shop assistant chased you off.

On the fateful day, we found ourselves wandering up Market Street, back towards Piccadilly Gardens. Just before Lewis's we turned right, down Fountain Street. About halfway down on the left, and just after The Shakespeare pub, was the Army Careers Office. We had a look in the front window, and were greeted by cardboard cut-outs of young blokes windsurfing, abseiling and generally having lots of fun. Another guy, looking suitably dirty, was firing a big bazooka, with a huge grin on his face. The last cut-out was of a bunch of lads, drinking in a bar, raising their glasses to the camera. I have to admit, it all looked pretty interesting, with one small criticism. All the civilian clothes that they had on were a bit 'seventies'. This was 1985, and to a lad like me, having the correct amount of Sergio Tacchini or Ellesse clothing was of critical importance. It didn't occur to me that the display was a bit out of date. I assumed that squaddies wore some sort of civilian uniform as well, that followed contemporary fashion with a seven-year time lag. I found out later, that this is a recurrent problem within the Forces. Torn between the need to recruit, and the reluctance to spend money on anything that doesn't actually kill people, they always tended to make a video/presentation/slideshow or cardboard cut-out and then use it for far too long. All the brochures and guides I was subsequently given to entice me featured blokes in flares with big sideburns. Only snooker players were dressing like that by the mid-eighties. Nevertheless, the display was alluring enough for me to want to know a bit more.

I said to Jimmy: "Should we go in?"

"Fuck that."

"Come on, we'll just ask a couple of questions."

"Go on then, you first though."

I laughed and made my way to the door. As I was pulling it open, there was a guy coming out. He was a big, bullet-headed, shifty looking fucker and I moved out of his way as he came through.

"Alright, lads? Don't do it, you'll fucking regret it."

"In you come fellas, don't worry about him."

The shout came from inside, and before I knew it, I was on one side of the door and Jimmy was on the other. The door was thick glass, I couldn't hear him but I watched his silent laughter as he walked off.

"Come in son, take a seat."

I looked toward the source of the voice. It was the same fat sergeant who'd been to the school a couple of months before. He was sat behind a large, highly polished, wooden desk, with a brass name plate facing towards me. Sergeant Pete Chapman, King's Regiment, it announced grandly. There were two flags on the wall behind him, a Union Jack and the British Army standard, that had a lion and crown on a red background. I shuffled towards the desk, and he stood up and offered his outstretched hand. I shook it. It was the first time I'd ever shaken anyone's hand and it made me feel older.

"What's your name?"

"Eddy… Eddy Nugent," I stuttered.

"Nice to meet you, I'm Pete Chapman – Sergeant Chapman, but you don't have to call me Sergeant quite yet. Sit yourself down."

We both sat down at the same time, and remained there in silence for a second or two before he opened with: "Thinking of joining us then, eh?"

I thought nervously for a second or two, before saying: "Nah, not really, just thought I'd have a look at a couple of brochures or something."

He started moving into what I presume was his tried-and-tested sales pitch.

"It's a great life you know, son. Twenty years I've been in, and I've enjoyed every last minute."

I looked at him dumbly, my natural resting expression, and waited for him to continue.

"I'm not saying it's easy, but it's a fantastic way of becoming a man and seeing the world at the same time."

"What parts of the world?"

"Oooh, all sorts. Germany, Cyprus, Belize, Norway, Ireland and loads of others." At the time, I didn't notice that he'd left the word Northern out when mentioning Ireland. Maybe he thought that by employing this subtle omission, he'd dupe potential recruits into thinking that a portion of their career would be spent fishing in Galway.

"How old are you, son?"

"I was 16 in January."

"So you'd be 17 next January?"

"Erm… yeah!"

"Well you're a bit too young to join up as an adult, but there are other options. You could become a Junior Leader or an Army Apprentice."

Both terms meant absolutely nothing to me, so I allowed my jaw to slacken a little more, giving him another cue to carry on.

"If you've got enough brains about you, and you look like a smart lad, you can get accepted for an apprenticeship. It will mean two years at an Army College and you'll come out qualified to take up a position in either the Royal Corps of Signals, Royal Electrical and Mechanical Engineers or the Royal Engineers."

"What are they like, these colleges?" To tell the truth, although I considered myself academically reasonable, I was never a big fan of school and wasn't very studious. The idea of another two years of it didn't appeal at all.

"They perform all the functions of an ordinary college. On top of that: you get paid; get to take part in lots of adventure training; and train as a soldier concurrently."

Now to my ears, that sounded pretty good, but I'd remember that description later on, usually when being fucked about for a minor indiscretion. I didn't realise it at the time, but he'd made no special observations about me that led him to suggest this career course. Everyone my age, who went in that week, would have been offered the same thing, to fill whatever the latest quota requirement was. If I'd gone in the week before, I'd have been a helicopter pilot, the week after, a Gurkha.

"Sounds alright," I ventured, trying to sound non-committal.

" 'Course, to go any further you'll need your parents' permission, but I'll give you all the usual bumph. You can show it to them and come back when you're ready."

He started to collect single pieces of paper and leaflets from drawers in the desk.

"So what'll happen next?" I was certainly interested enough to want to know that.

"Get your mum and dad's signatures, and come back to take some tests, then we'll take it from there."

It felt like a natural punctuation mark, so I started to stand up.

"Just a couple of questions to get out of the way before we go any further."

"Oh, okay."

I sat back down abruptly.

"Are you a homosexual?"

I looked at him blankly. I wasn't sure what answer he wanted, but I thought I'd better opt for the truth.

"No."

I wasn't really an anything sexual. I'd done a bit of wanking, and had begun to refine my technique using the only acceptable pornography in a Catholic household, my Mum's *Grattan* catalogue. At a stretch, I could have claimed masturbatory promiscuity, in that I occasionally preferred the see-through lingerie on page 186 over the basques on page 150. It constituted my sole experience to that date. I still don't know how I never got caught. Once or sometimes twice a day, I'd emerge furtively from the toilet, with an 873 page catalogue under my arm, and stroll nonchalantly over to put it back where it belonged, near Mum's magazine rack. I never went to the trouble of preparing an alibi, so I don't know what I would have said, if ever confronted with the question: 'What were you doing in the toilet with the catalogue?' I suppose 'Working out what I'd like for Christmas' would have been a truthful and vague enough answer to evade capture.

"Sorry to ask, but it's Army regulations. Wouldn't want any poofters sneaking in would we?"

I'm not sure how much sneaking would be required, to answer a question 'No' instead of 'Yes', but I understood the point he was trying to make.

He leant forward, and his face expression became earnest, "What about drugs, ever taken any?"

"No," once again a truthful answer. I presumed he meant hard stuff. Like most of the lads at my school, I drank and smoked, both in moderation. A packet of ten Craven 'A' would last me a week, and the under-16s football team I played for all used to go for a pint in the Crown in Hulme after our Sunday games. In hindsight, it seemed an unusual question. In the pre-ecstasy and (easily available) cocaine days, the narcotic progression, in order of severity, was weed, glue and heroin. Weed smokers used to talk a lot of bollocks and eat a lot of Kentucky, but it didn't seem credible that someone sitting there stoned, could suddenly get that Damascan moment, and float off to the Careers Office. I had no experience of glue but we used to have to run past the smack addicts in the Hulme flats every Sunday morning on our way to the football. We'd unconsciously conserve some of our energy during the match, to ensure fleet-footedness on the return trip. Once again, soldiering probably wasn't the first moneymaking scheme that sprang to a junky's mind, when he needed to make a few quid, quickly.

"Ever been in trouble with the Police?"

"What do you mean by trouble?" I asked guardedly.

"Anything serious; ever been arrested or charged with an offence?"

He had his pen at the ready, primed to write any response down.

"I got cautioned when I was 14, but not charged."

"What for?"

He jotted something down.

"Swearing at a Policeman," I admitted sheepishly. I thought I'd better come clean. They'd probably find out sooner or later anyway. It was nothing really. Every summer, they used to have an Ideal Homes Exhibition in the park. There was nothing there for kids really, except for those rubbish art stalls, where you could make your own pictures. After allowing you to squeeze a few blobs of primary-coloured paint on to a piece of paper, they'd stick it in a centrifuge and turn it on for a few seconds. Then, hey presto your masterpiece was revealed for the bargain sum of 40p. There were never any surprises. It was always a ghastly combination of the four colours, forming a representation of an enormous tropical insect, splattered on a windscreen. Other than the art stand, the exhibition was a great opportunity for fooling around and annoying the vendors. The trouble was they used to charge a pound for entry. Bearing in mind that that sum was enough to buy chips for six hungry men, it was considered a bit steep, so we used to sneak in. An open drainage outlet used to emerge in the park. It was 400 metres long, and you could gain entry into it, halfway down Brighton Grove. It was a pretty spooky affair. The tunnel was semicircular, about eight-foot wide, and six-foot at its highest point. There was a small river of polluted water running down the centre, about a foot wide. Either side of the water was a raised path which you could walk along. You would inch along the path, with either matches to light your way, or in complete darkness if you were feeling particularly brave. For all the kids I knocked around with, it was a real rite of passage. It came to be known as 'Witches Tunnel'. The first time I went through it, I was ten. I thought I was going to die of fright. I'll never forget the feeling of utter relief, when we rounded the last bend, and could see a stab of light coming from the park. Of course, by the age of 14, I was an old hand, and the tunnel was just a convenient means of access and egress. We even used to eat chips down there sometimes. To sneak into the exhibition, you simply emerged out of the end of the tunnel, hopped over a two-foot fence, and you were in. On this occasion, and by complete chance, a copper happened to watch us all come out of the tunnel. By the time we'd spotted him he had hold of me by the back of the neck. The rest of the lads were straight back over the fence and into the tunnel, disappearing into the darkness like rats in school uniform.

"You fuckin' bastards!" I shouted behind them. Unfortunately, the copper thought I was talking to him. Despite my remonstrations, he took me down to the station on Platt Lane and cautioned me in front of Mum and Dad. They were both mortified. On the way home, a walk of about a quarter of a mile, Mum wouldn't talk to me. They walked together discussing me and I had to walk a couple of paces in front of them. Every now and again, my Dad took a casual swipe at the back of my head with his right hand, cursing under his breath. My transgression hardly made me Clyde Barrow, but it was enough to get me to behave from then on.

"Well, I shouldn't have thought that'll set you back too far," he smiled, putting down his pen. "That's enough for now, son. Get yourself home and we'll see you for the tests when your parents have signed."

I stood up and we shook hands again. He gave me the various leaflets he'd assembled. I nodded, turned round and walked out.

Walking back towards Market Street, I was in a bit of a daze. Had I really just started the ball rolling with an application to join the Army? Royal Signals, Royal Engineers, what was all that about? In my naivety, I thought that you just joined 'The Army' then you could decide what you wanted to do exactly at a later date, when you'd had time to think about it.

I didn't say anything for a few days to Mum and Dad. I wasn't nervous or anything, just a bit uncertain about the whole thing really. This went on for about a week. After that, I just thought: 'Fuck it, I can decide not to proceed at any time.' That particular phrase was splashed all over the leaflets, apart from 'Fuck it!' Maybe they'd had people who'd thought they were conscripted as soon as they looked in the window, and the caring, sharing Army wanted to assure everyone else that this wasn't the case.

Mum and Dad were good about the whole thing. Dad started off his popular opening shot. "What the fucking hell do you want to go and do that for?" he shouted, slamming down the paper. I had no idea of the answer, so I let him get on with it. "A brainy lad like you shouldn't join the bleeding Army, it's for ex-cons and people who can't get on in life."

I'm not sure what he was using as his points of reference, but it seemed a bit outdated.

"But Dad, have a look at the leaflets, it's not like that any more. I'd be at the college for two years getting a trade and learning loads," I pleaded.

"He's right for once, Pat. It does look worthwhile. He can always come home if it doesn't work out."

Nice one, Mum. She was always the realist. She'd probably sussed that this was the one chance she'd have of pushing me into any sort of further education.

"Hmm."

Dad made a big display of ignoring the leaflets and going back to the paper. He conceded the argument quietly over the next few days. I saw his glasses on the leaflets one day, where he'd left them. Another time he was coming in from work, and I was on my way out. We met at the front garden gate.

"So you fancy this Army Apprentice thing then?" he asked quietly, looking at the handlebars of his bike.

"Looks alright, Dad. I wouldn't mind a go."

I looked at the side of his head hopefully. He looked up.

"I'll tell you why I've got misgivings, son. I've known a few soldiers in my time, both serving and retired. I'm not saying they're all the same, but most of the ones I've met were arseholes."

"What sort of arseholes?"

"Big mouths mainly, they've got a fucking story for every occasion. There was a lad I was working with last year, who used to be in the Artillery; they ended up calling him Tommy Two Shits. At tea break, if anyone was telling a story, he'd go one better, no matter what the subject was."

"Why Tommy Two Shits?"

He looked at me like I was a bit slow, "If you've had a shit, he's had two."

We both laughed.

"Give me your word that you won't turn out like him, and I'll sign the form."

"No problem, Dad, it's a promise."

We parted ways.

The form got signed and sent off. The next thing I got from them was an instruction to come for a written exam, back at the Careers Office.

I turned up at the date and time specified, and was led into a room full of desks, 14 or 15 of which were occupied by fellow potential field marshals. They represented quite a cross-section of Mancunian society. Most noticeable were several missing links, a bubble-permed, Brian May look-alike and a fat, camp chap with his glasses round his neck on a string. The rest were a selection of spotty teens like me, at various stages of an acne coup. I took my seat, and the show began.

The ever-present Sergeant Chapman came in and started handing out the question papers, whilst going through his hackneyed stand-up act.

"Remember lads, no cheating; you'd only be cheating yourselves. You can look down for inspiration and up in exasperation, but don't look side-to-side for information."

He explained that the Army currently had 170 career choices available. The worse your score on the test, the less choice available. Very straightforward. I don't remember the questions exactly, but it wasn't difficult. I handed in my paper, then went into another room and had a brew. After a while, all the papers had been collected and marked, and we got called in one by one. My interview was brief. I'd achieved the score required for my selected trade, and could continue to the next stage, which was the medical.

I got another letter about a week later. It contained instructions to attend the Territorial Army Centre on Lloyd Street, on the first of May, at 9am for my first medical examination. Attached to the back of the instruction was what was supposed to be a map, giving directions to the centre, but which actually looked like one of the clues off '3-2-1'. It made no sense whichever way I turned it. It just had a straight line representing Lloyd Street and a blob at the top which I suppose you had to assume was the city centre. I showed it to my Dad, who'd lived in Manchester all of his life, but he was stumped.

"Maybe it's an initiative test?" he said, whilst turning the paper for the fifth time. That hadn't occurred to me, so I examined it with renewed enthusiasm. After a while, Mum got sick of listening to us trying to work it out. She got the A-Z out of the top drawer in the front-room sideboard and after a minute or so, folded the book open in front of us, at the right page, with her finger pointing at the correct spot.

"Good thinking, Barbara," complimented Dad, with a wink. She went back to what she was doing, shaking her head slowly. Once Dad was looking at a proper map, he sorted it out straightaway. I was going to have to go on my own on the day of the medical, but he offered to show me where it was the next day, for a dry run. I took him up on it, and when the day of the medical arrived, I was outside the TA centre 15 minutes early with no map-reading problems. We'd been told to dress smart, so I had my one-and-only suit on. It was a blue, cheap-and-nasty affair that I'd had to wear to a cousin's wedding. It was too big for me, but I'd been told that I'd grow into it, probably when I was 42. The TA Centre was a big, Victorian building, with a huge set of wooden, double doors. There was a smaller door, cut into the right-hand one. As I was hanging around, a few more people showed up in ill-fitting suits. Each time someone new arrived, we all looked at him hopefully, expecting to get some instructions, until it became obvious that he was another potential recruit. Eventually, at five past nine, a soldier emerged from the smaller door, carrying a blue clipboard and began to address us.

"Morning fellas, I'm Corporal Smythe. Are you all here for your medicals?"

The group nodded assent, and he went through his list of names. There were six of us now. It looked like there was one no-show and as soon as the corporal was happy that he had the right number of bodies he put his pen away.

"Right, follow me."

He disappeared back through his little door quickly, so we set off after him. Once inside, the building resembled an old gym. This, he explained, was the drill hall. It smelt musty and could have done with a good clean. We walked through into a corridor, and were told to sit down on a bench that ran the length of the wall.

"Listen in for your names, and go through that door when you're called." He pointed down to the end of the corridor at a slightly-ajar, black, wood-panelled door. Once again he disappeared, leaving us alone with each other and our thoughts. I didn't know it then, but this was to be one of the major features of my military life. Regardless of what the situation was, be it a medical, inspection, meeting or operation, you would always be required to arrive at a predetermined time and place. Fulfilling your part of the bargain, you would turn up as expected, and then be left standing around, until someone in authority would eventually find the time to wander over with more instructions. The further instructions usually involved being told to wait some more, until somebody with further instructions arrived.

"Nugent." I was stirred out of my torpor, by the return of Corporal Smythe. He was stood in the corridor, near the open door, now armed with a green clipboard. I stood up and walked slowly towards him.

"Come on, son. Get a fucking move on or we'll be here all day." I sped up, as requested, and got level with him. He flicked his head in the direction of the door, "In you go, and just do as you're told."

I nodded, and went through the door, into an extremely old-fashioned looking office. Behind a desk, in front of a big bay window, was a very old man, who I assumed to be the doctor. I had been expecting someone of military bearing, but this guy looked just like Charles Laughton. I walked over to the desk and stood by the knackered wooden chair that was placed in front of it.

He looked down at a piece of paper on the desk, and scrutinised it for a few seconds, before stopping and taking a pair of glasses out of his suit pocket. He tried again, then looked up at me and said: "Edward Nugent?"

"Eddy, yeah."

"Let's get off on the right foot, Mr Nugent. I may not look like an Army officer, and I can't begin to tell you how pleased I am about that, but you can call me Sir from now on." His rebuke was delivered in a friendly tone, but I got the message.

"Yes, Sir."

"Take your shirt off, there's a good man."

I did as I was told, whilst he hobbled round the desk towards me, pulling a stethoscope out of another pocket. I got a better look at him then. He should have been about five feet six, but the hunched-over way that he walked took about four inches off the total. He had a big shock of white, unkempt hair that looked like it had been combed with a toffee apple. He was like one of those doctors that you used to see in old gangster films, a washed up, old turps-nudger that had been struck off. The only way he could get by was by illegally patching up shot-up mobsters, who couldn't use a hospital. He took so long to get round to me, that I'd started to get a bit cold. He started his examination, tapping his fingers on my back and listening intently, before moving round to the front and feeling my hands and arm joints. He then took a step backwards before muttering: "Good, good, now drop your trousers please."

I undid my belt, and my oversize strides flopped straight to the carpet.

"And the underpants please."

I complied immediately, exposing my tackle for his inspection. He cupped first the right, then the left testicle. During this little procedure, I kept my gaze firmly on the wall opposite me. Funny that isn't it? If he was putting stitches in my arm or checking my reflexes, I'd have been watching intently, showing an interest in what was going on, but the fact that a strange man was fondling my genitalia, induced in me an air of feigned detachment. Perhaps, in my mind's eye, taking an interest could have been misconstrued as a come on. From where I was standing, I could see out of the bay window, and right across the road to a row of shops. I could also see a painter and decorator at the top of a ladder, touching up the eaves of the building directly opposite. Thankfully, he was more concerned with not falling off the ladder, than watching me having my goolies groped.

The doctor finished the examination and instructed me to put my clothes back on. When I'd done so, he invited me to sit down in the chair.

"No problems at all there, young Nugent. I'll sign you off as fully fit, and you can continue with your quest to take the shilling," he commented, as he signed an otherwise unidentifiable piece of paper, with an elegant flourish.

"Pardon Sir?"

"Join the Army."

"Oh, right."

"Off you go then." He dismissed me with a wave of his pen, and I made for the door. Corporal Smythe must have been listening in to the conversation, because he shouted the next name before I got back out into the corridor. The doctor's next victim strode past me as I drew level with the corporal.

"In you go, just do as you're told," he instructed the lad, before turning his gaze to me and enquiring "Something the matter?"

"Sorry, I just wondered what I do next?"

He rolled his eyes theatrically.

"Go home. They'll get your medical results and contact you with further instructions."

"So there's nothing more to do today?" I ventured.

He fixed me with what he probably considered his hard-man stare. It wasn't a bad one actually.

"Are you still here?" he growled.

I took his point, and made my way out of the building. I felt good on the bus home, like I'd jumped another hurdle. Dad was in the living room, reading his paper when I got in.

"How'd it go?" he enquired, trying to pretend that he wasn't all that interested.

"Alright Dad. The doctor was a bit weird, but he said that I was fully fit and that I could continue with my application." I sat down next to him on the sofa.

"Fit as fucking fiddles, our family. You won't have any problems there, son." He started to go back to his paper, before putting it down again and continuing "Old Tommy Two Shits was at it again today. One of the lads from work, Dave, found a massive spider in his garage yesterday. He was telling me about it at tea break. You know who was listening in of course?"

"Tommy."

"Dead right."

'That's nothing that is,' he said, 'when I was in Malaya, during the emergency, there were spiders as big as dustbin lids; they used to carry off babies from the villages.'

'Really?' I said.

'Yeah, found one in me sleeping bag once, and had to kill it with a shovel.'

'That's interesting,' said Dave, 'I served in Malaya, but I don't remember spiders like that.'

'I think there were only a few, they'd been released from captivity or something.'

'And another thing, for you to have served in Malaya during the emergency, they'd have to have been taking recruits in at five years old. You're about ten years too young you daft fucker. Get your stories straight before you start dishing 'em out as fact.'

"I'll tell you son, I was laughing all afternoon. And even better, that foghorn was quiet as a mouse for the rest of the day."

We both laughed, then Dad picked up the paper, and started reading again, muttering something about 'fucking space shuttles'.

A couple of weeks later, another brown envelope arrived, with the MOD stamp on it. I took it into the kitchen and opened it. It started off by congratulating me on passing the medical, and then gave me a date to attend a selection course at the Army Recruiting Centre in Sutton Coldfield. Whilst there, I would be expected to perform various physical exercises, complete a written test, undergo a chest X-ray, and generally get fucked about for a day and a half. I'd be interviewed at the end and, if successful, would be accepted into the Forces. It was recommended that I trained for the physical exercises. These would be sit-ups, pull-ups, a standing jump and a one-mile run. I wandered over to the calendar on the wall, and thought: "Fuck me, that's only three weeks away!" Also in the envelope was a rail warrant to get me to Sutton Coldfield train station. I've always had the dubious talent of deciding where places are by the way that they sound. Nuneaton sounds like it should be in Scotland. Harrogate is somewhere near Brighton, and Sutton Coldfield is just outside London. It must fit in with some logic process I own, but as a practical ability, it's fairly useless. Fortunately for me, there was a badly photocopied map in the envelope, revealing the true location to be slightly north of Birmingham.

Over the next couple of weeks, I did a bit of training. It wasn't exactly *Rocky III*, but I did a bit of running, and checked to see if I could do sit-ups and pull-ups. I didn't even know what a standing jump was, but it didn't sound too difficult, so I omitted it from my strict regime.

As the day drew close, I got a bit nervous about it. I spoke to Dad, and after having a good look at the letter they'd sent me, he opined. "Nothing to it, son. There's nothing on there you won't be able to do, take my word for it."

I still wasn't convinced. "I just wish I knew more about what's going to happen, Dad."

"Listen, you're a clever lad and you're fit, medically and physically. You're as good as in, son. You don't think the Army can afford to be that choosy do you? How many people, with brains, do you think they get showing up at careers offices? Half the people on this selection thing will be thick as fuck, and fat as fuck and they're the only ones you've got to be better than, if you want to get in. If they've got any sense they'll have you in the day after you go on this little course."

Once again, his little pep talk had the desired effect, and I started to look forward to the challenge of the Selection.

When the day finally arrived, I was ready to go. I caught the bus into Piccadilly Gardens, then walked up the short hill that took you into Piccadilly train station. It was just after 9am. My train wasn't due to leave for another 30 minutes, so I'd have had time for a quick brew, but I was too nervous to relax. I made straight for the platform and sat on a bench near the train. This allowed me to maintain sight of it throughout my wait. I'm not sure what I was expecting it to do, maybe bugger off up the track as soon as I wasn't looking, leaving me stranded and potentially jobless. Nevertheless, it comforted me to keep it within my visual range. I felt a bit of a twat, sat there in shirt and tie, with a big green holdall on the floor between my feet. Once again, they'd instructed us to dress smart for the occasion. Ten minutes before departure time, the noise of air escaping drew my attention to the doors, which were opening slowly. I got on, stowed my holdall underneath a seat, and sat down. A few more people got on over the next few minutes, but didn't sit anywhere near me. I'd always been told that the way to get a double seat to yourself on any form of public transport was to give a wide smile to anyone who approached. People would generally assume that you were doolally, and move on. I employed the tactic to good effect, and was able to stretch out and put my feet on the opposite seat, as soon as the train pulled out.

The journey down to Birmingham was uneventful; I even nodded off for a while, waking up with a nice pool of drool on my shoulder, as we passed through Walsall. Once we got into New Street, I followed the instructions written down on another helpful leaflet, and made my way to the right platform, just in time to make the connection for the Sutton Coldfield train. This one was a bit busier, and I had to stand in the toilet area between two compartments. Once the train got under way, I had a quick look for a seat, through the window of the compartment to my right. Nothing doing. What was noticeable though, was the ubiquity of people very like myself. The carriage was full of lads and young men, with short haircuts, white shirts and nervous dispositions. Lots of blokes, lost in their own thoughts, dreaming up ways in which they were going to fuck this selection up for themselves.

The casual traveller might think he'd stumbled into a Jehovah's Witness day-trip. The train eased in to Sutton Coldfield station and everyone alighted. As I was making my way off the platform and towards the exit, the first military man of the day hove into view and earshot.

"Anyone who's here for the Army Personnel Selection Centre, make your way over to me please," he barked. He didn't mean the "please" bit, but I suppose he didn't want to scare us off just yet. As lads made themselves known to him, he swung his pen holding right arm back in a long arc, "On the coach, fill up from the back."

I looked in the direction of his pointing arm, to the vehicle he'd described as a coach. It looked like something from a Norman Wisdom film. A huge, green charabanc that didn't look capable of forward movement. People were clambering aboard, so I followed and made my way to an empty seat. Almost immediately, another lad, with shockingly wiry, ginger hair, parked his arse next to me.

"Alright, mate. Whatchoo here to join then?" he enquired in a comical, cockney twang whilst moving his feet to rest on the top of the seat in front.

"Hopefully the Royal Signals if everything goes alright, what about you?"

"Fackin' Greenjackets, mate. Best regiment in the Army."

I didn't have the first clue what a 'fackin' Greenjacket' was but I nodded and smiled in admiration.

As the coach filled up, the soldier climbed on, and stood next to the driver, facing down the aisle. He began to address us in a broad Yorkshire accent.

"Listen up everyone, my name's Sergeant Graham. I'll just go through the nominal roll and then we can get going."

He rattled through his list as quickly as our inability to answer would allow. When he got to the cockney's name, which was Jordan, the cockney replied: " 'Ere, Sarge."

Sergeant Graham glared at him and shouted: "If you think you're fucking clever enough to address me by rank, call me Sergeant, you little cockney cunt."

"Yes, Sergeant," he whispered in response.

"And get your fucking feet off that chair, or I'll make you eat this fuckin' clipboard."

The newly humbled Jordan did as he was told and dropped his head so he could stare at his knees.

'Jesus,' I thought, and this is treating us with kid gloves. I needn't have worried; Sergeant Graham was simply employing a tactic, used the world over, in every industry where lots of men work together. Identify the person with the biggest mouth, humiliate him in front of his peers and gain control of the entire group. Graham was perfectly polite to everyone else, after his little verbal firepower demonstration, and the journey to the barracks was as short and pleasant a drive as it could be through Birmingham.

As soon as we arrived, we were all ushered off the coach quickly. There were five or six Sergeant Graham clones standing around now, all shouting and cajoling at once. Eventually they corralled us into a fairly neat formation of three ranks, with each rank containing approximately 20 men. When this little operation was complete, the clones moved off to one side and stood in a row. The one at the end then detached himself and moved to the front of our dishevelled bunch. He identified himself as Sergeant-Major Jones, and welcomed us to the APSC. He then ran through a prepared briefing, outlining all the dos and don'ts to be observed during our stay, mainly don'ts of course. He managed to keep it quite light-hearted throughout, but the little details now escape my memory. One thing he did mention that has stuck with me was with regard to the use of the toilets.

"Now fellas, I'm not sure what you're used to at home, but we do get a bit of a problem with people leaving turds in the bogs. Don't do it. It's a disgusting little habit and someone's got to clean it. If, tomorrow morning, you happen to drop a log into one of our pristine little shitters, then flush it away please. If it's still there after you've flushed, then flush again. If it still won't go down, then pick the bugger up, break it over your knee and try again. If this fails, then you have produced something worthy of admiration. Grab a member of staff and we will take your turd and frame the fucker for display in the Sergeants' Mess."

Immediately after this we were marched to our rooms. I say marched, but what actually happened was that the clones did a lot of shouting, and our group sort of ambled in the direction they were walking. There were one or two lads who must have done some time in the cadets, as they were trying to march properly, arms swinging back and forth etc. They were wasting their time, and just succeeded in getting filthy looks off the rest of us, for trying to be fucking clever. Yet another funny thing… as I write, I'm discovering that some of the most important military lessons were learnt right at the start. Do not, on any account, try to show initiative. It's a lose–lose situation. If your attempt at individual mental enterprise turns out to be successful, you'll gain the grudging appreciation of the men in charge, and the hooting derision of your compadres. If it turns out to be a stupid idea, every bastard gets to laugh at you. Don't bother and save yourself some heartache.

The rooms were exactly as you'd expect. A long dormitory with ten double bunks spanning its length, on either side of a central aisle, containing a table with four orange plastic chairs.

"Pick a bunk, dump your bags and get back outside please lads," said the latest clone, positioning himself by the door. We did as we were told and were soon loosely assembled in our squad, awaiting further direction. This came from Sergeant Graham.

"You will now be taken to the cinema to watch a short film," he announced grandly.

We were shepherded over to a small cinema and filed in. Everybody took their seats quietly. The lights had been pre-dimmed and some identifiably military music was being piped through the PA system. When everyone was seated, the Sergeant-Major opened up. He was stood in front of the cinema screen.

"Right, fellas. If you look under your seats, you'll find a programme of what you're going to be up to while you're here. It's all very straightforward. Do as you're told and get where you're supposed to be on time, and we'll all get along fine." The implied threat was evident, and immediately taken on board.

"You will now be shown a short film about Army life, after which you will be taken to the gymnasium for your physical tests. Has anyone not done any training?"

The question was unexpected and nobody replied. He chuckled malevolently, "We'll see, we'll see. Enjoy the film, gents."

He moved to the side of the screen, simultaneously giving the thumbs-up gesture to the projectionist, hidden away behind us.

The screen flashed into life. It lasted for ten minutes, and was, in hindsight, hilarious. The whole film consisted of brief clips showing all the great, adventurous things we could expect to do during our tenure. There were people windsurfing, abseiling from helicopters, rock-climbing, sky-diving and scuba-diving. This was all accompanied by a cheesy, action soundtrack that sounded like the introduction to a Pearl and Dean cinematic production. We were treated to film of young, short haired men, lazing about sunbathing on a Caribbean beach. The same guys were then shown playing volleyball with local kids. Surely it couldn't get any better than this? I couldn't wait to sign up.

The last portion of the film was unforgettable. The camera cut to another bunch of blokes propping up the bar of what must have been a NAAFI pub. At first the camera was about 15 feet away from them, but then it began to pan into the group. When it got to within four feet of them, the central character, a dark-haired, fat-faced corporal, slowly turned to face us. He raised his three-quarters-full pint pot to us, winked at the camera and said: "All this, and pay as well!"

Over the ensuing years, I'd get to repeat that phrase a few times, usually through gritted teeth, and whilst up to my neck in the shit. As soon as the film finished, the Sergeant-Major moved back in front of the screen. He was smiling. "Right, lads. There you have it. I couldn't have put it better meself. Every man an emperor, every day a holiday, every meal a feast. I wish I was the same age as you lot, 'cos I'd get to do it all again. Now, get your arses back over to your rooms, get your PT kit on, and wait to get called."

Immediately, there was a flurry of activity and the clones roared into life again, ushering us all out of our seats, and generally harrying us until we were back in the rooms.

"Come on, fellas. Get a fucking wiggle on." Once again, our sergeant – Rogers this one was called – cooed words of encouragement concealed within a generally abusive patina. We were all moving as quickly as we could. Whilst I was getting changed, I was looking round at the other lads' progress. I didn't want to be the last one ready and therefore receive some unwanted verbal flack. Everyone was dressed very differently. There were a few lads, like myself, that had the usual footy shorts, footy socks, running trainers and plain T-shirt on. Apart from that, a huge variety of 'sports' clothing was on show: football tops; rugby tops; hockey shirts; tracksuit bottoms; rugby shorts; and the occasional bit of dayglo lycra. There were a few lads with pop band T-shirts on, and a couple of brave bastards had political comments. As each person got changed, they had to run past Sergeant Rogers to get out of the door and he had an absolute field day. The first bloke he pulled up got the full treatment: “Frankie says NO WAR! Frankie fuckin’ says NO WAR! Where the fuck do you think you are, son? Greenham Common? Get back to your fucking holdall and get a top on that doesn’t make me want to punch you.”

“I haven’t got another sports top, though,” ventured the lad.

“I couldn’t give a shit if you’ve got to do press-ups in a fucking sheepskin, son, get it off.”

As soon as ‘Frankie says’ spun round, another target presented itself to Rogers. One of the blokes was trying to jog past him with a pair of Union Jack running shorts on. They were the type that loads of people doing the London Marathon used to wear, but in no way did they float Sergeant Roger’s boat.

“What the fuck have you got on there?” he bellowed.

“Shorts,” came the bemused reply.

“They are not fucking shorts, son. They are a defacement of your country’s flag.”

The short wearer was brave enough to defend himself: “They’re just shorts.”

Rogers blew his stack and roared: “No they are fuckin’ not. They are your single-handed attempt at overthrowing the government, aren’t they?”

“Eh?”

“That flag has flown over some of the finest buildings in the world. It was carried by men in battles that they couldn’t possibly have won, but did anyway. And you think that that same flag should now be used to cover your shitty little arse while you run round the gym. Do you? Do you?”

Fuck me; he really went in off the deep end. I couldn’t believe he’d flipped his lid quite so spectacularly over something as mundane as a pair of shorts. It was another lesson to be learned over the coming years. Some people took all of that blindly patriotic bullshit quite seriously. Rogers was obviously one of them. The wrongdoer soon became aware of this. By the time the rant had finished, he was already back at his bunk, and changing into another pair of shorts. Almost everyone got varying degrees of abuse from Rogers as they moved past him. I got off quite lightly.

"You could have given them trainers a scrub, son."

That was it, no comparisons with war criminals or references to Genghis Khan. When we were all outside, we assembled loosely into our squad again. We were then jogged, *en masse*, over to the gym. I quite liked the jog over, it was the first thing we'd done which felt vaguely martial. Sixty men, all running, sort of in step. I was quite surprised that nobody broke out into one of those American 'Sound off, 1, 2, 3, 4' cadences. I'd be told at a later stage that the British Army simply didn't perform those 'let everyone know you're here' chants as it was considered vulgar. "And besides," as one physical training instructor put it, "if you've got enough energy to sing, you can fucking run faster."

We came to a halt outside the gym and were again addressed by the Sergeant-Major.

"When you get inside, do exactly as you're told by the PTIs. You'll know which ones they are. They've got big muscles and they're all extremely handsome. As long as you don't get between a PTI and his mirror, you'll have no problems."

With that we were ushered into a huge, hangar like gymnasium. Set up all over its floor were various pieces of apparatus. There were chin-up bars, ropes, medicine balls, benches and mats all strategically placed. Dotted around, numbering about 11 in all, were the aforementioned Adonises.

As described by the Sergeant-Major, they all appeared to be perfect physical specimens. Dressed in identical white plimsolls, blue stirrup pants and white vests with red piping, they all bristled with recently exercised muscle groups. There was something quietly sinister in this look. It conjured in my mind, black and white images of Aryans doing mass public displays of exercise at Nazi rallies in the thirties. I was quietly transfixed by their imposing presence and felt distinctly weedy in my thrown-together outfit, and twig-thin legs. The spell was broken when the lead hunk stepped forward and identified himself. Instead of the expected Bavarian accent, his words poured out in best Blackburn.

"Right, fellas. Welcome to my world. My name is QMSI Rixon. You're here to perform some basic physical tasks, so we can establish that you're not complete knackers. Failing any of the tests will seriously jeopardise your chances of joining the Army. You've all received advance warning of what to expect, so there is no excuse for not being prepared. Has anybody not done any training?"

He cast his eyes up and down the ranks assembled before him, but exactly like Sergeant-Major Jones, received no reply.

"Good, good, good. All magnificently trained and honed to perfection then? From here you will be assembled into groups of six and taken round the various apparatus where you will do your tests, and be marked accordingly. As per your instructions, you will be expected to execute seven sit-ups on an inclined bench, three underarm pull-ups on the beam, and an 18-inch standing jump. You will also be doing a one-mile squadded run in ten minutes, immediately followed by the same run done with individual best effort. The time limit for this portion of the run is 7 minutes."

He continued: "The run will be carried out tomorrow morning, immediately prior to your final interview. Any questions? Good. Listen in."

With that, the other PTIs sprang to life and ran over to us. They quickly set about dissecting our group into the manageable chunks of six that their boss had mentioned. Whilst standing there, one of the PTIs – a big, black guy – made a chopping motion next to my left shoulder, and swept me and the five guys to my right to one side.

"Right you're my lot. I'm Corporal Fox, follow me."

He turned on his heel and ran off, so we ran after him. Whilst running over to the first piece of apparatus – the pull-up bar – I had just enough time to weigh up the physical condition of my cohorts. Of course, we weren't in direct competition, as it was an individual physical assessment, but it was always a good morale booster, to have a Billy Bunter around, to make you look a bit better. No such luck this time round. The other five lads all looked pretty similar to me, pasty and skinny, but with no evidence of spare tyres anywhere.

He stopped us just before the bar, and pivoted round smartly. We were all panting slightly from the run, and waited for his next instruction, whilst gazing up at the bar, with slight trepidation.

"First three, up to the beam."

I was in the first three, so I moved forward and stood directly beneath the beam. Corporal Fox then proceeded to demonstrate exactly what to do. He dropped his clipboard, jumped up to the beam, and caught it, underarm, in a firm grip, with his arms shoulder width apart.

"When I give the word, you will dangle from the beam like so, making sure your arms are fully extended," he carried out this movement and continued: "When I say up, you will heave yourself up until your chin is above the bar." Once again he performed the activity as he spoke. "You'll stay there 'til I say 'down'. If I catch anyone resting their chin on the bar, I'll chop his fucking legs off. When I say 'down', you'll drop back into the start position. Complete that three times and that's you done."

With that, he released his grip and landed, cat-like in front of us. By cat-like, I don't mean that he started to lick his own balls, but that he landed gracefully.

"Okay, jump up to the beam."

I'd done a bit of training so I was quietly confident.

Our trio stepped forward as one. We jumped up to the beam, and proceeded to dangle in the prescribed military fashion. It seemed like an age before he gave the command to pull up. We did so immediately. I was the middle man so I was able to use my peripheral vision to check on my colleagues' progress. The first one was no problem for all three of us, but the second made the guy on my left struggle a bit, and pull a gurning face as he barely got his chin above the bar. He then made the mistake of resting his chin, just for a second, on the bar. Of course Corporal Fox spotted him immediately and proceeded to berate him.

"Fucking stop it you, or I'll you'll have me hanging off your legs for the last one."

The gurner quickly complied and we were instructed to drop down again. He left us dangling for what was only three or four seconds but felt like 15. When he called 'Up' again, I heaved myself into position and waited. The three second wait had done for the gurner, and he was trying to pull himself up in instalments. First he'd go up a little bit on his left arm then a bit more on the right. All of this was accompanied by loud grunts, more at home on a maternity ward. His legs were kicking frantically, as if riding an imaginary unicycle. Corporal Fox was completely unimpressed and stood in front of him looking up at his face.

"Are you pulling faces at me, son? I fucking hope not. Get up there you fucking waster, you're keeping your mates waiting," which of course he was. I'd been resisting the incredible urge to let my chin drop onto the bar for about ten seconds now, and my puny biceps were beginning to pack up. The bloke on my right, seemed to be going through the same sort of pain, and sounded like he was trying to pass a particularly large shit.

"For fuck's sake, get up there. Put some effort in. You're starting to embarrass me."

After another three or four seconds of primal screaming, the gurner finally got his chin above the bar, and we were allowed to drop down.

Corporal Fox stood in front of us, and scribbled quickly onto his clipboard. He then dropped it and pointed his pen, first at the guy on my right, then me, then the gurner. "Pass, Pass, Fail. You'd better work hard on the rest of the exercises, son, or you'll be fucked. Next three, up to the bar."

He redirected his gaze to the next rank, giving us our cue to shift out of the way and watch. They all completed their three pull-ups without incident. We then followed Fox round the gym to the sit-up bay. Although the seven sit-ups had to be performed on a bench, inclined at about 30 degrees, they were very easy, and posed nobody any problems. We then moved round to the standing jump. As explained in detail by Corporal Fox, this exercise involved a single jump. Each person, in turn, would stand on their tiptoes with the right arm extended, fingers pointed, palm flat against a small blackboard. The PTI would then make a chalk mark on the board, at the tip of the fingers. The 'athlete' was then required, to crouch down and leap straight up into the air, restriking the blackboard. The difference between the two marks had to be no less than 18 inches. I now know that this is used to measure explosive power, and can identify numerous physical shortcomings, but at the time I was totally perplexed. As an exercise, it didn't seem to make any sense, other than to establish your promising future as a basketball player. Maybe there was some sort of future military requirement for this skill, that hadn't occurred to us at the potential recruit stage. I had visions of a platoon of hard bitten Second World War British Tommies standing outside a house that they were trying to storm. They were trying to throw a grenade through a window, but it was just too high. From out of nowhere, came the regimental standing-jump expert. He positioned himself by the wall and crouched down. Then, in one balletic flourish, leapt skywards, right arm outstretched. The grenade was dispatched through the open window, and the day was saved. He landed amongst the cheers, congratulations and hearty backslaps of his comrades. I was shaken from my daydream, as usual, by somebody shouting.

"Don't you dare bob down, you little cheat. Full extension of the arm, on tiptoes," roared Corporal Fox at the gurner, of all people. He was trying to load the dice a little bit for himself, by trying to appear shorter. That hadn't even occurred to me. It would be a while before I understood the concept of 'skive to survive'. Just like in the Second World War, where it was every Allied POWs unwritten duty to try to escape whenever possible, it was every soldier's tacitly sworn oath, to skive whenever possible during a PT lesson. It was never done because of the soldier's lack of fitness, but primarily as a bit of a 'fuck you' to the PTIs. Secondly, during a ferocious PT beasting, you never actually knew just how much more you were going to be made to do. Therefore, it was simple common sense that you would try to conserve energy whenever you weren't being watched. Of course, the downside of this little tactic was that, should you be caught, no mercy was expected, or given. You would be given more exercise than everyone else, and your skive would prove to have been counterproductive. I managed my jump without too much drama, as did most, and that completed the tests, apart from, of course, the run.

We were herded back into the original group, and once again addressed by the QMSI. As he spoke, he was occasionally looking down at his clipboard and shaking his head. "Right, most of you have passed everything, but some of you are a shower of shite. Where's the bloke who couldn't do one pull-up?"

An arm, somewhere off to my right, slid up reluctantly.

"You, son, are a shabby excuse for a potential soldier. You should be fucking ashamed of yourself. My Granddad is 93 tomorrow. He's got Alzheimer's and diabetes and one of his arms is still on the Somme, but even he can do more pull-ups than you."

The arm crept back down ashamedly, as barely suppressed laughter, escaped from the ranks around him.

"That's it for the gym today. Next bit of exercise is tomorrow's run. Those of you who did badly in here had better impress me tomorrow or you'll be up the road."

We were then taken, *en masse*, for our chest X-rays. This happened in a scruffy white Portakabin, close to the cinema. By the time we'd all been through, it was about 3.30pm and I was wondering when we might knock off. Of course, we weren't quite finished yet, and Sergeant-Major Jones filled us in with the details of the next thrilling instalment.

"Okay lads. Last activity of the day. After you've got cleaned up, we're going to take you over to the main hall, where you'll do your written tests. After that, you'll be taken to the cookhouse for your tea. Then, until tomorrow morning, your time's your own. Your dormitory sergeant will show you where the NAAFI is. You can use the phone or get something to eat there. Those of you who are old enough can have a beer. Don't get pissed. If anybody turns up tomorrow morning smelling like a magic marker, he will not be allowed to do the run."

With that we were spirited off to the dormitory again. After a quick shower and change, we were paraded back outside, and taken over to the main hall. It was just like our assembly hall at school. As I'd just started my O-Levels, it had a very familiar look. Long rows of single desks, with lots of cheat-denying space between them. We were pointed towards the desks, which already had the test papers resting on them. Once everyone was seated, we were addressed by an officer, the first one I'd seen. He was an Education Corps captain and looked quite dapper. He spoke with a clipped, Home Counties accent.

"Hello, fellas. I'm Captain Turncroft. Hope you've had a nice day so far?"

No response.

"Yes… well then. Read all the questions before you start and stop writing when I tell you to. You have an hour."

After a suitably grandiose pause, he added: "You may begin."

I'm not sure what the tests were designed to identify, but they were not difficult. I don't remember any of the questions specifically, but it was all multiple guess. The worst case scenario gave you a one-in-four chance of getting the question right with a complete stab in the dark. I'm not particularly clever, yet I sailed through it, and I was left with 20 minutes of thumb-twiddling before the clock ran down. I looked round the room and spotted several stereotypical examinee types. There were the ones like me who'd finished early and wanted the world to know. They were tapping pencils on the desk or exhaling loudly, hoping someone would notice how smart they were to get done so quickly. Then there were those guys, fiercely protective of their own work. Despite the fact that there wasn't another person within eight feet of them, they were hunched over their desks, one arm writing, or rather crossing the correct box furiously, whilst the other arm shielded their precious output. Some blokes had the look of the damned to them. Sitting there like they'd been given a different paper to everyone else – one on quantum physics, or another subject they knew nothing about. They'd be staring at a wall or looking up at the ceiling, wondering what sort of a job they'd have to do now, now that they'd found out that they couldn't even pass an Army test. By the time Captain Turncroft coughed lightly and said "Five minutes," almost everybody had finished. One guy at the front was still intermittently chewing his pencil and writing. He was either a bit thick or being really thoughtful about his ticking style. The rest of the time drained away, and Turncroft reappeared, to say to nobody in particular: "Time up, stop writing."

The clones appeared from all directions, scooping up question papers as they darted between the desks. Then it was back outside again, and as the Sergeant-Major had promised, we were taken over to the cookhouse for our first taste of Army food. It was pretty good actually, a couple of choices of main course, a couple of puddings and as much bread and cordial as you could down. It was the first and only time that I was to encounter polite and affable cookhouse staff. The men and women of the Army Catering Corps are pilloried incessantly by the rest of the Army, for being responsible for more military deaths than any amount of enemy action. The old adage is that theirs is the hardest course in the British Army, because no one has ever passed it. As a result of all the abuse they get, they are turned into the bitterest of soldiers, without a good word for anyone or anything. They seek little victories over their customers by subjecting them to strict food rationing at the hotplate. Woe betide any man who tries to take more than one sausage at breakfast, or fancies helping himself to a couple of extra slices of bread. Obviously, the cooks had been briefed to be on their best behaviour at the APSC, lest they scare any of us off, and they couldn't have been more friendly. After feeding up, we were taken back to the dormitory and left to our own devices. It was only 5.30pm, but it had been a long day. I had a bit of a kip on my bed, then went down to the NAAFI to phone home. I joined a short queue at one of a line of four phone booths, and waited for a couple of minutes.

When it was my turn, I got in the booth, whacked a bit of change in and punched in our home number. After three rings, Dad answered.

"Hello."

"Alright, Dad?"

"Who's this?"

"Eddy!"

"Eddy… mmm I used to have a son called Eddy. He left home years ago."

"Dad!!!"

"Alright, son. How's it going?"

"Not bad, passed all the tests so far."

"Told you you'd be alright. What else is left?"

"Just a run tomorrow morning, then an interview."

"Piece of piss, get an early night and you'll scream round."

"Hope so."

"Everyone treating you alright?"

"Yeah, they all shout a bit, but I haven't done anything to attract attention to myself."

"That's the trick. There's always some other daft bastard who'll get himself noticed, and when he does, make sure you're on the other side of the room."

"Okay."

"Good luck for tomorrow then, son. Shall I put your Mam on?"

"Yeah."

He placed his hand over the mouthpiece but I could still hear his muffled voice. "Barbara, Barbara, it's our Eddy. Mummy's little soldier wants tucking in." I heard the footsteps tapping up the hall, then the sound of the handset changing owners.

"Hiya, son. Are you alright?"

"Fine, Mum."

"You've not been firing guns or anything yet, have you?"

"Ha, ha, no not yet."

"It's not funny Eddy, they're dangerous them things."

"I know Mum; I won't get my hands on anything like that until I actually join though."

"Good."

"Did you go and see Gran today?"

"Yeah, you should have heard her when I told her about you. 'Don't let any o' them buggers bully him Barbara or they'll have me to answer to.' Bless her."

"Jesus."

"When will you be back?"

"Sometime in the afternoon."

"OK, son. Take care, sleep well."

"Bye."

I hung up and made my way out of the booth, holding the door open for the next man. I followed Dad's instructions and after getting cleaned up, got an early night. I think I was asleep by about nine o'clock. I had a shit night's sleep. I think it was a combination of nervousness at the thought of the run and the stink and noise of my room-mates. There was some industrial strength snoring going on. The bloke in the bed directly opposite me, sounded like he was turning into a werewolf under his covers. Throughout the night, the snoring was punctuated by those loud, lazy farts which can only be ejected through a sleeping sphincter. They succeeded in making the smell in the room strong enough to start a windmill on an old Dutch painting. I was glad to be out of bed in the morning. After having another shower, I got into my PT kit. We'd been told to be ready by seven-thirty, but by twenty past, everyone was sat on their beds, nervously awaiting the arrival of the shouting men. They duly arrived, and verbally steered us outside.

The QMSI and his pantheon of gods were waiting for us.

"Right, good morning to you all. I trust you slept well? Good. Okay, you all know the score for the run, but for those of you with no brains I'll go over it again. From here we'll go to the start point at the parade square. We will then run, walk, run for one mile. This will take exactly ten minutes and will be considered a warm up. You will then have 30 seconds to sort yourselves out.

You will then turn round and run back over exactly the same route. This time, you will have seven minutes to complete the distance. This is not difficult and is only two-thirds of what we refer to as the Basic Fitness Test. One of the PTIs will run round in exactly this time. If you finish behind him you've failed. But what I don't want to see is a load of blokes jogging one pace ahead of him. Best personal effort, gentlemen. If I catch any fucker cruising, I will make him eat his own trainers. I'll be stood watching at the finish line. I want to see some aggression in those spotty faces. You should be trying to catch up with the man in front of you right up until the last second."

His speech just made me feel even more nervous. I'd done the training and knew I would make it round in the time specified, but I had no idea it was going to be like 'Chariots of Fire'. As soon as he finished speaking, we were assembled into the standard three ranks again, and we jogged over to the start line.

Without further ado, the QMSI pressed a button on a ridiculously large stopwatch he had dangling from a cord round his neck, and we set off. As we ran, it became apparent that it was going to be two laps of the camp's huge parade square. The first third of the test wasn't in the least bit difficult. There was a lot of nervous coughing, spitting and farting, but nobody appeared to be tired. I was about five back from the front of the left-hand rank, and could see the QMSI at the front setting the pace, running like one of those Spanish dressage horses. Lots of flamboyant knee-raising, all done for show and to demonstrate his superior physical prowess. We did our two laps of the camp and came to a halt, back at the start line.

"Right, if anyone needs a piss, have one quickly."

A couple of blokes nipped to one side to relieve themselves. The QMSI was studying his stopwatch intently. "Hurry up, hurry up," he shouted to the nervous pissers as they packed themselves away. His urgency was transmitted to the crowd. We were no longer in ranks, but all vying for pole position on the start line. There was lots of semi-polite elbowing and shoving. Fuck me, it felt like the Grand National or something.

"Remember, gents, best effort. Standby… GO."

We were off. The BFT, or Basic Fitness Test, as the QMSI said, is not difficult; that's why it's called basic. Though we were running a shortened version, it was easy to see that a young person with a modicum of physical fitness would have no problems running a mile and a half at around a seven-minute-mile pace. The trouble with the BFT is the start. Peer pressure makes everyone go off like greyhounds. This is alright for the cross-country runners who'll end up doing the whole thing no slower than eight minutes, but when you get a ten-thirty man, running off at the same pace, he's setting himself up for some serious pain. The trick was always to set yourself a decent pace, and pound that out for the first mile. Over the last half-mile, if you were feeling fit, you could open up a bit. Of course, whenever you spotted a PTI lurking, you were obliged to put in a bit more effort. You wouldn't actually run any faster, but you would create that impression by swinging your arms a bit more or contorting your face into an expression that looked like you were approaching the vinegar strokes of a vicious wank. I learnt all of this over the next few years of course, and like everyone else, sprinted like a bastard as soon as the QMSI said go. Of the 60 runners, I found myself in the lead group of about ten. The man right at the front was putting distance between himself and the rest of the group with every step he took. He was running so aggressively that from the side, he must have looked like a human Swastika. By the time we'd got halfway round the first lap, I'd already started to get knackered, and started to slow down. Quite a few people edged past me, so I just started to look at the floor and continued to plod on. By the time the start line came into view, I'd regained a bit of composure and was running okay again, and I was still in the top 20. There were lots of people around the area of the start line, shouting at the runners as they passed through for the second lap. The shouts alternated between encouragement and outright abuse.

"Come on, lads. One more lap to go, keep it going!"

"Get moving, you fat cunt!"

"Excellent, you in the red top. Now get after the next man!"

"Fuckin' hell, son. Douglas Bader could get round quicker than you!"

As I passed through I got my second wind. With only a third of a mile to go, I felt confident enough to start putting in some real effort and passed a handful of people on the way round. By the time I'd done another circuit and had entered into the home straight again, I was about 15th. I sprinted for the line. The QMSI was timing at the finish line and shouting the time out every ten seconds. As I crossed he was just shouting: "Five minutes, 50."

I stumbled to a halt and adopted the standard pose. I bent over double, standing with my head almost between my knees, with my hands resting on my thighs. I got a smack across the top of the head and looked up, startled, to find one of the PTIs growling at me.

"None of that bollocks; stand up straight and take deep breaths." I did exactly as I was told, though the temptation to crouch down was overwhelming. All round me, finishers were being discouraged from adopting a similar pose. Some blokes, who had obviously put in a bit more effort than everyone else, were vomiting copiously on to the floor. A couple were dry retching, producing nothing but a bit of bile and bulging eyes for all their effort. The PTIs were going mad at the spewers. "Don't you fucking dare be sick on a parade square," one PTI was roaring at a dry heaver. The lad was doing his best and had his hand over his mouth. The PTI warned him again.

"If you're sick, I'll make you pick it up and carry it back to your room." The potential spewee now had both his lips firmly clasped between his fingers, but started to relax when he realised he'd won the battle with his regurgitation reflex.

All the while, the QMSI was running down the clock. As the time got to seven minutes, we were all ordered to encourage the rest of the runners in. I turned in the direction of the home straight, and counted about ten men, some quite a way back. The QMSI bellowed: "C'mon, you fuckers. Six minutes 40! Six minutes 45!"

Those runners within earshot flew into a blind panic, and began to sprint like demons. As he was shouting 6.55, five of them crashed over the line in unison, collapsing in a sweaty heap the moment they'd finished. They were immediately upbraided by the assembled training staff. "NAAFI break is it? How come you lot are resting? The time you fuckers took to get round you must have already stopped for a brew?"

Only three blokes failed to make it within the allotted time. They were quietly taken to one side and had their names taken. After another 30 seconds of people standing around getting their breath back the QMSI piped up: "Not bad lads, not bad at all. Only three failures out of 60. Your results for this and all the other tests will be passed to the personnel selection officers for your final interview. You'll now be taken back over to the rooms to get scrubbed up. Then it's back in your best clobber for your interview. Any questions? Good. Get 'em away!"

The staff quickly assembled us, but this time were kind enough to walk our tired bodies back to the rooms. There didn't appear to be any reason to rush but, as usual, Sergeant Rogers hurried us along anyway. From the doorway, he displayed his command of swearing with aplomb. "Come on, you lot. Stop dragging your feet; you've only been for a little fucking run. Hurry up and get fucking dressed."

As soon as people started donning their shirts and ties, or suits, he warmed up. He spotted one bloke, in a musty looking, black, single breasted, two-piece that looked a touch on the small side.

"Fuck me, son. Did you get that off a dead body?"

Some lads had gone for shirt, tie and trousers, but most of us had opted for suits. As usual, they were either badly fitted, or garishly coloured and sometimes a combination of both. It was only a hunch, but I don't think anyone had been to a gentleman's outfitter. I donned the same suit that I'd worn to the medical. I'd had the opportunity to grow a bit more since then, so filled it out slightly better, but not enough to avoid Sergeant Rogers' sartorially critical eye.

"What's your name, son?"

"Nugent."

"Right, lads. If anyone's forgotten their suit, there's enough room in Nugent's for one more."

The bastard. I scuttled past him as quickly as I could and waited outside. I'd never get the chance to see how he dressed when off duty, but I'll bet he was no Cary Grant. Everyone knew the drill now, so when the entire complement were outside, we turned in the direction we knew we'd be going. This time we were walked over to a single-storey block, adjacent to the cinema. I have to admit that Sergeant Rogers was right about us though. We did look shit in our best clothes. The mid-eighties was not a good period for fashion, and there were some real crimes on show. Worst of all was the abundance of *Dynasty*-style false shoulders in the ranks. Guys who had looked like Charlie Drake on the run had been transformed into American footballers. The squeak of patent leather shoes must have been audible on the other side of the camp. It didn't help that most people were still sweating from the run and there was lots of finger-in-the-collar head twitching going on. We stopped outside the block and waited. Sergeant-Major Jones emerged and began speaking immediately.

"This is your final interview, lads. Please address the Personnel Selection Officer as Sir. Your future depends on it. Don't be nervous."

With that useless bit of encouragement he ducked back inside. When they shouted for the first bloke, it was obvious that it was going to be done in alphabetical order. I don't know about other organisations, but it was a real advantage in the Army to have a name beginning with one of the early letters of the alphabet. Nobody in the military had the imagination to do things differently, so the As and Bs got everything first. Pay, jabs, kit, rations, they'd get seen to before the rest of us. Of course, my middle-of-the-road surname wasn't too bad, but you were fucked if you were W or later. Everybody would be asleep by the time you got back to the room with whatever you'd been issued.

They got round to me after about half an hour. I went into the block and was pointed towards a slightly-ajar, badly veneered door, by one of the sergeants. I knocked, and entered. The PSO stood up and greeted me quite warmly, introducing himself as Sergeant-Major Robinson.

"How have you found it all then, Mr Nugent?"

Another first, I'd never been addressed as Mister before, unless you counted sarcastic History teachers.

"Okay thanks, Sir."

"I've had a good look through your results. You don't appear to have struggled on anything in particular. Good scores on the written tests and no problem on the physical. I watched you on the run this morning; you did seem to be cruising a bit at the end of the first lap?"

"I just wasn't sure of the distance, Sir, and I went off a bit quick at the start."

"Not to worry, you'll have plenty of opportunity to hone your pacing techniques."

You're down to join the Royal Signals as an Apprentice, correct?"

"Yes, Sir."

"I'm happy to tell you that based on your results, I'm prepared to offer you a place at the Army Apprentices' College, Harrogate."

Fuck me, that was it, I was in. In the couple of seconds before he started talking again, I went through a range of feelings. Delight, of course, quickly followed by horror, trepidation and excitement.

"Are you prepared to accept this offer?"

"Yes, Sir."

"Good, congratulations. The College has two more intakes this year. You can either join in June or September. Which would you prefer?"

"September, Sir". I may have been 16 and on the verge of an exciting period of my life, but there was no way I was missing out on the summer holidays. The Army could have me, after I'd had a couple more months pissing about.

"The paperwork will be sent to your parents for signatures. The only thing remaining is your attestation. This is where you swear allegiance to the Queen. It will be done at your local careers office between now and your joining date, which will be September the third. Have you any questions?"

"No, Sir."

"Well then Nugent, that's it."

He stood up smiling, and offered his hand again, "Well done, and good luck."

I shook the proffered hand vigorously.

"Thank you, Sir."

"You can go back home now. Transport to the train station will be leaving in a few minutes."

He picked another folder up from the desk and starting reading it, and I took my cue to leave. I was feeling slightly bewildered as I got back outside. Incredibly, I already felt a little bit different to the lads still waiting. I was in, and they weren't yet. You'd think I'd passed SAS selection or been promoted to General. I was directed on to the same, ugly, green bus that I'd arrived on. It was half-full and the lads scattered around were engaged in happy conversations. I presumed they'd all received the same nod as me. The gurner from the pull-ups bar was sat, on his own about three seats up from me, looking despondently out of the window. It was pretty obvious from his demeanour that he hadn't been so lucky. My counselling skills were at quite a rudimentary level at this stage of my life, so I thought better of saying anything to him, and contented myself with a self-satisfied, smug grin, which I wore all the way to the station. I made all the connections back to Manchester with no problems, and just had time at Birmingham New Street to call home.

"Hello."

"Hiya, Dad, it's me."

"Everything okay, son?"

"No."

"Eh? What's happened?"

"They said I didn't try hard enough on the run and to come back when I could show some more effort."

"The dirty bastards. Who do they think they are? I'll fucking go down there I will. Where is it?"

"Only joking, Dad. I've been accepted."

"Ha ha ha, you little bugger, wait until I see you. Well done, Eddy."

"I'd better go, me train's due."

"Right, I'll tell your Mam. See you when you get home."

Mum was a bit subdued when I got in. I know she was pleased for me, but she had the obvious heartache of losing her boy to the Forces.

I had a whole three months before my joining date and had a great time. I kept myself fit, usually going for a run every couple of days. Amongst my mates, I was one of the only ones who had got something sorted out. With school now over for most of them, the prospect of no employment hung over the less fortunate ones. In the time before I left, a couple more started the process of joining up, bolstered by my bragging into thinking it was a brilliant career choice. A few of my mates were going on to college. Despite the fact that they were the sensible ones, who were setting themselves up for success in later life, all they actually saw at the time was a further two years of school, whilst I was disappearing for a swashbuckling life of adventure on the open seas, or its land-based equivalent.

About six weeks before my joining date, I received an instruction to attend the Careers Office in Fountain Street for my attestation. As usual, I was told to dress smart for the occasion and to be there for one-thirty in the afternoon on the 23rd of July. This time, when I walked through the door of the office on the date specified, it was with a bit more confidence. There were a couple of lads hanging around outside, examining the shoddy, cardboard displays in the windows. I was cocky enough to tip them a wink, and say "Alright, lads?" as I strolled through the door.

As with my last visit, the first person I spotted was Sergeant Chapman, who was wedged into his seat, behind the desk. He got up and was just about to launch into his welcoming speech, before vaguely recognising me and stopping. He half closed one eye Columbo-style, and said: "Have you been in before, son?"

"Yes. I'm Eddy Nugent; I'm here for my attestation."

"Right, right. So you did it then? Well done."

"What do I have to do for the attestation?"

"Oh it's straightforward enough. You'll go upstairs and have a quick interview with the attesting officer and then you make a declaration, to serve the Queen and do as you're told. Let's have a look at who the attesting officer is today."

He glanced down at his desk, and ran his finger down a single sheet of white paper, stopping halfway. His brow furrowed slightly. "Oh… right, you've got Major Hathaway."

His tone worried me a bit, so I enquired: "Is that a problem?"

"Oh no, he's just a bit odd. He can get a bit short tempered. He's probably got a piece of shrapnel stuck in his brain or something. I'll tell you what, don't do anything to antagonise him, and you'll be out of there in five minutes."

Once more, a senior NCO's attempt to reassure me had had the opposite effect.

"Take a seat over by the stairs, and I'll give you a shout when he's ready to see you."

"Okay."

I sat down, feeling uncomfortable in my low quality suit, and waited. I nervously thumbed through a couple of leaflets which pleaded with me to 'Be the best you can be', and 'Pick a life, not just a career'. They were obviously preaching to the converted but there was nothing else to read. After a couple of minutes, Sergeant Chapman caught my attention from his desk, "You can go up now. Remember, be polite."

I nodded anxiously and walked up the two flights of stairs that led to the first-floor offices. I walked through a single fire-escape door that led to a short corridor with four doors on each side. I walked down slowly, glancing at each name tag, before identifying Major Hathaway's office, at the end, on the left. I straightened my tie, wiped the front of each shoe, in turn on the opposite trouser leg and knocked lightly on the door three times. There was no answer, so after a wait of about ten seconds, I gave another three taps, this time slightly harder, but there was still no recognition from inside. Maybe he wasn't in? I turned the handle of the door and pushed it open far enough to poke my head through. Shit, he was in there. He was stood with his back to me looking out of the window. His left hand was behind his back and his right was holding a big pipe. I was just about to sneak back out and knock again when he turned round, and I froze. He was one scary looking man. At least in his late forties, and about five feet ten, he had the same face as the straight man from the Laurel and Hardy films. I think he was called James Finlayson. You know the guy, the one who always turned to camera with one eye shut in apoplexy at being outwitted or injured by Stan and Ollie. That contorted, angry face was Major Hathaway's default expression. His face was topped off by a set of eyebrows in which you could have lost Dennis Healey. They were enormously bushy, and looked like someone had nailed two Yorkshire terriers to his forehead. Above the eyebrows, his head was dazzlingly bald, apart from a little Hitler moustache above each ear. I feared for my life.

"Who are you, boy?" he scowled. As he was an officer, I was expecting a posh accent, but he sounded like a cross between Brian Glover and Fred Dibnah.

"Eddy Nugent."

"A 'Sir' on the end of that is forthcoming?"

"Err… Yes, Sir."

"Where's your manners, Nugent?"

"Pardon, Sir?"

"In the Army that I joined in 1960, it was considered polite to knock on someone's door before entering their office."

"I knocked a couple of times, Sir." I stayed close to the door, ready to leg it if things turned nastier.

"I haven't served 25 years in this man's Army, in order that a limp-wristed, can't-knock-on-a-door-properly, little bugger like you can backchat me."

Despite the fact that he was six feet away from me, his tobacco impregnated breath was making my eyes sting. By now, he'd moved to stand behind his desk. On the wall behind his head was a picture of the Queen. She looked about 30 years old and, incredibly, the artist had managed to make her look attractive. He swung his arm in her general direction and said: "So you're here to take an oath of allegiance to her majesty are you?"

"I think so. Yes, Sir," my voice was trembling.

"You bloody think so? You're not joining the Cubs, lad. You better bloody know so."

He turned away from me and looked toward the picture. He stayed focused on it for a full ten seconds before turning back to me. He had tears in his eyes. This was not a well man.

"It's not something to be taken lightly lad. I took mine a quarter of a bloody century ago and I can still remember it like it was yesterday."

He placed both hands on the desk and stared at me intently. "What I want to know, son, is are you a quitter?"

"Pardon, Sir?"

"A quitter, are you a quitter?"

His accent made the word come out 'kerrwitter'.

"I'll not let anyone take the Oath of Allegiance if I don't think he means it. Too many of you lads joining now are only doing it for a laugh."

"I'm not a quitter, Sir," I ventured, timidly.

"Good, prove it to me then. Can you do star-jumps?"

I had no idea what he meant and told him so. He explained.

"A star-jump is a physical exercise where you crouch down and then jump up throwing your arms and legs out."

He walked round the front of the desk and demonstrated one for me. When he reached the arms and legs out bit, he looked like he was going to burst out with a big show tune or something. He stopped and fixed me again, with his deranged stare.

"Start pushing 'em out."

I should let you know, that the average soldier's experience of taking the Oath was, walk in, shake hands, read Oath of Allegiance whilst holding Bible, shake hands again, depart. This usually took three minutes. I'd obviously picked the wrong day and the wrong man. I'd already been getting bollocked for five minutes and now I was about to have an impromptu physical beasting, whilst wearing a suit. I started performing the exercise. After doing about five, I paused and looked at the major. He returned my gaze and with an alarmed look shouted: "Did somebody say stop?"

I carried on. I could feel myself starting to sweat through my suit. Each time I jumped up, my tie flapped around in my face. After another couple of minutes, I started to get tired. Instead of doing the exercises with the vigour demonstrated, I started to falter. He was quick to spot the downturn in effort.

"So you are a bloody quitter?"

He'd moved to stand right in front of me, and at the end of each repetition my face was level with his. I shouted back: "No, Sir."

It went on for another minute or so. By the time he said stop, I was completely fucked. I couldn't do a proper one at all now. I was just bobbing down a bit, then standing up whilst throwing my arms back, like John Inman feigning surprise. He put his hand on my shoulder and said quietly: "Stop, lad. You've done enough."

I was a complete mess. The top button of my shirt had fallen off, my tie was wrapped right round my neck, and my suit jacket was hanging off me. I looked like I'd been thrown out of a nightclub. Whilst I was stood there gasping like a newly-caught fish, he produced The Bible and the card with the Oath written on it. I was forced to recite it, whilst having to take a breath after every two words. I can't remember its exact content. Suffice to say, it involved agreeing to do exactly as you were fucking well told, no matter how stupid or needless the said order was. I'd have read whatever he put in front of me, if it meant I could leave once I'd finished. As soon as I'd completed it, he whipped both the items away and placed them in the top drawer of his desk. He then picked up his pipe and wandered back over to his window. He casually turned round and nodding sagely in my direction said: "You can go now, lad."

I straightened myself out, and made to leave. As I put my hand on the door handle, he called to me: “Nugent?”

“Yes Sir.”

“I hate quitters.” Oh no, I was going to get some more. I thought fast.

“Me too, Sir”.

He turned to face me again, and looked at me quizzically, exhibiting superhuman strength by raising one of his eyebrows, smiled and said: “Tell Sergeant Chapman to send in my next patient.”

I practically ran down the corridor and down the stairs. When I got to the foyer, there was another lad waiting in the seat that I’d previously occupied. I was just about to warn him, when Sergeant Chapman interrupted, from his seat behind the desk.

“Right, Morris, you can go up. Don’t antagonise Major Hathaway; he’s a bit short tempered. Just be polite and you’ll be out of there in five minutes.”

Morris got up and made his way upstairs, the poor bastard. Sergeant Chapman came round to stand in front of me. “What did he make you do?”

“Star-jumps. He’s fucking mad.”

“You were lucky. He had one lad running on the spot for 45 minutes last week. I didn’t want you to say anything to Morris. To tell the truth, you’re better off not knowing. So that’s you all done then.”

“What happens now?”

“You’ve got your joining date?”

“September the third.”

“A few weeks beforehand, you’ll get sent travel details and a train warrant to get you where you’re going.”

“Right.”

“Best of luck then.” He took my hand and shook it.

“Thanks.”

I made my way out of the office and back onto the street. I got the bus home and was still sweating from Hathaway’s treatment when I got in 20 minutes later. In my last month and a half of freedom, I continued to train, and did a couple of things that I thought I might find helpful. I got Mum to show me how to iron clothes, and I started setting my alarm clock early, to see what hauling myself out of bed at 6am would be like. It was shit, and something I could never see myself getting used to doing. I consoled myself with the thought that maybe all that getting up early and people saying 'You 'orrible little man', only happened in *It Ain't Half Hot Mum*. It would be safe to say, in hindsight, that the Sergeant-Major character that Windsor Davies played was a watered down version of some of the people I was going to meet.

About halfway through August, I received the hotly anticipated joining instructions and travel warrants. The assorted leaflets went into great detail about what to bring with me for recruit training. Ominously, it stated that I wouldn't need any of my civilian clothes for the first seven weeks, so not to bring too many. They must have had some real dimwits turning up, as they felt it necessary to list every little thing they wanted you to bring. 'Please ensure you arrive with adequate amounts of underwear' was one of the instructions. It suggested that you sew or mark your name in all of your clothing as well. I disregarded this bit of advice and was to regret it later.

A week before I joined, I went and exchanged my travel warrants for train tickets, at Piccadilly Station. I left them on the window ledge of my bedroom, and spent the rest of the week looking at them every time I went in there, with a growing sense of foreboding. It was only really dawning on me, right at the death, that I was about to take a huge step in my life, and it was beginning to scare the shit out of me.

My date to join was September the third, 1985. It fell on a Tuesday, and Mum and Dad had a party for me on the weekend before I went. It was round at the house, and the place was mobbed with various aunties, uncles, cousins and mates, all there to wish me well, and get pissed. By midnight, I had lots of watery-eyed relatives telling me how proud they were of me. My Auntie Mary told me that I'd make a great soldier, but I don't know how 30 years working in a biscuit factory had qualified her to make such a judgement. Her husband Jim had won the award for being the most sozzled bloke at the party. He collared me at about nine o'clock as I was coming out of the kitchen.

"Yer a fucking smasher, Eddy, 'ere you go."

He dug into his pocket, almost losing his arm in the process, and pulled out a two pence piece. He placed it carefully into my hand and closed my fingers around it, winking conspiratorially all the time. In his advanced state of drunkenness he must have thought he was back in the fifties, when two pence would have bought something more than a Bazooka Joe. By midnight he was asleep on the back lawn. He'd been trying to show my Dad a few disco moves. When he collapsed after a fourth attempt at a 360 degree spin, Dad just left him in the garden. Appropriately, his position was not unlike the famous John Travolta pose from the Saturday Night Fever posters, albeit lying down, with booze fumes emanating from him. I don't recall being able to see Travolta's bum crack either. Mum got a bit maudlin just before bedtime. I had to have a dance with her, and she started to cry a bit, with her head on my shoulder.

"Don't cry, Mum. I'll be back on leave after a couple of months."

"I know, son. I just worry about you, that's all."

"I'll be okay."

The next couple of days were spent packing and repacking my suitcase. It's always been a habit of mine, checking things that don't need checking. I'd packed the case myself, but I still went through the little inventory to ensure I'd remembered everything. I found myself doing this every four or five hours until Dad got sick of it on Monday morning and said, throwing down his newspaper, "For fuck's sake, Eddy. Give it a rest. If you check that case one more time before tonight, I'll shut you up in it."

For the rest of the day and evening I just sort of hung around, too nervous to do anything but pace around. On Dad's recommendation, I decided to get an early night and went up to bed at around nine o'clock. Mum and Dad were just getting ready to watch the news. I stood in the doorway and whispered quietly: "Night Mum, Dad."

They both looked round. I could see from Mum's eyes that she was holding back the waterworks and Dad seemed to be wavering behind his familiar stoics mask.

"Night, son," they said in unison, and I closed the door quietly behind me.

My sleep was incredibly fitful. I had all sorts of odd dreams that I couldn't recollect then or now. I remember lying on my back under the duvet, with both arms behind my head, willing myself to sleep. I must have got off at some stage though, because the next thing I remember was waking up. It was broad daylight and it was time to join the Army.

Chapter 2

The Four Feathers

Dad gave me a lift to the station. Neither of us spoke during the drive, and the silence was only broken by the music coming from the one working speaker of the cassette recorder. I don't think Johnny Cash was the right choice for the moment. I was extremely nervous about what was waiting to greet me at Harrogate, and Johnny crooning throatily about prisons and shooting people wasn't helping. We got to Victoria Station with 15 minutes to spare. Dad helped me to the platform with my bags. He had to be at work, so he couldn't hang around to see me off. He went to shake my hand, but when he took it, realised that something more than that was required. He pulled me close in to him and hugged me. We stayed like that for a few seconds and when he pulled back, he had tears in his eyes. I'd never seen him cry before and was taken aback so I tried to reassure him.

"I'll be alright, Dad."

He smiled with an effort.

"I know, son. Now listen. If this isn't for you, don't be bloody scared to say so. The world's full of people doing jobs they don't like. If it gets too hard, or it doesn't turn out like you thought it would, you can come home and try something else."

I nodded, and he continued, whilst picking up my holdall and moving towards the empty carriage.

"Mind you," he cautioned, "don't give up too easy. I can't imagine that it's going to be pleasant, but us Nugents have never been quitters." There it was, that word again. My recent trauma at the hands of the Mad

Major swooped into view and I gave an involuntary shudder. I climbed on with my suitcase, and put it into the luggage rack, leaving Dad at the door. I went back and took the holdall from him. As I shut the door, I pulled the window down to talk to him.

"Right then, Dad. See you soon, hopefully."

"Okay, son. I need to shoot off to work now anyway. Take care of yourself and keep your head down. Don't get noticed and you'll be alright." He ruffled my hair with his right hand.

"Go on. Get sat down or you'll lose your seat." I looked around and saw that the carriage was starting to fill up. We said our final goodbye and Dad spun smartly on his heel and strode quickly up the platform. I watched him get to the ticket inspection point, then I shut the window and made my way to the seat.

In the ten minutes before we left, I watched a few more easily identifiable Harrogate recruits, board the train. Even though they were camouflaged amongst the other passengers, commuters mainly, they stuck out like sore thumbs. New haircuts, uncomfortable shirts and ties, plus an over-abundance of baggage for 16-year-old lads made them difficult to miss. As the guard started making his way up the platform, shutting doors, a few were still saying goodbye. One lad had almost an entire football team of relatives seeing him off. He was being patted on the head, slapped on the back and hugged simultaneously. He pulled himself away like a pop star avoiding autograph hunters, and boarded the train one carriage down from me. Several other lads, cutting it fine and with no one to see them off, had to open doors that the guard had already shut, to make it on.

When the whistle finally went and the train pulled off, I still had a double seat to myself and tried to settle down, despite my nerves. I had my travel instructions tucked safely into the arse pocket of my trousers but still took them out every few minutes to check. The trip to Leeds would take about an hour, then we would change for the onward service to Harrogate. I spent the entire journey gazing out of the window, attempting to take in a bit of the scenery. Every now and again we went through a tunnel and my reflection stared back at me. It seemed to be saying 'You daft twat,' so I ignored it. The only other thing I remember from our crossing of the West Yorkshire countryside was a sign outside a farm. It was a large wooden panel, cut out to represent the front part of a pig, with some wording that had been done with a thick black paintbrush. All it said was: "Half a pig, fifteen quid." It helped to cement the feeling that I was moving from one world to another. When the train pulled in to Leeds station, there was the usual panicked rush to change platforms, to make the connection in time. According to my instructions, I had 20 minutes to get to platform 5C, but I ran anyway, blundering through the station with my bags, like an old lady with an eye on a jumble-sale bargain. The dash was pointless, leaving me with a quarter of an hour to kill. The train was waiting, but the automatic doors hadn't been opened. I found an empty bench and sat wearily. Over the next ten minutes, the platform filled with the same young faces, all nervously smoking, or introducing themselves to people, in the hope of getting a little bit of information about the forthcoming experience, that would help to allay their fears. Just before the train doors hissed open, I was joined on the bench by a lad who was struggling with six bags. I immediately started worrying about what I might have forgotten. I had a good look around the platform. Everyone's luggage was piled up, which made it hard to attribute bags to owners, but I took some solace in the fact that everybody seemed to be averaging two or three cases. Eager to befriend a fellow traveller, I nodded to the lad, a stocky guy with a ginger flat-top, and said: "Fuckin' hell, mate. You've got a lot of stuff there."

He looked at me quizzically and replied: "All essential gear, mate. You only got the two bags then?"

"I've got everything they put on the list," I protested.

"I didn't go off their list. Me Dad's in the Green Howards, so he told me what to take."

I was going to find out the hard way that being the first soldier in the family was going to have drawbacks. It was a big advantage to know someone who'd been through the same training, who could provide hints and tips that would help avoid the pitfalls that I was going to stumble into with every step.

We were interrupted by an automated metallic voice, coming from the train, informing us that the doors were opening. Everyone started gathering up his luggage and cramming it onto the two-carriage express. By the time I got on, all the seats were taken, so I stood by the doors and dropped my bags. The doors closed and the train moved off silently. The journey only took half an hour and as we travelled through Burley, Kirkstall, Horsforth, Weeton, Pannal and Oatlands the mood grew palpably more sombre and conversation dwindled to a few hushed exchanges. As the train slid into Harrogate station, everyone already had their bags in their hands waiting for the loco to stop. When it did, we all spilled through the open doors and on to the platform.

As I lumbered down the concourse, I noticed an old man in Army uniform. He was holding a clipboard, and directing some of the lads who had got off the train before me, to go outside. When I got nearer, I saw that the old codger had a name tag that read 'Lang' on his chest. He had a black cane with a metallic end under one arm, and a black arm band with the letters RP emblazoned on it in red, on the other. Soon I was close enough to ask for directions. I looked him up and down discreetly. He had the gaunt, craggy features of Old Man Steptoe.

He told the lad in front of me to get on the green bus outside and then I was next. I was shitting myself with nerves and before I could speak, the old coot looked up and barked: "Name?"

"Eddy. Eddy Nugent."

He scowled at me, and shot back: "Eddy Nugent, what?"

In a moment of panic induced confusion, I thought that he wanted me to give him more details about myself, so I said: "Eddy Nugent, from Manchester, er, Sir."

"SIR! Fucking, Sir! I'm not a fucking Sir, Nugent. I work for a living. Do you understand?"

"Yes."

"Yes, fucking what?" He screeched whilst pointing at the single chevron on his right arm.

I wasn't stupid, and I knew that he wanted me to call him by his rank, but I didn't have a clue what it was. My stomach was tied in knots with worry. I'd only been off the train for five minutes and I was in the shit already. So I just pulled a rank out of my head that I had heard in a war film at one time or another.

"Yes… Corporal."

"That's more like it you horrible, lazy, bastard. Now get on that fucking green bus in the car park, and I'll be watching you, lad."

It was extremely fortuitous that I said the correct rank, because if I had been wrong with the first one, the only others that I knew were Squadron-Leader, Admiral and Centurion. Although the latter was probably the mouldy old git's last rank, before he got demoted for having excessive dandruff.

I shuffled outside, put my bags in the luggage compartment of the bus and climbed aboard. The coach interior was very spartan, with uncomfortable, thinly-padded, green bench-seats that had metal rails for headrests. Everyone had a double seat to himself, and nobody was mixing or talking to anyone else. I too was silent, and my mind was awash with visions of terrible punishments for getting lippy with the old corporal. I kept thinking to myself it wasn't my fault. How was I supposed to know his rank! Oh, God! They're going to kick me out already! What if I can't find a job and have to become a tramp?!

Soon all of the double seats were taken, and the guys coming on board now were starting to fill up the gaps on the bus. A chubby kid sat next to me. At least there would be one person who I could beat on a run, I thought. It's amazing, what things can give you a bit of comfort when you think you are in dire straits. Once the bus was full, the driver started the engine and the old corporal climbed aboard. The pneumatic doors closed behind him with a hiss and he braced himself in the aisle. When what little conversation there was died down, he sneered: "Right, you little fuckers! You're in the Army now! So when I speak to you, you will call me Corporal. Do you understand?"

"YES, CORPORAL!" came the loud reply in unison. Although there was one voice that deviated from the required response. A tall lad, two seats in front of me, must have also noticed Lance-Corporal Lang's similarity to Steptoe Senior. Because instead of shouting "Yes, Corporal," with the rest of us, he called out "You dirty old man," in the manner of Harry H. Corbett. Unfortunately for the would-be comic, by the time we had said our bit his lone impression was still in full flow, and the "old man" part trailed away into silence, and then he realised just how badly he had fucked up. Lance-Corporal Lang turned scarlet with rage and he was about an inch away from having steam coming out of his ears, to the accompaniment of the noise from a locomotive whistle. The bus was deathly quiet aside from the occasional suppressed snigger, but the majority of us were shocked into wide-eyed silence. I was just thinking that this would be a smoke screen for my minor altercation, when Lang took a step forward.

"What's your fucking name?" he bellowed to the joker.

"Smith, Corporal."

"Right, Smith. Me and you are going to have fucking words."

Then to our surprise, Lang just sat down and the bus pulled out of the car park and headed towards camp.

I didn't take in any of the scenery on the drive, and I just stared at my troubled reflection in the window. I did, however, notice the transition from the light stone houses of the town, to the darker greenery of the countryside. Soon, we were climbing a foreboding hill that had a cross-junction at the top. Once there, we travelled down a straight and level lane that had a small housing estate and what looked like the huts from *Tenko* on the right. Then, after a while, the camp perimeter came into view on the left. It seemed to be in the middle of nowhere, making it extremely open to the elements.

Then – the moment of truth – the bus slowed and we turned in through the gates. I was in awe of everything, even the guy on the gate, because he had passed basic training and I hadn't.

I was snapped out of my gawping by the bus suddenly coming to a stop outside the guardroom. Then Lang stood up and shouted: "Right, Smith! You funny fucker! Get off the shagging bus!"

Smith didn't move at first and just looked around the bus as if one of us would offer some advice, but we were all as scared as each other and could be of no use. Then Lang called out again: "Come on, you cunt. Get the fuck off the fucking bus now!"

Smith slowly stood, and Lang harangued him all the way down the aisle.

"Take your fucking time, Smith! Don't hurry whatever you do, you cunt. I've got all shagging day!"

Smith sped up and jogged along the aisle and down the steps. Once outside and on the tarmac, Smith was subjected to Lang's full arsenal of insults. Then, to my horror, he was marched into the guardroom jail at a ridiculously fast pace.

A minute or so later, Lang came back out of the building, and on to the bus again. He looked very smug, and he shouted: "Any other comedians?" When there was no reply, the bus set off and turned right along the road, which ran parallel to the inside of the perimeter fence. We passed a large boiler house with a chimney, and a strange round building with a sign saying 'NAAFI' outside it. Then a series of four-storey accommodation blocks came into view. We stopped outside the corner of where two blocks met, and Lang read out a list of names, then told all the people who had been called out that they were to be in Scott Squadron, and to get off the bus. As soon as the Scott Squadron guys started to filter down the steps, they were verbally set upon by a group of young junior ranks, who shouted: "Hurry the fuck up," and "sort your fucking shit out!" They were then herded into one of the blocks and out of sight.

Then Lang read out another list of names, and when mine was called out, my heart skipped a beat. Although I was relieved to an extent, because he didn't berate me for my earlier altercation, he then said: "Right, you lot are Rawson Squadron, so get the fuck off the bus."

We all stood up and made our way down the aisle. As soon as the first of us stepped on to the ground, another group of blokes, about a year older than myself, came out from the block and started to shout abuse at us, that was identical to that which had been used on the Scott Squadron guys.

There was a mad scrabble for our cases from the belly of the coach, and as soon as I had my baggage, I just turned and followed the person in front of me. There were so many NCOs shouting so much abuse, and so loud, that – as we clambered up the stairs of the block – the hollering seemed to form one unintelligible downpour of swear words and threats. I didn't dare look at any of the instructors, for fear of some unspeakable reprisal.

When we reached the first floor, we were directed to our right, and through some brown double fire doors. We were then told to give our names, and were lined up along the wall in alphabetical order. Even though we were stood perfectly still and looking above the heads of the NCOs, they still shouted at us for some imaginary crime, whilst stalking the corridor and eyeballing us. Soon another coach load of recruits turned up, and they were integrated into our group through the same medium of loud swearing.

Once we were all there, we were each assigned a bed – eight of us per room. Then we dropped off our cases, and were herded back down the stairs into the quadrangle, which was formed by the accommodation blocks. After the palaver of trying to form three ranks, we were turned to our left and marched to the cookhouse for our first taste of Army cuisine. None of us was in step and the ripple effect of our pathetic attempt at marching resembled the legwork of a drunken millipede. After a short while, we were marching down a covered walkway, with grubby glass walls. This walkway was the approach to the cookhouse and it came in from several directions.

One of the instructors called for the squad to halt, and numerous comedy collisions took place, with some of us stopping dead, whilst the rest carried on marching. Our disorganised state earned us more grippings.

"You useless bastards! You cunts can't do fuck all. Now line up against the glass wall on the right, and get in single, shaggin' file!"

There was a scrabble as we attempted to obey the order and the transition from three ranks to single file was mayhem. I ended up in the middle of the line, and soon we started moving closer towards the cookhouse.

Once inside, I sneaked a brief look around. There was an illuminated hot plate with a line of cooks, wearing stained whites, standing behind it. Some of the tables had soldiers in uniform sitting around them. These blokes looked across at us and laughed whilst making the odd comment about us being a 'bunch of wankers'. One of the NCOs caught me looking and was immediately in my face.

"What the fuck are you looking at, you cunt?"

"Nothing, Corporal!" I replied. Luckily he had the same rank as Lang, so I knew what it was.

He pointed to the guys in uniform who were already eating, then hissed: "Don't you fucking dare look at them, you're not worthy."

I don't know what he expected me to do, if I wasn't worthy of looking at anybody who was out of basic training, then I'd spend most of my time with my eyes shut. Surely this would raise some serious safety issues, especially when undergoing firearms training.

To appease the situation, I just looked up and ahead of me, then said: "Yes, Corporal!"

Then he was away to grip someone else for an equally trivial crime.

After a while, I was bearing down on the hotplate. The meal itself was not too far removed from school dinners. There were the staple foods such as chips, sausage, pies, beans etc. However, the people serving the food were very different. As opposed to the red faced, friendly, dinner ladies that I had known in school, these people, whilst still red faced, were cantankerous, borderline psychotics with all manner of skin disorders. I made a mental note to stay clear of the Cornflakes at breakfast. As I moved along the hotplate, I was met with scowls from the chefs, and I felt like they personally hated me for making them have to work. So I just got my scoff as fast as I could, and took it to an empty table where I began to eat at a leisurely pace.

I had only got halfway through my meal, when the NCOs stood up and shouted: "Right, Rawson Squadron recruits. Get outside now!"

Not one of us had finished our food, and we looked around at each other in dismay. But the instructor, who had just shouted the order, reiterated his point by bellowing: "FUCKING GET OUTSIDE NOW, RAWSON RECRUITS!"

Spurred on by the level of the NCO's rage, we all made for the exits as soon as possible – even some of the blokes who were just coming off the hotplate with a tray full of food. Our first lesson had been learned: Get your food eaten as fast as possible, because the NCOs went through first, and as soon as they had finished their scoff, it was time to leave. This lesson meant that come the next meal, there was plenty of physical jostling for a good place in the queue. If you were last to get served, then table manners had to be suspended and you would just eat your scoff as you went down the hotplate.

Once back outside and in the covered walkway, we were put into three ranks again and 'marched' out past the back of the accommodation, where the bus had dropped us off before. From there, we went back down the road in the direction of the guardroom looking like Napoleon's retreat from Moscow. On passing the boiler house again, we turned right down towards a large, derelict-looking building and came to a shambling halt at its doors. I noticed the word 'CINEMA' above them – a seemingly ambitious claim, I thought. To the left of the main entrance was a wall-mounted poster, informing us all excitedly that 'Trading Places' was coming soon, only three years after everyone else had seen it. I wasn't used to the constant yelling, and jumped a little when one of the instructors roared: "Front rank, file in." Then there was a picosecond pause before he added: "Get a fucking wiggle on, you lazy fucking gobshites."

Harried, scared and nervous, the front rank did as it was told, followed by the middle and rear, under constant vocal bombardment. Glancing timidly left and right as we went through the foyer, I could see that, as cinemas went, it was a bare-arsed affair. Dour shades of purple and blue reigned, with none of the usual accoutrements like a popcorn stand or a gorgeous, thick-skulled ticket lady. We were herded down the central aisle and down to the front and were instructed via points, threats and grunts to file into the first empty row. Sitting down was bliss. Regardless of the abuse, it was enjoyable to take advantage of the surprisingly soft furnishings. As the rest of the intake moved into their seats, I took the liberty of having a look round. On the wall to my left was a collection of dark wooden panels, listing in gold lettering, the names and tenure dates of all the Commanding Officers of the College. On the right were similar boards giving the same information for the AT RSMs. Once sat down, our numbers seemed quite impressive. With the four squadrons' intakes combined, there were about 400 of us. The NCOs had all taken up position to the rear of the seating, lining the back wall like a row of evil usherettes. One of them spotted me staring and sneered: "Can I get you a fucking choc-ice or anything?"

I turned back round quickly and tried to disappear into my seat. He didn't get the chance to reprimand me any further, as a huge man came striding down the aisle. He was at least six feet three and marched so purposefully that he made it to the front in about eight paces. He turned and engaged us grimly. Our silence descended to a new level. He opened up in a Glaswegian baritone that sounded like he'd been gargling glass.

"Good afternoon, gentlemen." Without waiting for a response, he continued: "My name is Company Sergeant-Major Hendricks of Penney Squadron." He turned to stare at the Penney recruits who were sitting to his left near the back.

"Those of you in my squadron will get to know me very well over the next two years. I'm not very good with names, so those of you whose names I can recall will either have done something to impress me, or acted the cunt. Either way, you'll remember me."

Hendricks was scaring the shit out of me, at a distance of 40 feet. This was getting to be like a bad joke. Every newly introduced member of the DS was worse than the previous one. It was both well choreographed and utterly depressing. Hendricks' voice shook me out of my fugue.

"The rest of you will meet your company sergeant-majors soon. They are all as nice as me, so you won't be disappointed. You're here now to meet the two most important men in your life for the next two years. You will be addressed first by the RSM, and secondly by the Camp Commandant. When the RSM walks into the room, I will give you the command 'Sit Up'. You will then sit up so straight in your seats, that all your vertebrae will fuse simultaneously. Understood? Good."

He moved to the side of the cinema, and stood, poker straight, with his eyes looking expectantly towards the entrance. There was utter silence, punctuated only by a tiny, nervous fart from someone in front of me. I heard the foyer door being pushed open, and glanced at Sergeant-Major Hendricks, just in time to hear him shout his command. The entire room stiffened, and 400 sets of peripheral vision tried to clock the RSM as he boomed down the aisle. As he got to the front, he executed a perfect parade ground halt, no doubt doing additional damage to an already threadbare carpet. He then spun round, in a perfect about-turn and slammed his right foot down to complete the movement, almost putting it through the floor. It was a full three seconds before he spoke and he cast his gaze critically on a sweeping panorama of the room. He wasn't as tall as Hendricks, probably five feet nine, but he was more powerfully built, like an all in wrestler. His stable belt was wrapped round a prodigious beer-gut, which was straining to escape both above and below it. His pace stick was jammed tight under his left arm and his boots were shinier than it was possible for non-metallic objects to be. His head was all hat. He obviously subscribed to the little man–big hat school of thought and peered at us from under its enormous peak, denying us eye contact and increasing his aura of danger. His voice, when it emerged, took us by complete surprise.

"Good afternoon to you all. My name is Warrant Officer First Class, Regimental Sergeant-Major Banning, of the Coldstream Guards."

There was a trace of a Cornish accent, but his tone was light and almost too quiet to hear clearly.

"I am responsible for your discipline and well being, whilst serving at this training establishment. I am an extremely fair man, with high standards both given and demanded. If you try your hardest and endeavour to honour the words in your oath to Her Majesty the Queen, you will find me to be no enemy."

That sounded fair enough to me. His delivery was calm and measured and made me feel that perhaps there were small pockets of sanity existing in the place. But, of course, there was more, and it made my dread return immediately. He removed his pace stick from under his arm and pointed it in our general direction. With no change in his manner, he said: "If any of you besmirch the good name of this College, or bring the smallest aspect of the Army into disrepute, I will stick this pace stick right up your arse. It will need two strong men, armed with bolt croppers to retrieve it, and when they do, it won't be me that cleans the shit off it."

It was at that supremely inopportune moment, that someone coughed loudly. It may have been the nervous farter, or someone close by. The result was predictable. The RSM turned to face him, and asked him quietly: "Do you think it's polite to interrupt a Regimental Sergeant-Major while he's speaking?"

The guilty lad was beyond speech, and simply sat and stared, and waited for whatever was coming next. The RSM raised his voice to the Senior NCOs at the back of the room.

"Sergeant Bolton, please remove this man to the guardroom and ensure that he understands his folly."

For the capital crime of performing a reflex bodily action, the guilty party was ordered into the aisle and marched away, forever, probably.

As if nothing had happened, RSM Banning made a polite enquiry.

“Would anyone else like to cough?”

He took our terrified hush as a no.

“There you have it in a nutshell boys. Stick to the rules and you’ll have no problem. Fuck me or any of my staff about, and you will receive no quarter.”

He glanced at his watch and said: “The Commandant will be entering the building shortly. I will give the same command to sit up that Company Sergeant-Major Hendricks gave you earlier. Make sure your response is equally observed.”

He moved to stand by CSM Hendricks and adopted an identical pose. Despite all the fear that they’d managed to instil into me, it was at this point that I was able to start laughing at my predicament, internally of course. They looked such a pair of cunts stood there. You’d have thought God Himself was about to walk through the door, if their chin jutting, deadly serious expressions were anything to go by. I got the sneaking suspicion that thinking this way was going to be a useful release valve.

We were all anticipating the sound of the doors opening, and when they did, we made ready to brace ourselves up after the RSM’s command.

“Sit up.”

From the back, it must have looked like an attempt to break the ‘most people doing an impression of being executed in Texas’ record, as the Commandant moved quietly down to the front. As he neared the RSM, Banning sprang to life and made a show of marching three feet towards the Commandant before completing another exaggerated drill movement. In tones barely higher than whispers, the RSM informed the CO that the new intake were awaiting his instruction. The RSM then retreated to his initial position by the stage after being thanked by the CO. Whilst this short pantomime was being enacted, I checked out the Commandant. He was shorter again than the RSM, probably about five feet seven, and his build was slight. He was in Number Two dress and looked pretty snappy. A pair of well polished, brown shoes finished the look. The only person I'd ever seen dressed like this before was the Brigadier from *Doctor Who*. The CO removed his hat and turned to face his audience, knocking us completely off guard, by producing a huge smile.

"Sit at ease please, boys," he invited. I only relaxed a fraction, letting my shoulders slump slightly. He continued to smile without speaking, mentally preparing an off-the-cuff speech. After a few seconds, looking up and down the rows of shell-shocked faces, he began.

"Good afternoon, and welcome to Uniacke Barracks, home of the Royal Corps of Signals Army Apprentices' College, Harrogate. My name is Lieutenant-Colonel De La Tour and I am the Commandant of this fine establishment."

His accent was neither posh nor common, but hovered somewhere near 'wannabe aristocrat'. It did sound like he was having to put it on a bit, and that maybe his background wasn't quite as high-falutin' as he'd have us believe. I'd heard a teacher talking like that once. I'd had to drop off a note at the staff room and went in, after knocking, to find Mr Lever talking to his bank manager on the phone. When he was teaching us French, he had a slight West Lancashire accent, but the bloke at Barclays must have thought he was talking to a minor royal. It seemed like De La Tour was exhibiting a similar verbal idiosyncrasy. I could just imagine him going home after a hard day's commandanting, taking off his hat and coat and greeting his wife with: "Nah then, lass. Give us a great, big fooking kiss."

He looked at the RSM and then back to us.

"By now, you've met a couple of the personalities that make up our little family. The thing that you must always bear in mind is that we are here to help you in your undertaking to become trained soldiers. None of my staff are paid to mess you around unnecessarily and they will endeavour to help you find your way, without having to resort to threats or punishment."

Now I was confused. This didn't seem to tally up with anything we'd experienced so far.

"However, if you are failing to achieve the standards laid down by me, then I fully expect my NCOs and Senior NCOs to encourage you along, perhaps with some gentle chiding."

The RSM's face was totally inscrutable, but I could see that Hendricks was cracking into an almost imperceptible grin. Just like it's rumoured that the Queen thinks the world smells of fresh paint, the Commandant had a slightly lopsided view of 'his' College. As soon as he was around, the shouting and abuse stopped and was replaced by constructive criticism.

"There will be times when some of you feel homesick or that you are simply unable to continue, for many reasons. If you find yourself in this position, inform any permanent member of staff and you will receive a sympathetic hearing."

The light chuckle coming from the line of NCOs at the back was quickly strangled by a ferocious look from the RSM.

"Don't forget to try and enjoy this experience. You are embarking on an adventure that will see you emerge in just under two years, as trained soldiers and tradesmen in our esteemed Corps. It's not for the faint-hearted and no doubt a few of you will fall by the wayside, but those of you who complete your training, will have gained something to be fiercely proud of. I'll now leave you in the capable hands of the RSM, and would just like to congratulate you all on choosing a career in the Royal Corps of Signals. Carry on RSM."

"Sit up," bellowed Banning and we complied immediately, as the Commandant took a leisurely stroll back up the cinema aisle, smiling. As soon as he was through the double doors and out of earshot, the dark cloud that had temporarily been dispersed returned with vigour. Of course, it was Army policy that none of the NCOs or the RSM would publicly disagree with anything the Commandant said, particularly in front of junior ranks. Nevertheless, the sniggers and grins made it quite apparent, to anyone with the tiniest amount of perception, that they all thought he was spouting utter bollocks. He probably thought we were going straight back to the block, from the cinema, for a big sing-song with the NCOs.

We hadn't been sat at ease since the Commandant left, so the RSM left without requiring us to stiffen up theatrically. When he'd gone, CSM Hendricks waited for a few seconds and followed him without another word. The second the doors closed behind him, the braying returned immediately. We were 'encouraged along' and 'gently chided' by the NCOs until we got back outside the cinema. Once again, they optimistically tried to get us to march as a squad, presumably to give them some more abuse ammunition, as if they needed it.

When we made it back in front of the block, we were halted in the quadrangle facing the Squadron offices. At this point, all of the AT NCOs gathered in front of us. This was one of the things I'd never be able to reconcile myself with throughout my time at the College. I'd love to have met the bright spark at the MOD, who'd thought that it was a great idea to put 17-year-olds, who'd been in the Army a year, in charge of their younger colleagues. It was a revelation of man-management, straight from the William Golding school of social studies.

The AT NCOs loitered around, eyeing us up for an excuse to give us an ear-bashing. But we had already learned to avoid eye contact and to say fuck all, unless something was asked of us.

Then, after a couple of minutes, what looked like a werewolf in a dress and a tramp in uniform came out of the Squadron offices.

The tramp spoke: "Good afternoon, gents. I am Corporal Timms and I am in charge of the Squadron stores. So when you get your webbing, your lids, and all that, you will get it from me. I will also give you all of the shit that you need to keep the block clean. Is that clear?"

"Yes, Corporal!"

He then pointed a shaking hand to the cross-dressing lycanthrope, and said: "And this lovely lady is Dawn. She is the Squadron Clerk, and will deal with all of your administrative problems. So you will treat her with respect. Is that also clear?"

"Yes, Corporal!"

Corporal Timms was a scruffy bastard. His uniform looked like he had just pulled it off a dead body, and he himself had the appearance of having been on a dirty protest, with nothing to keep him company other than a year's supply of meths. His ensemble would have been complete, had he been using a length of electrical flex to hold up his trousers. My blind respect for anyone with rank had just taken its first knock.

Dawn, the Clerk, seemed like a nice enough girl. Although a bit timid, she was of a pleasant disposition. But fuck me was she hairy! Not the soft ladies fluff that's noticeable on some women, should you catch it from the wrong angle. No, this woman had proper whiskers that you could light a match off. If she'd been a man, she'd have been charged for not shaving.

Following the introductions by the cast of Carry On Screaming, two other permanent staff came out of the office. They were both medium-sized men, again in uniform, but they were carrying pace sticks and wearing a blue sash each that ran diagonally across their chests.

They looked like also-rans from a military beauty contest.

Both men also wore forage caps (more commonly known as 'twat hats'), with the peaks running straight down their faces, thus compressing their noses and obscuring their eyes. When they addressed us, they had to tilt their heads back and look down their noses at us.

The one on the right spoke first and out of the side of his mouth.

"Gentlemen!" his voice boomed, "I am Sergeant Atkins. And this," he gesticulated to the other sergeant with his stick, "is Sergeant Bailey. Soon you will be split into different troops, and one of us will be your troop sergeant, and from that moment forth you will fucking hate us. Do I make myself understood?"

"Yes, Sergeant!" We hollered. But amidst our call, a single whining voice could be made out saying "Yes Corporal."

All the instructors, both permanent staff and junior soldiers, heard it, and in a flash had congregated around a pencil-thin kid, who looked a bit like a girl.

"What the fuck did you call me?" screamed Atkins.

"Corporal, Sergeant," replied the quivering youth.

"WHY!? Do I look like a corporal?"

"No, Corp… er, Sergeant."

Atkins stepped forward until he was almost nose to nose with the unfortunate youth.

"What's your fucking name?" he hissed through gritted teeth.

"Rose, Sergeant." He was close to tears when he replied.

"Are you sure it's not Pansy? Do you play any musical instruments, Rose?"

"Yes, Sergeant. The guitar, Sergeant."

"Bollocks, you play the fucking pink piccolo, or is it the blue veined flute? You'd better sort your fucking shit out and stark fucking sparking, Pansy. Or you will end up in a world of hurt."

With that, Atkins, Bailey, and all the other non-recruits, moved off to the sides, and the final introduction of the Squadron hierarchy took place.

Three men walked out, the first, who was also wielding a pace stick, had a badge on the sleeve of his right arm. The other two had their rank atop their shoulders. The first man, with the stick, screamed a word of command: "SQUA', SQUAAAAAAAAA', CHAAA! Standstill!"

This unintelligible noise, like a sound effect from a karate film, made all the other people in uniform spring to attention. Then the smallest of the three men stepped forward, his rank was denoted by a crown on his epaulettes. He spoke in 1950s BBC English.

"Ah, yes, gentlemen. Welcome to Rawson Squadron. You will soon learn that this is the best squadron in this College, and that to let the standard slip would be a terrible error on your behalf. I am the officer commanding the Squadron, Major Tatchell. This is Captain Bassett, my second in command." He pointed to the other officer, who was much older and bigger and also had a broken nose. He looked like he had been in the Army since the Battle of the Bulge.

Major Tatchell then gestured to the third man who had come out with them and who had made the strange shouting noises. "And this is Sergeant-Major Horton. You will get to know him very well in the future gentlemen, just make sure that it is for all the right reasons."

SSM Horton could have been Tatchell's brother. They were both short slender men, with hook noses and hooded eyes and seemed to radiate an air of a wholly unpleasant persuasion. Like a couple of evil Smurfs.

Tatchell looked up and down our group of scruffy youngsters, then he sniffed the air, spun on his heel and called: "Carry on, Sergeant-Major!"

"SAH!" replied Horton, as he snapped up an immaculate salute. Then when both officers had gone, he turned to Sergeants Atkins and Bailey and told them to get us processed. Then he too returned to his office.

The two sergeants had a conversation with the junior instructors and Dawn, who then went up into the accommodation block.

Then Bailey spoke: “Right, gents. When I fall you out, get your lazy arses up into your shaggin’ rooms and get your documentation that you were told to bring. Then be out in the fucking corridor before I arrive, or there will be hell to pay!”

He paused, sucked in a lung-full of air then made the same kind of noises that the SSM had earlier: “SQUA, FAAAAAAAAAAALLLLLLL, ITE!”

As soon as he had given the word, the junior NCOs started shouting and herding us up the stairs, occasionally slipping in an assisting boot up the ring.

We sprinted up the corridor, panting and frantic. The corridor itself was split into three parts, each separated from one another by double doors, and containing three sleeping rooms, one set of toilets, one drying room and one set of showers and sinks. I was in the middle room of the corridor, so I got to my kit quite quickly. Luckily I had stashed my documents at the top of my bag, so I got back out into the corridor well within time. The NCOs had wedged the double doors back, so the corridor was open to its full extent and I could see Dawn at the far end, sitting behind a table laden with files.

When Sergeant Bailey came up the stairs, there were still some lads rummaging frantically through their kit to find their documentation.

Bailey went mad.

“WHAT DID I SAY? WHAT THE FUCK DID I FUCKING SAY? BE OUT IN THE CUNTING CORRIDOR, WITH YOUR FUCKING DOCS BEFORE I GET UP HERE. AND YOU CAN’T EVEN FUCKING GET THAT RIGHT! YOU FUCKING WANKERS! THIS IS A VERY FUCKING BAD

START GENTLEMEN, VERY BAD IN-FUCKING-DEED!"

I could feel a wave of trepidation sweep through us recruits. Bailey waited until the last man was out in the corridor with his documents. He then told us all to turn to our right, and the first man at the head of the line then dressed forward with his birth certificate, and Dawn processed him into the Army. After what seemed like an eternity, I was next in line. I gave Dawn my documents; she yawned and scratched her chin. It sounded like a path being swept with a stiff broom. I closed my eyes and shuddered, but all I could visualise was a big pig, rubbing its side up against a tree. I was pulled out of my hideous thoughts, when Dawn told me my Army number and also said not to forget it. So as I returned to my room, I just repeated the number over and over in my head, and it helped drive out the last remnants of the swine visions.

I was the first person to get back to the room, and I took advantage of the relative calm to remember my number. Once it was ingrained into my mind, I surveyed the room. There were two doors leading in. On entering from the first door, there was a bunk bed with two lockers on the right, on the other side of which was an identical arrangement next to the window. This layout was duplicated around the room, except for the back right-hand corner where there was a single bed with a locker. I didn't know who that belonged to. It was made up, unlike the bunks which were bare of even mattresses. My exposure to the other guys in the room had been negligible, as we had only briefly passed each other as we dropped our bags off, or picked up our docs. But soon they started to filter in.

They were all just nondescript kids, like myself. Most of them were, like me, scrawny, although one of them was a bit overweight. We were all quiet and engrossed in our own troublesome thoughts, when one of them piped up in London accent: "Alwight, lads. We've got to get to know each uvver, so I'm Paul, Paul Jones."

I followed next and just told them my name, then the rest of the lads took it in turns. The fat kid was called Alistair McKenzie and was from an obscure village in Hampshire. There was Steve Keets from Nottingham, Tom Galbraith from Glasgow, Colin Mortimer from Newcastle, and finally, two friends who had joined up together in Warrington, Barry Nash and Neil Moody.

The initial conversation between us was brief and nervous. Cockney Paul, as he had been before, was by far the loudest and most vocal. He seemed very confident, and had, along with Alistair been in the Army Cadets before joining up. Inevitably, both of the ex-cadets, on finding out that none of the rest of us had any similar experience, took on an air of superiority, and started trying to give an impromptu drill lesson to the rest of us. It was a waste of time really. I just gazed miserably at them, as they marked time on the spot, shouting at themselves. It just looked like one of the things I was never going to get the hang of. The display was cut short by the instructors screaming for us to get out into the corridor again. Once out there, we were told, with another fanfare of shouting, that we were now to be issued our bedding and shown how to assemble our bedblocks. What the fuck was a bedblock? Whatever it was, I was already betting it wouldn't be something pleasant, to help make our lives easier. No doubt, we wouldn't be kept in suspense for too long. We were taken down to the bedding store, which was adjacent to Corporal Timms' grotto. Twenty minutes later, we were back in the room with our newly issued kit. It consisted of two pillows, two sheets, two pillowcases, a counterpane and four grey blankets. None of the items looked remotely inviting. Both my pillows had decorative slobber stains. The counterpane had a hideous orange, seventies pattern. The blankets were almost too painful to carry. They were bristly enough to feel like a scratchier version of loft insulation. I ditched them all on my bed. I'd opted for the bottom bunk near the door. The mattress was clean and white and had green stripes running the length of it, making it look like a Pacer. Steve Keets took the top bunk and started to put his gear on the mattress. Barry and Neil, being mates, buddied up in the nearest bunk, with the two ex-cadets, Paul and Alistair deciding it would be a good idea to share. That left the last bunk to Tom and Colin. Tom asked the question that was on all of our minds.

"What's a bedblock then, Paul?"

In his capacity, as temporary military attaché to Room 4 Recruit Troop he began to explain: "It's just another thing to fuck us about with. It's a way of folding your blankets and sheets for inspection. It looks like a big liquorice allsort and it's a cunt to get the hang of."

Just as he was about to go into a bit more detail, the 'corridor' shout came again, and we rushed out of the room, dropping everything. Neither of the permanent sergeants was around now, so we were entirely in the hands of the AT NCOs. There were six lance-corporals, three corporals and a sergeant. The sergeant's special status was defined by a red sash and pace stick, and he quickly introduced himself.

"Afternoon, tossers. I'm AT Sergeant Bramhall and my sole job in life for the next 14 weeks is to fuck you about until you hate me so much you'll want to kill me."

I'd only known him for eight seconds, and I'd have happily done him some serious physical damage, if I was quite a lot harder; he couldn't see my face, and I could blame someone else.

"Tonight, your room NCOs will be in charge of you. Sergeant Atkins will be going round the block at eight o'clock tomorrow morning, and your rooms will be fucking spotless. If they're not..." he trailed off for a second and smiled, "well, we'll see what fucking happens. Before tea, Corporal Edgeley will come round to your rooms, one by one, and show how to get your bedblocks ready for the morning. When I say 'go,' get back to your rooms. Oh, by the way, if I catch any fucker sitting on a bed or leaning against a locker, between now and December, I'll throw him out the nearest window. GO!" We ran back into our room and tried our hardest to stand around in a military fashion. It seemed a bit unfair about the bed and locker thing. There were only four chairs round the table, so those of us that didn't get one had to just stand around, like drunks waiting for a pub to open.

Twenty minutes later, Corporal Edgeley wandered in with a permanent sneer on his face.

"Right, the lot of you round the table in a semicircle now." Of course we weren't quick enough to respond to the command, and found ourselves pushing out the press-ups for a minute or so, until he got bored and stood us up again. He pointed at Tom.

"Have you been issued your bedding?"

"Yes, Corporal."

"Fucking hell, not another sweaty sock. Go and get it and bring it over here. Quickly."

Tom ran to his bedspace, even though it was only five feet away and he could have made it over there in one step. I suppose he was just showing willing. He returned with his full complement of bedding, and was reprimanded immediately by Edgeley.

"Did I say bring your fucking counterpane, did I?"

The changes in Tom's expression took place in an instant. His first reaction was one of consternation. 'You told me to get my bedding, so I brought the lot, you cunt.' His mind quickly computed that this wouldn't have been a clever answer. It altered immediately to one of vacant capitulation, as he – like the rest of us – started to learn the game.

"Sorry, Corporal." He managed to make it sound genuine, even though we all knew that he was punctuating the words internally, with the phrase 'you fucking wanker'.

"Right then, get it on. You can be the ghost of the counterpane." For the rest of the display, Tom wore the counterpane over his head and looked like a psychedelic trick-or-treater. Edgeley assembled the bedblock with ease and a running commentary. Even as I watched him folding blankets and sheets to millimetre perfect dimensions, I knew that this would be the first of many things where I would fail. He used three blankets, separated by the two sheets to create the bulk of the block. He then employed the fourth blanket as a sort of wrapping to the whole affair, folding it in such an ingenious way, that I stopped trying to suss it out immediately. The whole process took him about three minutes and when he finished he was left with a solid chunk of best Army bedding, trussed to the point of bursting.

"This is a fairly quick job. What I want yours to look like is this." He left the room for a second and returned with another bedblock and placed it on the table. It was a complete set up. It must have taken somebody days, equipped with elaborate measuring tools and a banding machine, to produce such perfection. It had been compressed so tightly and neatly, that it was two-thirds the size of its cousin. I had the feeling that if anyone pulled at one of the sheets, there would be an almighty explosion and people would be picking pieces of bed linen out of their hair for days.

It felt like one of those 'Generation Game' displays, when they get an expert on to perform a task he's been doing for years. It's then the turn of some a badly dressed bloke from Solihull to try to emulate the expert. After a 30-second tutorial. Edgeley continued with the lesson.

"You'll place your bedblock at the head end of the bed, with the pillows on top. Any questions?"

Tom's muffled voice emerged from beneath his disguise.

"What about the counterpane, Corporal?"

"Oh yeah, forgot about that. Give it here, Spooky." He took the counterpane off Tom's head and dragged it over to his bed. He then covered Tom's mattress with it and began to tuck it in.

"What I'm doing here are called hospital corners. This is the way you'll make your bed for the rest of your military careers, those of you who are here for more than a week, that is."

That bit looked fairly straightforward, and when he'd completed pulling it tight, from underneath the bed, he placed the bedblock and pillows on top.

"Da daaa! There you go. Piece of piss." He looked at Tom.

"What's your name again, Jock."

"Galbraith, Corporal."

"Well yours is all made up already Galbraith. Looks like it's your lucky day."

"Yes, Corporal."

"Is it fuck!" He then proceeded to dismantle Tom's bedblock down to component level, taking special care to shake the blankets out thoroughly. I'm sure that his reasoning was that he didn't want to lend Tom an unfair advantage and not that he was just an utter cunt, taking great pleasure in making lesser mortals miserable. When he'd finished, Tom's bunk looked like a Moroccan carpet shop, with blankets hanging from the lights and lockers. He then left, heading for Room 5 gleefully, with the perfect bedblock under his arm, to repeat the display. As soon as we could hear him shouting next door, we knew the coast was clear, and started talking quietly. Colin helped Tom get his bedding down as we discussed the finer points of the bedblock.

"What a fucking gobshite," said Tom, folding his blankets back to their original size.

"The bad thing is, I think they're all gonna be like that, mate," added Paul.

I ventured my opinion too: "I'll tell you what, I've got no fucking chance of making one of them things." This brought a laugh of assent from Steve.

"I'm with you there, Eddy. I reckon we'll get shat on tomorrow morning."

Paul cut in again.

"Don't worry about it, lads. We'll get shat on however well we do."

And there it was, though I didn't know it at the time. The secret of basic training. There is no correct answer. The sooner you learned it the better. It took me a couple of weeks. Some got it in days. Others went through the entire three months thinking they'd done something to personally upset the instructors. All punishments and prizes were preordained. How an inspection went was not down to how much cleaning or polishing you'd done – the staff had already decided, over a brew, exactly what standard you'd achieved. The inspection was academic – a smokescreen to justify whatever punishment they had in mind for that day. For the fortunate ones who learned the secret early, it took a lot of the pressure off. Only you knew if you'd tried your hardest to do something correctly – an NCO screaming in your face on a flimsy pretext wouldn't change that.

The next corridor shout came about 20 minutes later. We were told to put all our spare civilian clothes, less underwear, into our suitcases and stow them in the case room. That left me with just the clobber I was standing up in, until we were issued our uniforms. Putting your civvies away seemed like a far more emphatic step towards being in the Army than signing papers or chanting attestations. All the instruction and running about took us up to teatime, and we were quickly assembled back outside for a piss-poor march to the cookhouse for the evening meal. The food maintained the same ropey standards of the lunchtime meal, although this time it was slightly different. Still shit, just different. Instead of chips and sausages we got chips and pies. And it transpired that to ask 'What's in the pies, Chef?' of one of the slop-jockeys would see you rewarded with a four-letter barrage for getting lippy.

On our arrival back at the block that evening, we discovered who else would be sleeping in the other bed in our room. Lance-Corporal Baker was one of the junior instructors. He was about seventeen and a half, which – when you were a 16-year-old recruit – put him somewhat on a pedestal. Baker was about six feet tall with dark hair and a permanent shadow on his jaw that meant that he needed to shave every day. Unlike the rest of us, for whom, although we were forced to shave on a daily basis, it was by no means a task that was born of necessity. It transpired that Baker would sleep in the room and be the first line of discipline. He started his introduction as he meant to go on, by telling us to 'shut the fuck up' and to 'listen the fuck in' and to 'start shagging sparking'. Then he continued: "Right, gents. I will be your room NCO during basic training and to that end I am responsible for the state of you fuckers and this room. So for the rest of the shagging night you are going to be taught how to clean the room, the corridor and the ablutions. You will also be taught how to behave when a senior rank enters the room, and how to lay out your lockers. At the end of the night you WILL write a shagging letter home telling everyone how fucking great it is here, and you WILL have your shagging heads down at 2200 hours local fucking time! Do you understand?" He had a stronger Mancunian accent than mine, but I couldn't see us being mates for a while.

"Yes, Corporal!" We shouted as loud as we could.

"LOUDER YOU LAZY BASTARDS!"

"Yes, Corporal!" We shouted back at exactly the same volume as before.

"That's better! Right, firstly you've got to learn room etiquette. If you see an NCO walk into the room, then the first thing you do is stand to attention and shout

'UP!'" He bellowed the 'up' part. "Right, we'll practice that for a bit."

I could here sporadic shouts of "UP!" coming from the other rooms; no doubt their etiquette lessons were already in full swing.

Baker scowled and left the room. We all looked at each other bemusedly and before we could say anything, he had come in through the other door right next to Alistair McKenzie, who in-turn just stared back at him and gawped, open mouthed and frozen with fear. On seeing Baker, I went rigid and shouted: "UP!" All the other lads did the same, but Baker was bearing down on McKenzie in a rage. Before addressing Alistair, he shouted to the rest of us: "Keep fucking shouting it! You're going to need the shagging practice!" So we continued to shout rhythmically at the tops of our voices. I felt like a bit of knob, but if it stopped me getting a gripping, then it was worth it. Baker was really going to town on McKenzie.

"Why the fuck didn't you shout when I entered the room?"

"I don't know, Corporal."

"Well you'd better start knowing, Goat Jugs. Or you're going to shit out!"

"Yes, Corporal!"

"Right, the rest of you shut up. McKenzie, carry on."

All eyes were on Alistair as he started to shout. "UP! UP! UP!" He was very self-conscious and was close to tears. Despite this, Baker showed no sign of letting up.

"Come on, McKenzie! Get some air in those pudgy pregnant dog tits and get shouting."

Eventually, Alistair paid his penance, and for the next 30 minutes the NCOs spent their time just wandering in and out of each other's rooms to keep us on our toes and ensure that we could grasp the concept of standing up and shouting.

When Baker came back into the room, he started to take us through the basics of not just keeping the room tidy (which was about all I was used to at that point), but also the intricacies of 'bumpering' the floor with sickly smelling yellow floor wax and an ancient looking manual bumper. The bumper consisted of a solid lump of metal, with a soft brush base and a long wooden handle that protruded from the top of the weight. Baker described how we could use the bumper to bring the brown lino floor up into a shine.

"Right, gents. Get a cloth each, with a good fucking scoop of wax, then get on your shagging knees in a line and smear that fucking shit into the deck in a circular motion."

We did as we were bid and – after a while – Baker continued with his instruction.

"USE YOUR FUCKING NOGGIN, GENTS! ONCE YOU'VE COVERED THE AREA IN FRONT OF YOU, MOVE BACKWARDS UNTIL THE WHOLE FUCKING FLOOR'S COVERED. JESUS FUCKING H FUCKING CHRIST! IT'S NOT FUCKING ROCKET SCIENCE!"

Once the floor was covered the wax was left to dry, and when we returned the method of getting it shiny was very simple. Just push and pull the heavy bumper over the wax, very fast, for a very long time, whilst under a constant verbal assault from Baker. Those of us that weren't on bumper duty were cleaning the washrooms and the toilets. It was relatively straightforward as all it involved was scrubbing and polishing everything in sight. The other jobs – like cleaning the showers, the corridor and the drying room – were shared amongst the other two rooms in our section of corridor. Every now and then we would have to swap over and take turns running the bumper in the room. I was very nervous about doing this, as Barry Nash and Neil Moody had already done a stint, and when they staggered from the room, they looked like they had just been released from the Bastille.

I was to be no different. Each push and pull of the vile instrument drained my strength. The fact that I was as skinny as the bumper handle itself didn't help matters and each motion released new pains in my arms and my now sore hands. Every time the bumper was swung out and pulled back again, it made a 'ka-chunk' noise and after a while it made it easier to build up a rhythm. I could also hear the other recruits wielding their own bumpers and the noise reverberated down the corridor accompanied by the encouragements from the NCOs.

"I fucking love bumpering, Nugent." said Baker as he sat on his bed. "Do you?"

"Yes, Corporal!" The two words were broken up by gasps for air.

"Do you know the one thing that I like more than bumpering, Nugent?"

"No, Corporal!"

"Watching people bumper for me! Now that gives me wood! Does it give you wood, Nugent?"

"Yes, Corporal!"

"Fucking good man, Nugent! Right, repeat after me at the top of your voice. One two three four, I must bump the floor!"

I repeated everything he wanted me to chant and each one got more bizarre. The final slogan was done to the tune of 'I love to love but my baby just loves to dance'. So for the final five minutes of my bumpering odyssey I sang: "I love to bumper, 'cos it gives Corporal Baker wood."

By the time 9.30pm rolled around, we were all knackered and smelling like a school janitor's cleaning cupboard. I couldn't believe how spotless the room was, but Baker told us that it was in 'bog order' and looked like 'the main stage at the world shit-juggling championships'.

Despite his criticisms, Baker made us all sit down and write a letter home. I didn't really know what to put on the paper so I just said that I had arrived safely and that the food was okay. My mind was in a bit of turmoil and that must have been evident in the banality of my writing.

Once we had all finished, Baker took the letters and we all went to bed, with an enforced lights out at 10pm. We whispered quietly for a bit. Hushed questions shot back and forth to find out where guys were from and what they thought of the Army so far. When I wasn't involved in a conversation, my mind would wander and I took stock of my current predicament. In the middle of one of my thoughts, Tom was describing life in Scotland, and after completing a swear-word-laden sentence, he finished off with: "D'ya ken what I mean?"

After 30 seconds of silence, Paul's cockney accent cut through the dark like an 18-certificate Dick Van Dyke, "Who the fackin' 'ell's Ken?"

Like myself, Paul had never heard this strange Scots colloquialism before.

Tom replied: "It's no a fuckin' bloke's name, it means 'D'ya know what I mean?' D'ya ken?"

I dropped off as Tom continued to explain the origins of Glaswegian gibberish. I was woken, three seconds later, by Baker, smacking the shit out of Steve's and my bunk with one of his mess tins. The metal on metal clanging was horrendous and woke the entire room immediately.

"Come on, you lazy tossers. Hands off cocks and on socks. Get out of them fucking scratchers. There's work to do." I jumped out of bed and checked my watch. It said 5.30am, but I couldn't believe that I'd been asleep. A shocked Steve climbed down quickly from the top bunk, obviously with the same thought in mind. Within three or four seconds, all eight of us, in a selection of unsightly undercrackers, were stood at the end of our beds, shivering slightly, whilst we waited for Baker to say something else.

He started laughing, "Look at the fucking state of you lot. The Army's had it, I tell ya." He had a point actually.

Standing there to attention, thrusting our chests out, dressed only in Y-fronts, we were a sorry display of manhood. Tom Galbraith was stood on the other side of the room, directly opposite me. He had his eyes fixed on a point somewhere above and behind my head and had failed to notice that his right spud was hanging outside his gruds, in mid-air, like a turkey's wattle. I averted my gaze quickly and watched Alistair McKenzie trying to keep his gut sucked in, giving the impression that he had a 48-inch chest. All our bodies were of a uniform hue. There was no sign of a tan anywhere. Col Mortimer, whose skin had been subjected to 16 years of sub-zero Geordie winters was horribly white. Tippex painted on to his chest would have been rendered immediately invisible.

After shaking his head a bit more, Baker continued. To nobody in particular, he shouted: "Stand up straight, you fucking dregs. Right, it's half-five, you've got until seven to get this place in order. You'll then be taken down to breakfast. At eight o'clock Sergeant Atkins will be round. If you've got any problems or you need help with anything ask someone who gives a fuck." With that, he retreated to his bedspace. He opened his locker door and lay down on his bed. Leaving the door ajar created an effective barrier between him and us. Paul Jones, as usual, was the first to speak up.

"Let's get scrubbed up first, then we'll get on with it." I grabbed my towel and wash-kit and followed the rest of the lads into the ablutions. Rooms 5 and 6 shared the sinks and toilets with us, so 24 blokes were waiting on eight washbasins and three showers. I got in line and had to witness a poor lad with acne having his first shave. He looked like he was going to need a transfusion when he was finished and when I got to the bowl after him, I was sure I could see little lumps of flesh in the plughole. I had never shaved in my entire life, but mindful of the joining instructions, I'd arrived, equipped with a couple of Bic razors and a big can of shaving foam. '*It is an offence not to be cleanly shaven in the British Army. All personnel will arrive with adequate shaving equipment for day one of basic training.*' The trouble was, I didn't have anything to remove, not even a bit of bum-fluff. I lathered up my face until I looked like Father Christmas, then went through the motions, somehow managing not to slit my throat. By the time I'd had a quick shower, got back into the room and got dressed in my day old civvies, the time had moved on to just short of six o'clock. Baker made an appearance from behind his door.

"I'll tell you what lads, I'm not hearing many cleany-cleany noises. You'd better get a fucking move on. Nugent, what are you doing, you fucking knob-gobbler?"

I was just making a start on my bedblock, and told him so. Using the method familiar to all recruits, I replied by looking at the ceiling in the middle of the room and shouting as loud as was humanly possible for my underdeveloped lungs.

"I'M DOING ME BEDBLOCK, CORPORAL."

"Well, it's fucking shit. Sergeant Atkins is going to love you," replied Baker.

Over the next hour, we all flitted around from bedblocks to sweeping to dusting to cleaning to polishing to bumpering to cowering to worrying to bedblocks again. By breakfast time, we'd achieved a sum total of fuck all. Paul and Alistair's bedblocks looked alright and they'd tried to help a bit with the rest of us, but the short time we had didn't lend itself to the lengthy instruction we needed. We were browbeaten down to breakfast by Baker and his mates. I was pleasantly surprised by the cookhouse's morning offering. With only the experience of the previous day's lunch and dinner to go on, I wasn't expecting much. In a radical departure, the food looked okay and tasted of something. The choices were, always had been, and always would be: cereal, toast, a big greasy fry-up, or a combination of the three. Feeling quite hungry from my room cleaning exertions, I went for the fry-up. Moving my way along the hotplate, I could see various trays, holding bacon, sausages, fried eggs and fried bread. Each tray had a set of metal tongs lying on top of the food, inviting you to help yourself. There was a steaming cauldron of baked beans at the end. Within two seconds I'd made the biggest mistake it was possible to make in the slop-jockey code of practice. I picked up two sausages and put them on my plate. I went back in for a third, but as soon as the tongs hit the skin of the frazzled banger, one of the cooks appeared from nowhere, and stuck his head through the counter until we were nose to nose.

"Two sausages only, you fucking stroker."

He was absolutely fuming – a reaction totally out of proportion to my 'crime'. Perhaps he was paid in sausages and I was eating his wages. I dropped the tongs immediately and scuttled down the hotplate to get away from him. He glared at me as I carefully removed one piece of bacon, one fried egg and one piece of fried bread from their greasy homes. I couldn't decide whether one or two ladles full of beans was the correct amount, so opted for none, the only safe bet. The rest of the lads from the room had managed to get round one table, and I squeezed on to the end after helping myself to a brew from a silver 'Burco' boiler near the entrance doors. The room NCOs had allocated us 45 seconds to eat our meal, so conversation was at a minimum. Barry had enough time to lick his plate, but I was just tucking into my second sausage when the shouting started. I managed to gobble it down as we were herded back outside. Baker was waiting for us when we got back to the room. He was shaking his head ruefully.

"Half-seven lads. You'll just have to tell Sergeant Atkins that you were too busy filling your fat fucking bellies at breakfast, to get the room done properly."

We spent the next 25 minutes trying to get the room up to the imaginary required standard. By 7.55am, my bedblock was still hopeless. It sat there, on the end of my bed, like a dead badger. A quick look round the rest of the room, confirmed that no one else's was much better.

"Right, stop fucking about now. You've had as much time as you're gonna get. He'll be round in a couple of minutes, so stand by your fucking beds." We did as we were told whilst Baker continued.

"Nugent?"

"YES, CORPORAL."

"I want you to stand outside the door. When Sergeant Atkins has finished with Room 3, I want you to stand to attention. You will then shout 'ROOM, ROOM, SHUN,' to bring the rest of the lads up. Do you think you can do that?"

"YES, CORPORAL."

He turned to the rest of the room.

"When Nugent shouts 'ROOM, ROOM, SHUN,' you will all stand up straight as your spongy little spines will allow. Understood?"

"YES, CORPORAL." I was quite impressed by just how loud seven blokes shouting at the same time could be.

"We'll see." He turned back to me.

"You will then say to Sergeant Atkins: 'Good morning, Sergeant. Room 4 Recruit Troop ready and awaiting your inspection', and that's when the fun starts. Got it?"

"YES, CORPORAL."

I waited for further instructions but the only one forthcoming was: "Well, fuck off then."

I positioned myself outside the room door and looked along the corridor. To my front I could see one bloke from each of Rooms 1, 2 and 3 adopting an identical stance to my own. I didn't dare look around, but presumed this was being duplicated down to Room 10. Before Atkins arrived, I had a couple of minutes to go through my lines. There wasn't much point really. I knew I was going to fuck it up, I was that nervous.

When he came through the double doors adjacent to Room 1 he was accompanied by Corporal Timms, who was carrying a clipboard, self-importantly. It was hard to eavesdrop, whilst trying to stand perfectly still, but the guy outside Room 1 seemed to say the right things and the entourage moved inside, followed by the room NCO. For about five seconds there was relative silence and I thought maybe it was going to be alright. Perhaps they'd go easy on us, it being our first full day and all that. The first sign that this wasn't going to be the case was a bedblock being thrown into the corridor. It was followed by Sergeant Atkins roaring at the owner. Even when it landed in the corridor, it still looked better than mine. The guy outside Room 2 looked round at us and the expression on his face said it all. He looked like he'd seen a ghost and simply mimed the words "Oh, fuck." I had to stifle the urge to laugh, despite my growing sense of dread and the fact that Atkins was only three rooms away. The destruction of Room 1 took about three minutes. I heard the same process being repeated eight times. First there would be a couple of questions from Atkins, the volume rising dramatically with each word. There would be a short nervous answer, interrupted by what sounded like a bear roaring. The unmistakeable noise of furniture being up-ended was next, followed by a short period of silence as Atkins moved to the next bunk. The system was employed identically in Rooms 2 and 3. As soon as they'd moved in to next door, Baker came out and stood beside me.

"You'd better get it fucking right, Nugent."

I was shaking like a leaf. I felt like I was going to be sick and drop a dog egg into my underpants at the same time. I counted eight sets of the, by now familiar, banging and clattering and readied myself for the onslaught.

Atkins emerged from Room 3, red-faced and angry. He made a beeline for me and stopped no more than a pace away. I looked at him and started breathing in to say "Good morning."

"Don't you fucking look at me, sunshine. Do you fucking fancy me or summat?"

I switched my gaze to a point above his head and shouted: "Good morning, Sergeant." I stopped, because he was shaking his head angrily.

"What I think you're trying to say is ROOM, ROOM, SHUN."

Steve and the rest of the lads responded immediately to the authority in Sergeant Atkins' voice. I realised my mistake and started to shout.

"ROOM, ROO…"

"Too fucking late, don't bother. And never mind the 'good morning' bollocks either, you've already fucked it all up, beyond redemption."

He turned to Lance-Corporal Baker.

"Get a grip of your blokes, Corporal Baker, or I'll get a fucking grip of you." He moved past us both and into the room. Baker followed him, shooting me a filthy look as he went by. I hadn't really dropped him in the shit, it was all just a big blag between the DS, but I wasn't to know that. I was just starting to feel sorry for myself, when Atkins screamed.

"Whose fucking bedblock is this?" I didn't really need to look, but I did anyway. He had impaled the offending article on the end of his pace stick and was inspecting it with grim fascination.

"MINE, SERGEANT. NUGENT"

"Jesus Christ, this is the worst one I've seen so far. It's like a fucking elephant's nest. Did you have boxing gloves and a blindfold on when you did this?"

"NO, SERGEANT."

"Well you should have done. You might have done a better fucking job. Bad start, Nugent. Bad fucking start."

He lobbed it over his shoulder, like a farmhand shifting straw bales. It bounced off my head and onto the floor at my feet. He continued to move through the room, voicing unsurprising opinions about our hygiene, stupidity and genetic make-up, all done at town-crier decibels. Only Col Mortimer came in for a similar amount of flak as me. He'd had the great idea of disagreeing with Sergeant Atkins.

"Whose is this one?" said Atkins, prodding Col's bedblock.

"MINE, SERGEANT. MORTIMER."

"Think you've done a good job do you?"

"ERM, YES, SERGEANT."

"Well, I think it's shite."

He pointed to a bulge at the back of the arrangement, that shouldn't have been there.

"What the fuck's that? It looks like you've trapped Arthur Askey in there. So you think that's up to standard do you."

"YES, SERGEANT."

"So, I'm a fucking liar am I?"

"What? ERM, YES… NO SERGEANT."

The rest of us were shouting silently 'Shut the fuck up, Col,' but he'd already stitched himself up. Atkins continued with the theme.

"So, what you're saying is you know better than me. A spotty, little Geordie gobshite, who's not even been in the Army for a day, knows better than me, a sergeant in the Royal Corps of Signals with 12 years service under his belt?"

"NO, SERGEANT."

"I'll be fucking watching you, Mortimer. No one likes a smart-arse. Especially one with a grid like a pizza. Corporal Baker, sort this fine bunch of wankers out."

He left the room, with Timms in his wake, urgently scribbling on his clipboard. As the mêlée began in Room 5, Baker debriefed us.

"Fucking cheers, lads. That's me in the shit. Well fuck youse lot. When I'm in the shit, you're in the shit. I'll get you sparking, don't worry about that. Right, put your stuff back together and wait for the next corridor call."

We started reassembling our bedblocks and putting the mattresses back on the beds. It looked like we'd been burgled by gorillas. Baker got called out by the NCO from Room 3 and left us to our own devices. We were all in our own little worlds, panicking about what might happen next, when Paul Jones shouted across to Col.

"I carn't fackin' believe you called 'im a liar, Col."

Before Col could protest, we erupted into laughter. Fuck, did we need it.

"What about me, I've got a fucking elephant's nest," I added.

This got them all laughing even louder. When Alistair reminded us of the insult Atkins had levelled at him, about his weight, we were giggling like schoolgirls. He did quite a good impression of the Sergeant as well.

"Fuck me, McKenzie. You're a bit of a fucking blimp aren't you? When you go to the zoo, do the elephants throw peanuts at you?"

It relieved a bit of the pressure and by the time the next corridor shout came, I was feeling less depressed. This time we were taken down to the M.R.S. for our medicals. The med-centre consisted of a 20-seat waiting area, a couple of examination rooms, a small dental clinic and a ward with eight beds for inpatients. It should have been a fair assumption that a medical practice might have been a repository of human kindness on the camp, but that idea was quickly dispelled by the staff. It was run by an old Scottish dragon. She was a major in the QARANCs. She wore a pair of horn-rimmed specs, suspended on a chain around her neck. She introduced herself in unfriendly, 'Miss Jean Brodie' tones.

"Welcome to the Medical Reception Station. My name is Major Lines. You're here for your medical today and we will process you presently. For the rest of your two years, this is where you will come, should you ever need to report sick. I am well aware that our services are often abused by skivers and malingerers, who always report here in large numbers, whenever a cross-country run is looming. You may rest assured boys, that if you report sick and I, or the doctor, find nothing wrong with you, you will be for the high-jump. And in this instance, the high-jump will not be a preferred alternative to long distance running."

She had a small self-satisfied giggle to herself. Eighty blank faces stared at her. The first 20 lads were seated whilst the rest of us filled up the space behind the chairs and the entrance corridor. Whilst Major Lines was talking, a little man had appeared behind her. I suppose he was a soldier, since he was in uniform, but he had the military bearing of Ronnie Corbett. He wore a pair of shiny black shoes and dark green, barrack-dress trousers. He also wore a starched white, short-sleeved smock of the sort that dental nurses wear. A single, silver-metal chevron on the right sleeve indicated his rank. He can't have weighed more than seven stones and most of that was hair. He had a classic comb-over, a haircut which, fortunately, was sliding into extinction. In the absence of the raw materials required for such a 'do' he looked like he'd been combing it out of his ears, such was the pube-like nature of the finish. Major Lines nodded to him and said: "Lance-Corporal Nesbitt will make sure order is kept whilst you are waiting. When I call out your name make your way to the examination room."

With the roll being called alphabetically, I was the last one from our room to go through. The medical was fairly standard and was conducted by a disinterested, septuagenarian doctor, as the Major looked on and took notes. I did all the same tests that I'd completed prior to joining, presumably to make sure I hadn't blagged my way through. With the treatment we'd been receiving, it was beyond my comprehension that anyone would consider cheating to get in. It would have been like someone pushing into the queue for the guillotine. As soon as I'd finished, I got dressed and made my way out into the waiting area as Major Lines shouted out the next name. Baker clocked me straight away.

"Back up to the room, Nugent. Carry on tidying."

When I walked in, all the lads were gathered round the window, looking down on to the parade square. A squad of 30 lads were being drilled by a sergeant. They were moving in perfect unison and responded to his commands with complete precision. It looked fucking cold that square, though. It was roughly the size of a couple of football pitches laid side to side, with a small inspection dais on the left. When the squad was stood still, the flapping of their trousers indicated that the wind was tear-arsing across the barren expanse of concrete.

"That lot looks pretty difficult," ventured Steve.

Paul replied: "Nah, mate, just takes a bit of getting used to. We'll be that good in no time flat."

I appreciated the confidence he was placing in me, but watching the skill levels required on the square, I assumed correctly that drill would be something I could place on my list of 'things that I am shit at'. I asked nobody in particular "What's happening now then?"

"Baker told me that we'll be getting our kit issued, in the indoor arena."

I liked the sound of that. It would be nice to actually stick a uniform on, if only to make me feel like I belonged a bit more. From all the running about in the same set of civvies, I was getting some major BO fumes from my shirt.

Baker turned up 20 minutes later and fell us in downstairs with the rest of the troop. The indoor arena was adjacent to the gym, and as we halted outside it a squad of about 15 apprentices were coming in off a run, in Army PT kit. In their red, v-neck tops, huge blue shorts, green socks and white plimsolls, they looked like the winners of the 1926 FA Cup Final.

Sergeant Atkins had made another appearance and gave us a brief talking to, just before we went in.

The inside of the arena was huge – about a third the size of the parade square, with rows of supporting pillars up to a three-storey-high ceiling. Lots of large blue crash mats were propped up against the far wall to our right. At the bottom end of the building a line of tables ran its full width. Each table was piled high with lots of items of clothing and kit, in varying shades of green.

We filed forward, one rank at a time. I was approximately in the middle of our group. The storemen who were dispensing the clothing had obviously been through the same kind of traumatic experience as the cooks. They were surly bastards who treated the items to be issued as their own personal belongings.

The first bits of kit I received were two sets of camouflaged trousers and jackets. The man behind the table scrutinised me for about a second, then spoke some clothing sizes and handed me my outfit. It was painfully obvious that they wouldn't fit me. Even at an initial glance I could tell that they would be too wide and too short and had been designed with Bella Emberg in mind.

Next came two pairs of olive green trousers and jumpers, followed by a dark blue beret that was the size and shape of a freakishly large cow pat.

Adjacent to the berets was a stack of shirts. Although they were the same dull green as the jumpers, they gave off an occasional glint, as a sharp piece of the fabric – that had no place in any kind of garment – caught the light. This had me worried straight away. When the shirts were placed on top of the clothing pile that was now perched on my outstretched arms, I placed my chin on them for support. It felt like having fibre-glass ground into my neck. It was the most uncomfortable cloth I had ever felt. The only reason I could think for manufacturing such a vile thing was to use up unwanted sandbag stock-piles from the Second World War. Maybe the Army tested them on Trappist monks. Any shirt that the monks could endure would be rejected on the grounds of being unnecessarily comfortable, and lobbed into the seconds bin, where it would be used to scrub the hulls of Navy frigates clean of barnacles when they were in dry-dock. It must have been spun from a mixture of rusty barbed wire and hedgehog pubes.

The amount of items being supported by my spindly arms was now reaching critical mass, so it was with some relief that the next desk was piled high with kit bags. These would enable us to carry all of our clothes with a modicum of ease. However, my heart sank when I realised that the kit bag or 'sausage-bag' as it was known, was to practical carriage as the KF shirt was to comfortable clobber. After the sausage bag came the holdall, into which I deposited my stockpile of items (including the sausage bag itself), swiftly followed by a plethora of towels, eating irons and Robin Hood-style green thermals. Finally we were given our PT kit, which comprised one white and two red T-shirts, two pairs of shorts and a pair of white road-slapper plimsolls. This footwear had a sole so thin, that it offered no cushioning whatsoever. You could get bruises on your feet just by walking on an insect.

Once fully laden, I felt like a pack mule and was bent double under the weight of all my kit. My arms were overflowing with green clothes and the holdall was slung over my shoulder. This didn't cut me any slack with the NCOs. As soon as I came out into the daylight, I was harangued back to the block by Baker and his mates.

Eventually the rest of the lads filtered back to the room, and they were all in the same state as myself, panting and wild-eyed. Five minutes later, Baker came in and took us through the process of laying out our lockers. He folded everything perfectly and placed it on its predesignated spot on the shelves. After half an hour of demonstrating this, he set us to the task of doing it ourselves. The results didn't satisfy him and he called us 'idle fucking wankers!'

He shouted as he emptied every shelf from every locker, "Do it again, and this time, try to make your shagging lockers look a bit less like a thalidomide jumble sale!"

By the third time our kit had hit the deck it was lunch, so we marched to the cookhouse again, only this time armed with our own knifes, forks, spoons and porcelain mugs. After the meal we were halted outside the accommodation, where the troop sergeant shouted: "Right, gents. You've got one minute to get up those shagging stairs, get your diggers washed and get out into the corridor for an inspection!" He surveyed us, "Well don't just stand there! Get fucking moving!"

The whole squad did a bomb-burst and charged up the stairs. Some lads were trampled underfoot as we surged on like a herd of startled wildebeest. There was a scuffle for the taps to clean our utensils, then we were out into the corridor and stood to attention. The NCOs moved up and down our line, inspecting every knife, fork, spoon and mug. The majority of the pot mugs were sent smashing to the floor. The other diggers were scattered the full length of the building.

"You minging bastards! Next time get the fucking things dried and cleaned properly!" one of them shouted. Soon the lessons would be learnt and it wasn't long before we could get all of our items cleaned and dried in a minute. There were always a few trample-victims after every basic training meal, though.

The rest of the afternoon was spent queuing, yet again, for more equipment issue. This time it was from the Squadron stores. The inside of Corporal Timms' domain was dark and foreboding, and had a slight aroma of Bell's Whisky.

The shelves were stacked with various items of stout green cloth webbing, helmets and sleeping bags, all of which were issued to us as one big pile. We were then taken outside onto the grass, where we were shown how to assemble the multitude of belts, straps and pouches.

The webbing was incredibly archaic, '58 pattern' indicating its year of design rather than its revision. It was virtually impossible to adjust in size and any exposure to moisture would cause it to triple in weight. Aside from this, it had a negligible carrying capacity. When we were given the list of items that we had to pack in the various pouches, I couldn't help but think that unless the inventor of the TARDIS had designed the stuff, then we would be shit out of luck. This would become more apparent on our first training exercise.

After a tussle with assembling the webbing, we were shown how to pack and unpack our sleeping bags. My bag was suspiciously light, and when I unfolded it, not only was it the size of a moth pupa, it was also as thin as a sheet of used toilet paper, with a similar scent. I checked the cloth with a growing sense of dread for any signs of a material that might provide some form of insulation. After scrutinising the entire length of the sleeping bag (all three feet of it), I found the grand total of four feathers that were supposed to stave off the cold of a North Yorkshire winter!

I looked around despairingly. It seemed that there was a direct correlation with the bag sizes and their new owner. The smaller the guy was, the bigger his sleeping bag, and vice versa. It appeared that I would spend the next two years of exercise sleeping in an involuntary foetal position.

The icing on the cake for the afternoon's issues was our helmets. They were identical to those issued in the Second World War. The moment one of these lids was donned, an instant transformation took place, turning every one of us into Private Pike, the loveable *Dad's Army* fuckwit. They were also equipped with the novel invention of an inch-and-a-half spike that protruded downwards from the inside of the helmet's centre towards the skull. I stared at the spike in disbelief, surely this was some mistake? The trauma was softened somewhat by an item known as 'The Spider', which looked just like its namesake and clipped inside the helmet and onto the spike. It consisted of a central hole for the spike, with eight evenly spaced plastic 'legs' that ran down the head, so that the helmet would be seated properly on your noggin. The spider was good for two things. Firstly, it reduced the spike penetration into your head from an inch and a half to just half an inch. Secondly, you could place it on your head by itself and run around pretending to be a pre-war American footballer. When accompanying the spike protrusion with the bouncing caused by the elastic chinstrap, it would make running in the helmets feel like having an enraged woodpecker stuck to your head.

I didn't even bother to check my respirator. After the trauma of the helmet, I imagined there to be something equally hideous inside the gasmask. I'd had enough shocks for one day, so I just put the 'resi' into its relevant pouch and bundled everything together.

It was with a relatively heavy heart at the prospect of two years of torture, that I carried the last of my issued kit up to the room.

The evening was taken up by demonstrations of kit preparation and actually sorting the stuff out ourselves.

Baker used Alistair's uniform to demonstrate ironing techniques. He was meticulous in starching perfect creases, so that the shirts and trousers he had been working on were immaculate. Once he had completed his lesson, he looked around us and said: "Got the hang of that, gents?"

We all nodded blankly, not wanting to rock the boat by asking any questions. Baker must have known this because he added: "Well, we'll soon see. You scruffy cunts'll probably turn out like The Billy Smart's Clown Liberation Front."

His gaze then fell on Alistair.

"I bet you're chuffed to have a set of decent working dress eh, McKenzie?"

"Yes, Corporal!"

"Well I'd better sort that out then!"

Baker then ironed a massive set of tramline double creases down the front of Alistair's trousers. "I tell you what, McKenzie. I'm a right cunt, me. Those will be a bastard to get out!" He quickly buggered off and left us to it.

From then until lights out, we took it in turns on the iron, and when we weren't doing that, we polished our boots. Baker had offered us plenty of advice about breaking the boots in so that you didn't get blisters. He suggested that we mark time in a bath full of water for half an hour or fill them full of piss. This would ensure that the leather would be supple. It turned out, that these particular hints had been handed down through generations of soldiers, and only really suited the boots of squaddies that were taking part in the relief of Ladysmith.

To familiarise us with the various types of uniform, the NCOs used the evening to take us through quick-change parades. These were exactly what they sounded like; we would be told a certain dress code, for example PT kit, and then given a certain timescale in which to get dressed. This was normally abbreviated into the command: "One minute, PT kit, GO!" On this, we would then rush to our lockers, and scramble into the required clothing and parade back into the corridor, only to be met by "Too slow. One minute, combats, GO!" And so it would continue. I suppose it served a purpose, but once the dress code became a bit more cosmopolitan then the whole thing went a bit of course. The more exotic parades were in 'Robin Hood dress', which entailed green thermal top and bottoms (tucked into green socks), green waterproof poncho cape and green cap comforter (a rolled up piece of cloth that looked like the old commando head dress). This one wasn't too bad, and it paled into insignificance next to 'mess tin order'. This was a green Army belt worn around the waist, but also looped through the handles of both mess tins, one of which would cover the arse and the other the wedding tackle; and that was it. Admittedly it was easy and quick to get into, but it let the wind in something fierce, not to mention the hygiene issues that it raised.

As soon as Baker woke us up in the morning, we were instructed to put on our 'combats'. I'd heard that word, during the blizzard of quick changes, so it must have been one of the dress permutations we'd adopted, however briefly. I couldn't for the life of me, remember which bits of my newly issued kit were required for this particular outfit, and stared helplessly into my locker. Steve Keets was no good to me. Instead of rummaging around his locker, he was just gawping at me with an 'I hope you fucking know, 'cos I don't' look on his face. Only Paul had started to get dressed and, of course, Baker quickly spotted this. Exasperated, he started shouting.

"Fucking hell, is Jones the only of you knobbers with a memory? Combats, you cunts."

He caught me sneaking a look over at Paul to get a couple of tips.

"Stop eyeing him up Nugent, he's not your bird. I'll say it one more time. Combats. This includes, one pair of Army socks, one pair of boots-combat-high, combat trousers, combat jacket, shirt KF and that farcical fucking excuse for a beret."

As he was shouting it out, I was pulling it on to the floor of my locker so I couldn't forget. Baker chivvied us along with his brand of tough love and five minutes later, we were all dressed in the requisite outfit. We looked various degrees of ridiculous. As usual, Paul and Alistair looked okay, but the rest of us looked like DPM tramps. Either we'd shrunk as we slept, or the uniforms were living things, and had spent the night growing a couple of sizes. It was hard to say who looked the silliest as we all stood to attention at the end of our beds, trying to project some military bearing.

My clothes were the most ill-fitting. Barry Nash won the prize for the worst shaped beret. The rest of us had opted for the 'plop it on your head, then smooth it down over your right ear' look. This gave off a sort of martial Frank Spencer vibe. Barry had spent so much time smoothing his down, that it nearly touched his right shoulder. The band of the beret should have been just above his left ear, but his over-enthusiastic preening left a gap of about four inches. I'd seen photographs of Second World War Tommies wearing them like that, but it was safe to say that that style was no longer in fashion. Baker started laughing when he saw it.

"Jesus, Nash. What the fuck is that?"

"Don't know, Corporal."

"Neither do I. You look like you're just back from El Alamein. Get it fucking sorted out."

Barry did as he was told, and pulled the band until it was directly over his lug. This made the bit that was touching his shoulder stick out until it was parallel with the ground. The 'improvement' had managed to make him look a bigger twat. You could have landed a small helicopter on it. As Baker checked the rest of us out, he continued to chuckle. Not benevolently though, that would never have done. It was the laugh of someone who revelled in his post as Critic-in-Chief. After he gave us the nod, we clumped into the corridor and outside for a recruit troop parade. I don't suppose the boots were especially heavy, but I'd never worn anything like them before and had to consciously think about each step I took, lifting my legs in the exaggerated fashion of an astronaut walking in zero gravity. When we were all on parade, in three ranks, the effect was no less unimpressive. It seemed like everyone had someone else's uniform on. We looked like the North Yorkshire detachment of a badly equipped, central-African rebel force. All of the Apprentice NCOs were there. They were dressed in boots, lightweights and navy blue sweatshirts, with a Royal Corps of Signals cap badge embroidered over the left tit. I presume they were dressed differently, so that nobody could possibly mistake them for recruits. Given the state of us, it was highly unlikely. When Sergeant Atkins and Sergeant Bailey appeared, they were attired similarly.

"Good morning, gents," said Sergeant Bailey.

"We're going to take you on a run round camp now. Don't worry about it; it's not a test or anything. We'll use it to get you used to running in step and to point out the various buildings and areas that you'll be using. Do as you're told and pay attention when you're given information. Listen in to my word of command."

He was just about to shout something, but then realised that we didn't even know the basics of drill yet, so instructed us in a more conversational tone."

"Turn to your right, and keep fucking still."

Three or four blokes managed to fuck this simple order up. As I turned to my right, the bloke to my left spun the wrong way, and stood there, facing me. For a second, you could see him thinking 'Maybe I'm the only one that's right.' The torrent of abuse from the NCOs soon clarified matters for him. Sergeant Bailey then moved to the head of the squad and stood beside the front-left man and shouted: "By the right, double-march," and set off.

As the sergeant had promised, it wasn't a physically demanding run. We ran round the camp at a pace only slightly faster than a walk. I did like it though. It was the first time I'd felt remotely 'soldierly'. There's something indefinably enjoyable about running along in a squad, even if it looks like a band of SWAPO rejects. Maybe it's the powerful sound of 80 heavy boots hitting the ground at the same time. More realistically, it's probably that – if you're in the middle rank like I was – you're cushioned slightly from the abuse. As the AT NCOs continually bemoaned our lack of coordination, Sergeant Bailey occasionally brought the squad to a shuffling halt, before pointing out a feature of the camp. Using this method, we got a whistle-stop tour which would aid us in finding our way round.

The main camp was a rectangle of about a kilometre by half a kilometre. The parade square was bang in the centre and most of the buildings clustered around it, on all four sides. To its west were the accommodation blocks where ours and three other squadrons' recruits suffered. Behind them were the cookhouse and Baker Block, where the single, permanent staff below the rank of sergeant lived. To the south of the square were the four, three-storey education blocks where we would learn our trades. To their left was the gym, the swimming pool and indoor arena. Tucked in, neatly behind the indoor arena, was the outdoor arena and assault course. The all important NAAFI was at the north-west corner of the square. The cinema and guardroom, which was adjacent to the camp entrance was at the north-east corner. The camp's most distinctive geographical feature ran flush to the square's western edge. There were three churches running along the perimeter, all triangular in shape. In the centre, forming a huge wigwam of glass and concrete was the C of E church. To its north was a much smaller Catholic version and a similar sized chapel to the south catered for interdenominational services. Behind the churches were the playing fields, bordered by the Officers' and Sergeants' Messes. Out of the camp, and up Pennypot Lane, was another area where we would receive field-based telecomms training, but Bailey didn't trust us on a public road and opted for a brief description of that location. Throughout the run, Sergeant Bailey offered unsettling glimpses of the purpose of each landmark he pointed out. Of the NAAFI, he pointedly observed: "Don't fucking worry about remembering this place, you won't be spending much time in it."

He simply scowled as we jogged past the Officers' Mess, but brought us to a halt outside the WOs' and Sergeants' Mess and spoke reverently.

"Think about it, fellas. Keep your noses clean and in ten years or so, you may get to enjoy all the things the Mess has to offer."

It wasn't very Churchillian, in its power to inspire. Never mind a decade, all my powers of concentration were focused on lasting the day. He took great pleasure in showing us the assault course. It consisted of all the usual obstacles. A set of monkey bars, a wall, a bigger wall and an even bigger wall, with an extra-big wall behind it. Right near the end was the comedy sketch staple, the rope swing, which traversed a deep pool of pungent looking water. Throughout the remainder of my years in the Army, this would be the single point on every assault course where the spectators would congregate. The opportunities for belly-laughter were bottomless. The rope swing would always be the penultimate obstacle, so that when the soldier arrived there, he was generally ballbagged, unless he was a racing snake. He would run up a small grassed ramp to a brick edged wall. The soldier who'd already made it across would be on the other side, still holding the rope. The idea, as demonstrated by the PTIs was that the soldier in possession of the rope would let go of it, giving it a bit of forward propulsion as it went. When it reached the other side, the recipient was to grab the rope with both arms about a third of the way up its length, quickly getting both his legs round it as well, for extra support. He would then swing athletically across releasing his leg grip as he reached the other side. Landing with a comforting, two-footed thud, he would keep hold of the rope and wait for the next man, whereupon, the exercise would be repeated. It sometimes worked like this, but regularly didn't, hence the expectant crowd. There were various ways it could go wrong, all resulting in observers crying with laughter and a fall into a shit-stained pool for the unlucky acrobat. In the 'Marcel Marceau', the rope despatcher was a little too vigorous in his throwing technique. Holding the rope by the bottom, he'd bring it back over his shoulder and chuck it powerfully towards his mate. This would put a kink in the rope, which would usually flick it upwards just before it got to the other side. If he hadn't predicted this, the jumper would have already leant forward to grasp something that was no longer there. All the way down to the water, his hands would still be holding an imaginary rope. Even if the throwing part was done correctly, there was plenty more that could go wrong. For a textbook example of 'The Reluctant Fireman' the rope was generally quite wet from use or weather. If the jumper didn't grab it tenaciously, he'd just slide right down it, usually over the centre of the pool. This would result in a couple of hefty rope burns on the hands, which would be quickly soothed by being dunked in four feet of borderline sewage. If he caught the rope and didn't slip off he might make it across, but only if he didn't catch it too high or too low. Too high, and he'd perform 'The Town Hall Clock'. This involved just swinging back and forth with no chance of making it to either bank. Eventually he'd come to a stop and then resign himself to the inevitable. Too low, and the jumper would demonstrate a 'Queen Mary', ploughing through the pool, leaving a wake like one of Cunard's finest before halting at the far wall, and sinking without trace. The sturdy bloke who avoided all these pitfalls was still left with one to beat, 'The Stretch Armstrong'. If he didn't time his leg release perfectly, he was up shit-street. If he let go too late, the return swing would have begun and he'd be left with his toes gripping the edge of the wall for all they were worth, whilst his arms held on to the now immobile rope which left him suspended right over the water. A strong lad could hold on for a good 30 seconds in this position, but as his arms started to give up, his toes would be trying to burst through his toecaps to gain a bit more purchase. You'd have thought there was only one course of action here. Surrender and let your feet fall into the pool, quickly followed by the rest of your body. I did see someone try an alternative once. He let go with his hands first. With his feet hooked behind a course of bricks, his body formed a lovely arc as it swung back and twatted the wall, leaving him knocked out and still dangling, with his head underwater. As a couple of his mates hauled him out, preventing his certain death, the assembled crowd shrieked with amusement at his stupidity.

After the tour, and just before Sergeant Bailey fell us out for lunch, he informed us that we would be getting our first drill lesson that afternoon, in working dress. Thankfully, Paul was able to remember what we had to stick on. Stood outside in boots, lightweights, shirt, jumper and beret, we waited to commence our long and painful relationship with the square and the myriad joys of marching up and down in straight lines. The two sergeants took the lesson, with the AT NCOs assisting. Predictably, we were utterly hopeless and smashed all previous 'wrath incurred per second' records. We weren't the only squad on the parade ground that day. All the other squadrons' recruits were undergoing a similar baptism of fire. The indiscriminate roars of drill sergeants came from all directions. To begin with, it was hard to tell which sergeant was shouting at which squad, but it didn't take long for us to pick out Bailey and Atkins' individual styles, like a brood of newborn chicks identifying their mother's call. The concept of the lesson sounded easy. Being our first time, all they wanted to do was basic foot drill. It didn't even involve marching. Standing easy, standing at ease, and standing to attention was all we had to learn. As usual, there was a broad spectrum of competence on display, with the ex-cadets showing strongly. The only way I could judge my individual performance was by mentally measuring the yells I received, on my internal 'screamometer', in comparison to my peers. This simple yardstick put me in the bottom ten. With the permanent staff giving all the commands, the AT NCOs took on the responsibility of monitoring the recruits from their own rooms. Steve Keets and I took the most shit off Baker.

I don't know what it was about drill – maybe my heart was never in it. We had it repeatedly explained, that it was the most efficient way of moving a large body of men from point A to point B. I couldn't argue with that, but there always seemed to be an unnecessary amount of fucking about, taking in the rest of the alphabet before finally getting to the second letter. Even at its most basic level, it was an easy thing to get wrong, consistently in my case. 'Standing at ease' was a slight misnomer. It involved standing with legs shoulder width apart. The arms were behind the back, with the right hand being held by the left, at the base of the spine. The chin was supposed to be slightly raised. It wasn't the stress position, but I could think of more comfortable ways of standing. Leaning against a convenient wall or lamppost or simply standing with the arms folded, would have looked and felt quite good. I never chanced suggesting it to an NCO though. From here, you could go one of two ways. With the command 'Stand Easy', you could relax your shoulders and drop your chin a bit. This was as indolent as drill got in the British Army. There was never any further instruction to 'Just chill out for a bit, lads.' It was a reasonably comfortable stance but, of course, absolute silence was a rule. Anyone caught coughing, sniffing up a greenie or shuffling around would be rounded upon and subjected to a bombardment of verbal brickbats. The insults levelled were always vulgar and funny to all but the recipient, and represented the first level of punishment on the drill square. If you fucked any movement up, the first reaction from the staff would be insults from a distance. Further transgression merited a more personal approach, and you would be shouted at from point blank range. If this wasn't enough incentive to get your act together, you would be taken out of the squad and humiliated slightly. You would be made to demonstrate your atrocious drill in a 'here's how not to do it', display. The ultimate punishment, reserved only for those who were beyond drill redemption was to be jailed. Going to prison for not being able to move your legs or arms as instructed seemed slightly excessive, but it was done in the best interests of the recruit, apparently. It was a brand of tough love that took a bit of getting used to. Whichever blackguard had annoyed the drill instructor to this extent was deemed to have 'had it coming'.

Watching somebody being jailed always made for great entertainment, coupled with the optimistic hope that the instructor might have now got his anger out of his system. The prospective jailbird would have been subjected to levels 1, 2 and 3 before being awarded the top prize. The first indication that he was going away was a barely intelligible shriek from the drillpig to 'Stay where you fucking are.' The recruit would attempt to halt, usually badly, compounding his error. The instructor would then accuse him of deliberately sabotaging the lesson before shaking his head and turning to one of the AT NCO pissboys, with the immortal words 'Get him off my square.' The recruit would immediately be dragged out of the squad and told by the AT NCO to remove his beret and belt and hold them in his left hand. I'm not sure why. It might have been that he was no longer fit to wear his headgear. It was more likely to be that it made him look a bit more of a tit. With the words 'Listen in to my timing,' the recruit would be marched to jail at 40 miles an hour. The horrendously quick pace, reserved for people on their way to jail, was known as 'pokey drill'. When he got to the jail, he was handed over to the reviled RPs who would have a list of shitty jobs for him. He'd stay there until the end of the lesson, usually an hour or two. At the end of his punishment, one of the AT NCOs would come and get him and pokey him back to the squad.

The other option from the 'Stand at Ease' was 'Attention'. Prior to beginning the movement, you would usually be 'Stood Easy'. The correct method from here was as follows: The instructor would roar the word 'SQUAD'. In a millisecond, 80 chins would jut up and 160 shoulders would brace up. He'd then repeat the word, this time in a strangled, elongated fashion. This was to let you know that an executive word of command was shortly to follow and no action was to be taken, other than to ready yourself for further instruction.

"SQQUUAAAAAAAD."

A second or so later, the word 'SHUN' would be screamed. In a lightning fast response, 80 right legs would lift, until the thigh was parallel to the ground, before slamming the foot back down, to rest adjacent to the left, with both feet forming the 'ten to two' position. Simultaneously, the arms would move from their position at the back, to be pinned tightly at the sides, fists clenched with the little finger to the rear, and the thumbs pressed tightly on the index fingers.

Each drill instructor had his own way of delivering the 'SHUN'. It allowed them to express themselves creatively, within the strictures of the parade square. Some would just shout extra loud for that bit. Others used to raise their voices, going from tenor to falsetto in the space of a single word. The strangest ones, Sergeant Bailey included, opted for a complete disfigurement of the word, paired with the high pitched delivery. The instruction would come out as 'SHHOOOWWNNNAAA', and just needed the word 'muthafuckers' on the end to complete the 'New York pimp' effect.

Our lesson didn't go as Bailey and Atkins planned, and they got progressively more angry at our inability to do anything correctly. We started pissing Sergeant Bailey off right from the start.

"SQUAD," he roared unexpectedly. Some of the troop reacted within the allocated time, but most of us braced up a full two seconds later.

"AS YOU WERE." This was our cue to go back to the 'Stand Easy' for another go.

He abused us for a few moments.

"When you hear the command 'SQUAD', I want shit-off-a-shovel reactions. Let's try again."

Without further warning, he shouted again.

"SQUAD. AS YOU FUCKING WERE. Right, you wankers. You're starting to grip my shit."

He then went through a blur of commands which were impossible to keep up with.

"SQUADASYOUWERESQUADASYOUWERESQUADASYOUWERESQUADASYOUWERESQUADASYOUWERESQUAD."

At the end, none of us was sure of what position to stand in. I initially opted for standing easy. A furtive glance left and right gave the impression that everyone else had gone for standing at ease. Like one of the kids on the eighties TV show *Runaround*, I changed my position, to go with the majority. We spent 20 minutes on that particular movement, with Bailey getting redder in the face with our continued sluggish reactions. In the gaps between the shouting, I felt the injustice of it. How were we supposed to know all this stuff, right off the bat? I had the urge to complain to the Drill Ombudsman. I managed to tick off the first two levels of abuse, in that first portion of the lesson too. I'd already been shouted at from a distance a couple of times and had instinctively shrunk to make myself a smaller target. Whilst I was formulating the words to my official complaint, I missed another shout, and braced my shoulders nearly five minutes after everyone else. This made Bailey as mad as a bastard and he stormed over to me and bellowed at me, nose to nose. I could smell his breath. It was that combination of low quality hot beverages and high quality tabs, producing a heady concoction that smelt like shit.

"What's your fucking name?"

"NUGENT, SERGEANT."

He prodded me in the chest with his pace stick.

"Start getting it right, Nugent, you cock. I've seen quicker reactions from a waxwork."

"YES, SERGEANT."

With that, he retreated, taking his demonic breath with him. By the time we moved on to 'Coming to Attention', both sergeants were at an increased level of animation. The AT NCOs mirrored their mood, throwing in continuous barbed criticisms of every lacklustre knee raise or tardy brace. Knowing that I'd progressed through levels 1 and 2, Baker focused his attention on me, finding increasing fault with everything I did. It was a tactic borrowed from professional football. I was the defender on a yellow, with Baker as a striker trying to get me sent off. I thought I was doing it right, but it wasn't long before Bailey had me stood out in front of the squad, demonstrating my shoddy drill. Whilst performing, I was compared to a variety of old-fashioned, camp stereotypes including Liberace, Danny La Rue and Larry Grayson. This was due to my inability to make much noise when my right boot slammed into the concrete, on the completion of the movement. As I continued to repeat the actions, as instructed, Bailey addressed the rest of the lads.

"I want to hear a noise like a fucking shotgun going off when I shout 'SHUN'. Not like this cunt." He thumbed over his shoulder at me, carrying on regardless.

"I could make more fucking noise banging me bellend off the armoury door. Get back in the squad, Nugent, you're on your last chance."

I marched back into the anonymity of the squad as quickly as I could. From then on, I made a superhuman effort to do everything correctly. My problem was that the spirit was willing, but the flesh was weak. I wasn't the only one fucking up and it was a toss up between me and a few others as to who would be the one to push Bailey over the edge and get sent to jail. The question was answered half an hour before the lesson finished, when my beret fell off. It had been a bit windy, but not enough to remove headgear. The constant drill movements and flinching had caused the band to ride up from my left ear. I was too scared to adjust it. I spent a couple of minutes trying to manoeuvre it back into position by waggling my ears, but that didn't work. At the same time as I completed my millionth 'SHUN', a small gust of wind caught the underside of the band and tipped the beret off my head, onto my right shoulder and then down to the ground. It rested by my foot, stolidly refusing to jump back on my head, despite my telepathic command. As soon as Bailey saw it lying there, he used his powers of deduction to affirm that it belonged to me and screamed: "Nugent, not you a-fucking-gain. I've had enough of you, you fucking leg-iron. The only thing you're good at is being shit. Lance-Corporal Baker, get him off my square."

Nobody in the squad actually moved, but I could feel them all pulling subtly away, isolating me, to eliminate any potential for guilt by association. If it had been allowed, they'd have all been looking in 80 different directions, whilst whistling in a carefree fashion. Baker appeared with undisguised glee.

"Right, Nugent, pick your beret up and get it in your left hand." I obeyed as quickly as I could, hoping it might earn me a reprieve. Unfortunately for me, my fate had been decided as soon as my cap hit the floor. Baker continued: "Listen in to my timing. By the left, quick march."

With that, we were off. Baker's timing turned the words into one, barely understandable racket.

"Lefrighlefrighlefrighlefrighlefrighlefrighlefrighlefrig hlefrighlefrighleffft."

I was trying to match his pace and swing my right arm in time, which was impossible. I must have looked like Charlie Chaplin. It was a march of 200 metres to my final destination, and we got there in less than a minute. Baker's shouts must have alerted the trolls in the guardroom, and they were waiting to greet me.

Foremost, of course, was Corporal Lang, and he beamed, revealing a set of teeth that I would later hear described as 'like a fighting patrol, all blacked out and five metres apart'.

Baker and Lang had a brief conversation, as I stood there panting. They discussed the reasons for my jailing, and the appropriate punishment. Once Lang had established that he had me for 30 minutes, I was released into his custody. He wasted no time.

"Right, you little shagbag, get in that fucking guardroom. There's some bumpering to be done."

I started to march, but Lang told me to run or he'd kick me up the arse. Needing no further persuasion, I ran into the guardroom, where a couple of fat, old lance-corporals were reading tabloids and eating hardboiled eggs. A bumper appeared immediately, and Lang shouted: "Right, fucking get on with it. I want to see my face in this floor when you're done."

I couldn't think why. He was a grotesque little cunt, but I wasn't arguing. Having done my share the previous night, I was confident that bumpering was at least one thing I'd be able to do without criticism. Frankly, it didn't seem like a punishment. I was now off the square and away from Bailey and Baker's beady eyes. Sharing personal airspace with Lang wasn't pleasant, but distinctly preferable. I should have realised that the Army was far too clever to make a punishment more desirable than regular work. I was already doing the standard bumper sweeps, when Lang stopped me. His tone was scarily amiable.

"No, no, no. That's not how you do it. Let me show you."

He then positioned my hands correctly. At that point I realised that I wanted to go back on the square. I was now stood with my left hand at the top of the bumper handle and my right at the bottom, just above the bumper itself. It was an extra long handle, and I had to be at full stretch to implement Lang's orders. He said: "Lovely, carry on like that and you'll do a great fucking job." He then sat with his egg eating mates and enjoyed the show. I spent the remaining 25 minutes of my punishment walking up and down the room in this agonising position. It was phenomenally back-breaking and I was sweating through my jumper within a couple of minutes. It was difficult to tell from the angle I was at, but it didn't seem to get the floor any shinier either. Occasionally, Lang or one of his cronies would give me a bit of condescending encouragement. There was a big clock on the back wall, and every now and again I'd get a glimpse of it. Its ticking was interminably slow, and by the time my ordeal was over, I felt like I'd been there a week.

When Lance-Corporal Baker came to get me, Lang told me to stand up. I released the bumper handle but found myself locked in position. I straightened myself up, letting out an involuntary yelp as my back snapped back into line.

"Never mind that, you fucking girl," Lang said, before adding: "Come back anytime you like."

By the time Baker had pokied me back to the lads, they were just about to be marched off the square. Sgt Bailey greeted me cordially.

"Ah, Nugent. Enjoy the hospitality in the guardroom?"

"YES, SERGEANT."

"Good. They aim to please. Think on for next time."

I joined the back of the squad and we were taken back to the block, where I was debriefed by the rest of the lads. Like the kid who gets the strap at school, I found that my punishment had accorded me a bit of celebrity status. I went into great detail and it made my room-mates shudder and laugh in equal quantity.

That evening was a simple repetition of the one before. The only change was that the standards expected were now higher, as we were now such veterans. We also had to start ironing our uniforms as well. Mum's impromptu lessons helped me out here and I was able to show a couple of the other lads how to do it. It was the first time I'd felt useful since arriving. There is a method to some of the madness though. Our joint tribulations were already succeeding in us sticking together as a room. By lights out we'd achieved what we judged to be a decent job. Baker's opinion was less effusive.

"Better than last night, but still fucking shit. Call it a hunch, but I don't think Sergeant Bailey will be impressed. Get a good night's sleep anyway fellas, you've got PT tomorrow."

Baker's intuition proved to be spot on and the room was turned upside down again. It was a good demonstration of the law of diminishing returns. The room-trashing was expected this time so it didn't bother us so much. For the second time in two days, my bedblock bounced off my head before falling to pieces on the floor. As soon as they moved on to Room 5, we started straightening the place up, on auto-pilot. Baker was out of the room, so we indulged in a bit of our own banter. Paul shouted across to me.

" 'Ere, Eddy? What's the facking score wiv' you an' that bedblock then?"

"Fuck knows, mate. I reckon someone's nobbling it while I'm having a shave."

"Yeah, that'd be right," shouted Tom. "Industrial fucking espionage, that's what I reckon. When I went for a shit last night my kit was spotless. I got back and some cunt had ironed it all wrong, behind my back."

This brought roars of laughter. Tom was going to be the tramp of the room, of that we were assured. He couldn't iron and he always looked like he'd slept in his clothes. Fortunately for him, he didn't worry too much about it, and left that for Baker and the other NCOs. The other accolade he'd won for himself, even at this early stage, was the room's farting champion. Everyone was at it of course, and people went out of their way to inject both volume and aroma into all their anal output. I considered myself quite schooled in the art, but Tom was a master. I have never smelt farts that stank as bad as Tom's. He was an honest man though, and would always inform the room immediately prior to a delivery. Because of their incredibly rank qualities, they had to be smelt to be believed. If he dropped one nearby, it was impossible to resist taking a tiny whiff before plunging headlong for the nearest door or window. Smell isn't enough to create a true flatulent hero, and Tom didn't disappoint in its other discipline. He must have had an uncanny control of his sphincter. He could produce eerily high-pitched, 15-seconders that brought a tear to the eye, both his and yours. At the other end of the scale were huge explosions that would have caused tissue damage to a lesser man. Some of these were so powerful that he would hold the end of his knob before beginning, so he didn't inadvertently piss himself during the display. He even practised in his sleep. I'd come back from having a pee the night before. I snuck back into the room, just in time to hear his snoozing flourish. It was a four-second, apathetic trump that sounded like the start of 'Night Boat to Cairo', by Madness. His performances would prove to be an invaluable source of morale throughout training, even if they did make you feel a bit sick.

When Baker came back in, he screamed at us to get into our PT kit, and we scrambled around in our lockers with the now familiar panic-tinged haste.

Once attired in our baggy shirts and shorts, our green issue socks and plimsolls, we looked ready to take on Roger Bannister on a cinder track of his choice. There was no time for flights of fancy though, as Baker was already herding us outside, along with the rest of the rooms. We were fallen in outside the Squadron offices, and marched down to the gym. On arriving at the end of the 400m walk in our paper-thin daps, every man-jack of us had shin-splints.

The NCOs left us in our shit-scared silence outside the gym and in a couple of seconds, a pack of knuckle-scraping PT instructors filed out of a side door and descended on us in an ominous manner. This was it; this was the beginning of *Planet of the Apes*. Obviously a bunch of silverbacks had escaped from Twycross and were masquerading as the camp's PTIs. However on closer inspection, they turned out to be just ridiculously heavily muscled psychopaths, suffering from acute narcissistic rage. I found this out as one of them, in a white and red-piped gym vest, put his broken nose to mine and whispered: "You're fucking weak aren't you?"

"No, Corporal!" I lied.

He glanced at my arms; I looked like the poster child for a Red Cross famine appeal.

He snorted in disgust and moved on to the next lad to dish out an equally unnerving insult.

The air was broken by a Scouse accent.

"Right yous' guys, I am QMSI Johns, and I run the physical training on this camp. In a minute you will be fallen out into the gym, for your first PT lesson. Once that happens, you are the property of my instructors. One piece of advice, gents. Never walk during a PT lesson."

Then, with a 'carry on' to his troop of simians, he walked back into the gym.

The largest and angriest of the instructors stepped forward.

"Listen in. When I give you the command 'Fall Out', you will turn to your right, march three paces and get into the gym as fast as your pathetic bodies will carry you."

His already huge chest filled with air, and he bellowed:

"FAAAAAAAAAALLLLLLLLLLLL OUT!"

Before we had even started our turn to the right, the shouting started.

"Come on, you lazy cunts! Get in that shagging gym! Are you walking!? Are you fucking walking!? You'd better-fucking-not be!"

This took us by surprise and everyone tried to make a runner for the gym at the same time. It was bedlam and we ran like a nest of startled woodlice, scurrying for cover. The squeeze through the gym door was horrendous and we were all treading on each other in the effort not to be last to fall in. The simple result of this was that every set of white plimsolls was covered in dirty footmarks.

We all thought that once we were in the gym, we would get beasted, and that would be it. It would be horrible, but predictable. As usual, we were sadly mistaken as there was an inspection first. Unsurprisingly, the NCOs went howling mad at the state of our kit. Given that we had been half crushed to death whilst entering the gym, I thought we weren't too badly turned out. It goes without saying that I didn't air my views.

The chief ape walked out in front of us. "You idle fucking bastards! You are the worst turned-out group of recruits I have ever seen, and you are going to pay the price, gents, you mark my words! Tonight, you will parade back here at 1800 hours, with your kit ironed properly and your fucking pumps whitened! Do I make myself clear!"

"Yes, Corporal!"

"PT lessons are a parade ladies! And as such, you lazy cunts will be well turned out. Now, I was going to give you a nice easy lesson to get you used to the gym, but seeing as you can't be bothered to turn out in good order for my class, I can't be bothered to take things easy on you. NOW GET ROUND THE FUCKING GYM AND TOUCH ALL FOUR CORNERS, GO!"

Then it began. Everything we did, be it press-ups, sit-ups or whatever torture the instructors could think of, the order would come as: "Exercise… begin! TOO SLOW,

DO IT AGAIN! YOU'RE NOT IMPRESSING ME, GENTS!"

After the third time that an individual was deemed as 'not impressing' the PTIs, they would be sent to hang off the wall bars until they saw the error of their ways. At one point or another during the lesson, everyone had done a stint on the bars. My turn came whilst in the middle of my hundredth nodding-head, arse-thrusting, straight-armed press-up. The instructor told me that I wasn't trying hard enough, and that he had my number. After that, it was a matter of seconds before he lost his temper with me.

"Get on those fucking wall bars you idle cunt, Nugent!" I tried to run to the bars, but I just staggered across the floor as if I had done ten revolutions at a game of 'spin round the broom handle'.

I had actually been trying my best at the time of the gripping, and this punishment taught me the benefits of 'skive to survive', immediately.

From then on, if the instructors weren't looking, I rested. As soon as they turned around, I grimaced dramatically and put on my best vinegar stroke face.

At the end of the session, everyone looked ravaged. We were all sweating profusely, red of face, and the previously pristine v-neck of each of our PT shirts had now stretched to form a huge 'U' that was exposing at least one nipple.

The worst thing was that we had to get back to the block, sort our kit out, and go back to the gym to suffer it all again.

Our return trip to the gym that day was not as physically demanding as before, but ten times worse all the same. During the first PT lesson, it had begun to rain, and when we returned at 1800 hours, it was lashing down. They kept us standing in the rain for ten minutes. By the time two of the instructors came out the whitener had begun to run off our daps, and was making a white river on its way down to the drains.

"Well, gents. Seeing as you can't get your clothes clean, we may as well get them dirty for you! Now fall out and start running around the assault course!"

So we set off on our adventure. We didn't actually attempt the obstacles as – like before – we were clad in only T-shirt, shorts and daps. What we did do though was run up and down the side of the course until the mud became ankle deep. We were then made to get into the prone position and crawl up and down until we looked like 1950s B-movie, mud-monsters.

With our lesson in the importance of PT kit maintenance thoroughly drilled home, we were marched back to the block where we scrambled to get our washing done in time for the next lesson.

On arriving back to the room, Baker was waiting with his arms folded and shaking his head. He summed up his feelings about our current plight in one word: "Cunts."

I went to sleep that night, feeling heartily sorry for myself. There was absolutely no way on this planet that I was going to be able to withstand these levels of abuse for 14 weeks. Like every other recruit in history, I nodded off, safe in the knowledge that I was easily the biggest arsehole to ever have graced the uniform. However, the Army had always got this bit right; we were all in it together. The camaraderie created by mutual adversity got me, and various other deadlegs, through. As the days went by, things seemed to get incrementally better. You wouldn't be able to plot this progress on a graph, and normal measuring techniques would have been equally useless. It was in the little things, that I began to see the light at the end of the tunnel. Baker's use of the word 'cunt' was as frequent, but seemed to lose some of its venom with each repetition. I found, to my immense surprise, that my body did actually have the building blocks of co-ordination, and that occasionally I could march in a straight line and halt at the same time as everyone else. I hesitate to say it, but by the time I'd been there a couple of weeks, part of me was starting to enjoy the training.

We were lucky in Room 4, as all the other rooms appeared to have a duty fuckwit. It was the duty fuckwit's task to inadvertently spoil everyone else's hard work. On room inspections, it was his appointed duty to forget to do something important, therefore bringing the wrath of the DS down on his mates. Room 6 had the biggest fuckwit. He was called McDaid and hailed from somewhere in the far north of Scotland, that was closer to Russia than it was to Harrogate. He had the endearing habit of leaving shitty undercrackers around. Never considered to be a particularly high social grace, in a recruit troop setting it was apt to get the entire room murdered, when discovered by a nosey sergeant. As soon as his little habit was discovered, Sergeant Atkins always paid special attention to McDaid's locker, on the hunt for 'brown treasure'. He struck dark gold one morning when 'Skiddy', as he soon became known, had dunked a pair of particularly clinker-infested gruds into one of his boots, in the couple of seconds immediately preceding the 'Room, room shun.'

"Where have you left 'em this morning, McDaid?"

"Pardon, Sergeant."

"Do I have to go fishing with my pace stick, or are you going to give me a clue?"

After a couple of moments, Skiddy sighed and said: "Ma right boot, Sergeant."

Atkins shuddered, and shouted: "You dirty bastard. I don't know what it's like in fucking Latvia or wherever it is you're from, but in the British Army, we do not keep our soiled underwear in our boots, or anyone else's for that matter. Right, get 'em on your 'ead and you can wear them all morning."

On that morning's drill lesson, Skiddy was conspicuous as the only man who appeared to be wearing a turd-hardened cravat.

Tom Galbraith was the closest we got to a fuckwit, but his brilliant sense of humour and superlative farting skills compensated well for his shortcomings. He always made me laugh, even when I didn't know what the fuck he was on about. He told me one of the jokes from his Scottish cabaret, whilst we were cleaning the bogs on a bull night and I didn't get it until the next morning.

"Hey, Eddie, ya cunt. You'll like this 'ain. What's the difference between Bing Crosby and Walt Disney?"

I was concentrating on removing a particularly adhesive bit of shit with the back side of the scrubbing brush, and replied impatiently: "I dunno, mate. What?"

"Bing sings, and Walt disnae." He roared with laughter slapping me on the back when I just stared at him, dumbfounded.

"Ya miserable fucker ye'. Walt disnae," he implored.

I carried on with removing shit from the toilets, for Queen and country.

It was mildly comforting to know that the Army did not expect us to endure our hardships without any kind of reward. To that end, we were paid the princely sum of ten pounds per week. However, in typical Army fashion, obtaining and spending the money was not made easy.

Our financial reward was administered on an official pay parade at the end of every week and took place in the block. The Squadron 2IC would be sat behind a table at the end of our corridor, flanked by Atkins and Bailey, like two vultures just waiting for one of us to fuck up. In front of the officer would be a tin of money, a pen, and a register of our names. We in turn, would be lined up in front of him in single file. At his behest, the recruit at the head of the line would spring to attention, march forward, halt in front of him, salute, give his name and number, accept the ten pounds, check it, announce "Pay correct, Sir!" salute again, about turn and march away, all to be carried out with regimental pauses of 'one-two-three-one'. It all sounded straightforward enough, but the reality was a different matter.

Any mistakes would be picked up by Atkins or Bailey and the offender would be sent to the back of the line where he would wait 15 minutes for his next turn. Should someone be unlucky enough, or just totally shit at drill, to be picked up three times, then they would be sent to jail. 'Grippable' offences would include a lacklustre spring to attention, a step on the march forward or away that had an inadequate heel-dig or arm-swing, and sloppy saluting (of which Skiddy was particularly guilty, as he saluted like a depressed New Romantic sweeping his flick from his eyes). We would even be gripped for not checking our money properly. I was jailed for this on one occasion, and after that I would snap my head down to look at the tenner in my hand, and bring it up again as smartly as possible.

Once armed with our fortune, we still had to purchase our boot polish, plimsoll whitener, boot-bulling cloths, starch and all other manner of kit maintenance stuff from it. Which left a negligible amount of change for anything else.

Any trip to the NAAFI was only to be done by one person per room, and they were not allowed to buy any confectionery for themselves or the rest of the chaps. To enforce this, the room NCOs would search any NAAFI run bags when the designated shopper returned. This led to most of the guys developing the ability to drink a freshly opened 1.5 litre bottle of Irn Bru and eat ten Mars bars in one minute. It meant that you would be burping up fizzy pop sick for the rest of the night, but it was worth it for the sugar fix. Although I was more of a litre of Coke man myself, as the orange hue of Irn Bru always reminded me of the bottles containing strange liquids that tramps would leave under park benches.

Another weekly routine was the Sunday church parade. The Army considered itself religious and in the spirit of tolerance and acceptance, if it was religious, then so were you. Atkins and Bailey would have us all outside at nine o'clock for an inspection. God demanded that we be in our best clobber, so we wore what was known as barrack dress. It was pretty much the same as working dress, but instead of the dreaded KF, we wore the far more civilised, brown Number Two dress shirt. In addition we wore barrack dress trousers, in place of our lightweights. They were a horrible bit of kit, their only plus point being that they didn't take much ironing. This was due to their being fashioned from some sort of weird plastic-textile-hybrid material. Once pressed with a suitably hot iron, they held their crease for three or four years. Walking round in them felt like having your legs rubbed with a Brillo Pad and marking time for more than a few seconds would leave you with severe carpet burns on your thighs.

All recruits had to attend, but the rest of the apprentices only had to go every four weeks, whenever Rawson was the duty squadron. It was the only time we mixed with our seniors. Although they didn't have to wear a military uniform to church, they might as well have. A rigid dress code was enforced. It must have been a reaction to the styles of the time. Petrified that everyone would be showing up in cameo cod-pieces or Spandau Ballet suits, the college hierarchy decided that each squadron would have a civilian uniform as well. Rawson's was probably the worst. Shoes and smart 'get-you-into-a-club' trousers had to be worn, as well as a white shirt. They were topped with a fetching purple jumper and purple tie. The jumper had a yellow eagle motif on the left tit, and the tie had diagonal yellow stripes of smaller eagles running across it. All assembled for the march over to the church; they looked like they were off for a couple of rounds with Tarby and Brucey, at a pro-am golf tournament. To add insult to injury, these items had to be purchased from the PRI with a significant portion of the apprentices' meagre wages. Just before we set off, we were split up into our respective religions. Three-quarters of the recruit troop fell into the C of E category. This included anyone who wasn't sure and all the atheists who didn't want an argument. The rest of us were Catholics, or as Sergeant Atkins put it, Ratcatchers. Conveniently, Sergeant Bailey was also a 'Roman Candle', so he always took our squad. The C of E service was taken in the big church, by the College Padre, whilst our mass was taken in the smaller church to its left, by a priest who drove in from Harrogate. Mum and Dad weren't regular churchgoers, so my exposure to the Catholic rites had mainly been courtesy of school. My memories were of boredom and the unsubtle sabotage of popular hymns. The simple replacement of the word 'light' with 'shite' had always reaped huge dividends. It was made pretty clear by Sergeant Bailey that impromptu amendments to songs wouldn't be tolerated in the Army. As we filed into the chapel for the first time, I was a bit slow in removing my beret, which caused Bailey to growl: "Take your hat off in the house of the Lord, Nugent, you cunt."

Once you were inside and sat down, sanctuary was achieved for the duration of the proceedings. For 30 minutes, you were left alone with no one to shout at you. As long as you didn't fall asleep or fuck about, it was a well-earned break. As the priest droned on, it was possible to drift off and relax. He would relate anecdotes about life in Harrogate, but because it was outside the camp gates, he may as well have been talking about Kathmandu. I used to take the opportunity to look at some of the eye candy on show. Permanent members of staff would bring their wives and children to the services. Most of the wives were on the big side, but some of the daughters provided a welcome change from having to look at squaddies all the time.

An unsettling aspect of the service, which a theologian could have written a dissertation on, was that the priest was a grass. If he ever spotted anyone, especially a recruit, nodding off, he would bring it to the attention of one of the sergeants hovering at the end of the pew. How a man of the cloth could do this, in the safe knowledge that the sleeper would soon be undergoing punishment far outweighing his crime, was beyond me. After every service, as he shook hands and smiled at his departing parishioners, five or six lads would be doing star-jumps on the grass behind him, whilst one of the SNCOs berated them for not displaying the Christian value of being good listeners. Our mass always finished a quarter of an hour earlier than the C of E, so we were allowed to go and have a cup of tea in the refectory next door, whilst we waited for the rest of the troop. It was a nice skive and it was quickly spotted by the other lads. As the weeks went by, a conversion took place that Billy Graham would have been proud of. Six weeks into training, almost half the troop were declaring themselves Catholic on a Sunday morning. Atkins and Bailey had never bothered to count numbers, but they started to get suspicious by week ten, when only Atkins and eight recruits were heading over to the big church. A glance to the left allowed them to witness the massed ranks of unbaptised Catholics squeezing in next door, all eager to enjoy a sneaky brew, with only their immortal souls as payment. They put a stop to it eventually, by checking names against a list of everyone's official religious beliefs.

A few weeks into training we were introduced to the primary role of the Army; military training. This covered all aspects of what I envisaged soldiering to be. It was a heady mix of weapon handling, including stripping, assembling, loading and unloading various rifles. All of this led to the natural conclusion of firing them on the ranges. As the range day drew closer, my trepidation grew at an exponential rate. We had been filled with all sorts of stories on how the SLR was an elephant gun and that if you didn't hold it properly when firing, it would dislocate every bone in your body. It was all the normal shit that people who have done something feed to those that haven't. Once we were all deemed competent with the rifles, we were loaded onto four-tonners and whisked off to the sunny climes of Whitburn ranges on the North Sea coast, or 'Whitburn-sur-la-Merde' as it should have been known.

We were all sat down and broken into two groups. One lot who would be shooting first and the others who would be operating and repairing the targets. This second group was known as the 'butt party', which drew several laughs.

I was in the butt party first off, which only made the build-up to shooting even more ominous. I shouldn't have been so nervous, but I had never fired anything with a calibre larger than an elastic band in my life and I just didn't know what to expect. So when the first 'crack and thump' of the rounds whipping over head snapped me out of a tit-and-fanny daydream, it only threw fuel on the fire of my anguish.

Still, it wasn't all bad. Colin Mortimer tried to cheer me up by pointing to a 6-inch diameter glue pot, and in his thick Newcastle accent said: "How, Eddie man. Ya see that pot 'o glue? Well, that's your arse, that is!"

We were in the butts for the morning, and it soon became monotonous. The guys would shoot, we would tot up the scores and then repair the targets, and so it would continue. It soon occurred to me that shooting first would be better, as you would have all afternoon to get your weapon clean. Not that it would make much odds, because any instructor who inspected your rifle would say that it was in 'bog order', regardless of its actual condition and you would be sent away to reclean it. If it was clean you wouldn't bother to touch it again. When you took it back for reinspection, the instructor would say: 'That's fucking better! Why didn't you do that properly in the first place, you lazy cunt!' But that was neither here nor there.

The transition from butts to shooting took place at lunch and we all congregated behind the firing line, near an old hut. The hut was staffed by an old guy, who was the range warden. He looked like a Wookiee with mange and at first I thought that he stank to high heaven, but it later transpired that the god-awful smell was coming from a small kitchen inside his hut. One of the instructors asked him what the source of the whiff was, and he replied: "Don't you worry about that, son. I'm just cooking up a few starfishes for me dog." With that, he pointed down to his side, but there was no dog there. The man was obviously insane.

Our lunch meal had been driven out from camp and consisted of two large food containers, one containing stew and the other containing tea. Unfortunately, the last time that they were used, they had swapped roles, but had not been cleaned. So the tea tasted of stew and vice versa.

The moment of truth eventually came at two o'clock that afternoon. I got into the prone position behind my long black rifle and followed all of the instructor's orders to load and make ready. It was just like being in the classroom and I soon forgot my worries, until I fired the fucking thing! It kicked like a barge mule and leapt back in my lack-lustre grip whereupon the rear sight split my eyebrow open in a flash of white pain. Needless to say I held on to it for grim death after that. When I dressed away from the firing point, one of the instructors noticed my bleeding eye and called me over. I explained myself and he offered the encouraging words of: "Well you won't fucking do that again, will you, you dickhead?" He was right – I never did.

We were also taught field craft, the art of seeing without being seen, which is similar to the effects of being drunk, when you could be dancing naked in the street but be completely convinced that you are invisible. We also covered practical and written lessons, in first-aid and nuclear, biological, and chemical warfare. Instruction in the latter culminated in us being gassed in a small chamber that was filled with CS. When it was my turn to remove my respirator, I held my breath as long as possible. Soon, the instructors bombarded me with a series of questions that resulted in me taking in an involuntary lung full of the horrible substance, and spending the next five minutes choking and spluttering, with two 12-inch-long snot strings hanging from my beak.

The only other time I caught the full force of CS was during the 'canister change' drills, when I panicked. Despite my best efforts to get the filter secured back in place by cupping my right hand over its mounting hole, it still got cross-threaded on reattachment and I got a full hit of gas inside my respirator.

The whole mil training extravaganza was overseen by a group of moustachioed instructors, who were only one step down from the PTIs on the 'angry-at-the-world-ometer'. Their rage would peak every time one of us fucked up on a test, and the most common example was the magazine loading. This was a practical exam that involved kneeling with an empty magazine between your legs, and an upturned helmet full of 20 rounds on the floor in front of you. When the instructor said go, the panic began and it was a desperate, shaking finger scramble to bomb up the mag with the loose rounds, in the allotted time. The last couple of rounds were the worst as you would have to chase them around the inside of the lid, and forcing them into the magazine would result in skinned fingers and knuckles.

We were split into sections for the mil training and ours consisted of my room-mates and, much to my horror, Skiddy McDaid. Our instructor, Corporal Havers, was a large, but relatively reasonable man. Unfortunately, Skiddy's inability to carry out even the most basic instructions often saw Havers flip into a rage that resulted in our section running around camp with our rifles above our heads. It wasn't until Tom and Barry threatened Skiddy with a good shoeing, that his level of competence rose from 'no use to man or beast and an affront to God and nature' to the dizzy heights of 'dreg of society'. One of Skiddy's more memorable fuck-ups was on our first ‘contents of webbing’ inspection. The crux of packing your webbing was for everything to be as compact and portable as possible. To that end, for a shaving kit, everybody would pack a brush, a soap stick and a razor inside their mess-tins. Skiddy, however, rocked up with a 33% extra free, 1 litre can of Erasmic moisturising shaving foam. The can was coloured in the well known camouflage combination of red and white, and it stuck out of his kidney pouch and up his back like a full-size barber’s pole. Once again, it caused Havers to lose his rag and another jaunt around camp was on the cards.

All of our military training came to a head with our basic training exercise, when we packed our hopelessly inadequate webbing, clambered aboard the four-tonne trucks and headed off to Catterick Training Area. As soon as we got off the four-tonners, another flaw in the webbing came to light. We were told to lie down in the all round defence formation. As soon as I went prone on the deck, my backpack rode up and pushed on the back of my head, forcing my face into the ground. I couldn’t see more than two feet in front of me, and that was only by rolling my eyes up as far as they would go. Eventually I had to rest the front lip of my helmet onto the rear sight of the rifle. This was beneficial in two ways. Firstly it took the bone breaking pressure off my neck. Secondly it increased my field of vision from two to three feet. Even so, I was no use in this position. If we had been attacked, the order to open fire would have to have been: “Don’t shoot until you see the blacks of their toe-caps.”

We were taken to an area known as Rabbit Wood, where we were shown the basics of building ‘bashas’ out of our ponchos. The example that Havers built was perfectly formed and looked like a proper tent. Our attempts, on the other hand, were more like a shanty-town on the edge of Sao Paulo’s worst favela.

As we were now deployed on exercise, we had to cam-up with shit-smelling, brown 'cam-cream'. The lesson for this always follows a rigid pattern. The instructor explained that you could use too much, too little, or just the right amount of cream. He then press-ganged three recruits and did a practical. I was fortunate enough to be the 'too little' person and looked like an American quarterback, with a single dark line under each eye. Tom dipped out and got the 'too much'; he looked like Al Jolson, and Havers took great pleasure in grinding the cream into Tom's ears whilst singing 'Mammy'. Barry was 'Mr Right' as Havers called it. Once the cream was applied he had about half of his face covered in short brown smears, and he looked like, for the first time in his life and to everyone's surprise, a soldier.

Once we had rebuilt all of our bashas to an acceptable standard, and were all cammed-up, we were taken through compo rations. These field rations came in tins, and as a general rule were bland to the extreme. The only glimmer of hope was in the sundries pack that came with the box, because there was the familiar site of a packet of Rolos. These were a massive morale boost, although I was a bit dubious of their authenticity, given that all the writing on the pack was in Arabic. The other sweets in the box were some Fox's Glacier Fruits. They were impossible to separate from their wrappers and were invariably consumed with at least half of the plastic still on. Other delights from the boxes included a horrible processed cheese that became known as 'cheese possessed' and baconburgers that were simply a solid lump of fat and scrag meat. There was also a single slop-like substance that in one tin was called 'chicken curry' which would reappear in identical form in another tin, but called 'chicken in brown sauce'. The king of compo food, however, was steak and kidney pudding or 'babies' heads' as it was affectionately known, due to the soft indented feeling to the pastry, when cooked.

The cumbersome tins of compo stretched our already overloaded webbing to its limit. This meant that the only available storage space for the Rolos and other sweets was in the respirator pouch. This was dicing with death, as we were told from the start that nothing, but nothing other than NBC equipment was to go in the pouch. It seemed a shame, as it was large enough to house a family of Vietnamese boat people. The sweets in the pouch thing worked great until the first afternoon, when Havers threw a lit CS tablet into our harbour area and roared: "GAS, GAS, GAS!"

There was a flurry of activity from all of us, and in my attempts to avoid the effects of the gas I pulled out my respirator with all of my strength from its pouch. Sweets were scattered over a ten-foot radius; it was like an explosion at Willy Wonka's factory (although there were no charred oompa-loompa corpses strewn around the area). As soon as I had my respirator on I attempted to pick up the sweets from the floor before Havers noticed them and put the boots to me. When I started scanning the deck for the stickies, I noticed that the vision in my left eye was blurred and tinged brown. I figured the outside of the eyepiece must have been dirty, so I rubbed it, but to no effect. I stared quizzically at the stain for a second before the true horror of the situation hit me. There was a melted Rolo stuck to the inside of my respirator eye-piece, and there was CS gas everywhere, so I could do fuck all about it. Driven on by blind fear as to what Havers would do to me if he saw the offending sweet, I tried desperately to shift it. I started by contorting my face, hoping that the movement of my grid would shift the respirator and dislodge the sweet, but to no avail. Next I tried nodding and shaking my head furiously, but again my efforts were fruitless. In a desperate last-ditch attempt, I tried to stretch and blink my eyelids forward at the same time as a head-nod, in the hope that I could catch the offending chocolate in my lids. Quite what I would have done, or how painful it would have been, had I been successful I dread to think. But it was irrelevant, as after a minute or so of doing this, all I had achieved was to invent a mad dance routine that was suited only to a Northern Soul all-nighter. So I gave up my mad head motions, accompanied by the residual body gyrations, as they were only serving to draw attention to myself.

I spent the rest of the time avoiding the instructors, or if there were any around, I just tilted my head away from them.

When the gas all clear was given, I whipped off my mask and cleaned it as quickly as possible. It had been a close shave and I had been shitting myself throughout the whole embarrassing affair. And although I had come out unscathed, I had certainly learned a lesson.

The rest of the day was taken up with practising section attacks. This entailed alternate members of the squad running in leap frogs to attack an imaginary foe. It was knackering, especially when trying to avoid sheep-shit and puddles when hitting the deck.

Come last light, we had the mandatory stand-to and then we cooked our compo evening meal. It wasn't the best tasting food ever, but the hot chow did the trick on our weak and tired bodies.

That evening, a guard roster was drawn up, and we settled into night routine. However, at around 2100 hours, the heavens opened and we got drenched.

At one point I was lying in my sleeping bag, and I could feel waves of water lapping against my body. In the light of day we surveyed the harbour area, and it was 4 inches under water. Everyone, including the instructors, was soaking wet, as was all of our kit. It went without saying that morale was at rock bottom. Virtually no one was talking, and any words that were passed were in the form of a massive whinge. I think most of the guys must have been thinking the same as me, which was: "Fucking hell, if all exercises are going to be like this, then it's going to be a nightmare." To that end, it was decided by the DS that we would go back to camp. It was, after all, only supposed to be a two-night introduction to the field jaunt, and they would have two years to beast us over the various training areas of Great Britain. There was some consolation to be drawn from the fact that the whole of North Yorkshire had been subject to flooding in one form or another.

On returning to camp, Baker gave us the now inevitable hard time and told us that in his day they would not have been brought back in. He tried to justify his statement by giving us hugely inflated tales of hardship and exercises so cold that the flame on his lighter froze. But the whole fabrication fell on deaf ears. The last remnant of exercise life came in the form of 'compo shits', which were large dungs caused by the arse-blocking effects of the rations. They hit most of us about 12 hours after being back in camp. The strange thing about them was that they all smelled the same. One such cack was so huge that we were paraded into the corridor, then marched into the toilet one at a time and forced to look at it. It was incredible, like two cans and one bottle of Newcastle Brown Ale end on. It would have been three cans of brown, only the bottle is better shaped to give the natural taper of the log. The shit was massive, and so girthed that it wouldn't pass down the U-bend; there was no way it could have come from a human being's arsehole. Inevitably the blame fell on Skiddy, and he was given the dubious task of disposing of the beast. By all accounts he had to chop it up into manageable pieces before it would flush.

As Christmas drew closer, so did the end of training. In the last few weeks, we endured a constant ratcheting up of expected standards. Our admin skills had improved beyond recognition and the AT NCOs and sergeants increased their nitpicking to combat our new-found abilities. Baker took the lead in these matters, excelling in the discovery of things that weren't there. Even with Tom Galbraith's ropey contribution, we were on top of our game, and the room was generally gleaming. In the absence of any real problems, Baker simply invented them. During one inspection, he brushed his hand carefully across the top of my locker. When he brought it down, he inspected it, before gleefully showing its contents to me.

"What the fuck is that, Nugent?"

A solitary pubic hair nestled in his palm. It was obviously a plant. The colour match with Baker's hair was nearly perfect. I had a quick mental flash of him stood in the toilets just before he came into the room, selecting which pube to pull out. It wasn't worth challenging a person who would go to these lengths to drop you in the shit.

"It's a pube, Corporal."

"Oh, fucking really? And there's me thinking it was a fucking guitar string. What the fuck was it doing on top of your locker?"

For a fraction of a second, I entertained the notion of replying "You brought it in with you, you weird fucking bastard. It's one of yours, freshly plucked from your bush five minutes ago, you scary halfwit."

Instead, I replied: "I must have left it up there and forgotten about it, Corporal."

He wasn't sussed enough to realise that I was taking the piss, but Steve Keets couldn't stop himself from emitting a short, loud laugh. This caused the entire room to join in for the briefest of moments, before Baker screamed for order.

"Fucking funny is it, Keets?" He was blazing mad, and from our experience, was apt to do anything.

"No, Corporal."

"Like Nugent's pubes, do you?"

"No, Corporal."

"Well, you can have it. Here you go." With that, he stuck it to his forehead. Steve's anxious sweat held it in place perfectly. It looked like a comedy frown line.

By that stage of the game, impromptu pubic hair decoration seemed like a minor indignity and Steve didn't seem to suffer any ill effects.

Under threat of punishment, time was set aside for us to write home. Though not physically censored, we were always encouraged to write about the more positive aspects of the experience. This made for extremely short letters and I used to pack mine out with whining. Moaning about my circumstances was cathartic but probably made quite grim reading to Mum and Dad. They used to write their letters jointly, and they took on an almost conversational tone, as Dad would respond to comments further up the page by Mum. Also, for some reason, the pen would run out at least once during every single letter from them. Instead of stopping as soon as the ink began to wane, my Dad always wrote something like:

'Bloody hell, this pen's abo…' before recommencing with a completely different coloured pen. The running commentary wasn't essential but it always made me smile.

Getting letters from friends and family was fundamental to maintaining a modicum of mental health. The training staff were well aware of this and loved to piss people about on the weekly mail calls. The whole troop would be paraded and Sergeant Atkins would stand there with a huge pile of mail in his arms. The letters were in no particular order, so he'd just shout out the name and the recruit could run up to receive the highly prized item. The whole thing took about half an hour. Some recruits would get upwards of ten letters, but as the pile dwindled those yet to get a letter would start to get twitchy. I usually got one or two a week. The regular missive from Mum and Dad would occasionally be accompanied by a note from one of my mates. Gran wrote from time to time, but her bad eyesight and terrible spelling meant that I couldn't read them without an Enigma machine. Barry Nash obviously had three or four girls on the go, and by the time he went up to collect his eighth letter of the week, he would be getting scowled at by the less fortunate. One lad, Dave Norrington, hardly ever got a letter and Atkins used to love winding him up. The tricks were the same every week, but due to Nozzer's undiminished optimism, he fell for them every time.

"Norrington," Atkins would shout, holding an alluring blue envelope. Dave ran up like the excited schoolkid he'd recently been. As Atkins passed him the letter, he would deliver the blow, smiling and to a big roar from the troop.

"Give that to Nash, will you?"

As Atkins got to the last bits of post, he'd shout Dave's name out once more.

"Norrington?"

"Yes, Sarnt?"

"No mail."

If you were stood behind him, you could watch him deflating. It was that unsettling combination of funny and cuntish that made you feel a bit of a twat for laughing.

In the pre-mobile phone days, the only other form of contact with home was strictly rationed phone calls. It was a privilege that was withdrawn at the drop of a hat, but as a reward, it used to make us work our bollocks off. We didn't get anywhere near for the first six weeks, but during week seven our entire room was allowed down to the two red booths that stood outside the cinema. Chaperoned by Baker, we were allotted ten minutes each, 'and no fucking more'. I'd spent most of my money on polish and Brasso anyway, so keeping it short wouldn't pose a problem. When it was my turn, I went in and stacked a small pile of ten pence pieces on the top of the phone and dialled home. As soon as the connection was made, I heard my Mum's voice say 'Hello', and it affected me more than I thought it would. Though my Dad's use of profanity was liberal and inventive, it was an unwritten rule that I didn't swear in front of Mum. Unfortunately, having spent the last month and a half in a cursing workshop, where every second word and sometimes every single word was 'fuck', I couldn't help myself. It was great to hear the tones of a friendly female who meant me no harm.

"Hiya, Mum. It's really nice to hear your fucking voice," I replied.

"Pardon?"

I was horrified with myself and blushed hard enough to steam up the inside of the booth.

"Sorry, Mum. I'm not thinking straight."

"I hope that's not all they're teaching you, son?"

"No. Sorry Mum, everyone swears a lot round here."

"Maybe you can teach your Dad some more new ones when you come home. That'd be nice."

I got to speak to them both on five or six occasions before the end of training. It took Herculean efforts to keep the conversation expletive free. The calls were always short and sweet but never failed to put a spring in my step. Mum's concern for my wellbeing was comforting and Dad always had me laughing with stories about work and his eccentric views on current affairs. On one occasion, Gran was round having her tea when I rang. She tied up my whole ten minute allotment, telling me details about the death of a cat that belonged to a woman that I'd never heard of, before hanging up because her food was getting cold.

The two main bullshit factors of basic training were the drill badging parade and the Squadron Commander's block inspection. Both would be overseen by the evil troll-like OC, when he took a couple of days off from goat-bothering and emerged from under his bridge to plague the recruits one more time.

The purpose of the badging parade was to ensure that every man-jack of us could not only perform adequate drill, but also recite Corps history at the drop of a hat. Presumably, this was preparation for the unlikely event that one of us made it onto *Mastermind*, choosing 'Uninteresting facts about the Royal Corps of Signals' as our specialist subject.

Our reward for passing badging would be the Royal Signals cap badge that we could put in our berets to help us to stop looking like new members of the French Resistance.

At the start of the parade the OC stood at one side of the square, with our entire squad facing him at a distance of 20 paces. Two recruits would then come to attention, march forward out of the squad, salute to the left, salute to the right, halt, and salute to the front before answering a barrage of questions about the Royal Signals. With the job done, they would salute again, about turn, and march back into their original places leaving Bob as their uncle. However, in classic Army fashion, if the bloke you were partnered with were to fuck-up then you both failed. To that end I spent several minutes each week praying that I would not get saddled with McDaid as a partner. My reasons were twofold. Firstly, Skiddy was complete dog-toffee at drill. Secondly, the downwind hazard presented by the aroma of Skiddy's soiled kegs could prove to be slightly off-putting when trying to march.

The day of the parade was unseasonably hot and sunny, with a slight heat haze rising from the square. We were lined up in our pairs and I was partnered with Barry Nash. The OC started to appear in the distance, slowly getting larger. It took him ages to fully come into view and the scene was reminiscent of Omar Sharif coming out of the desert in Lawrence of Arabia.

Barry and I were in the best place to be for any kind of drill – in the middle of the group. This gave the kind of anonymity only dreamt of by right-hand markers and people whose surnames began with an A or a Z. No doubt, had there been a recruit Aardvark or Zimmerman, then they would have happily traded places with us. Tucked away in the centre of the pairs, Barry started to arse around. When the OC was in his final approach to the examiner's position, Barry began to talk quietly out of the side of his mouth, in a high-pitched voice.

"Hello, my name is Major Tatchell, and I am an evil troll!"

I started to giggle, but Barry carried on regardless.

"I live under a bridge and eat goats, just after I've bummed them to death!"

My laughter convulsions reached an uncontrollable level. The more I thought about how much trouble I would be in should I get caught, the more I chuckled. Barry continued.

"If your drill is not up to standard, young Nugent, that would be a very grave error on your behalf! Because you too shall receive a good bumming! Now march over my bridge, because I am a troll wanker!"

In between my giggles I whispered: "For fuck's sake, Barry! Shut the fuck up, you cunt!"

Luckily Barry stopped and I had composed myself by the time it came round for us to do the test. It went swimmingly with no slip-ups on the drill. The OC asked us the generic questions that we had been told to memorise. He asked me to name the slow and quick marches of the Corps and he got Barry to describe the cap badge in intricate detail. After our successful attempt, we had the opportunity to watch the rest of the guys go through their paces. As predicted, Skiddy fucked up monumentally. He saluted to the left when it should have been to the right, and vice versa. His halt, instead of a precise check pace, one-two, was just a random sequence of flailing legs that would have looked more at home in *Riverdance*. This, accompanied by Skiddy trailing a semi-perceptible brown cloud like a wounded swimmer, made for a highly amusing spectacle.

Two days later, we had the bull night for the OC's inspection. The brown lino floors had never been so shiny. We all armed ourselves with a tin of dark tan Kiwi Parade Gloss boot polish, then got on our hands and knees in one long line and polished the floor like a giant boot. Everyone worked their plums off and anyone going into another room without a good reason was met with anger and possible violence for the capital crime of fucking-up their floors. We pretty much worked the whole night through without stopping, save for an interim inspection by AT Sergeant Bramhall at ten o'clock. The inspection was unnecessary as we all knew the score with bull nights by this point, but Bramhall insisted that it go ahead, and who were we to protest? At the appointed hour, he sauntered into the room leaving scuff prints on the deck, whilst we all stood to attention and watched our work go down the tubes. He checked absolutely everything and could find no fault. In a last-ditch attempt to dig up a grippable offence, he picked up the metal waste paper bin and peered inside. It was spotless, but nevertheless, he went into an insane rage.

"Who the fuck was supposed to clean this?" he called.

Alistair stepped forward.

"Me, Sergeant. McKenzie, Sergeant."

"Come here, you lazy fucker and look in this fucking bin."

Alistair did as he was told and Bramhall continued.

"Well, Goat Jugs. What the fuck do you see?"

"Er, I don't know, Sergeant."

Alistair's reply was cautiously quizzical because there was not a spot of dirt in the receptacle. The bin was surgically clean.

Bramhall roared.

"Well I'll tell you, you shitdick! FEZZ! That's what it is, it's fucking FEZZ! Look!" He then forcefully up-ended the bin onto the white surface of a table and lifted it, expecting to see a pile of dust and dirt, but the table surface remained clean. So he repeated the action, only this time he followed it up by striking the base of the upside down bin with his pace stick. Again, his efforts were fruitless. At this point he went scarlet with anger and on his third attempt at shaking loose any dirt, he began thrashing the bin in a frenzy of long looping blows. When his arms became tired he stopped and stared at the now pockmarked base of the bin, which looked like an aerial photograph of Ypres. On lifting it, he took on the appearance of a vindicated man, because on the table was a flake of paint that his assault had knocked off the inside of the bin. The flake was about the size of a mouse's claw, but regardless of this, Bramhall felt that it justified his tirade.

"Right, McKenzie. Get your lazy fat arse into the corridor and bring in the large bin from the ablutions."

Five seconds later, Alistair returned with a normal family sized round metal bin. Bramhall then made Alistair stand to attention with the upside down bin over his head, and then subjected it to the same deranged attack that he had done previously with the smaller waste receptacle. I swear that each time the stick hit the bin, Bramhall's feet were off the floor. It was apparent, that some of his punishment ideas were cartoon-based.

The next day's inspection was carried out again by Major Tatchell, but this time it was done when we weren't there. We were given a run down on his findings when we returned from mil training that afternoon. Our room had come top, and the only thing he could find wrong was that one of the beds was missing a spring, no doubt shaken loose by the vibrations caused by years of masturbation. This was the final hurdle, and later that day we were awarded our cap badges, which had the strange design trait of having three lumps of metal that protruded through the inside of the beret and dug into the wearer's forehead. The NCOs were kind enough to emphasise this point by making us stand to attention in our berets and hitting the cap badges with the palms of their hands. After this we all had three small dents in our noggins, to remind us of the momentous occasion. Having the cap badge seemed to make a huge difference to our status. From the moment we were 'badged', we zipped up the food chain, all the way from amoebae to plankton. Although the bollockings and punishments still came thick and fast, the emphasis started to shift. There was a subtle perception that those who had got this far were likely to make it through basic and take up positions as apprentice tradesmen. Even strokers like Baker went a little bit easier on us. I presumed that there was an element of self-preservation to this stance. As soon as we finished training, his rank would mean pretty much fuck all and the desire for recriminations might surface. I didn't think I was capable of taking him on physically, but Tom Galbraith was relishing the prospect. One of his favourite topics of conversation was what he was going to do to Baker if he ever saw him in a pub.

"I'll tell ya', lads, if I ever get the chance to sort him out, he'd better hope there's someone walking round Harrogate with a bollock-donor card."

He was a great laugh, Tom, but I wouldn't want to have been in his bad books.

As we moved into December and closer to the passing off day, we seemed to spend more and more time fucking about on the square. Although my drill was adequate, I took a bit of pride in the fact that I wasn't much good at it. There were a few lads in the troop who loved it, and they could be seen practising on their own in the corridors, in the hope that one of the AT NCOs might spot them and award them a few arse-licking points. The rest of us saw it for what it was – one great big ballache, which we'd do our best to forget as soon as we didn't need to know it.

Getting through basic training was a process of continual assessment, so there were no big exams towards the end. The instructors had us convinced from the start that we could be kicked out just for farting at the wrong time. The reality was different and as long as you generally tried to do as you were told and didn't fuck up royally all day every day, you would probably get through. As we trudged through the three months, our numbers did diminish for various reasons. Some lads decided that the Armed Forces just wasn't for them and took the opportunity to voluntarily discharge themselves. Another handful disappeared when medical problems surfaced that hadn't been picked up in the selection process. With a couple of compassionate discharges and one disciplinary sacking, our numbers were reduced to 62 by the end. The troop sack-of-shit, Skiddy, sailed through to everyone's amazement. In hindsight, he was the perfect bloke for the Army, less the dubious personal hygiene habits. Despite his ability to mess up any given task, he never gave up trying and earned, from upwind, the grudging respect of the staff.

A week before pass off, we were paraded for our recruit troop photograph. As with everything else in the Army, the photograph was structured by rank. The OC and the recruit troop officer were sat plum centre, flanked by Sergeants Atkins and Bailey and the AT NCOs. To maintain symmetry, a couple of short-arsed recruits were placed in the seats on either side, to bulk up the front row. The rest of us were arranged in order of height to give an even look to the photo. Basketball players were bang in the middle of the back row then the size gradually diminished until it got to the Cornish contingent on the ends. The photographer took a couple of shots whilst everyone tried to give him a hard-man stare. Straight after, in an attempt at state-controlled fun, we were told to 'mess about', so that the snapper could take a jokey photo. For most of us, turning a photo from serious to humorous involved the simple action of exposing the right or left plum through an open zip, preferably resting on the head of the man in front. Before anyone thought of it, Atkins ruled it out as an option. This left us with the hilarious choices of putting our hats on back to front or winking at the camera.

In the last week, we were allowed to phone home every night. Mum, Dad and Gran were coming over for the pass off. All our conversations were taken up with the massive logistical operation that would see three people travelling from Manchester to Harrogate on a train. Mum was full of questions that I didn't have an answer for. 'Should I wear a hat?' 'Are all the other mums going?' 'Can we take pictures?'

Dad was more laconic and simply wanted to know if he was going to be able to buy me a pint after. Gran's main concern was over royalty. She'd made the assumption that one of the royal family would be in attendance and was disappointed when I gave her the news – that the highest dignitary would be the big, fat Mayor of Harrogate.

"Ooooh, that's a shame, Eddy. Are you sure?"

"Yeah, Gran. We had a look at the plan for the ceremony yesterday. There'll be a couple of colonels and a brigadier, plus the Mayor and his wife."

"You'd think one of 'em would have made the effort, the lazy buggers. What about that Princess Michael of Kent, you know, the Jerry. She's never doing anything, except pretending to be nice. She could have popped up."

"Sorry, Gran."

"Not to worry, I'm sure we'll have a nice time. I can't wait to see you in your uniform Eddy."

I had visions of her ruffling my hair in front of my new mates, or cleaning something off my cheek, by gobbing on a hankie.

We were dragged on to the square every day for more drill rehearsals. Once we were sized off for our pass off positions, I managed to secure myself a nice cosy berth in the middle rank, with Col and Tom close by. We were told what would happen on the day in fine detail. The four squadrons of recruits would form up closest to the flimsy, wooden, inspection dais, which would be struggling under the combined weights of the Mayor and his missus. Behind us would be four squads of back up troops, comprised of older apprentices. They were there solely to fill up the square a bit and reduce its barren wasteland appearance. To their rear would be the college band, a ramshackle collection of drummers, pipers and sick-bay rangers. Throughout my time in the College, the band was synonymous with skiving. 'Bandrats' got out of all sorts of duties and sometimes exercises. They were always disappearing out of camp for some performance or another. The downside was that it was a deeply uncool thing to do. In the overwhelmingly macho world of the Army, being in the band would mark you out as lacking in moral fibre. They only attended one of the rehearsals and that was two days before the event. We followed the boringly familiar routine. Our four squads marched on first, closely followed by the support troops. The band wheeled round to the back and halted. The RSM was on the square to check that everything was being done properly. With him around, the seniors were jittery and blokes were getting gripped and jailed, left, right and centre. There was a constant trickle of comedy marching over to the guardroom throughout the practice. With us all in position, the Razzer explained that we would be stood there for 45 minutes, whilst the Mayor did his inspection. He would stop to chat every now and again.

"If he stops to talk to you, speak to him clearly and look at him. I will be stood right behind him, so if anyone tries to give him a smart fucking answer, I'll be on hand to throw them into prison. Just think how much your mummies and daddies would enjoy watching me marching you away."

It was probably correct to assume that if we were getting a specific warning not to do something, it was because someone had done exactly that in the past. I'd love to have met the bloke who was that determined to be a smartarse, despite the massed brass of the College being on hand to hear him. I hoped it had been worth the jailtime.

To keep the crowd entertained, the band would play a medley of tunes during the inspection. They went through their repertoire for us and – try as I might – I couldn't find any running theme or connection in the tunes. They started off with a bagpipe solo of 'Amazing Grace'. It was supposed to bring a lump to the throat, but I was never a bagpipe fan, so it just gave me a headache. It was followed, inexplicably, by 'The Age of Aquarius' by Fifth Dimension. I was expecting soldierly tunes that would exhort me to puff my chest out, but we got, in quick succession, the theme tune from *Coronation Street*, 'Eye of the Tiger', the Corps quick march, 'Louis Louis' by the Kingsmen, 'Colonel Bogey', and 'Rio' by Duran Duran. I'd not heard a military arrangement of the synth-pop classic before and it took me a minute and a half to 'name that tune'.

The inspection finished, we came to attention and did a march past of the dais. On the day, the crowd would be directly behind the platform and this would be their chance to get a few photos. The march past complete, all that was left was the clichéd inspirational speech by the Commandant. For the practice, the padre pretended to be Lt Col De la Tour, and took the opportunity to do a bit of holy rolling to his captive audience. With that, we marched off to the haunting strains of the 'The Lion Sleeps Tonight'. It was an imaginative rendition, with the tuba player contributing the 'wim-a-way' sounds and the rest of the brass section playing the tune. I felt a bit cheated. Where were all the military classics? They never played any of this shit before kick off at Wembley.

The last night before pass off was a bit of a non-starter. Because Mum and Dad were only a couple of hours away, they were just going to travel over on the day. The parents of lads like Skiddy from the frozen North, and blokes from the West Country, were filling up Bed and Breakfasts all over Harrogate. Anyone who had folks coming that night was allowed out to have dinner with them. If the rest of us had known this, we'd have all been lying like NAAFI watches about where our families were staying. As they were all slipping out the door at seven, the rest of us were in the corridor getting on with a half-hearted bull night. Skiddy passed us in his best clobber, trailing a cloud of Blue Stratos behind him. He had a white shirt and grey suit on, and it was tight in all the wrong places.

Paul Jones shouted: "Fackin' 'ell; it's Alexei Sayle."

Steve Keets chipped in: "Apparently, you can't tell his Mum and Dad apart."

"What do you mean?" I enquired innocently.

"Fucking hell, Eddy. Let's put it this way. If you come from the same place as Skiddy and your mum, wife and sister add up to more than two people, you're not a local."

Although that was bollocks, Recruit McDaid did have that distinctive 'hillbilly' look to him.

Amazingly, that evening, Baker tried to ingratiate himself with us a bit. Nothing spectacular, but when he entered the room and I shouted 'Up' he waved his hand and said: "Don't worry about it. That's all finished with now. Just get the room squared away and we'll leave it that."

Cue seven bemused faces. When he went out about an hour later, we talked about him.

Tom Galbraith said: "You know what? I take back all I said about Baker. That one act of generosity has changed my opinion of him completely… he fucking wishes! What a cunt. Does he think we've all got goldfish memories or something?"

That was the thing with Baker. He hadn't really been any more unpleasant than anyone else. Getting bollocked, shouted at and punished for nothing were all part of the game. We understood that implicitly, and wouldn't be holding grudges against everyone. The subtle distinction with Baker was that you knew he really got off on the power trip. I'm sure he went off for a hand shandy every time he shouted at someone.

The last thing to do for the evening was to press our kit for the parade. The best outfit you could wear in the

Army was your Number One dress. It looked smart as fuck and was issued with a guarantee that said you would look sexy in front of gullible women. Trouble was, you only got to wear it at weddings, or if you were going to meet the Queen at the Palace. It had a black jacket with gold buttons and a collar worn high around the neck. The trousers were also black, with a red stripe down the side. We didn't get that one. The next outfit down was the Number Two dress. Aside from the toilet connotations, it was quite snappy. It was a sort of muddy-greeny-brown colour, and was worn with a brown shirt and tie, which didn't make it sound too hot. Once it was accessorized with collar dogs, silver buttons, a lanyard and white belt, it looked the bizz. Instead of a beret, the twat hat was worn with this two-piece and it made for a rather fetching look. We didn't get to wear that one either.

We were yet to be issued our Number Two dress and twat hats, so were left with the dreaded barrack dress. The only embellishment for the parade was a black plastic belt that was worn with a silver Corps buckle. The belt had to be cleaned with a special shaving foam, available only from the NAAFI at hyper-inflated prices. They were tossbags in that shop. They had a hotline to the squadrons and anytime you needed something desperately, you could catch them changing the price stickers when you got in there to buy it.

It rained on our pass off. It didn't rain enough for them to change the programme to the indoor arena, but it rained enough to get us all wet and miserable. It was still exciting, and when we formed up out of sight of the crowd, we were given a pep talk by the RSM.

"Right, gentlemen, you've earned this, so enjoy it. Let's see bags of swagger out there today, and please don't make me jail you."

All our drill was spot on, and we got into our positions without a hitch. For the expected 45 minutes of the inspection I tried to spot my Mum and Dad and couldn't. They must have got here late and had to stand at the back or something. It can't have been any easier for them. In the reduced visibility of the drizzle, the recruits must have been impossible to tell apart, at a distance of 40 metres. The Mayor and his wife went straight past me, but spoke to the next man. The band were just launching into their third tune, but I could earwig on the conversation. It was scintillating stuff.

"So, young man, where are you from?"

"Bedford, Sir," the recruit – Bloxham I think it was – replied.

"Oh, we love Bedford. We have friends there."

Bloxham left it for five seconds before realising he was supposed to reply.

"Smart, Sir."

The RSM glared at him, but the Mayor had already moved on, oblivious to the sarcasm. When the inspection was over and we were piss-wet through, we did our march past. We went past the dais twice, chucking up the obligatory eyes-right both times.

Before we were marched off, the Commandant got up and made his speech. It was jam-packed with clichés, leaving little room for sentiment or specifics.

"Recruits of 85C. I say to you 'well done'. You've all been through the mill in the last three months and have come up trumps. Your parents and I are all very proud of you today. But the proudest people here should be yourselves. You've grasped the bull by the horns, and stuck it through to the end," blah blah fucking blah. He went on like that for five minutes, including every sporting and military metaphor in the popular canon. I stopped listening after a bit and finally caught sight of my parents. There they were, right on the end of the third row of the stand. I couldn't work out how I hadn't pegged them before, then realised it was because Dad was wearing a suit. It wasn't something he did often, and he hated putting one on. Gran was to his right, talking to someone in the row behind. The RSM calling us to attention, snapped me out of it again, and we marched off, taking the opportunity to join the tuba during the 'wim-a-ways' this time.

As soon as we got off the square, we were dismissed, and we all ran to the NAAFI to meet up with our families. I found my three straight away. When Dad spotted me he waved, putting his pint down. He looked more excited than me. I made my way over to them and a group hug ensued. The scene was being repeated all over the NAAFI. Soldiers were getting their hair ruffled whilst they were rubbing lipstick off their cheeks. Shouts of 'Ooh, don't you look smart', and 'Can you get me a jumper like that?' bounced off the walls.

After the initial few seconds of adrenaline had died down, Dad reverted to type and searched for something to find fault with, whilst Mum and Gran twittered around me.

"Ahhh, look at you, Eddy," said Gran. She planted a hairy kiss on my face, before continuing: "I'll bet there isn't a smarter looking boy in the whole Army, eh, Barbara?"

Mum smiled, nodding. As she was about to speak, Sergeant Atkins came up and introduced himself.

"I was Recruit Nugent's troop sergeant for his basic training." He was all smiles and just about stopped short of putting his arm round my shoulders. It made me feel queasy. My Dad insisted on buying him a pint, whilst Gran asked him bone questions. He replied to them all professionally, but as soon as Dad returned with his beer he made his excuses and moved on to the next family. Whenever I spotted one of the lads from my room, I got them to come over and say hello. They were all politeness personified. Tom Galbraith nearly charmed the bloomers off Gran.

"What a lovely lad he was. So mannerly," she commented as he walked away. I didn't bother to tell her that he'd been flicking tagnut encrusted pubes at me a couple of days ago.

After a couple of beers and a few more impromptu speeches from various Squadron personalities, we were allowed to shoot off. Whilst Mum and Gran sat in the car, Dad gave me a hand getting my gear from the room. He took quite an interest in the room and had a good look round. The only comment he could think to make was uncannily accurate.

"Bloody hell, nine of you in this little room? It must have smelt like an open fucking drain."

I had two whole weeks off, and at the start of my leave it felt like the camp and all its horrible inhabitants were a million miles away. I spent significant chunks of my holiday boring the tits off my mates, with alcohol embellished-anecdotes about my newly acquired warrior status. They were all pleased to see me and interested in the stories to begin with, but as soon as I started using sentences entirely comprised of military abbreviations, their attention naturally wandered. Any time I saw this happening, I simply ramped up the fabrication percentage of each tale until they listened again. It meant that the 'Rolo in the eyepiece' incident had become a life-threatening event, with the CS gas being replaced with a far more noxious compound which I simply invented on the spot. I think they knew I was bullshitting, but at the time it was slightly more interesting than sixth form college.

I really did see myself as being far more grown up than my civilian contemporaries, but in hindsight I was probably just being a tosser.

I took full advantage of the relaxed home regime. Mum and Dad were probably expecting me to leap out of bed before them every morning before doing all the ironing, but I immediately reverted to my pre-Army, slovenly ways. I stayed in bed until lunchtime every day, waking up to an empty house. Whilst Mum and Dad were at work, I tried my hardest to clean out the fridge, whilst watching the finest soaps that Australia had to offer. I'd have tea with them when they got in, then ring round my mates, trying to persuade them to come out. A few beers later I'd roll in with a bag of chips, which I'd promptly fall asleep into, before beginning the cycle again. It was a pattern of behaviour that wouldn't change for my entire Army career, and my Dad could never understand it. Surveying my Beirut style bedroom, he'd make the same point.

"There's no way they'd let you get away with this in the Army."

He was absolutely right, and it was precisely why my room was a tip. As soon as I got home, the last thing I wanted to do was be tidy. Mum had to regularly pull me up about my language, as I used military level cursing to cope with any domestic crises. I couldn't find my door keys before going out one night, and had already broken the world record for using the word 'fuck' before I spotted Mum's horrified stare and stopped. Swearing was, however, not the most embarrassing habit that Mum picked me up for. On several occasions she would say something on the lines of 'Eddie, leave yourself alone!', at which point I would look around the room and reply "What?" On closer inspection I would realise that I was walking around the house with both of my hands down the front of my tracksuit bottoms, cupping my plums soothingly. I would then adopt the 'How did they get in there' facial expression and slink off to my room.

One night, I went out for a game of snooker with Dad. He was a lot better than me and augmented the difference by cheating whenever he thought I wasn't looking. It was little stuff like giving himself an extra point, or pretending not to notice that he'd nudged a red with his elbow. Whilst we played, he asked me about Harrogate.

"I have to tell you, son, I didn't think you'd stick it, you know. When I was putting you on that train you looked too little, and it seemed like it was going to be a bit too much for you."

"It wasn't that bad, Dad. After the first couple of weeks, it was the same old shit, and it was just a case of hanging in there."

"I must say though, I'm bloody proud of you." He was about to take a shot, but paused.

"I know I don't say much, but you should hear me go on about you at work. They're all sick of me reading out your letters."

"Even Tommy Two Shits?"

"Especially him. He doesn't like anyone stealing his thunder. He reckoned basic training was a lot harder in his day. Apparently, they ran 15 miles a day, in boots with no laces."

I laughed, as he missed an easy blue.

"Most of the sergeants are like that. Everything was done much faster when they were young, and they didn't have luxuries like food and water."

As he went to mark up his score he said: "So what happens with you now?"

I noted that he'd awarded himself five for a red and green. It must have been a hard red. I replied: "I go into trade training for a year and a half, then graduate from the College. I can do pretty much what I want from there."

"How do you mean?"

"The trade that I'm doing, Radio Telegraphist, is really well spread out through the Corps, so I can apply to be posted almost anywhere in the world. I've got to qualify as a tradesman first though."

I lined up a pot as he spoke.

"Don't you worry about that, son. They won't want to let you go after they've trained you up. Looking at some of them Cro-Magnons in your squad, I don't think you'll find it too hard to keep your head above water."

I hoped he was right, but we had been warned that passing through basic training was only the beginning of the Harrogate experience.

Christmas and New Year came and went really

quickly, and before I knew it, I was packing my bags to go back to camp. I shouldn't have been too bothered. It wasn't as if I was going to be one of the newest blokes there any more. A new intake would be arriving as soon as we got back, and all the DS's attention would be focused on them. I would have preferred a bit more time off though and it was quite a solemn train ride back to Yorkshire.

Chapter 3

Last Month's Razzle and Old Sven Hassel

Although not as nerve-wracking as my first journey, the return trip to Harrogate was still fraught with worries. My main concerns were whether or not I would be any good at trade training, and what my new room-mates would be like. The reasoning behind the latter was that after basic training our entire troop would be disbanded and redistributed amongst the rest of the Squadron. We would be spread randomly through the rooms occupied by older soldiers. Some of us would be lucky enough to end up with a couple of friends, the less fortunate might find themselves to be the only new boy in a room of hairy-arsed mentalists. My worries were slightly allayed once I got into camp and checked the Squadron orders board. My situation was in the middle ground of fortune. I was lucky enough to be in a room with Barry Nash, but I didn't know any of the other occupants. It was a who's who of unfamiliar names, McInerney, Ellis, Barnard and Collins. The room NCO was AT Lance-Corporal Derby.

The older blokes didn't really pay us much attention, but every now and then, Barry and I would be referred to as 'stroppy rooks'. As time went on, we were gradually accepted and integrated into the room pecking order. The natural life-cycle of the College continued and after a couple of weeks another recruit troop was in progress on the lower floor, meaning that we weren't at the bottom of the food chain anymore. As bad as it may seem, it cheered me up to see the new recruits getting beasted. From my recently acquired moral high ground, I couldn't believe how shit they were at drill and everything else for that matter.

As the lads gradually accepted us, we came to know them as individuals. They were all just older versions of the characters from my recruit troop. Paul McInerney was a mad jock and very similar to Tom Galbraith, but without his farting ability. What he lacked in flatulence, he more than made up for in tattoos.

The most morally bankrupt member of the room was Graham 'spud gun' Ellis. Spud was a porn fiend extraordinaire. His repository of filth was quite outstanding, particularly considering the lack of years he'd had on earth to accrue such an esteemed collection of 'art', as he called it. Many a time I would be snoozing on my bed, only to be awoken by Spud holding open the Readers' Wives section of a *Fiesta*, an inch from my face.

"Look at that, Eddie. Look at it. Now that is hot!" he would enthuse.

I'd move the magazine out from my face so that I could focus on the picture. Staring back at me would be 'Rita, from Tamworth', legs akimbo, airing her prestigiously furred display of genital topiary. Spud would continue: "What do you reckon to that fadge? Look at the state of the bastard; it's like a hairy nappy! Not bad eh? Hey, Eddie, it's like a wolf with its throat cut! Here, if you like that, look at page 42, there's two fat lezzas having a baked bean and custard fight."

This behaviour was only a scratch on the surface of Spud's depravity. His most notable idiosyncrasy had been the thing that had spawned his nickname. He had a scrotum that, when stretched to its full extent, was of record breaking proportions. On undoing his zip and flopping it out, it looked like someone fluffing up a duvet. The opening trick of his routine was to stretch his ballbag over the top of a pint pot and play it like a tom-tom drum. Anybody not suitably impressed by this could not help but be bowled over by the finale. Spud would get hold of one of his testicles, stretch it as far as it would go, then fold it back under his legs and push the plum up his arse. Any spectators that hadn't passed out at this point would be treated to him firing the bollock out of his ring piece with a large fart. The nad's exit would be accompanied by an x-rated Birdseye Peas ad 'plop' noise. I often wondered how he'd discovered this talent in the first place.

Spud's polar opposite was Nick Barnard, an ice-cool customer with the ladies. Even at 18 years old, his trapping skills were legendary. I'm almost certain that he never had to resort to sticking his bollocks up his arse in a last ditch attempt to get some fluff. It was quite the opposite in fact. Nick would just stand at the bar, like a Greek god with a badly-drawn bulldog tattoo, and let all of the ladies do the work. The pinnacle of his tupping came when he was promoted to Apprentice Sergeant and given his own room. It was like giving an American postman his own gun shop. Nick's already illustrious tupping exploits went through the roof, mostly because his latest conquests didn't have to worry about seven other blokes watching the action. The icing on the cake came when the orderly sergeant discovered him, firing one up one of the female permanent staff. In a world where shagging a woman was a major event, getting some action off a decent looking instructor was enough to promote a young lad to the hall of fame. Even the Sergeant-Major gripped him half-heartedly. The badge couldn't help but quiz him on the size of the woman's breasts and her techniques, then compliment him on his conquest.

Andy Collins was a bit of an enigma. He was quiet enough to be considered a grey man within the room. Ironically, he seemed to spend half of his time in the grey bar hotel, under the watchful gaze of Lang and his cronies in the guardroom. Andy's problem was that every time he got beered up, a David Banner metamorphosis would take place. Once drunk, if Andy wasn't pissing his own bed, it would be someone else's. If he wasn't fighting with bouncers, it would be with the police. He was otherwise a good soldier and that was the only thing that stopped him getting booted out. It was strangely admirable that he never offered any kind of viable excuse for his actions. His defence always followed a set pattern. When asked why he had committed these acts, he would just shrug and say: "Well, Sir, somebody's got to do it. These beds won't piss themselves you know."

He even used it after being caught having an affair with one of the instructor's wives. In his normal fashion he told the OC, with a perfectly straight face:

"Well, sir, somebody's got to do it. These marriages won't wreck themselves you know."

We never really got to know Lance-Corporal Derby. He kept himself to himself, drawing his blanket curtain across his bedspace as soon as he got in from trade. Spud reckoned he was a bit religious, and frowned on the various excesses on display in the room. He didn't bleat about it though and never attempted to convert any of us.

All in all, it wasn't a bad room and most of my anxieties were put to rest. This certainly did not leave me devoid of troubles though. I had the remaining 18 months of my training to get through yet.

The college year was split into standard terms with a nice big leave period separating each one. Leave coincided with the normal school holidays.

The syllabus was absolutely jam-packed. Each term was crammed with an intimidating amount of telecommunications trade training, education lessons, external leadership courses, military training exercises and telecomms exercises, known as 'Mercuries', which would put our trade knowledge to the test under field conditions. All of this was topped with a light dusting of mandatory hobbies, weekly bull nights and enough PT to slake the thirsts of even the most self-obsessed PTIs. It made for a richly-diverse stay.

Trade training filled a sizeable chunk of the curriculum. During term, when not on exercise or EL, most of our time was spent trying to absorb the skills that would turn us into competent tradesmen and more importantly, earn us the extra pay that came with qualification. The College taught various trades but the main split was technicians and operators. In its simplest terms, the techs fixed the radios and the operators broke them.

My particular trade was Radio Telegraphist. It was a mish-mash of all the operating skills and well regarded in the broader Corps. Most of our training took place in the operator wing and was conducted by a variety of instructors. Half were serving SNCOs with the remainder comprising JNCOs and civilians. The civilians were usually retired soldiers who never forgot to remind us that things were much harder in their day.

We were taught how to use all the radios in the Corps portfolio. Even in 1985, the Clansman range was beginning to look a bit dated. When we were first shown round the 353 room, I assumed we were in a museum. The VHF radios looked archaic and made peculiar noises whenever you flicked a switch or turned a dial. The HF range was no better. The internal whirring and clattering that accompanied any operation was comparable with a difference engine. Notwithstanding their aesthetic shortcomings, all the radios were robust and functioned as they were supposed to do, unlike the apprentices.

We were taught the cabalistic intricacies of British Army voice procedure. At face value it all seemed straightforward enough, but it was incredibly easy to say the wrong thing at the wrong time. The VP instructor was a retired YOS and always took great pains to remind us of the potential consequences of our actions. Of course it was true that a grid reference or name sent in clear language, on an insecure net, constituted a security breach, but his overreaction made us want to do it more. We would sit in his class, separated into little booths, with our headsets on. After being given a call-sign each, he would tell us what to do.

"0, I want you to direct the net and get an acknowledgement from D30. B10, I want you to then ask permission from 0 to send a long message to A20."

With that, the 45-minute lesson would commence and voice traffic would fly back and forth, with constant interjection and advice from Mr Brimble. As soon as someone made a mistake he would be up on his feet, pointing at them.

"You, son, have just had men killed. You sent a grid reference in clear. As we speak, one of Ivan's missiles is heading right for that spot and everyone one there will be dead. How do you feel about that, eh?"

Mr Brimble's first problem with his students was training bad habits out of them. These had all been learnt from films, and would have him constantly screaming.

"We don't say 'over and out' in the British Army. How many fucking times?"

It was his misfortune that Vietnam films were getting quite a showing in the cinemas around that time. He endured a constant battle against enthusiastic apprentices trying to call in airstrikes on villages or informing him that 'Charlie was behind the wire'.

One of the other disciplines to learn was the sending and receiving of Morse code. We were told constantly that in the event of a nuclear war, the first form of communication to be re-established would implement this century old skill. Learning it was a major headache and I used to dread the lessons. It wasn't particularly difficult, but I always felt that my napper was being damaged by weekly exposure to this repetitive noise. Sending was a doddle in comparison to receiving, and at least it gave you the opportunity to do something with your hands. Our instructor was a grumpy bastard who'd served on Arctic convoys in the war. The lessons always ran like clockwork and we'd start as soon as we walked in the door. He was the only ex-Forces member I have ever met who could not be distracted by questions about his service. We'd try every week, to no avail.

"Hey, Sir. It must have been really interesting in the Second World War."

He'd just ignore us and start piping Morse into our headsets, and we'd wearily begin jotting the translation onto message pads. One year, on our last lesson before Christmas, in a great display of magnanimity, he replaced the Morse tape with a Johnny Mathis Yuletide medley. It was the only time in the two years that I missed the Morse.

Another skill that the radio telegraphist had was the ability to type at 36 words per minute. Trying to square this with one's self-image as a warrior was a difficult task. The instructor, Sergeant Warnell, tried to convince us unsuccessfully.

He'd lecture us whilst we sat hunched behind medieval T100 teleprinters, waiting for the lesson to start.

"Don't knock typing, lads. The ability to produce a long message without errors, under enemy fire, is not something to be scoffed at."

Perhaps he was right, and the age of the typist was moving away from a secretarial monopoly. The two things – soldier and typewriter – just didn't fit together, though. I'd never seen one used as a weapon in any war film. We were taught on keyboards without embossed letters, so that we'd learn to touch-type. According to Warnell, this was so that we could type in a 'lights-out tactical situation'. Two or three lessons in, I made a mental note of never mentioning it to anyone who I was trying to impress.

One of the more interesting lessons was Antennas and Propagation. In the classroom we learnt all about the characteristics of radio waves and how best to use their idiosyncrasies to our advantage. All our practical work was done near the football pitches behind C block. The instructors were all radio hams and watched our attempts at antenna construction with undisguised horror. As they shook their heads, we'd try to assemble half-wave dipoles out of copper wire slung from 12-metre masts. The chief A and P instructor was a big Yorkshireman who'd just left the Corps after 22 years service. My efforts at putting up a sloping wire earned the following accolade from him.

"Fookin' hell, Nugent, it's all ovvert place. Like a crazy woman's shite."

As with every syllabus, the easiest lessons were the ones we enjoyed most. There were lots of little subjects that only took a term or so to learn and they came under the umbrella of 'basic signalling skills'. The two lance-corporals who took the lessons were a proper double act, who didn't really give a fuck. In the two years I was there, nobody failed one of their tests, primarily because all the answers were given out prior to the exams. This allowed the lance-corporals more time to drink brews and smoke tabs at the back door of the classroom whilst we arsed about waiting for the lesson to finish. The only thing I remember was something called the 'back of the hand test'. My memory is sketchy but it was a way of testing to see if a vehicle was electrically live or earthed appropriately. Before climbing into a box body or wagon you were supposed to brush the back of your hand against the outer skin whilst your feet were still on the ground. If you were going to get a shock, the perceived wisdom was that when your muscles spasmed, your fist would clench but not grab hold of anything. Do it with your palm and you would end up gripping the door handle and holding on until you died or someone brayed you with a GS shovel.

Once a term, our new found knowledge was put to test in the field. Mercury exercises were a combination of trade and military training. They all had the same basic format, but concentrated on different skills. Some focused on HF and Morse, others on VHF and RATT. They were all equally traumatic and an abject lesson in sleep deprivation. Every exercise was preceded by an equipment check. Because all Mercuries were conducted with the additional comforts of working from a vehicle, it would have been reasonable to think that the kit list wouldn't have been quite as important or exhaustive as on other manoeuvres. If only. The instructors approached the kit inspection with the fundamentalist vigour of crusaders. I'd be standing in line with my entire exercise kit laid out in front of me, shitting myself, as the corporals went down the line screaming at any kind of deviation from the sacred list.

"What the fuck is this?"

"My sewing kit, Corporal."

"I know that, you fucker! Why have you got two needles and one pin, when the list clearly states three needles! And another thing, why aren't your PT daps properly whitened?"

"Because we are going on exercise, Corporal. I didn't think…"

"Exactly, you scruffy, idle, bastard! Now get your shagging gat above your head and get round that football pitch until you see the error of your ways!"

And woe betide the man whose water bottle wasn't full to the lip.

Even if you had all of your contents down to the last item, you would get gripped for a purely fictitious infringement of the rules.

Paul Jones spent weeks preparing his clobber for these exercises. He went to extreme lengths and had even vacuum-packed some of his gear to ensure waterproofing. This still wasn't good enough. He got picked up for the fingers on his gloves being too long. Added to that, his packing technique had supposedly ruined the non-existent insulating properties of his military clothing.

When it came to the list, we were all born with original sin.

The bread and butter of exercise life involved operating the radios from the backs of the vehicles. Every 12 hours or so we would tear down and move location, setting up again immediately on arrival at the new destination. Sometimes the next location was miles away, but at other times it was only a matter of inches. Moves of less than ten feet were a sure sign that the instructors were pissed-off with you. The regular moves combined with the enormous task of staying awake whilst listening to white noise for hours on end, made for a decidedly unhealthy lifestyle.

Moving location may sound relatively straightforward, but it was the mother of all fuck-arounds, and its pain-in-the-arse factor was increased tenfold when performed at night. On tearing down the detachment, all camouflage netting, generators, 12-metre masts, tents and tools had to be packed away and all the trenches had to be filled in. Once we were packed up, our instructor would drive us to our next spot. If it was a bit of a distance, you got the chance to get your breath back and maybe catch a five-minute doze. Our hearts would sink on the short moves. We'd all jump in and he'd start the engine. We'd set off and everyone would have their fingers crossed hoping for a good long drive. Immediately after completing one rotation of the wheels he'd cut the ignition, and shout: "Right! Out you get, you fuckers. Get set up."

The worst application of this torture happened to us on Mercury Four. We spent almost the entire exercise in full NBC kit including respirators. The exercise took part in a particularly hot June, and we baked inside our noddy suits. All of the detachments spent the entire week and a half of the exercise in one field. The location changes were synchronised. Each time the radio message was sent for the move, every detachment would up sticks and move to the spot that their neighbour had just vacated. For ten days we literally just went round in circles, the depression increasing exponentially each time the call came. I don't think that such an act of soul-destroying suffering and banality has been perpetrated before or since. The whole spectacle took place under the watchful eyes of the instructors and the merciless sun.

The heat in my respirator was unbearable and it was filled with the stench of cam-cream, CS gas and perspiration. The sweat had worked itself into a lather and it made the mask slip around on my face. Putting up a 12-metre mast in those temperatures was hideous. But although the mask magnified the problem, it also provided the anonymity to whinge and look downtrodden without the instructors noticing. At first I thought it was just me who felt like this, but I walked past Colin Mortimer once, and all I could hear coming from his respirator were angry mutterings. He was hammering a mast stake into the ground badly and was whining to nobody in particular: “Howay, ye bastad. I divn’t like this fookan’ respur-reat-a one bit, like!”

Col was a constant source of amusement to me, he was always mumbling to himself and even though I only understood half of his rants, I still found them hilarious. I remember after watching *Karate Kid* in the camp cinema, he did an impromptu crap karate display whilst walking back to the block. He then turned to me and said: “How, Eddy, man. I reckon I’ll buy me sel’ one o’ them bonsai trees, like. Ye knaa, like that owld Jap blerk off of that film.”

“But aren’t they expensive?” I replied.

Col looked at me like I was retarded and answered: “Nah, man. They’re ownly small, like!”

As well as having to tear down and set up the detachments on a regular basis, the radio networks always had to be active. The permanent staff constantly monitored the nets to ensure that pointless traffic was being sent regardless of the situation.

The biggest nightmare on the location moves was the manipulation of the cam-net. It was an absolute bastard to deal with, particularly when wet. I’m still convinced that it was woven from the Devil’s arse-hair.

Its mesh like attributes meant that it would catch on anything it could. The most frequent hang-up points were all clothing buttons and weapon sights. Once caught up, the only way to get free was to wail pathetically until one of your oppos came to free you. Struggling only worsened the situation and it was possible to find yourself snared in eight or nine different places. I remember watching Spartacus and thinking that a net was a bit of a poncey weapon to have if you were up against a bloke with a trident and sword. As soon as I'd spent 15 minutes trussed up by my webbing and rifle, I reviewed my opinion.

I used to have nightmares whilst on exercise that I was snared in the nets or even worse, that the flywheel to the generator had caught the net and had sucked all of our cam into its engine. Like some unhinged 'Nam vet, I'd wake up with a jerk, but would quickly realise that I shouldn't have been sleeping in the first place, because I was on radio watch. I'd then have to check my watch to see how long I'd been asleep for and insert fraudulent entries into the radio logbook to account for the relevant time period. I was once in the process of such an act of counterfeiting when one of the training corporals, called Brady, came charging into the back of the wagon. He accused me of being 'a lazy spotty bastard' who'd been 'gonking on stag'! He backed this up by saying that he had been calling me over the net for the last ten minutes. As cool as a cucumber, I told him that I had been out checking the generator for petrol and that I had informed the net of my intentions. I struck lucky as he must've been having a wank or a shit, or maybe both at the same time, during the period that I'd sent my fictitious radio message, because he didn't question the authenticity of my statement. Luckily, he fucked off straight after our verbal exchange, because five minutes later the generator packed up, rendering my lie completely transparent. I knew he hadn't believed me and he got his revenge later in the exercise.

One night, we filled the detachment's metal wash bowl with compo and had a big stew cooked over a kero heater. It tasted lovely, but the burnt-on charcoal–food hybrid on the base of the bowl was physically impossible to clean. We used tons of Scotchbrite and parts of our weapon cleaning kits, but we couldn't shift the caked on baconburgers. Barry Nash even tried hitting it with a shovel, but the deposit was as hard as diamond. In a desperate attempt to minimise our gripping from Brady, we decided to lob the bowl away and say that we had lost it on the last move. Losing kit in a tear down was far more forgivable than getting it into the shit state that it was in. Our location at the time was called Bishop Monkton and we were right on a riverbank. It was decided that in the dark, we would chuck the bowl into the raging waters and let mother nature dispose of the evidence. Colin Mortimer did the honours and on returning to the tent he told us: "We wivn't see that fookan' thing again, man!"

We waited with confidence for the morning inspection by Brady. As soon as he turned up, he had us parade outside the vehicle and face the river. What had looked like a fast running torrent the night before, seemed more like a millpond in the cold light of day. Floating directly in the centre of its glass-like surface was our washbowl in all of its shitted-up glory. I remember a hot blast of adrenaline lighting up my stomach, as I realised the 'bang to rights' nature of the situation. After making us all swim out to the bowl and back in full combat gear, Brady had us move location every hour for the next day totalling an exact distance of 24 feet.

Although the Mercury exercises were necessary to prepare us for the job we were actually going to do when we left training, I preferred mil training. Although it was hard work, I felt like a bit more of a soldier going through the disciplines common to every member of the Army.

With our only previous foray into mil training exercises taking the form of a one-night-shortened baptism of water, it was with some trepidation that we went onto our next – and reputedly hardest – battlecamp. Exercise 'Warrior Dig' was a one-week trench digging exercise with a combined 'potential accumulation of sleep' rating of about five hours. This was not good, and the nightmare stories that the older lads fed us with, only served to heighten the feelings of dread amongst our still fresh-faced intake.

It was the arse end of February and we were all lined up in the boiler house car park, with our kit spread out in front of us, as the instructors went howling mad during the inspection. The weather was atrocious. Raging sleet and snow storms lashed us, as we held out one item at a time for the scrutiny of instructors.

The only consolation was that most of the lads from the basic training room were still in my section. Col was standing next to me, which was good for two reasons. Firstly, he was a good laugh, his dry humour never failing to cheer me up. Secondly, because he was upwind of me, he was bearing the full force of the snow. All the flakes that had my name on them were coming to rest in his right ear. He was shaking violently and there was a large stream of snot hanging from his hooter. Every now and then he would mutter to himself through gritted teeth: "Aaaahh howay, ya fookan' bastad! This is nee laffin' matta!"

I never thought that I would be glad to get on a Bedford four-tonner, but by the time they all rocked up, I was so cold that even their torn and useless canopies offered welcome sanctuary from the elements. Once all of the wagons were static, Corporal Havers shouted: "Right, gents. Get on the shaggin' Robert Redfords!"

As we climbed on, I could see that Colin's right cheek was bright red and a mound of compacted snow sat in his lughole, like a rudimentary hearing aid.

I managed to nod off on the drive to the training area, and woke up feeling like dog-egg. Still, it was all sleep in the bank for the forthcoming week.

Catterick training area had changed not a jot since I had last seen it, only this time it had a liberal sprinkling of snow. This served only to hide the bleak tufts of moorland grass that constantly caused marching soldiers to go over on their ankles.

We were rousted into our sections and set off one group at a time towards the platoon harbour areas. Every now and then someone would stumble and mutter 'Ya fuckin' bastard!' as they lurched to their feet with their ankle tendons screaming foul play.

After an hour of walking and falling we arrived in the exercise area. The plan was to spend the first day digging our trenches, bashering out that night in the woods. We would use the following day to complete the excavation. Once we were in position, we brewed up and waited for the instructors to take us to the trench locations. That time came much more quickly than I would have liked. It seemed like I had just finished my brew when Havers dropped an armful of picks and shovels in front of us, and with what could only be described as 'a shit-eating grin' said: "Right, ladies. Pick a shovel, any shovel, and follow me!"

He took us to an area that was about half a mile from our bashers. It was completely exposed and overlooked a valley.

We paired up and I stayed with Colin. We were then allocated an area each in which we would dig our trench. It was with considerable happiness that I noticed a familiarly shaped dent in the ground, right next to our allocated position. The indentation indicated that an old trench was there, which usually meant loose, easily diggable earth.

I looked at Colin, who obviously shared my thoughts, as he was smiling from ear to ear. So it transpired that by the time we were waist deep in our new house, the majority of the other lads were only down to their ankles in the rock-hard stony ground and it wasn't long before we had dug to the required depth.

We stood there for a while leaning on our shovels, looking at the other lads cracking on. There was no finer job in the world than watching other people work and we warmed to our task, making witty comments about everyone else's shortcomings. The slowest progressing hole belonged to Skiddy and Rose. Both of them had only got through basic by the skin on a mosquito's ballbag, and they were hacking at the soil with the ferocity of charging slugs, getting nowhere fast. Rose looked red faced with emotion, as they had already been gripped by Havers on a number of occasions. The last time he'd been past, he'd thrown a big clod of earth at Rose, shouting: "You'd better get that shaggin' hole dug, Pansy. Or I'll have you using shit for cam-cream. Now geldi-fucking-geldi!"

His use of different languages in his motivational speeches always impressed me.

When enough trenches were dug, we were shown how to use a kip sheet. A mesh of pegs and string were bashed into the ground at one end of the trench, through which would be woven the sheet itself. The whole thing was then covered in dirt. The theory was that a well installed sheet could cope with having a Land Rover driven over it. Rumours were rife that we would all have to take it in turns, cowering under our shelters whilst the instructors tested the manufacturer's claims. Colin articulated all of our concerns with a shout of: "Fuck that!"

The vehicle stress test didn't actually happen, but the instructors did jump up and down on top of the shelter whilst one of us sat underneath it. Although not ideal, the thought of having a size-ten pair of leather personnel carriers landing on your head was preferable to being crushed to death by a three-quarter-tonne vehicle.

By the end of the day, only half the trenches were finished and we traipsed the half mile back to the basher location. There was the normal guard roster to be carried out. Colin and I got the midnight-'til-one stag. Not the best, but by no means the worst. We spent it talking in hushed tones. Strictly speaking, it wasn't the brightest tactical move, but it was better than falling asleep on stag and getting a shoeing off Havers. Our conversation was typical of young blokes of the time. Colin told me how Sam Fox 'needed it', and that in his professional opinion, the blonde one from The Human League could beat the dark haired one in an imaginary fanny licking contest. Her equally imaginary 'prize' would be a severe tupping from himself. The subject then turned to the good old 'what would you do for a million quid?' favourite. Colin killed it off by going that little bit too far. The subjects had been getting more and more bizarre, until Colin, in an excited chatter said: "Oooh howay, Eddy. Worra boot this then man. How's aboot, reet, how's aboot letting Sinita, ye knaa that bord offa *Top'o the Pops* reet. Would ye let 'er shit on a plate reet, then freeze the bastad, then when the log is aal frerzen would ye let 'er stick it up yer orse leek a reet big broon dilder an' that?"

My shocked expression made Colin realise that he had got completely carried away, so he immediately countered: "Er… 'cos I wouldn't like, I mean I just thought that you, well ya knaa I didn't know if… Anyways, I reckon The Toon might win the cup this year!"

The uncomfortable silence could only have been bettered had there been a lonely cricket chirping in the background.

I shook my head and eventually replied: "Jesus Christ, Col. When God gave out common decency, you must have been wanking in the bogs and late for the parade."

As outlandish as the discussion became, it did the job of keeping us awake. One of the later stags had been less vigilant, and we were awoken by a barrage of thunder flashes being thrown into the harbour area. Some twat had wobbed out on shift, so there had been no reveille. The DS went fucking rhino, and although it was the fault of only two blokes, we were all beasted to near death. They were fuming and increased our trepidation by warning us angrily of the trauma about to come. For the first time in my career, the reality was actually worse than the possibilities that my mind could conjure up. We were made to don full NBC kits and then given a PT session the QMSI would have been proud of. The pinnacle of the punishment was what seemed like an endless run in respirators over the moors. I was really chinstrapped and I tried to get more air by sucking in as hard as possible through the canister. This only impeded the airflow and induced near panic and collapse simultaneously. It was with great mental effort that I controlled the urge to remove the mask and managed to regulate my breathing enough to keep my major organs functioning. It could have been worse though. Alistair McKenzie yakked up in his mask. No one realised until the rising vomit lake became visible, sloshing around in the eyepieces of his respirator. He eventually tore his mask off, and the honk spilled out like the breaching of the Moehne Dam. Despite this, the instructors still gripped him for taking off his resi without permission and he received additional punishment.

After this, the rest of the exercise – although filled with fatigue, cold and damp – didn't seem so bad. The beasting had been terrible enough to create a talking point for years afterwards. Next to it, standing in a trench freezing your plums off, up to your ankles in mud, was a comparative pleasure. On reflection, it was a good thing to have been treated so badly. The remaining mil training exercises had their moments, but they were easy to cope with, when put into context against the 'Great Resi Run of 86' yardstick. It was a mildly comforting thought, but comforting nonetheless.

The only other type of exercise we went on was External Leadership, or EL as it was unsurprisingly known. Initially it sounded like a bit of a skive. The prospect of a break from military and comms training for a week in the Lake District or Cairngorms seemed to be like a prepaid holiday. During the course of my apprenticeship, I was scheduled to go on three different leadership exercises. They were loosely described as canoe, rock and snow. They were one of the highlights of my time at Harrogate, despite the instructors' best efforts to spoil them. The first one I went on was 'snow'. It was meant to be a week of skiing near Aviemore. I was really excited about it. I'd never skied before and had visions of myself 'Franz Klammering' down lethal slopes. In the week prior to deploying, we had to go to the EL stores to be issued with our clothing. Those that were lucky, rich or smart enough supplied their own equipment. The rest of us took our chances at the storeman's hatch. Huge strides had been made in the development of outdoor clothing in the early eighties. Breathable, waterproof garments were freely available. Rucksacks were becoming lighter and more comfortable, with fresher, more ergonomic designs every week. Companies like Berghaus and Karrimor were designing boots that moulded to the foot of the wearer, providing a snug, blister-free walking experience. All of these innovations had passed by the Army Apprentices' College, Harrogate, without so much as a glance backwards. It appeared that there were only four design parameters to which the manufacturers had adhered. All the clothing had to be capable of holding comedy amounts of water. It all had to be garish in colour and capable of third-degree chafing. Finally, when the whole outfit was worn, it was important that the apprentice looked like an overgrown Austrian schoolchild. We were given orange 'windproof' smocks; red, knee-length socks; and grey, corduroy breeches. An enormous, grey, woollen balaclava topped off the natty ensemble. The walking boots that accompanied the outfit were ridiculous. Each weighed the same as a car battery and had laces 18 feet long. The only other bit of kit we were given was an ancient blue rucksack, fabricated with maximum discomfort in mind.

There was a huge kit list to go through. It would have been easier for them to tell us what not to bring. Of course, all of it had to go into the blue rucksack. There seemed to be more room in the balaclavas, but, they had to be worn.

On the first morning of the exercise, everyone going on the adventure paraded on the familiar testing ground of the boiler house car park at 6.30am The EL staff then turned up and performed a kit-check that went down to the last sock and shaving stick. The DSs of the three exercise disciplines must have been trying to outdo each other, in achieving higher and higher levels of pedantry. I never did understand the EL staff's attitude. Here they were with perhaps the best job in the Signals, but they were always miserable. For 48 weeks of the year, they didn't wear uniform and got to enjoy some of the best climbing and walking terrain in the world, yet they still wore the expressions of people who'd discovered dog shit in their pockets. I think that we cramped their style and they didn't appreciate it. We were the annoying little brothers to their teenagers and they were saddled with us for a week. After the kit-check and the obligatory bollockings for those of us who'd forgotten those all important things like a ninth pair of underpants or a spare pair of laces, we got ready to board the coaches. Stood there, in our post-Edwardian clothing, if we'd had a few huskies we'd have been mistaken for members of Ernest Shackleton's ill-fated Antarctic expedition.

Driving up to Scotland in those bone-crunchingly uncomfortable coaches took forever. Those with a bit of initiative had brought books to read, but the rest of us were reduced to examining the contents of our deathpacks for the 12-hour journey. Every now and again, someone at the back would read out a particularly juicy excerpt, from the letters page of a bongo-mag, which would raise morale for a short while. If the sound levels ever went up too far, one of the instructors would shout lazily from the front to 'keep the fucking noise down' – more out of duty than anything else. Why did people in positions of responsibility always sit at the front of the coach? Was there a practical reason, or were they just big kids who liked to pretend that they were driving? We stopped once, at a nondescript motorway services near Newcastle. We were given the opportunity to get off the coach and stretch our legs and get a brew in the canteen. Everyone got off and had sneaky slashes in nearby bushes. Nobody wanted to go into the main building, as we looked like such twats. For the rest of the trip, most of the lads got their heads down. By rotating my balaclava until the hole was at the back, I fashioned myself a bit of personal airspace and slept until we arrived.

The snow exercise was remarkable only in that there was no snow. Someone had obviously forgotten to book this integral ingredient of the downhill experience. Ever resourceful, the instructors simply replaced all skiing activities with huge walks through the mountains. The Cairngorms were absolutely beautiful and, although the hiking was extremely hard work, I loved it. Because it was the middle of winter we hardly met anyone and it felt like our group of eight were the only people in the hills at some times. When we did come across anyone, they'd always smile politely and say hello. As we slogged past, it was easy to see the pity in their eyes as they gazed at our low quality threads. Throughout the walks, our instructor would ask us challenging, map-related questions, which we invariably got wrong – but he didn't seem to mind too much. He'd show us the map and ask us to pinpoint where we were, using the landscape as our guide. After 30 or 40 wild guesses, with us jabbing his map like inquisitive primates, he'd give up and show us.

The only activity we did, that nodded in the direction of winter sports, was an hour's ice-skating in Kingussie. When I handed over my boots to be swapped for a pair of ice-skates, the assistant couldn't get both of them in the pigeonhole and had to leave them on the floor, assuring me unnecessarily that they wouldn't be stolen. I'd never skated before and kept falling over. Some of the lads spent the hour chatting up the local girls, despite being dressed like identical tramps. After whopping my head off the ice a couple of times, I spent the rest of the hour in the café nursing a cup of tea.

I enjoyed wearing the skates though and I was a bit gutted at the end, when I had to swap them back for my clodhoppers. The girl behind the counter had to lift them one at a time. As I was putting them back on, I noticed that a Recruit Karloff had written his name on one of the insoles.

The rock climbing and canoeing ELs were a great laugh. Both activities were extremely draining, but both being solitary disciplines, allowed for a bit of individual flair. I was a bit of a natural at the climbing, being in possession of the perfect 'skinny but strong' physique. The only thing that prevented me from a successful career in the sport was the dreaded 'disco leg'. It was a right bastard and always affected me at just the wrong moment. I'd be perched on the rock, just about to make the crux move in the climb, when my left leg would start shaking so badly, it looked like the opening bars of 'Jailhouse Rock' were about to kick in. It wasn't a nervous thing and was just down to tired muscles, but to the bloke doing the belaying on the ground it looked I was shitting myself, and the directing shout of: "Ten o'clock, disco leg, Eddy Nugent" would go up followed by roars of laughter from everyone on the deck. The twats.

You could look quite cool whilst canoeing. Anytime I walked around in shorts or trunks, I was painfully aware that my legs were hanging down from my arse like a pair of matchsticks with shoes on them. But in a canoe, everyone had the same build. I had a fairly strong upper body and got the hang of the stroke quite quickly. On the first day of the canoeing week, and before they let us row anywhere, the staff organised a confidence test. Each canoeist, in turn had to capsize his canoe, 50 metres from the shore. This was done by rolling the canoe clockwise until you were submerged. The confidence part of it was that you weren't allowed to right yourself and had to slap your hands on the bottom of the canoe until someone came to your rescue. I was one of the first to go. Once underwater, I was in complete silence and time disorientated. It only took 20 seconds for someone to get out to me, but by then I was beginning to shit myself and puff my cheeks out to conserve air. Once I'd done mine, I had the pleasure of watching everyone else. It was an ideal opportunity for the staff to take out any grudges they'd been holding about particular apprentices. Dependent on where their name appeared on the scale of cuntishness, people could be left drowning politely for anything between ten seconds and a minute. It was always funny to watch the tapping on the bottom of the canoe becoming more and more frantic as the seconds ticked away. A couple of people always lost it and emerged coughing and spluttering before the rescuer could get to them. Their lack of bottle was plain for all to see and their shame was compounded by the loud cheers coming from the shore.

It was obvious to the college authorities, that subjecting us to an academic syllabus entirely consisting of Morse code and lessons about radios had the very real possibility of sending us mad. In an attempt to break things up slightly, the officers of the Royal Education Corps were drafted in to try to inject more interesting information into our reluctant brains. The lessons were, to some extent, a blessed relief from the death by viewfoil tedium of trade training. We were schooled up to City and Guilds standards in various subjects, including English, Maths and General Science. Most of the lads were sporting a slack handful of ‘O’ Levels anyway, so it wasn’t too challenging. The lessons had the capacity for boredom but the education centre had a trump card. It had a complete monopoly on good looking female instructors. In a camp where the only other women soldiers were the soup dragons in the cookhouse, the pretty lieutenants and captains of the Ed Corps caught everyone’s attention. There wasn’t a man-jack on camp who had not thrapped whilst thinking about them. They would give lessons where their entire classes learnt absolutely nothing. Instead, 15 unlikely scenarios were being concocted in our heads, all with the same ending. There was a particularly attractive captain who taught maths. She was explaining an equation to me once and had leant over my desk, exposing the briefest glimpse of bra strap. This was wankers’ paydirt and instead of listening to the figures being clarified to me, all I could hear was a voice in my head repeating the words “Must-see-the-rest, must-see-the-rest.”

The lessons were all conducted in C block. The rooms were identical to the trade theory classrooms, save the odd dog-eared poster. The blocks were orientated in such a way that the sun came blasting through the windows at around mid-afternoon. On hot days it made it very difficult to pay attention and was very conducive to wobbing out mid-period.

On top of the usual subjects, we were also exposed to the new fangled world of computer studies. I’d done a tiny bit at school, but the one computer we had was the holy grail of local burglars and it usually went missing once a month. As soon as the insurance had paid out, the school would buy and proudly unveil its replacement. Word would hit the street within a couple of hours and the duty junky would be going in through the window shortly after the caretaker had gone home.

There were no such security risks at the College. The computer room was a secretive bunker with darkened windows, and it housed the latest BBC machinery; huge cream coloured machines like props from *Blake's Seven*. They were shite, to put it mildly, and used almost all of their processing power just to start up.

However, the BBCs did have one redeeming feature, in that it was very easy to make them display line after line of obscenities. It was the first lesson learnt by apprentices and the only one remembered by most. You simply typed in a swear word of your choice on line 10 and then instructed line 20 to "Go to 10". A swift tap of the 'run' key and hey presto, you were provided with an infinite number of lines of your favourite adjective from the dockers' dictionary. This was best put to use at the end of a lengthy 'programming' lesson. As soon as anyone made the mistake of going to the toilet, his hours of painstaking work could be deleted by his next door neighbour. When he returned from the traps, he would be greeted with a pleasant "Fuck off, you wanker" streaming up and down the screen.

All in all though, education was just viewed by the lads as a lovely doss and a break from the more important aspects of training. The Rodneys from the Education Corps were soft touches. We were used to being shouted at and threatened with execution, and their more cerebral approach was open to abuse. They were primarily teachers and the uniform was just an occupational necessity. Enforcing discipline didn't sit well with their self-image and it was always amusing if one of them lost it and tried to bollock someone. We'd been gripped by the best and it was impossible for mild-mannered tutors to reach the standards set by tattooed Glaswegian sociopaths.

To my mind, the combination of theoretical instruction and field training constituted a more than ample workload. The college authorities were keen to minimise any spare time and filled it with as many jobs and chores as possible.

Every four weeks, we took our turn being Duty Squadron. For those seven days, once a month, we did all the college jiff jobs and guards. On Sunday evening, the board would go up in the office window, detailing everyone's fate. Duties were meant to be divvied up equally, but you could be guaranteed one of the shittier jobs if you'd fucked-up in the preceding month. As soon as the duties were posted, we'd all be hovering round the list, hoping for something undemanding. There was a sliding scale of cushiness. The easiest job possible was the WRVS NCO and the most onerous, the much feared Sunday cookhouse. Sandwiched between the two extremes were fire picquets, weekday guard, weekday cookhouse and weekend guards.

It was a great when you realised you'd only copped for one WRVS. All you had to do was report to the WRVS woman at seven o'clock in the evening and be there to give her a hand with anything until she knocked you off at ten. At the time, the Women's Royal Voluntary Service had old biddies stationed all round the world, serving hot beverages and homespun philosophy to the Armed Forces. Three WRVS women came and went during my time and they all looked like Mary Whitehouse. They were always accompanied by a Yorkshire terrier, the annoying dog–rat crossbreed favoured by the elderly. I don't know if they were issued with one on the completion of WRVS basic training, or they passed the same dog along to their replacement, in an elaborate ceremony. The WRVS at Harrogate was only used by apprentices that had no money. The delights that were on offer, like table tennis and bar billiards, only attracted the serially skint or terminally bored. It made for a simple duty. You just had to sup cups of tea, whilst ensuring that no fights broke out over the billiards. It was obvious that the club hadn't had any money spent on it since the sixties. The posters placed on the bare walls, in an attempt to 'get with it', were of bands like Abba and the Brotherhood of Man. A quick look in the box next to an ageing turntable, confirmed that choices were limited to records that were unlikely to set the charts buzzing.

It was unusual to be dealt the prize hand of a single WRVS though. I generally found myself with a couple of guards to do during the week. The ten apprentices that constituted the guard had to parade outside the guardroom just after tea, to be inspected by the duty sergeant. The severity of the inspection depended entirely on the recent sexual successes or failures of the SNCO working his way up the line. It was a custom in training establishments of the time to have a thing called the 'stick man'. Whichever apprentice was the best turned out got knocked off and escaped the duty. As an incentive, it was flawed. You could be guaranteed that one of the ten was going to be the clear winner. This would be spotted as soon as the names went up. There were a few blokes who had the family connections, or thieving abilities, to ensure they had loads of spare clobber. They could afford to have a set of ridiculously starched combats hanging in their locker, waiting to be whipped out when duty called. The rest of us would be trying to press creases into trousers that had spent two months at the back of a top box, folded to the size of a matchbox. As soon as the stick man was thinned out, the guard roster was drawn up by the duty corporal and the stags began at 6pm. They always worked a two-hours-on, four-hours-off rota. Three of the guard would look after the front gate, taking a two-hour turn by the barrier, whilst the other six did prowler in pairs. Prowler was a better option. The book said that you were providing a 'visible security deterrent to any potential intruder, and a first line of defence in the event of a terrorist attack'. It sounded pretty impressive, but the reality was a bit different. It was a big camp with lots of nooks and crannies that provided comfortable harbour to the serious skiver. On the early evening shifts, up to NAAFI closing time, you had to be on the ball, as there were lots of people milling around. When the clock struck 12, the idleness could begin. My favourite hiding place was the kit store next to the outdoor arena. The lock on the back door was buggered. It still looked okay, which meant that nobody had ever fixed it or knew about it. The store was full of crash mats. My prowler buddy of the evening and I would lie down on one of the mats and pull another over the top of us and simply snooze there until 15 minutes before shift end. We were at the end of a radio, but the duty corporal could be relied upon to be too lazy to come out and physically check up on us. Every few minutes we'd be disturbed by a radio check, asking us for our location. I'd rub sleep out of my eyes and speak into the handset: "This is D10, we are at the assault course and heading for Bradley Squadron." This would satisfy him and he could go back to reading one of the month old *Razzles* or old Sven Hassel books that could be found in any guardroom drawer.

The front gate was a trickier prospect for the career layabout. The box, about the size of an average lift, was situated 20 metres from the guardroom. It had windows on all four sides making the occupant available for easy scrutiny. A two-hour shift lasted for approximately three months. There was absolutely nothing to do, except to keep awake at all costs. This was made doubly difficult by the presence of a radiator that was permanently fixed on full blast. There was a telephone and a button for raising and lowering the barrier and that was it. At night time, incoming traffic dropped to zero and you were left with your own limited imagination for 120 minutes. Masturbation, the great ennui reliever, was off limits to all but the most accomplished. There was subtle graffiti, but it only took a minute or two to read and was all 'cry-for-help' themed: 'Why the fuck am I here?', 'This place is fucking shit', 'I agree wholeheartedly', 'Who fucking asked you?', and 'Fuckoff, then'.

In my two years I did the gate three times and fell asleep once. I was on from 4am to 6am. It was freezing outside and as soon as I got into the warmth of the box, my eyes starting getting heavy. I held out for 15 minutes, the nodding-dog cycle becoming more pronounced with each passing moment. I drifted off and was woken, what felt like a second later, by a tooting horn. I peeled my face off the inner window and jumped up in my seat. It was one of the cleaners on a moped. I slid back the window and said: "Morning. Can I help you?"

She showed me her pass and I raised the barrier. I watched her go over a couple of the speed bumps and prayed to God that she was going to turn left for the Officers' Mess. Unluckily for me, the old bag couldn't wait to get to the guardroom and bubble me. She had a brief conversation with the corporal – it was Chester, from the gym. Five seconds later he burst out of the door and headed straight towards me. I smartened myself up, just before he banged on the window.

"Out here, you."

I came out and offered him my best creeper's grin.

"That cleaner says you were a-fucking-sleep when she came to the gate."

There was no way on this planet that I was going to admit it. Falling asleep on guard was one of the biggest no-nos possible. There was a principle at stake. Nod off on a poxy camp college gate and get away with it and you would be sure to be get all your mates killed at an unspecified point in the future.

"No, Corporal. I wasn't."

"You fucking liar; she said she waited there for five minutes watching you, before she bibbed her horn."

"I wasn't, Corporal. She must have been mistaken."

I was bricking it, but couldn't go back. The tremble in my voice was obvious, but really it was going to boil down to my word against a 79-year-old, fat dwarf from

Knaresborough. Chester knew this. He hadn't been watching me or he'd have said. He'd probably been pulling the head off it in the toilets, taking advantage of the quiet time. He jabbed his right index finger at the name tag on my combat jacket and glowered.

"Right then, Nugent. I'll have to give you the benefit of the doubt. But I don't fucking believe you for one minute. Your face needs ironing and you've got slobber on your collar. The next time I get you in the fucking gym, I'm going to beast the fuck out of you."

He was true to his oath, but it was a small price to pay.

In between shifts we had to sleep in the back room which we shared with the fire picquet. Fire picquet was a bit of a laugh as a duty. You spent the whole week living in the guardroom, turning up there after tea each evening. There was no work to do as such. You were on standby to react to any fire that occurred, as a stopgap before the emergency services arrived. There were lots of hydrant points around the camp and every evening the duty officer would call out the picquet for a drill. If you happened to be walking past at the time, it provided great entertainment. Eight blokes would come flying round the corner, frantically pushing a big red handcart. As the Duty Officer timed and supervised them, they would try to get the hose fixed to the hydrant. The exercise was over when they got water coming out of the end of the hose. It was a classic example of 'too many cooks'. They'd all be shouting and telling each other what to do without actually accomplishing anything. Somebody would be rooting round in the boxes on the cart, trying to find the correct lump of metal that provided the link between hose and hydrant. When it was located, he'd hold it up like the FA Cup, to a big cheer. As soon as it was fitted, someone else would turn the tap on, sending water spuming forth straight from the hydrant, having blown the incorrectly attached hose 15 feet down the road.

When they fucked-up like this, the Duty Officer would call them out a couple more times that night to hone their skills. It's a matter of divine providence that they never had to tackle a real blaze.

The guardroom sleeping area was horrible. There were 14 blokes in there at any one time, in varying states of unconsciousness, kipping on green, sweat-generating, rubberised, piss-proof mattresses. The stench in there went right off any available graph. Fourteen sleeping bags, 28 feet and 14 sets of cigarette-induced halitosis concocted a murderous smog, which was almost impossible to sleep in. I'll carry the smell with me to my dying day, in my hair and clothes.

The job to be avoided at all costs was the weekend cookhouse. It was an appalling experience from start to finish. Unlike the weekday version, where you just worked the mornings and evenings, you had to be there all day, from 6am until the last chip pan was sparkling, usually somewhere around 9pm. Blokes would do anything to get out of it. Claims of a family bereavement or self-amputation were common. I was only ever stung for one Sunday during my stint, but that was more than enough. I don't know what I'd done to deserve it, but when I saw my name scrawled in blue chinagraph in the appropriate box, the blood drained from my face. Worse still, I was on with Dave Preston, the biggest 'sex-liar' in the Squadron. Not only was I going to be elbow-deep in gristle and gravy all day, I was going to have to put up with Dave's eccentric stories. I met lots of sex-liars down the years. They were always the same. Superficially good-looking, they gave off some sort of female-repulsing pheromone that made all women run a mile. In the same way that nobody ever saw a cat having a shit, nobody ever saw a sex-liar cop off. Terry Waite was getting more sex than Dave Preston, but if you listened to the tales of his leave adventures, it seemed like his knob was doing overtime.

The worst thing about the cookhouse was the cooks. It wasn't so much the head chef or any of the seniors. They were quite aloof and spent most of their time ignoring you. The real fuckers were the privates and lance-jacks who gave you jobs to do. They hated everyone, but reserved a deeper vitriol for the apprentices. They'd made the wrong choice at the careers office and knew that they were sentenced to a military career in suffocating heat surrounded by the permanent smell of fried eggs. The duty was the one time we were allowed a glimpse into the hell of their normal life and boy did they love showing us.

Dave and I turned up at the hotplate promptly at 6-am. Dressed in shirtsleeve-order working dress, we were ready to go. The head chef met us and after checking his watch, said: "Morning, ladies. Report in the back to Private Greenwood and she'll give you your jobs for the day."

We went round the back of the hotplate and looked for our taskmaster. The tiled floor had a light film of grease and our boots slid uncomfortably as we moved across it. There were six or seven sloppies moving back and forth, carrying breakfast items to and from the hotplate. Greenwood was moving past us with a tray of streaky bacon, when I spotted her nametag.

"Private Greenwood?"

She ignored me, and carried on to the hotplate. After depositing the tray into its requisite cavity she came back drying her hands on a manky cloth.

"Are you two the cookhouse bods for the day?"

"Yeah," I replied.

"Yes, fucking, Private. Right?"

"Yes, Private." I'd forgotten that absolutely everyone outranked us on the camp, even fat, female, Danny Devito look-alikes. She really was a bit of a gronk. Clearly a graduate of the 'one for you, one for me' school of cookery, she must have been pushing 12 stones despite being five feet fuck all.

The first job she had us both doing was cleaning all the empty trays as they came back in from the front. Armed with wire wool pads and Deepio cleaner, we got to work. The huge, stainless steel sinks were full to the top with almost boiling water. Any cooler and it would have had no affect on the congealed grease from the substandard food products which had been superglued to the trays minutes before. The water was too hot to bear for more than a few seconds, so I had to 'sprint-scrub'. I'd identify a particular part of a pan that I was going to go for and plunge both arms into it. After a few moments of frenzied scrubbing, I'd pull them back out, before the skin on my forearms sloughed off like a debutante's glove. Dave seemed to have lower temperature water or a higher pain threshold and paddled merrily whilst working.

"What do you reckon to that Greenwood then?"

"She's a fucking Yeti, Dave. Why?"

"I did someone who looked just like her on my last leave. I did her mum as well."

Without any encouragement Dave continued with a Baron Munchausen approved anecdote, that finished with a healthy percentage of the female population of Torquay having been serviced by him.

Every time we got the pan pile down to zero, Greenwood showed up with more and it was a good two hours before we got finished. My hands were translucent by this time and the Deepio had softened my nails worryingly.

Greenwood sent Dave off with a mop somewhere and made me peel potatoes for three hours. I had to work my way through a four-foot pile of spuds in one of the back rooms and turn them from dirty and skinned, to clean and ready to be turned into chips. It was another experience I hadn't banked on having. I thought that disrobing spuds by hand had finished with National Service. I was in bits by the time she let me back out for a different job. The paper-thin skin on my hands was now full of cuts from the peeling knife that I'd been wielding so hamfistedly. Greenwood went bonkers when she saw the results of my carving.

"What the fuck is this?" she shouted.

She was holding up one of my finished articles between her thumb and forefinger. It had started life as a King Edward as big as a volleyball. Due to my over-enthusiasm I'd pared it down until it looked like an albino conker.

"Right, you fucking tossbag. If peeling spuds is too difficult for you, I've got a better job."

Keen to dispense summary justice, Greenwood dragged me to another room. There were three black plastic bins, the household variety. Two were empty and one was full of breakfast cereal. Smiling benignly, she said.

"Some daft bastard's mixed up the Frosties with the Cornflakes. You can sort them out until teatime."

She walked off laughing as I worked out the best way to approach my noble task. I spent five minutes thinking of elaborate, scientific methods that might be employed, conjuring images of contraptions, purpose-built for the undertaking. After much deliberation, I settled on a foolproof method. I picked up a single flake, examined it for the presence or absence of sugar frosting, then deposited it into the relevant bin. A clock in the back left-hand corner of the room ticked loudly as I worked. It wasn't all bad. I was sat down and I had Frosties on tap. I'd always loved them as a kid but they were reserved as a treat by Mum and Dad, placed in the same food group as Lucozade, Ribena and Aeros. Now I could eat as many as I wanted and selected only the most coated ones for consumption. When Greenwood came back to send me for my tea, I wasn't hungry and my pupils were heavily dilated.

Tea was followed by three more hours of panbash. Cracks were beginning to appear in the skin between my fingers and the Deepio was getting into the spud peeling cuts. I asked Greenwood if I could have some gloves but her reply would have made a navvy blush.

By the time we were finished I thought I was going to need arm transplants. It felt like I'd been using them to transport uranium. My clothes were ruined as well. My boots and lightweights were covered in a thick layer of sludge. When I tried to put some polish on my boots that evening, it just slid off. I stank of the cookhouse for over a week, despite obsessive showering. As we were leaving, I commiserated with Dave.

"God, that was fucking awful, eh?"

He winked at me and pointed down to his ball-sack area: "I don't know about you, mate, but I enjoyed it." He leaned in closer as we walked along and said: "I only shagged that Greenwood one, you know."

Every Duty Squadron after, it was the first box I looked at and I always breathed a sigh of relief when some other poor get's name was in there.

The head-sheds were aware that any leisure time would be spent wastefully. With the main pastimes being masturbation and soap-watching, sometimes simultaneously, it was their opinion that our youthful energies needed to be channelled positively. They contrived to limit potential hand-shandy time by making us attend 'hobbies night' every Tuesday and Thursday between 6 and 9pm. Tuesday night was compulsory, with a failure to attend punishable by instant, overnight jailing. Thursdays were ostensibly voluntary, but it was Army voluntary, which meant compulsory. Any apprentice who was caught 'up the block' on a hobbies night was right up shit creek.

At the start of each term, the troop sergeants would assemble everyone and force them to choose a hobby. The popular ones were instantly oversubscribed. Cycling, archery, sailing and clay pigeon shooting had an abundance of volunteers and you had no chance of getting in unless you knew the instructor. As the options dwindled, Barry Nash and I were trying to decide which would be the least bad. The big board posted up outside the Squadron office had a list of subjects down the left-hand side, with room on the right to place your name. It was a bastard of a decision to make as they were all as bad as each other. It read like a roll call of 'interests likely to get you ostracised'. Chess, guitar (non-electric), war-gaming, radio ham, bagpipes, woodwork, computers, painting and bird-watching. The more you looked at the list, the harder it was to choose. It was the troop sergeant's job to ensure everyone was given a slot and he would start making decisions for us, selling the subjects with the enthusiasm of a circus barker.

"Right, AT Gantry. You look like a musician to me. Just think how much you could impress the birds if you tell 'em you can play the guitar."

"Yes, Sergeant."

"Lovely, I'll stick your name down then. Report to Mr Kelly in Room 5, C Block. Nash and Nugent, you can fucking join him."

That was that. You were allowed to swap round at the end of each term, which meant we were lumbered with learning the guitar for three months. We should have been grateful to the instructors. They gave up their spare time for free, two evenings a week, to teach unwanted skills to unresponsive teenagers. There was no getting out of it either. Mr Kelly took a roll call every time and if you weren't there you were reported to the Squadron. There were 24 of us in the guitar lessons and learning was a slow process, hampered by a militant lack of enthusiasm on our part. By the time it came to change round, all he'd managed to teach us was the first four lines to 'Morning has Broken'. I can still play it, but have yet to find a situation where it can be used.

At each change round, the tough lessons learnt in the previous term made you determined to pick a decent or skivable one. In the weeks running up to the swap, an informal intelligence network sprang up, weighing up the relative pros and cons of each hobby. Was the instructor a pushover? Could you arrive late and leave early? Could you make a baseball bat in woodwork? All the info helped you towards a decision.

It was my intention to pick bird-watching next. Apparently, it was quite interesting and Mr Harrop only kept you there for an hour. At the parade, I waited to see if any space had become available in the hobbies on the 'A' list. If they'd asked, I'm sure that they'd have got volunteers to be archery targets or clay pigeons. People – and rightfully so – would go to any lengths not to learn the bagpipes.

Before I could stick my name down in the empty box set aside for the twitchers, I was stuck in the chess group, with the comment that I 'looked like a fucking egghead'.

I knew enough about chess to know that I didn't want to know any more and the instructor was a proper bastard. Mr Henly was an ex-RSM who taught radio principles in the operator wing and he was always out to drop people in the shit. Unfortunately for him, he picked the second week of that term to have a massive heart attack and die. Admittedly, it's cruel to take pleasure at someone's death, but at the time we were all doing guilty backflips. In the haste to backfill his official position and get him buried, his hobbies group was completely forgotten.

We had 12 weeks of doing shite all. We turned up at six o'clock every Tuesday and Thursday as required, safe in the knowledge that, barring miracles, we could piss off after half an hour, our duty done. I got caught up the block a couple of times that term, once whilst watching Star Trek and another time on my way back from a leisurely thrap. I dropped my wanking manual and toilet roll, as the duty sergeant appeared out of nowhere and roared: "What the fuck are you doing?"

The evidence was plain to see and before I could answer he followed up.

"I can see what your real hobby is but why aren't you at fucking chess?"

As agreed with the rest of the class, I stated simply that I was in the chess club and that we'd finished early.

"Right, I'll check with the instructor." He stormed off looking for someone else to catch out.

By the following term they'd managed to find another leader for the men of chess, but by that time I'd moved on again. I managed to get myself into the cycling club by schnecking unashamedly with Major Danby from the Education Corps, who took us for English. He ran the hobby and every time I was in his lesson, I used to try and drop hints that I was born to ride bicycles. It worked and he made the casual suggestion that I should stick my name down. I was in like a shot and stuck with the bike riding until the end of my time at the camp. We didn't actually ride them on Tuesdays and Thursdays. That was all done on the Wednesday sports afternoons. On the two evenings we did maintenance. Most of us just farted around whilst the more serious members got on with oiling chains and pumping up tyres.

Eighteen months can pass remarkably quickly when you are in a routine, and this was borne out by my remaining stay at the camp. The regular beastings in PT, combined with the weekly hobbies and bull nights, made time pass with alarming speed. The weekend hangovers, united with the comical highs of catching people wanking in the bath, and traumatic lows of someone vomming on you during a run, helped the weeks elapse unnoticeably.

Once each term, the senior term of lads would graduate and our intake would always do our bit as back-up squads. It had the effect of punctuating each incremental rise up the food chain. Seniority amongst the apprentices was mainly due to time served. There was a ranking structure that mirrored the non-commissioned table, but any rank attained was lost on graduation.

Horror stories were always circulating around camp about apprentice sergeants who had forgotten to show appropriate deference in their new working units. All the anecdotes finished with the upstart being given a shoeing by a liney. As the old lads went off one end of the conveyor belt, we moved along and a new intake of 16-year-old civvies would appear, cowering at the beginning.

Each night before graduation, the outgoing troops would sweep through the rooms like a herd of buffalo that had been drinking from a watering hole contaminated with woodpecker cider. They'd tip all the new boys out of their beds and destroy all manner of fixtures and fittings. The first time I experienced it, it was quite alarming, but after a new recruit troop had moved upstairs I had nothing to fear as the sprogs would take the full force of the beatings.

It wasn't until Nick, Spud and a whole host of other characters left that it dawned on me that soon it would be my intake's turn. Spud's departure was as gross as one could imagine. At his leaving do, he did his farting bollock trick for a final time. In an obviously prerehearsed fashion, he took a stack of ten pence coins and forced them into his foreskin. He then proceeded to rhythmically thrust his hips forward so that a coin flew out on each upstroke. He called this ritual 'tank slapping', and with each swish of his knob, he enthusiastically encouraged us to try and catch the warm coins. Naturally we gave it a miss, restricting our compliments to shouts of 'Ole'.

As with all 16- to 18-year-old lads, socialising played a large part in our lives. Saturday night was the main event, as mad drinking on a Friday wasn't considered wise. On Saturday mornings we had compulsory sports and anyone smelling like a magic marker was heading for the pokey. Every Saturday night there would be queues of several hundred youths waiting to book out of camp or catch a taxi. Most were dressed in grey slip-ons, white socks, chinos and shirt with the occasional Colonel Abrams/El Debarge-style padded shoulder suit. The over dressing wasn't a lifestyle choice the lads had adopted, but was a compulsory dress code imposed by the College. It was a rule that some guys would go to extraordinary lengths to get around, including climbing the fence or wearing jeans and a T-shirt under their hideous 'wedding outfits'. The guardroom corporals never noticed that guys would go out looking like they weighed 14 stone, and come back dressed in different clothes and noticeably lighter.

This formal dress code was a uniform in itself and made it incredibly difficult to blend in with the locals. I have to say that making conversation with a Harrogate girl whilst denying being in the Army was an almost impossible task, when surrounded by a Spandau Ballet impersonator's club. I found that I wasn't too bad at chatting up girls. Always nervous to begin with, after a couple of beers I could hold a decent conversation without making too much of a plum of myself. My attempts were usually futile though. Even if I was doing well, the final nail would be driven into the chat-up coffin by Barry Nash. Just as it looked like I was getting somewhere, he'd appear and put his arm around my shoulder. The Union Jack T-shirt with 'These Colours Don't Run!' emblazoned on the front meant that no further introduction was required.

His torpedoing would generally go like this:

Barry: "Wheeeyyyy, get the fuckin' beers in, you cunt!"

Me: "Er!"

Girl: "Who's that?"

Me: "Er, I don't know, I've never seen him before in my life!"

Girl: "He looks like he's in the Army."

Me: "Yes he does a bit, doesn't he?"

Barry: "What are you talking about, Eddy? You daft wanker!"

Girl: “Eddy? But you said your name was Dave!”

Me: “Yeah, Sorry about that.”

Girl: “I suppose you’re not really a deep sea salvage diver either!”

Me: “No.”

Girl: “And the house in the Cayman Islands?”

Me: “Sorry.”

Girl: “You squaddie bastid!”

Barry: “Here, Eddy, where’s your bird going?”

Me: “I tell you what, Barry. One of these days I am going to bray you.”

Barry was a good egg, but he loved getting blokes blown out. He would normally wait until the guy went to the toilet and then tell the girl that the chap who had been chatting her up used to own a cheese shop, but when his goat died of an acute strain of Malaysian Syphilis, the business went under. When the potential suitor returned from the trap, they would find Barry with a beer in one hand and the absent girl’s drink in the other.

Any town with a camp of junior soldiers nearby will always be troubled with violence between the locals and the military. In a garrison town with soldiers that were grown men, the sides were evenly matched, but we were the only military unit in the vicinity and short on punching power. Unfortunately the Army environment made lots of the lads think that they were infinitely harder than they actually were. It goes without saying that some skinny, flame-haired, 16-year-old jock, who is built like a Sudanese Locust and has had a sniff of the barmaid’s apron, is no match for an 18-stone piss-tank-warrior brickie from Leeds who is out for a few beers after work. This didn’t deter some of the more foolhardy from gobbing off. When they did, it was usually to completely the wrong bloke and they would often return to the block with black eyes and loose railings for their troubles. The injuries would be explained away, fraudulently. The victim would claim to have successfully fought off dozens of knife and chain-wielding nutters.

Many of the past clashes with local youths had attained legendary status, details being added with each telling of the stories. One such anecdote had probably had its origin in a bout of normal Saturday night fisticuffs. By the time I heard it, it was an epic tale of blokes being tied to a pool table and pushed out of a second story window. All of which had apparently resulted in the entire college booking out, dressed in boots, lightweights and PT kit, then being ferried into town by four-tonner and tearing the place apart. The fact that the local papers had not deigned to cover this momentous event never dented the enthusiasm of people recounting it to wide-eyed listeners. It was obviously a fabrication, as the duty clutch would never get off his lazy, fat arse to perform such a task. Secondly, the Commandant would never put his MBE at risk by legitimising violence. Finally, it had supposedly happened on a Saturday, but this wouldn't have been possible as everybody's uniform would have been in the wash.

There is no denying that my nights out in Harrogate were good fun, although a little frustrating due to my inability to tap off. The cheesily-named, local hot spots of Champers, the Kings Club and Christies were a laugh, and certainly chocker with enough skirt to fire me up for a milk when I got back to camp. Some of the guys were more successful with the ladies though, and those who didn't have the fieldcraft training to smuggle their partners on to camp, would find a quiet bush, or use the band stand in the Valley Gardens Park to do the Lord's work with their birds.

Four months before graduation, we were given the opportunity to select our postings on completion of training. The selection involved the completing of what was known as a dreamsheet. Trying to decide where you wanted to go in the world was a thrilling choice, but there was an element of the illusion to it. It wasn't called a dreamsheet for nothing. It was your right to pick any three units in the world, but you had absolutely no guarantee that you would achieve your desire. Like hobbies, it was blindingly obvious that everyone was going to go for the prime places like Cyprus and Brunei and a lucky handful would strike oil. The majority of lads would spend weeks humming and hawing over which sun-kissed part of the planet they'd choose only to find that manning and records had completely ignored their request and were packing them off to an armoured div near the East German border. As always in the Army, it was purely a matter of head count. If someone in Akrotiri was struck by lightning at the exact moment your request hit the posting officer's desk, you might get the dream draft. Otherwise you could expect to be trying to hide from a German winter behind a malfunctioning kero heater.

All round the walls of the trade block, were displays about specific units in the Corps. There were quite a few interesting ones. 30 Signal Regiment were known as the 'Globetrotters' and were always going away on UN operations. 249 Signal Squadron were ski-troops and spent considerable time in Norway, refining their Arctic warfare techniques. Both seemed interesting, but the one that really caught my attention was 5 Airborne Brigade Signal Squadron. They were a mainly parachute trained unit, whose job was to supply the Brigade with comms, jumping out of planes with radios. It made no bones about what was required of you on the display. Anyone going to the unit had to attempt the physically demanding P-Company course. On successful completion they would be awarded the coveted maroon beret, before going on to get their wings on the parachute course at Brize Norton. There were a couple of instructors who'd served time at the unit, and they walked round camp in their maroon lids and parachute smocks looking, in my opinion, the dog's bollocks. That was enough for me and I stuck my name down. Because it was a volunteer unit, they were always short of blokes and there was no danger that I'd be turned down. It would mean I'd stay in the UK, as they were based in Aldershot. As well as the prestige of serving in such a unit, it would mean I didn't have to disappear into the vortex of a BAOR posting.

As we came to the end of training we went through the trade board. All of the skills we'd learnt over the last two years were formally tested. The stakes were high. Anyone who failed would have to stay at the College for a course of remedial training prior to a reattempt. It was hard, but if you failed you would be treated like a major duffer by all and sundry. There was loads of cheating going on. People were entering into reciprocal agreements with colleagues who had the opposite strengths and weaknesses to themselves. Crib sheets and whispers were the order of the week and most of us got through, sometimes with the tacit assistance of a benevolent instructor, who couldn't be bothered with the hassle of retesting apprentices.

When the time came to leave, we'd been issued our Number Two dress. I was really looking forward to moving on, and speaking to Mum in the run up to graduation encouraged me further.

"We're so proud of you, Eddy. You've done really well to stick with it."

"Thanks, Mum."

"Even your Auntie Mary and Uncle Jim are coming across for the parade. Your Dad's hired a little minibus."

I hadn't realised I was the focus of such proud attention and it had to be a special day to prise Mary away from the McVitie's factory in Levenshulme.

The day of the graduation was great. It was the back-end of July and unlike the pass off, the sun put in an appearance for the whole show. I always found the camp unfamiliar on sunny days, it was almost pleasant. We were all excited about the parade, but feigned indifference to maintain street cred. We were sent down to collect weapons an hour before and queued impatiently outside the armoury. Lance-Corporal Lang was on weapons duty that day and he came in for a stack of abuse, from the anonymity of the queue. He was trying to keep order in his endearing way.

"Keep the fucking noise down, or there'll be no weapons and no fucking graduation."

He was wasting his time. It had been two years since he bollocked us at Leeds train station and the interim period had given us all time to figure out where his place was in the pecking order.

"Fuck off, Lang, you coffin dodger," someone far braver than I had shouted from the back. Lang was furious and ran up and down the line, demanding to know who'd insulted him. The wall of blank faces told him he'd get no answer. There was great pleasure to be taken in having one up on the little Nazi. He realised he was wasting his time on blokes who, two hours from now, would be able to give him a dig in the NAAFI, if he got lippy. He turned back towards the armoury door, and the same voice from the rear encouraged him to get back to work.

"Just give us our guns, you jittery old knacker."

He stopped for a moment, then thought better of it, moving behind the counter with previously unseen speed.

As we got into our twos dress in the block, the cameras started doing the rounds and people started adopting unnatural poses for the viewfinder. Men in various states of undress were pointing rifles menacingly around the room in the hope they'd look hard in the picture. Blokes who didn't smoke were dangling lit cigarettes from their lips to increase the delinquent effect. Of course, the unit 'photograph spoiler' was on hand to lower the tone and quality of any snaps. I recently dug out my Army photo album at Mum's and had a good look through, recounting the circumstances of each exposure. What I did notice as I flicked along was that every single photo had been spoilt by someone in the background. Every single one. It must have been an Army thing. My Mum's albums are full of smiling people, gathered at various family occasions. All the subjects behave impeccably. I started rooting through my album, trying to find one photo that didn't have someone doing rabbit ears behind someone's head, or exposing a hairy spud for all to see. Time and again, an otherwise good study was ruined by something going on behind the unwitting posers. One of the photos taken on the morning of the graduation was the worst. I'd managed to assemble our entire recruit troop room for a portrait before we all went our separate ways. All kitted out, ready to go for the parade, we looked the business. The eight of us stood there, whilst one of the lads from the intake below used my camera to get a couple of photos. After getting the film developed a few weeks later, I sat on a bench in Piccadilly Gardens to examine them. The one of Room 4 Recruit Troop was the best of the bunch. Stood there, with our laughable, hard-man stares, there was a real bonhomie to our little group. There were a couple of lockers behind us and it was only then that I noticed that someone had managed to climb on top of them and drop his kecks. Pulling his cheeks as wide as they would go, he was exposing his anus perfectly. I don't know who it was, but he must have had some photographic training, as his ricker was plumb top-centre. It was going to rest on Paul Jones' head for eternity.

We formed up for the parade in the road near Bradley Squadron, hidden from the stand and viewing platform by Penney Squadron's accommodation. As soon as the band started playing, the support troops marched into position and awaited our grand entrance. Listening in to the orders being roared by the RSM, we moved onto the square to the tune of the Corps quick march. Once we halted, we treated the spectators to a display of static weapons drill. We had it boxed off fairly well, and each crisp movement drew ‘oohs’ and ‘aahs’ from our families. After that came the obligatory ‘standing still for an hour’. It was a new mayor doing the inspection and he really took his time, revelling in the opportunity to dress like Henry VIII without attracting the attention of mental health professionals. The bandmaster was keen to show that his finger was on the pulse of any recent popular music developments. As well as the familiar playlist we were treated to a bizarre, brass version of ‘The Final Countdown’. The sun took its toll on the ranks. Eight blokes collapsed in all, two from our squad. We’d been told to rock back and forth gently within our boots, to keep the circulation going, but the heat and inactivity bred prime conditions for fainting. Every five minutes or so, my ears were drawn to a banging and clattering as another apprentice bit the dust. Whenever it happened, a couple of seniors ran on to the square and grabbed hold of the bloke under the arms, before dragging him off and taking all the precious bull off his boots simultaneously. If they could have got away with it, I think the Army would have liked to charge people for fainting, citing some obscure legal transgression like ‘showing disrespect to the Queen by hallucinating and breaking all your teeth in front of the colours’. Instead, the fainters had to endure the derision of those who’d managed to stay on their feet. I was feeling a bit wobbly myself and breathed a huge sigh of relief when the inspection party finally moved back to the dais.

It was great to get moving again and we completed the march past. When we got to the corners of the square furthest from scrutiny, discipline broke down slightly and discussions took place about any eye candy in the crowd.

“Did you see that blonde one with the big knockers in the Smiths T-shirt,” shouted someone behind me.

“That’s my fucking sister, you,” came the irate reply.

“Sorry, mate. She has got big knockers though, eh?”

"Fair one."

All was quiet again as we marched past for the second time, doing a snappy eyes-right as the Commandant saluted and the mayor tried to salute.

When we came off the parade ground we were marched behind the stands. After a count of three, everyone threw their hats in the air with a heartfelt cheer. That sort of thing always looked great in the films, but I spent the next five minutes looking at the names in scores of lids until I found my own. Several people took advantage of the situation to swipe hats that were in better condition than their own.

The Nugent gang descended on me as soon as I was spotted. Auntie Mary reached me first and smothered me in kisses, laughing and crying at the same time.

"Eddy, you were brilliant. I told you you'd make a good soldier."

Her prediction, written in the biscuits, had been accurate after all. Uncle Jim and Dad were stood behind her, smiling benignly. Gran had brought a 'gentleman friend' with her. He was an old soldier called Alfie Silver she'd met down the British Legion and he'd clearly enjoyed himself. He stepped forward and shook my hand firmly. He had a chest full of medals above the breast pocket of his Royal Engineers blazer.

"Well done, son. That parade was splendid. Takes me back to 1940 it does."

Before he could get started on his wartime record, Mum interrupted.

"Come on, Alfie, let me get to him."

She hugged me and kissed me gently on the forehead.

"Well done, Eddy. I'm so proud of you."

Dad joined her, putting an arm round both our shoulders.

"It was smashing that, son. I'm not sure about the music, but all that drill with the weapons looked the bee's knees."

I said my goodbyes to the lads, and we swapped earnest but ultimately doomed promises to keep in touch from our new units. We climbed into the minibus and headed for home. Dad had brought a crate of beers and we drank and sang all the way back to Manchester. The journey only took a couple of hours, but Alfie took full advantage of the free ale on offer and was boozed-up and waffling by the time we got to Leeds.

The chest full of medals he displayed, testified to the contribution he'd made during the Second World War, but he couldn't resist colouring in his stories a bit. With all the eye-witnesses out of the picture his imagination had free rein. Pointing to one of his brightly coloured gongs, he said: Do you know what I got this one for, Eddy lad?"

"No, Alfie. I know they're all Second World War medals but I don't know what each one means."

For the rest of the run in, he told me amazing stories about his adventures in the war. Some were heartbreaking, others hilarious. I can't recall the details now but one of his anecdotes had what is possibly the best opening line I've ever heard. "I was on the piss in Nazareth," it started.

It was impossible not to be captivated by the charming old codger, reliving memories of his youth. It was unimportant that he was making some of it up, and when my Dad pointed out that El Alamein and the Dieppe raid happened around the same time, he was shouted down by the rest of us and Alfie continued with his story.

I had a whole month before I had to report to Aldershot. I trained almost every day, following the curriculum suggested in my joining instructions. I ran in the mornings and did some work with a Bergan in the afternoons. There were no hills in our part of town, so I was reduced to running back and forth over a railway bridge near the local B & Q. I looked a knob and got regular abuse from schoolkids. I never responded, mainly because I agreed with all their comments.

I didn't let the training programme get in the way of my number one pastime and managed to fit in plenty of beer drinking. Now that I was receiving trade pay for my qualifications, my wages had gone up and I didn't have to sponge off Mum and Dad as much. Despite having busy working lives they tolerated my drunken behaviour with good grace. Dad only saw red with me once. I came home from a club one Saturday night at about 3am. When I realised that I didn't have my key, I tried to climb in the downstairs toilet window. I'd managed to squeeze my way through the small aperture. It was usually left open as Dad always liked to drop a depth charge just before bed and Mum thought that the draught might stop the paint from peeling.

I got my hands either side of the sink that sat just below the window and started to bring my legs through. Just when I thought I'd cracked it, I caught the bottom of my jeans on the handle of the window. I couldn't get it free or push myself back up. I struggled for five minutes before giving up with my head resting in the sink and my feet still outside. There was only one thing for it, and I meekly started shouting for help, the call muffled by the porcelain. I heard the lights upstairs being switched on followed by the noise of Dad stomping down the stairs. When he opened the toilet door he was hopping mad, and was just about to launch into a hefty bollocking, when he saw my predicament and started laughing.

"Fucking hell, Eddy. What time of night is this to be washing your hair?"

He grudgingly helped me down and went back to bed, but marked my card the next morning. I made sure there were no recurrences and concentrated on getting my fitness up for the trials ahead.

Chapter 4

Battery Bombs and Kentucky Muggers

I travelled down to Aldershot on a Thursday morning, as usual, by train. The rail warrant that I'd been issued with took me all round the houses. From Manchester, the usual route was: Piccadilly to Euston; tube from Euston to Waterloo; then Waterloo to Aldershot. Whoever had sorted my ticket out had decided to treat me to a tour of all the nondescript, dormitory towns which are dotted all over Network South East. Years later, I had a heated, regionalist argument with a mate from Woking. He was busy slagging off northerners for all he was worth. When I sought to counter his thrust by listing some of the achievements that citizens of Manchester had accomplished, which were now of benefit to the entire world community, he shrugged me off with that annoying combination of a faux cockney accent and an inability to pronounce his 'r's.

"Fack off, Eddy, you're talking wabbish."

"Go on then, name one thing that Woking can be proud of?"

He stopped, and pondered thoughtfully for a few seconds before saying proudly: "We've got the biggest cemetery in Europe."

The accuracy of that statement is unimportant. The fact that he considered it a more significant contribution than the invention of the computer was a real testament to his civic pride.

When the train finally emerged at Aldershot station, I hauled all my belongings off the luggage rack and struggled through the exit doors and on to the approach. I had no idea how far it was to the camp so I walked over to a taxi driver, who was leaning on his car, smoking, whilst waiting for his next fare.

" 'Scuse me, mate. I'm looking for Arnhem Barracks."

"Do you want directions, or do you want me to take you up there?"

"Is it far?"

"It will be with all those bags," he chuckled.

"Fair enough," I conceded.

He popped the boot and I slung my two holdalls and daysack in. I climbed in, and off we went. It was only a short journey but he managed to give me his life story. Like lots of garrison towns, Aldershot was extensively populated with old soldiers who left the Army but not the town. The ties that bound them to the place, namely the social circuit and their marriage to a local, meant that, regardless of their point of origin, they couldn't think of a place they'd rather live. My driver had been in 3 Para for 12 years, before leaving in the mid-seventies. He was quite fat now, no doubt due to the standard cabbie's diet of kebabs and Coke, but he still looked quite capable of handling himself. Close cropped hair, number two all over, and a selection of tattoos on his arm that looked like they'd been done with a blue crayon, helped him to transmit a reasonable amount of menace. Looking in the rear-view mirror, he interrogated me.

"Arnhem barracks, eh? What are you then, Signals?"

"Yeah that's right, first day today."

"You just out of training then?"

"Yeah, I've been at the Army Apprentices' College in Harrogate for the last two years."

He wrinkled his nose up at that one.

"Sounds a bit wank all that, mate. Are you here to do P-Company?"

"That's right; I'm posted in to the Signal Squadron, but as a volunteer for Airborne Forces."

"Fit lad, are you?"

“Not bad, I’ve been doing a lot of training?”

He smiled, and shook his head slowly.

“You’d better be ready for some pain.”

During the conversation the taxi had headed out of town and up a short rise called Hospital Hill. At the top of the hill was Knollys Road roundabout. He went straight on into Queen’s Avenue. About 100 metres down on the right was a huge Victorian building, and he pulled up next to it. He looked over his shoulder at me, whilst simultaneously indicating towards the building with his thumb.

“That’s Maida gym. You’ll get to see lots of grown men crying in there, yourself included,” he chortled. He then pointed down to his left.

“That’s the NAAFI on the left, and if you look a bit further down on the right, that’s the Sig Squadron offices. That’s £2.60 please, mate.”

I gave him three quid and told him to keep the change. I got all of my gear out of the boot and deposited it by the side of the road. He gave me the thumbs-up and a wink, before spinning the car round and heading back into town.

I stood there for a moment, getting my bearings. Looking into the camp, it seemed enormous. From where I was standing, it looked like a badly designed, sixties housing estate. Way down on my right were a collection of three-storey concrete squares with windows in them. These were the accommodation blocks. In the direction that the taxi driver had pointed, were various two-storey buildings, all made out of the same ugly material as the accommodation. A huge building across the road from the NAAFI later revealed itself to be the cookhouse. At that time, there was no fence around the camp, and you could walk on to it at any point. A year or so later, there was an escalation in terrorist activity on the mainland which resulted in an equivalent escalation in camp security. Over a couple of weeks, a two-metre fence was erected around the entire camp. For months after they put it up, people were cutting through it. Not terrorists of course, just pissed-up squaddies who didn't want to have to walk the long way round after a night out. One particular patch of the fence was breached and repaired almost on a daily basis. It was right by the 9 Para, Royal Engineers living quarters. They ended up having two poor bastards sat in a 9 x 9 tent, watching it every night, until the practice stopped. Unfortunately for the fencewatch personnel, they weren't a great deterrent. Blokes from 9 Sqn would just turn up with a set of bolt croppers and snip a big chunk out of the fence right in front of them, offering to snip a big chunk out of the guard if they said anything. When the guard commander came to check on them during the night, he would rightfully want to know why there was a huge fucking hole in the fence when it was their job to prevent that precise event from occurring. Rather than grass on the fence cutters, the guard would have to pretend that they hadn't seen anything and had only noticed the hole when the guard commander had pointed it out to them. This would all be done silent movie-style, with lots of exaggerated eye-rubbing and hands on hips incredulity. Eventually 9 Sqn started walking round to the back gate like everyone else, and the short lived and completely ineffectual 'fence-picquet' were stood down.

I gathered my bags up and walked down towards the Signal Squadron offices. It was just after lunch, so lots of blokes were coming in and out of the NAAFI. I saw a few Signals cap badges and several others, medics, engineers, REME and a couple of Ordnance Corps blokes. The only thing that everyone had in common was the maroon beret, which I found myself gazing at in admiration. I found out later, that a hugely controversial rule had just been passed within the Brigade. Prior to the regulations changing, only those personnel in the Brigade who were parachute-trained, and – by extension – had passed P-Company, were entitled to wear parachute wings and the maroon beret. Anyone else serving in the Brigade was obliged to wear their normal headgear until the courses were passed.

The new rule was that anyone posted in to the Brigade would wear a maroon beret. In defence of whoever had had the bright idea, it was probably done with the best of intentions (e.g. make everyone look the same, and engender a good *esprit de corps* within the Brigade). Of course it had the diametrically opposite effect. Soldiers who had earned the beret prior to the rules changing, bitterly resented other soldiers wearing it without having to go through exactly the same trial. Many soldiers who had just arrived, had volunteered for the Brigade in a bid to gain something considered coveted, and objected to having to wear the beret just as bitterly. Of course there were quite a few that enjoyed getting to wear the gear without having to do anything for it, and they further inflamed the situation. Fat blokes walking round in badly shaped maroon berets, were absolute punch-magnets and would regularly get assaulted without ever understanding why. The only way that the beret kept its cherished status within the Brigade was with the introduction of an unwritten rule. Anyone in the Brigade could wear the bog standard, stores-issued beret, but only parachute trained soldiers could wear the higher quality, leather-banded affair, available for purchase at the Victor's shop in Aldershot. It wasn't an ideal solution, but I'm sure it kept a lot of lard-arses from getting a good kicking.

I carried on past the NAAFI and walked over to the Signal Squadron. I stopped at the base of a flagpole that had an Airborne Signals flag fluttering from it, and dropped my bags. There was no one around so I had a good look about. I was standing on a parade square about the size of half a football pitch. Behind me was another two-storey building. An external spiral staircase gave entry to the first floor. Dotted all over the building were blue doors marked with blue and white squares. The writing on the squares gave details of the pleasures to be had inside. Clothing store, bedding store, armoury, QM's department, Squadron offices. On the opposite side of the parade ground was the side wall of the cookhouse. The third side of the square had another row of two-storey offices. The signs on the doors read from left to right, Line Stores, Alpha Troop and Bravo Troop. There didn't appear to be too much more to the place. Whilst I was stood there, wondering what to do next, the door marked Alpha Troop opened, and a very large man came out and headed towards me. By the time he'd completed the walk of about 50 metres, I'd had enough time to identify his rank – Sergeant – and demeanour – threatening. Unlike everyone in the Apprentice College, he didn't have a nametag on his jacket.

"Who are you?" he snapped. Throughout my time in Aldershot, this was the standard opening shot in any conversation with a stranger. It was meant to put the respondent on the back foot immediately and was very effective. I learnt later, that the correct response to the question, leaving both parties with honours even was: "Why, who are you?"

At this early stage in my education, such a response would have been folly, and would have probably resulted in some sort of physical pain, so I opted for burbling nervously: "Sig Nugent, Sarnt."

"Posted in?"

"Yes, Sarnt, from Harrogate."

"Craphat then, yeah?"

"Err, yes."

"There's no fucker about at the moment. Everybody gets back off block leave on Monday morning. I think Kenny Rogers is over in the stores, stocktaking or something. If you go over and see him, he'll sort you out with some accommodation. Do you know who you're supposed to report to?"

"Staff Sergeant Herbert."

"Right, well that's a bit fucked up. He's on leave 'til Monday as well." He stood there for a second, wondering what to do with me before saying: "Go see Kenny, and get your bedspace. Get him to show you around a bit if he's got time. Other than that you can do your own thing 'til tomorrow morning."

He crooked his thumb in the direction of the door he'd just exited from.

"Come and see me at eight o'clock, in normal working dress, and I'll find you some jobs to do."

"Right, Sarnt."

With our conversation complete, he moved off back towards his office, before stopping and shouting back.

"Nugent?"

"Sarnt?"

"Try not to talk to anyone, you'll only annoy them."

"Errr, right, Sarnt."

He moved off and left me alone. Leaving my bags where they were, I headed towards the bedding stores door and knocked. Predictably, the shout that came from inside was not Texan, but deepest, darkest Brummie.

"What the fuck do you want?"

Slightly taken aback, I shouted through the closed door: "It's Sig Nugent from Harrogate. The sergeant told me to come and see you to get some accommodation sorted out."

"Which sergeant?"

"I don't know his name. He was a big guy, a Scouser."

"Bryson?"

"I don't know."

"Fucking wanker; thinks I've got nothing better to do." There was a brief sound of footsteps before the door to the store started the long process of becoming unlocked. It sounded like three padlocks then bolts, top, middle and bottom being undone, before the door finally opened. I had to check to make sure it was the bedding store, and not a repository for some priceless antiquity.

Kenny Rogers emerged, or rather his head emerged from behind the door. He was a bit of a gargoyle. He had a skinhead which exposed the various lumps, bumps and stitch-marks on his skull. An oft broken nose and a set of bad teeth completed the look.

"What is it you want then?"

"Sergeant Bryson said to get a bedspace."

"Fuckin' did he?"

"Yeah."

He softened slightly

"Sorry, mate, not having a go at you. I've got loads of work to do and I know for a fact that that fucker is just sat up in his office looking at himself in the mirror, and it's his fault that I'm the only fucker not on leave at the minute."

"Why's that then?"

"He brought a mattress in last week and tried to exchange it, but I wouldn't let him. He tried to say he'd spilt a brew on it, but you could tell he'd pissed it."

"How did you know?"

"The only way that could have been a brew stain, is if he'd been drinking out of the European Cup. The whole fucking mattress was piss-wet through. Only the corners were still white. If it was tea or coffee the stain would have been brown, but it was as yellow as a Post-it. So I billed him the 15 quid for a new one."

"And he didn't like that?"

"Did he fuck. Whilst he was signing the chit he says to me, smiling: "I'll be doing the guard roster for the block leave period today, Rogers." So that was me fucked".

Whilst he was talking, he'd opened the door fully, and was now going through the elaborate process of making the door secure from the outside.

"Sorry to hear it, mate."

"Ahh, it's not too bad, I've caught up on a lot of me work, and I get to fuck off as soon as the rest of 'em come back. It's always mad here the first week back after block leave, so it'll be good to be out of the way."

He moved the last padlock into place and snapped it shut, before turning back to me.

"Right, I'll take you over the block. Probably stick you up on the top floor. There's a few more coming from Harrogate isn't there?"

"Yeah, five I think."

"Yeah? I'll stick you all on the top floor, you'll be a bit more out of the way, and the meatheads might leave you alone."

"Meatheads?"

"Meatheads, cassette heads, empty heads, Aldershot orphans, call 'em what you want. It's all the blokes who never go home. They've either got no parents or family, or no parents or family who like them. All they do is work here, and go down town and get pissed at all other times. They hate craphats, and they like to pay visits when they're leathered. Nothing too bad really, usually just a bit of drunken fist waving, and the occasional bit of mayhem. If I stick you on the top floor, they might be too drunk to make it up that far."

"Are you a craphat?"

"No I'm fucking not," what do you think these are?" He pointed at the set of parachute wings, sewn neatly on to his jumper at the top of the right sleeve.

"Sorry," I replied. After what Sergeant Bryson had said, I was very scared of offending anyone, but Kenny started laughing.

"Don't worry about it. I tell you what though, a lot of people are really touchy about who is and who isn't, especially since all the hats are wearing maroon lids. You'll find all this out. There are some blokes who will flatly refuse to speak to you if you aren't Para-trained. Most blokes will tolerate you, but would rather have someone Para-trained in your slot. Then there are blokes like me who don't give a monkey's who I work with. I've passed the course so I've got nothing to prove to the meatheads, but I can't be arsed being shitty with someone just because they haven't got their wings. The best thing I can suggest is you get Pre-Para and P-Company out of the way as quick as you can. Then you don't have to worry about it."

"I think Pre-Para starts next Tuesday."

"Yeah, that'd be right. Have you been training?"

"Quite a lot, yeah."

"That won't matter. It'll still be fucking murder," he smiled, "wouldn't want to go through that again."

In the time it took to have the conversation, we'd walked across the square – picking up my bags along the way – past the cookhouse and down a short path, with accommodation blocks either side; six in total. We stopped outside the second one on the right. It was a forbidding looking building.

"Here you go, Prisoner Cell Block E. Rumour has it that the architect who came up with this scheme is doing time for designing a load of flats that fell down in Bradford."

"Seriously?"

"Don't know, might be a load of bollocks, but if this camp is anything to go by, he'll be getting buggered in strange ways in Strangeways, ha-ha! Like I say, I'll stick you in one of the eight-man rooms on the top floor. When any of the other Pre-Para lads show up, I'll send 'em in the same direction."

He bent down, picked up one of my bags and turned to the door. I grabbed the other two and followed. There was a rudimentary, push button combination lock on the door. He ignored it and pulled the door straight open.

"Don't know why the fuck they bother with them. The combination is always the same, 1-2-3-4, but you still get blokes who are too thick or pissed to remember, so they just boot it off with a size-ten master key. It gets fixed every Monday and smashed every Friday." He laughed, shrugged his shoulders and headed up the stairs. The stairwell seemed quite clean and tidy, and I was beginning to get my hopes up that the interior was going to be more welcoming, after my first impressions from outside.

"Seems quite clean, Kenny?"

"This is the best you'll ever see it. Before any block leave, there's a big clean-up. The head-shed threaten you with keeping you back unless it's done. The razz man comes round, the morning of knock-off day and inspects. It's the only time anyone bothers their arse. All the shit gets crammed into lockers, into the false ceilings and under beds. He usually just has a bit of a skim round, makes sure there's no blood on the walls or bodies in the drying room. I tell you what though, if he opened one of the lockers, he'd get killed by a shit avalanche."

"So there's not too much bullshit then?" I asked hopefully.

"Nah, mate, it's not that sort of place. They concentrate more on running and tabbing than drill and inspections."

Well that was one thing at least. After Harrogate, it was going to be nice not having to worry about shiny boots, but unfortunately Kenny continued.

"Anyway, you'll be that ballbagged from getting beasted all over the training area, you wouldn't have the energy for drill if they tried to get you to do it at gunpoint."

I got that queasy feeling in my stomach. What had I got myself into? I was pinning my hopes on Kenny feeding me a bit of a line to scare me, but he didn't seem like that sort of bloke.

We climbed four flights of stairs and reached the second floor. Kenny turned right and opened a fire door leading into a short corridor revealing more doors. He pointed.

"You want the first door on the right. Just pick an empty bedspace and sort your locker out."

"Cheers, Kenny."

"No probs. Wash area's through on your left, and there are three other rooms up here. You'd better stay out of them. All the lads are away, but you don't want anyone catching you skulking around their kit. I can tell you for a fact that they won't be very understanding. I'll see you about."

With that parting shot, he left me to it. I went through the door, this time lugging all the bags and opened up the room door. It was fairly big. There were four beds in the side of the room I was in. Each had a locker, top box and side drawers set up next to them. All the beds were stripped, with a clean mattress on each, awaiting their next occupants. To my left there was a small walkway that led to the other half of the room, which duplicated the furniture exactly. A partition separated the two halves, and each had a large square window, which opened outwards on centrally fixed hinges. It all looked okay and I was going to be afforded about the same amount of privacy as I had in Harrogate, i.e. none! I chose one of the beds nearest to the window and dropped my kit next to it. After a brief gawp out of the window, surveying my new domain, I emptied all my gear and started putting it in the locker. The locker was exactly the same as the ones at the College, with the addition of some weird graffiti. On the inside of the left-hand door, just below the mirror were the words 'Clash, Cash, Hash, Gash, Keith and Sarah'. I'm mulling over it again, years later, and I still haven't got a clue what it means. A list of Keith and Sarah's needs, in order of importance perhaps? After I'd done my locker, I lay on the unsheeted bed and had forty winks.

Until the Squadron came back in its entirety, the next few days were boring and strange. I'd never been on an empty camp before. It was mind-numbing enough for me to make a mental note not to drop myself into deep enough shit to get me held back during block leave. I did a bit of work for Sergeant Bryson, painting a couple of Land Rovers in an imaginative combination of black and green. I went to every meal in the cookhouse, where an industrially fat, slop-jockey corporal dished out heavily fried food, to the slack handful of blokes that were knocking around.

I took walks into town on Saturday and Sunday – during the day, of course. I'd heard enough about the nightlife not to attempt a boozing spree single-handed.

Over the weekend, the other five Pre-Para lads showed up. I was able to help out a bit, showing them the various parts of the camp that I'd discovered, or had shown to me. By Sunday night, all six of us were in the room, sitting on our beds, apprehensively discussing what lay in store for us. Other than Davey Bovan, Willie Edwards and Scouse Marriott from Harrogate, there was Joey Donaldson from 30 Sigs and Shuggy Tennant from 211 Signal Squadron in Germany. During any conversation of this sort, everyone is secretly trying to establish that they are not the most unfit, haven't done the least training, and are not the most disorganised.

I was alright on the first two points, but lagged behind the rest of them when it came to organisational skills. Davey, Willie and Scouse had all done a lot of training at Harrogate and during the big summer leave, and were raring to go. Joey was on the Corps cross-country team and had wanted to serve with Airborne Forces for five years. This was his first chance. Shuggy on the other hand, had a beer gut. It came out during the conversation that he'd only volunteered to get out of Germany.

"How do you mean?" asked Scouse, perplexed.

"Well it's a volunteer posting innit," replied Shuggy, "I was fucking sick of Germany. I've been there six years, straight out of training and I had another two to go before me next posting. They call it the Iron Triangle, 1 Div, 3 Div and 4 Div. Once you're in you never get back out. Thing is, if you stick your name down for a volunteer unit, and pass the course, they've got to let you go."

"There's one little flaw in your plan there, mate," said Davey.

"What's that?"

"Pre-Para and P-Company are a cunt to pass. We're going to be getting ran absolutely fucking ragged for the next six weeks. Are you up for all that?"

"I should be alright, I've done a bit of training, and I can pass me BFT and all that."

It sounds tight to say it, but I was heartened by the fact that I could be 100 per cent certain that somebody was going to be behind me on some of the runs. At about ten o'clock people started sorting themselves out for bed. The general consensus was that an early night might be beneficial. At about a quarter past, the door opened and a short man squeezed himself through into the room, smiling slightly. He was about five feet six tall and had a similar width around the shoulders. He was dressed in boots, lightweights, shirt and maroon beret. Round his waist, looped through the top of the lightweights was a Signals stable belt, with an Airborne buckle. He also had a green and yellow lanyard on instead of the normal Signals blue. His short sleeves allowed him to display his extensively tattooed and muscled arms. He looked friendly enough, in a no nonsense way. He also looked capable of beating us all up with one hand tied behind his back.

He took his beret off, to reveal a number two, the choice of the discerning paratrooper and introduced himself, in a strong Northern Irish accent.

"Evening, lads. I'm Staff Sergeant Herbert. I'm the training wing staffie and I'll be taking you for Pre-Para for the next three weeks."

We gathered round him, leaving a bit of a respectful distance.

"There are seven more on the course. Two officers and five lads who failed the last one. I hope for your sakes, you've done a lot of training."

This received some nods in agreement and a comedy gulp from Shuggy.

"Well, we're starting tomorrow, so I hope so. I want you all formed up on the square at 0730 hours, underneath the flag. Dress is red PT tops, lightweights and boots. No watches, no jewellery, no make up."

He had a quick glance round.

"Looks like we'll have a haircutting party tomorrow as well." He looked over at Davey and shook his head.

"You've got more hair than Bonnie fucking Tyler. Not to worry, we'll sort that out. Make sure you've all got a white material patch on the front of your shirts with your name clearly visible."

This had been on the joining instructions and I had three shirts, two issued, one proffed, all with a nice big name tag in the middle, made from a ripped up pillow case.

"Tomorrow morning it will just be a light run and a bit of battle PT, to see what sort of condition you're all in. You'd best get some sleep."

He stuck his beret back on and trundled back through the door, leaving us to ruminate on his words. I was bricking it a bit to tell the truth. I just had no idea what to expect, and would rather have just got started then than wait until the next morning.

From then on, everyone was quite subdued, and went back to sorting their kit out for the morning. The last sidelight went out at about 11. I slept well considering that I was nervous.

The alarm was set for 0630 hours and I jumped out of bed as soon as it went off. I got shaved and cleaned-up and got into my gear for the run. Breakfast was at seven o'clock, but I didn't fancy it. The idea of running around with a load of pigswill sloshing around my guts didn't appeal one bit. At 7.15am we all got together and walked over to the square. The camp was bustling with activity. All the units were back in from block leave now, and there were people milling about all over. We were immediately identifiable in the red PT tops as Pre-Para fodder. In the short time it took to get to the square we attracted quite a lot of looks, mainly of the pitying sort. By twenty-five past, all 13 of us were stood in front of the flagpole. The two officers had white PT tops on, and looked like standard Sandhurst, rosy-cheeked teenagers. A couple of minutes later Staff Sergeant Herbert came out of the first-floor offices and down the stairs followed by two, younger, but bigger blokes. They were wearing the same outfit as us, but with a maroon T-shirt instead of the PT top and no name tag.

When he got in front of us, he introduced himself again.

"For those of you who didn't get to meet me last night, my name is Staff Sergeant Herbert. I will be looking after your mental welfare for the next three weeks."

The two other men stood slightly behind and either side of him. He swept his hand to the left indicating a tall, ginger man with more tattoos and even less hair.

"This is Corporal Griffiths, and this is Lance-Corporal Frankson."

The other chap had slightly fewer tattoos but was both taller and harder looking than the other two. All the time that Herbert was talking, the two corporals glared up and down our lines, daring anybody to make eye contact. Nobody did. Herbert continued.

"You all know what you're here for so I won't give you any long speeches. Passing Pre-Para will entitle you to attempt P-Company. We're not in the business of sending people to Depot Para who we don't think will pass. It makes us look bad. Pre-Para is not an easy course but lots of people have passed it so it's not impossible. Turn to your right and listen in."

We did exactly as instructed, immediately. Staff Sergeant Herbert walked to the front man and addressed him.

"Stay with me. Stay exactly half a pace behind me. If you get any closer, I'll assume that you all want to run faster."

Without further fanfare, he started to run and we followed, for three weeks. The whole of Pre-Para was a blur of mud, pain and launderettes. Right from the first morning, they set out to murder us. They were working on the unscientific premise that anybody who was left standing at the end would consider P-Company as a bit of time off. The light run that Herbert had mentioned the night before, consisted of an eight-mile, cross-country, slog. The route we took became achingly familiar within a couple of days. Under the Arnhem Barracks archway, down the road past Normandy Barracks, over Pegasus Bridge, and down past the Wellington Memorial and onto the training area. The training area was like a twisted version of Alton Towers. It was a massive expanse of MOD owned land covered in hills and intertwining paths. Unfortunately, in place of the rides you'd normally expect at a theme park, they'd put little physical tests designed to further deplete the visitor. The first one we encountered actually sounded like a ride, and was called 'Spiders'. By the time we got there, we'd already pegged it two miles and were starting to feel the pace. Herbert called us to a halt at the bottom of a small hill. Well, he said 'halt,' but what he actually meant was for us to stop running forwards, and to start marking time at the double.

"Get your fucking knees up," screamed Frankson. They weren't happy until we looked like a mad, Irish dancing troupe. Spiders was so named because of the myriad paths that ran over and around it. I suppose that from the air, it must have resembled a large arachnid, albeit with 15 or 20 legs. The usual script is that one of the instructors will run up and down the paths, crossing the peak of the small hill regularly for about five minutes. He'll then swap with another instructor who'll take the next shift. Of course, unlike the instructors, the students don't get to take a rest, and are thoroughly chinstrapped after a couple of goes round. The most horrific thing about it was the fact that it didn't count towards anything. You didn't get any points or backslaps for completing it. It was just something you did on the way out to the training area. After our introduction to Spiders, we simply formed back up in a squad, and carried on with the run. Unless the instructors were in a hurry, there would always be time for a bit of a beasting on Spiders. If you were particularly unlucky, you'd do it on the way back in as well. As we got closer to Spiders after a hard run, you could almost hear a gentle praying in the squad. Hoping that Herbert would forget it was there, you would get a horrible sinking feeling in your stomach, as he veered off the metalled road and ran in its direction. Since leaving, whenever I hear someone utter the expression 'I'm scared of Spiders,' I get a flashback and have a little shudder to myself. Various other rides in the theme park were Hungry Hill, Miles End Hill, Flagstaff, Zigzags, Long Valley and the Mulberry Bush. Funnily enough, they all involved running up and down hills until you thought you were going to regurgitate your heart and lungs. When I wasn't looking at my own feet, I'd occasionally look around me frantically, hoping there would be a big cliff that I could just jump off, or a nice pothole in which I could break my ankle. The first morning's run was just the start. We covered every fucking blade of grass and dog turd on that area. Sometimes in PT kit, sometimes with Bergans, sometimes carrying each other, but always knackered. As well as the joys of the training area there were the gym sessions. These would usually last somewhere between an hour, and an hour and a half. You'd run into the changing rooms in Maida gym, and get into the ridiculous clobber that they called a PT kit. Whilst you were climbing into your 'Tupper of the Track' shorts you would start to hear the roars from inside the cavernous gym, emanating from an increasingly impatient Frankson or Griffiths.

"Come on you lot, hiding won't do you any good".

"The longer you take, the worse we'll make it".

Joey Donaldson was the fittest lad on the course, he sailed round all of the runs, but the gym sessions had a weird effect on him. When the corporals started screaming at us to get in from the changing rooms, he'd get all upset. He'd start jogging on the spot with a look of horrified panic in his eyes.

"What do you think we'll do today?" he'd ask, in the hope that someone would say that volleyball was down on the timetable. The answer was always the same. We would get crucified. The sessions would always consist of a warm up that left me more fucked than any complete PT lesson we did in Harrogate. Then came the kneeling gun drills. If ever an exercise was designed by the Devil it was this one. I believe it got banned eventually, because it turned peoples' knees to mush. Originally it was for Artillery gun crews and would assist in getting them fit for the arduous drills required to fire a fucking great lump of metal at something over the horizon. Some sadist from another unit in Aldershot must have caught sight of it, and recognised its misery inducing potential and hijacked it for 'all arms'. We started off in the kneeling position, left foot planted flat, right foot tucked under right arse cheek. From there, keeping the head and back straight at all times, we would leap gracefully until our feet left the floor, before dropping down into the original start position, but with the feet reversed. Then simply continue, until dead or dying. Very quickly, our thighs would turn to concrete and despite all the instructors' protestations we would find our leaps becoming less and less graceful with each repetition. After a couple of minutes we were reduced to looking like we were trying to tie our shoelaces and have a shit at the same time. Sometimes Frankson didn't think this was hard enough and would occasionally have us doing the same exercise, but on a crashmat.

After the gun drills, they would just run us up and down the gym doing shuttles, for what seemed like an eternity. Every possible permutation of this was employed. Press-ups, sit-ups, star-jumps, burpees, sprinting on the spot, bunny-hops, seal-crawl, leopard-crawl, monkey-crawl. By the end of the lesson, we would have usually stopped sweating, and would be staring, bug-eyed at the instructors waiting for the next task. The necks on our red PT tops would have undergone their usual transformation, to the gaping U that displayed both nipples and belly button. And we'd have all that lovely white cack round the outside of our mouths, that can only usually be found on marathon runners, or people who have just been saved after being buried for a couple of days beneath a collapsed building. At the end of the session, Herbert might give us a word of encouragement, but all I could ever hear was a big thumping sound in my head where my brain was trying to escape. The instructors' favourite trick in the gym was to knock us off to get changed, before calling us back because somebody had been seen to commit a minor transgression, like not running properly out of the gym or failing to hallucinate correctly. We would then be hauled back for another ten minutes of punishment, usually on the ropes. Anyone caught trying to cheat on any of the exercises, for a couple of seconds of respite, would be dangled from the wall bars, and made to hold on with both arms and raise the legs until the body formed an 'L' shape. When we finally escaped their clutches and got through the double doors into the changing rooms, people would fall on to the benches and wonder how the fuck they were going to summon up the energy to take their clothes off to change.

Of course, the meat and drink of the Airborne Forces is Bergan humping, and Herbert and his staff made plenty of time for it. We would generally be expected to run, walk, run between six and ten miles every afternoon, carrying a 35 pound Bergan and a drill weapon of about ten pounds. With water and everything else, it usually totalled around the 50 pound mark. The weapon always had to be carried in the high port with the index finger of the right hand over the trigger guard. The carrying handle, despite its name, was never to be used. It didn't make sense, but I don't remember anybody, during the whole three weeks, being argumentative about anything. The Bergans had to be filled with useful items. Unfortunately, the Bergans were tiny and – by useful items – they didn't mean car-jacks or housebricks, but kit you could use if you got stranded on the training area. Packing the Bergans in the block was always done in the best Laurel and Hardy tradition, with people jumping up and down on them and trying every method to cram another boot in there to make up the weight, before a buckle snapped with a comedy twang. When you finally got it shut, it generally looked like an ill-fitting corset.

The tabs took the same routes as the runs, but were obviously much harder with the additional weight. The pace was slower, but it was always much more difficult to stay together. The squad would always get strung out after a few miles and would resemble a line of refugees attempting a border crossing. Other physical activities would form regular punctuation marks between the gym and the training area. We would be taken round some of the P-Company events, notably the steeplechase and the assault course. The steeplechase wasn't too bad, a two-mile cross-country run, but with lots more mud and a good chance of catching Weil's disease. It was two laps of a route marked by white ringed trees, through the woods to the rear of the football pitches. There were knee-high hurdles all the way around it and huge water jumps. Next time the Olympic steeplechase is televised, watch the runner take the water jump. Imagine that, instead of landing in three inches of clean water, he gets totally submerged in what looks like drinking chocolate but smells like cow shit, before emerging like the creature from the black lagoon, with a child's bike wrapped round his neck. This will give you a bit of a feel for the course. We had 18 minutes to get round twice. At the end of the run, we stood in a row waiting for our time to be shouted out. We were caked in so much mud, that we looked like disinterred corpses, with about as much energy.

Rumour had it, that the assault course had been designed by a committee of psychologists and fitness experts to ensure that runners were stretched to their physical and mental limits. Presumably, they were out-of-work Nazis doing a bit of post-war freelancing. It wasn't the worst assault course I've done but, fuck me, I knew who my mates were whilst I was on it. We had seven minutes 30 seconds to do three laps. There weren't any big gaps between obstacles, so the only way to overtake people was to barge them out of the way or climb over them. The first obstacle was a six-foot wall, and when the shout went to start, everyone hit it at the same time. Best mates were gladly hauling each other off and stepping on heads to get a quicker start. From there, it was a case of clattering round as best I could. Every now and again Frankson or Griffiths would berate me for not overtaking the man in front. Fortunately, by the second and third laps, all the wood on the course was good and wet from everyone's boots. At some stage, the guy in front would go flying when his feet hit something slippery, allowing me to breeze past without having to break his nose. The same thing would happen to me on the next obstacle and a kind of status quo would be maintained and the training hounds would be kept at bay. For safety purposes, we had to wear helmets on both the steeplechase and the assault course. The trouble was that you were more likely to do yourself a serious injury whilst wearing one. With the constant jumping up and down, the front of your helmet would always start going over your eyes, leaving you with a good chance of running into a tree. The pace throughout the three weeks was relentless.

One afternoon, halfway through the second week, Herbert informed us that instead of a tab, we were going to go swimming. We turned up and got changed at the pool, in the Royal Engineers barracks at Cove, thinking that at last we'd been given a bit of a break. The optimism of fools knows no bounds. It was just as terrible as the gym. The shuttles were exactly the same, only water based. Until that session, I didn't think it was actually possible to sweat in a swimming pool. It went on for an hour. Anytime we got out of the water we were not allowed to use the bar to aid our climb. We were supposed to haul ourselves up and out using only our arms, with the right leg swinging on to the poolside at the last second. This was okay at the beginning, but by the midpoint of the beasting, the only way to climb out was by hoping a freak wave would wash us ashore. The last thing they had us doing was a pathetic attempt at the butterfly. My method was to give it a quick spin of the arms before going under, whilst swallowing as much water as I could. Just as I was about to drown, I'd summon enough energy to kick and push my head to the surface. Another lacklustre attempt at the arm movement would follow, and another quick breath before heading for Davy Jones' locker again. It took me about three minutes to complete a length at this rate, and I came second.

An average day consisted of a six- to eight-mile run first thing in the morning, straight into the gym for a beasting, get changed, have a weapons lesson followed by lunch, and then a Bergan march in the afternoon. It was a macabre version of Groundhog Day. Every morning at about 7am, our squad of the living dead would assemble in the ablutions and get washed and shaved whilst staring at ourselves in the mirror, trying to summon the mental rigidity required to get through day. To their credit, the instructors were quite inventive. As soon as you thought you'd been subjected to every possible agony, they would produce another. One afternoon we were doing battle PT on Queen's Parade. We were doing fireman's lifts: 50 metres there, 50 metres back, then swap and get carried by your oppo. I was carrying Willie and dropped him. Frankson went berserk.

"Nugent, Edwards, fucking get here."

We ran over as fast as we could.

"Right, you funny cunts. Think it's a fucking joke do you? See that big tree?" He pointed back over our shoulders. I turned round. I looked for a big tree but couldn't see one. Queen's Avenue is a vast grassed area, usually covered in football pitches. Then I did spot a tree. He couldn't mean that one could he? It was about half a mile away. But it was the only one, so it had to be. I quickly turned back round and said: "Yes, Staff."

"Good, round the tree and back again, GO!"

We ran off at a sprint, but the pace dropped off as soon as it appeared that the tree wasn't getting any closer.

"Where the fuck is it, Eddy?"

"Right by the fence, you can just about see it."

Despite being 200 metres away, Frankson's superhuman hearing picked our voices up and he screamed like Duncan Norvelle's twisted younger brother.

"Got time to fucking talk have you? Don't make me chase you."

We picked up the pace, and eventually ran the mile it took to get back to the squad. Frankson was waiting for us, smiling.

"Too slow, go round again".

Of course, we did exactly as we were told, and to tell the truth, it was the first time that I managed to laugh on the course. Once we were near the tree, we were well out of even Frankson's aural range. I said to Willie, between ragged attempts to breathe: "I've never been this fucked in my life, mate."

He took a deep breath before producing his reply.

"All this," another breath, "and pay an' all."

It was enough to get a bit of a giggle out of me. The three weeks was a tough experience, but – like anything in the Army – we managed to laugh at our own misfortune. It was a volunteer posting, so we had no business complaining. There were no bullshit inspections. As long as your boots and kit were clean and ironed, that was enough. Every evening after tea, we'd head down town as a bunch and chuck all our laundry at the woman in the Posh Wash on Grosvenor Road. Whilst she attempted to remove all the skids, and half the steeplechase from our kit, we'd nip off to the McDonald's. Despite having just eaten our tea, we'd be hungry again and would usually find room for a couple of Big Macs and a skipful of chips. This would leave just enough time to down one or two pints of Guinness before picking up the washing. Straight back up Hospital Hill and back to the block. By the time we'd got all our ironing done, it would be about ten o'clock and time for some lovely sleep. I've never slept so deeply before or since. I would shut my eyes, and what seemed like two seconds later, my alarm would go off at 6.55am. I used to feel completely cheated, until Davey came up with a great idea. It sounds daft now but at the time it made perfect sense. We used to set the alarm for 3.30am. As soon as it went off, we'd sit up and revel in the fact that we had another three hours kip before Herbert could get his hands on us again. When justifying it, Davey said it was like the story of the bloke talking to the old tramp. The tramp tells him that he wears a pair of shoes that are four sizes too small for him. The bloke asks him why and the tramp replies that the only pleasure in his sorry life is taking the fuckers off at night.

When we finally finished each Friday, we had the weekends to ourselves. This was a couple of days to recharge failing batteries for the following Monday and it was conducted in the time-honoured tradition of getting leathered. Herbert recommended that we go for a couple of light runs on Saturday and Sunday to keep the joints oiled but we had another form of lubrication in mind. So what if it meant additional suffering. I think a few of us would have cracked up if there weren't a few beers to look forward to, after spending a week working harder than Esther Rantzen's toothbrush. Great care had to be taken whilst on the pop in Aldershot though. It wasn't a welcoming place for the non-Para trained. All the pubs were divided between the various units in the Brigade. Anybody wandering in off the street, either not from the unit or not friends with someone in the unit was likely to be challenged, and – if lucky – just chucked out. If it was a bit later on in the evening and people were pissed, or if the trespasser had a particularly punchable face, then a bit of a kicking might ensue. It was primitive in the extreme, but as long as you knew the rules, you could avoid trouble. There were only a handful of pubs that weren't off limits to craphats like myself, the most popular being The Queen's and The South Western. The Queen's was the first pub you came to on your way into town and was pretty good. All the units used it. There was usually a disco on each weekend night and lots of loose women could be expected to attend. The South Western was right by the train station and a right dive. It was always three-quarters empty and was in severe need of redecoration. The important factor for us in both pubs was safety. We could get pissed, and were not likely to bump into, or offend anyone serving with the Brigade.

Paras love a fight – an absolute fact! They don't care who they have a fight with. Being outnumbered doesn't bother them. After a night on the ale, the slightest provocation – actual or perceived – can result in a big scrap. The local newspapers used to get so much copy from events in the Aldershot pubs. They commonly referred to it as a Wild West town. Local folklore used to recount the time when riot police turned up to try to prevent Paras from destroying the town during Airborne Forces weekend in '86. It was said that the police formed up at one end of a road, and faced off with an equal number of soldiers about 100 metres away. The police went into their usual routine of shield beating, before advancing menacingly towards the mob. Unfortunately for the police, these tactics were designed to intimidate the wavering rioter. A crowd of drunken paratroopers were a different prospect. They simply saw the shield beating as a bit of a challenge and performed their own advance. Instead of the rigidly disciplined movement of the coppers, this was more like a Highland charge by a pack of wild gorillas. Apparently, the police line broke and retreated immediately, leaving helmets, batons and shields scattered everywhere. In the absence of an easily identifiable enemy, blokes from the Brigade would turn inwards and fight each other. Lads would pick fights with other guys from the same unit just for a laugh. Whilst we were on Pre-Para we all managed to avoid trouble but I witnessed at least four fights a night.

The black dog of depression would begin to descend somewhere around Sunday afternoon, when we realised that our next beasting was less than 24 hours away. The evening would be spent putting white zinc tape all over our blistered feet and the various places on our backs where the Bergans had rubbed skin away. It was good stuff, zinc tape. It covered up all the injuries, but it was an absolute bastard to remove. It would almost form a second skin and taking it off took persistence and an unfeasibly high tolerance to pain. The only thing that hurt more was tincture of benzene or 'tinc-benz'. It was absolutely brilliant for foot blisters, but the pain involved in administering it was beyond compare. The procedure was supposed to be carried out by a medical professional, but you could get hold of the required gear yourself and do a bit of 'DIY'. The procedure is as follows:

Lay the patient down on the floor. Remove the boot and sock from the required foot. Insert the toe end of the boot into the patient's mouth and ask him to clamp his teeth on to it. Puncture the blister with a sterile hypodermic needle and draw out any liquid from the area of the blister. Remove the needle and eject the fluid. Suck up a couple of mills of tinc-benz from the bottle. Instruct four large blokes to get hold of one of the patient's limbs each and ask that they pin the fucker down and hold on for dear life. Inject the tinc-benz into the blister cavity. Retreat quickly whilst the four men try to contain the boot-chewing patient who has now turned into a bucking bronco.

It worked like a dream though. You would never get another blister on that patch of skin again, so the pain was worth it.

As the three weeks drew to a close, it was apparent that most of us were going to pass this phase. The two Rodneys and Joey had no problems and were at the front for everything. Then there was a group of seven, including me that struggled like fuck for the duration of the course, but had managed to stay with it enough to get the nod. Three lads failed. Two of the blokes who were on their second attempt, gave up halfway through the second week and were quickly posted back to their units. Then of course there was Shuggy. Right from the start he was lagging behind. He was last on everything. Every time we went on a tab, he was getting dragged along by his Bergan straps after a mile or two. I think he earned the grudging admiration of the training staff by flatly refusing to jack it in, despite it being obvious that he was never going to be fit enough to attend P-Company. He must have really hated Germany. He did manage to introduce a new word into the local dictionary though. We were doing a BFT round Queen's Parade. Shuggy went off like a shot and was matching Joey Donaldson pace for pace. For about 300 metres. His speed deserted him as soon as his lungs started burning, and the rest of us, pounding out the distance at a more regular pace, soon closed up with him. As I passed him he started to vomit. I say vomit, but nothing was actually coming out. He was just making horrible retching noises with every couple of steps. In a timed event like the BFT, you don't have the luxury of pulling over for a spew, so Shuggy attempted to keep running whilst his digestive tract went into spasm. Each time he made a renewed effort to bring up his entire diaphragm, his right knee slammed up, to his chest, involuntarily. He would stumble on for a few paces before repeating the movement. He looked like the victim of someone with a Voodoo doll and an itchy pin finger. He did this for a couple of hundred metres before his constitution settled down. Ever after, if someone was afflicted with a similar complaint, he was said to be 'shuggying' (verb 'to shuggy'). I'm sure it made him quite proud, and served as some consolation when Herbert gave him the bad news and despatched him back to the loving embrace of the 'Iron Triangle'.

On the last Friday of the course we were treated quite well, and after a farewell punishment session in the gym, we were addressed by Herbert.

"Ok, lads. Well done over the last three weeks." It was the first and only time he gave us any indication that we'd pleased him. He quickly qualified his praise.

"You've not been the worst, but you've certainly not been the best. Having said that, ten is a very good number to be sending down the road to Depot Para. You've all done enough to prove you can pass P-Company, but you'll have to graft. Remember it's only three more weeks and you're finished. Don't make the mistake of failing; you'll only have to do this all over again."

The thought horrified us all, and the squad visibly shuddered.

"Have a good weekend, and standby for Monday."

He knocked us off and we had from Friday lunchtime to Monday morning to ourselves. We had a good piss up on the Friday night. Everything from nine o'clock onwards was a blur of beer and pizza. We spent the rest of the weekend getting our gear together, and by Sunday night we were all ready to go. Sitting around on our beds at 10pm, we discussed what our fate would be.

"Do you reckon it'll be much harder than Pre-Para?" said Scouse Marriott.

"That isn't possible," replied Davey.

Joey chipped in: "Our kid did it about five years ago; he said it wasn't too bad."

"Yeah, but I bet he was a fucking racing snake like you? What about the rest of us slugs?" Willie had a low, but realistic, opinion of his abilities.

Scouse said: "Like Herbert said, I'll be fucked if I'm doing this again. Just keep ticking off the days, lads."

In the morning, we had to be there for 7.00am. We got all our kit together and wandered down the road. The Parachute Regiment depot was straight across the road from Montgomery Lines so it was a short walk. Two guys from 1 Para were manning the vehicle checkpoint at the front gate, and had a good snigger as we approached them.

"P-Company is it, lads?"

"Yeah."

"Ha ha ha, fucking scaly craphats; you'll be back by tomorrow night."

"Yeah, with a lovely big payslip," retorted Scouse.

"Wankers," said the 1 Para lad who'd mouthed off. Before he could take it any further a car started coming up the road and they had to get back to work. One of the bugbears that other units in the Brigade had about the Signals was that we got paid loads more than them. It was a bit of a misconception. Some of the techs were on a really good wedge compared to your average infanteer, but the rest of the trades didn't clear too much more money than their opposite number in an Infantry regiment. Still, it was always a good way to wind someone up quickly, and Scouse had used it to good effect. We crossed Alison's Road, past the Second World War Dakota aeroplane that stood guard outside the barracks, and walked into 'Depot'.

P-Company was fundamentally similar to Pre-Para, in that it involved getting run into the ground and shouted at a lot, but it differed in some ways. There were a lot more people involved. There were 90 candidates from all over the Army. RCT, Ordnance Corps, RE, Signals, Artillery, REME. There were even two guys from the Pay Corps. I could just see them parachuting into some hot spot in the middle of nowhere, with a Bergan full of money for the lads. It was nice to know that the Army were providing the facility to get yourself into debt, no matter how remote the location. All the instructors were senior NCOs from the Parachute Regiment and were uniformly mean and moody. I can't remember any of their names. As with Sutton Coldfield, with the passage of time they've all sort of morphed into a single character in my mind's eye. Six feet tall, light heavyweight boxer's build, Freddie Mercury moustache, black hair cut in the same style as an Action Man. Their dispositions were all frighteningly similar. Whenever approached by a student, they would answer his question politely. Underneath, and visible to all watching, they would be barely concealing the desire to beast them for having the audacity to engage them in conversation. They had all found their perfect niche in life. Getting paid for behaviour that could and would get you sectioned in another industry. Aside from that, as I said, Pre-Para and P-Company were alike. All the days consisted of runs, tabs and gym sessions. The pace was the same, but you couldn't skive in the gym. There was a big balcony at the back, where extra training staff would assemble. They would be assigned a few of us to watch, and as soon as the lesson began they would be screaming at anyone seen not to be trying. On the first morning, there were 23 of us hanging from the wall bars, wailing like prisoners in a medieval dungeon.

The staff had room inspections in the mornings, but they were only looking for big stuff, turds in lockers for instance. There were no white gloves and they didn't give you a really hard time. This was all reserved for the tabs, which got longer and faster each day. On the Monday of the second week, we were taken in coaches, to the South Downs. It came as no surprise that we weren't going to take in the scenery for a while and go home. That day's work was a 15-mile speed march. I never got to the end – not on foot anyway. The halfway point was called Chalk Hill. The squad was mostly still together by this stage, but one of the REME lads in front of me was getting loads of jip from one of the instructors.

"Number 44, get hold of that fucking weapon properly." We all had numbers, painted with pump whitener, on the map pockets of our lightweights. It saved the P-Company staff having to remember anyone's name. Mine was 38. The REME bloke was obviously feeling the pace and had started to exhibit an unusual characteristic that I'd seen on a few guys, as they started to get more and more exhausted on a tab. His neck and head seemed to be getting further and further from his Bergan. Whether it was from the weight of the Bergan pulling itself off his shoulders a bit, or whether it was a subconscious attempt to distance himself from the thing which was causing him such intense misery, I don't know, but he'd started to resemble a tortoise on its hindlegs, stretching for a lettuce leaf that someone was holding, just out of its reach. Unfortunately for the lad, he was starting to drop down to a tortoise's pace as well. The instructor further berated him. Coming right up to his earhole, he shouted: "You, you annoying fucker, are making the people behind work harder. Catch up with the man in front, or I'll fucking launch you." He was now three or four yards back on the man to his front, when he should have been right up his arse – nose touching Bergan. The instructor planted a hand into the back of REME's Bergan and shoved him along until he caught up. It was fruitless; within a couple of seconds of catching up, the lad was lagging again. After four or five more cycles of getting pushed, then dropping back again, you could tell that he was close to jacking it in. From my point of view, this was all quite beneficial. The little tableau to my front was taking my mind off my own exhaustion.

The instructor spotted and assessed the lad's mental state pretty quickly, and said, more quietly this time: "Fucking quitter are you?" I was instantly transported back to the Careers Office. I was glad I wasn't having to do this tab in a suit.

"No, Staff."

"Get in the fucking jack wagon, you're slowing everyone down."

"NO, Staff."

"It's not a fucking request 44. Do as you're told. Fall out, Bergan off, and wait for the wagon." The instructor was getting more and more irate. But the REME lad knew the consequences of jacking and didn't want any of it. On P-Company they had a black mark system. It probably changes from time to time, but we were told that if you got three black marks you were RTUd. Failing to complete an exercise, or coming in outside the time required for a particular event, got you a mark. I'd already got up to two; one for not finishing with the squad on the first tab and the second for dregging on the Mulberry Bush run, the previous Friday.

"Fuck off, I'm alright," he screamed back, which tipped the instructor over the edge. He grabbed the lad by the back of the Bergan and spun him round, presumably hoping to extricate him from the squad, and fill him in. Number 44 realised he'd given the wrong answer and started trying to escape a hiding by losing himself in the squad. This might have worked if we all had 44 written on our trousers, and shared his surname, which was emblazoned across the front of his chest. The rest of us were still tabbing along, staring open mouthed at the Buster Keaton scene to our front. Number 44 got about a yard away from the instructor before he was grabbed again. The instructor was screaming unintelligible expletives at Olympic pace now, but 44 was still struggling. All of a sudden they both went over on their arses and we all piled into them. It was like Becher's Brook. I found myself at the bottom of about six bodies.

By the time we got up and got moving again, I was way behind the squad. They seemed to be moving under some sort of different speed mechanism to me as I crawled up behind, like a slug in a Bergan. By the time I got to the rest point at the top, the rest of the squad was getting ready to move again and the medics looked bored. One gave me a lukewarm brew as one of the instructors approached with absolutely no fanfare to inform me that my number was up. There was a similar lack of ceremony back at the depot. They'd seen thousands of abject failures and processed me with appropriate apathy.

So that was P-Company finished for me. Four weeks for nothing. I was out of Depot Para by the end of the day. Scouse and Willie helped me carry my gear back to Montgomery Lines. They didn't say much, just dropped the gear by my bed and before they left, gave the universal shrugged shoulder movement that means 'Tough shit, mate,' before heading off down town to do their washing.

Truthfully, it was a blessing in disguise. I don't think I had the mental rigidity required to get through P-Company. It wasn't just a fitness course, otherwise the whole Brigade would have been manned by cross-country runners. The course had been designed to test people's ability to keep going whilst under lots of additional pressures and I found myself lacking in this department.

The next morning I had to report to Staff Sergeant Herbert at 8.15am. He was less than sympathetic.

"Go on then, let's hear it," he called across his desk sarcastically.

I explained what had happened in brief, whilst Herbert rolled his eyes, tutted and shook his head, and fixed me with a 'heard it all be-fucking-fore' stare. He held his hand up to silence me before growling: "There are two types of soldier in this unit, Nugent – Airborne and non-Airborne. If you're Airborne, that's great. If you're not, then nobody wants to hear your excuses."

"Right, Staff."

"It's just tough shit. You'll get sent down again, if and when we let you. We've just had word from Manning and Records that you've been posted in, so pass or fail, you're with us for the next four years."

This was news to me. I assumed I'd be posted out for failing. It turned out that units were short of blokes of my trade, and Para-trained or not, I could operate a radio and do Morse code.

"You'll be in Bravo Troop, otherwise known as Bongo Battery. Go over there now and stick your feet in Staff Sergeant Jeans' in-tray." He dismissed me with a wave of his hand and he went back to inventing new forms of torture.

So that was me, posted in. Aldershot was going to be my home for the foreseeable. After what Kenny had told me, I wasn't too sure that it was what I wanted. I needn't have worried. Despite the fact that I never did pass P-Company and get my wings, even after another attempt, I had a great four years. I got promoted – just; got fit; and learnt that there was plenty of fun to be had, once you'd escaped training and got into a working unit. As soon as I got over to Bongo Battery, Staff Sergeant Jeans welcomed me with the words: "Fucking great, another craphat. I'll stick you on one of the RATT dets. Go down and see Tin Can Ally and ask him where RATT Delta is."

"Yes, Staff." I quickly excused myself and walked down the stairs. I opened the door into the Bravo Troop locker stores and was confronted with a handful of blokes jumping into action. It was quite apparent that they'd been sat around skiving until they heard me on the stairs. Not knowing that there was a new boy posted in, they must have assumed I was Staff Sergeant Jeans and they were all trying to look busy. One guy had grabbed a broom and was feverishly sweeping a perfectly clean floor. Another was more inventive. He'd obviously been kipping on a rolled up cam net which had served as a very comfortable bean bag, but as soon as I walked in, he started jumping up and down on it, as if trying to cram it into a smaller space and make the place look more tidy. The second they caught sight of my 18-year-old sprog features, they stopped the charade and fell back into their previous positions. I piped up.

"Is Tin Can Ally around?"

The cam-net squasher shook his head in remonstration.

"Fuckin' 'ell, mate. Don't call him that if you want to see another NAAFI break. It's Corporal Allinson to you."

"Sorry, Staff Sergeant Jeans told me to ask for Tin Can Ally."

"Yeah, well he can get away with it, you can't. He's out the back sorting out one of the Rovers. 18 GB 64 I think."

I thanked him and left him to his important task. I walked through the locker stores and through a set of blue double doors, which led out to a Land Rover bay. Looking to the left and right, I could see a row of about 15 of the three-quarter-tonne, DPM painted vehicles. All of them had trailers attached and looked like they were ready to be driven out of the compound. Dotted sporadically around the Rovers, were soldiers in green coveralls performing various tasks. Some were painting, some were checking tyre pressures and others just seemed to be hanging about, like the guys in the stores, ready at a moment's notice to burst into action, whenever a figure of authority appeared. The Rover marked 18 GB 64 was directly to my front, and a large, coverall-clothed arse was sticking out of it. I tapped on the side panel of the vehicle and said: "Corporal Allinson?"

The guy inside jumped, and there was a fizzing noise, before he emerged rubbing the back of his head with a filthy right hand.

"For fuck's sake, mate. Never bang on a wagon when someone's doing batteries." He climbed down and shook my hand.

"Pete Allinson."

"Eddy Nugent, sorry about that. Staff Sergeant Jeans told me to come down and see you, to get put on RATT Delta."

"This is Delta." He crooked his thumb back over his shoulder to the vehicle he'd just been working on.

"I'm the Det Commander, so it looks like you're me new sprog."

He smiled. Looking closely at his face, it seemed like he'd been in the wars. His nose was squashed flat and his whole head looked slightly out of shape. I found out later from one of the other blokes, what had happened to Pete to earn him his quite snazzy nickname. He'd been working on a trailer, one lunchtime, trying to get a chain fitted near the towing eye to hold the split pin. Once the trailer was connected to the towing hook on the Land Rover, the split pin would hold it in place. The trailer was disconnected from the Land Rover, and was being kept upright by a water jerry can, whilst Pete lay underneath it. Whilst moving around, Pete had accidentally kicked the jerrycan causing the front end of the trailer, to come swinging down, pinning him underneath. The towing eye had hit him right in the face and was now lying on top of him with just his nose and mouth protruding from the centre circle. There was no one around because it was lunchtime, so Pete was reduced to calling for help from the confines of the eye. Due to his face being so compressed, his screams were reduced to a quiet "Hoooouuullp."

After 15 minutes, a troop staffie coming back in off a lunchtime run had stopped by the compound to warm down, and heard someone calling. He later said that it had sounded like a Dutch child. When they got the trailer off him, Pete was fairly bashed up, and had to have extensive chunks of steelwork put into his face, to keep it all together. He never got called the nickname to his face, mainly because he was on the Army boxing team and was quite capable of doing trailer-style damage to the face of anyone brave enough to call him Tin Can Ally. He was a spot-on bloke, and looked after me on the det until he got posted out a couple of years later.

Life in the troop was fairly easy going. A standard day consisted of turning up for parade in normal working dress, which consisted of boots, lightweights, shirt and jumper in the winter and boots, lightweight and shirt in the summer. The decision to change from winter to summer dress and vice versa was always taken without any regard to the weather. It would just appear on orders that the following Monday, May the first, summer dress would come into effect, regardless of the fact that a thunderstorm was expected that day. Blokes would be walking round in the pouring rain, with a flimsy KF shirt on, and nipples like a fighter pilot's thumbs, whilst others would be hiding under cam-nets in the troop stores, trying to conserve their body heat. At the end of the summer, the reverse decision would be made, and everyone would don jumpers in a heatwave. Any work carried out at all, would result in dinner-plate sized sweat patches emerging underneath your arms, due to the amazing, heat retaining qualities of the jersey, heavy wool.

The first parade of the day was usually at 0815 hours. The troop would form up, and there might be a cursory inspection, just to make sure that nobody was in a really shit state. It was a bit of a lottery really. You could take the chance of not pressing your kit or polishing your boots, gambling that there might not be an inspection. If the call went out, from Staff Sergeant Jeans, "In open order, right dress," you'd be in the shit. You could expect a handful of extra duties or a shitty job for the day. Occasionally you'd do your kit and still get extras. Just before parade, we did area cleaning – scooping up the pizza boxes and beer cans from the night before. If the big wheelie bins were a bit full, we'd have to climb in to stamp some of the rubbish down. This would leave your boots and the bottom of your lightweights, covered in aromatic bin juice, and all primed to get a rifting for not being smartly turned out. After the parade you'd be fallen out to do first works parade on the vehicles. This is what I'd seen them all doing on the day I first spoke to Pete Allinson. It was a bit of a joke really. You were supposed to do various checks on the wagons – lights, oil, brakes, indicators etc. It was just a job creation scheme for the serially inactive. There isn't a lot that can go wrong on a Land Rover that has been stationary for 24 hours, but – by fuck – we'd make certain. The most common fault was the theft of your indicator lenses. People were always accidentally breaking them. Solution: unscrew the fucked one; toss casually over the shoulder; approach the next wagon in the row; look round furtively; unscrew your new lens; look round furtively; and put it on your wagon.

The victim would usually find out the next morning and shout: "Who's nicked me fuckin' rubies." He would be met with blank stares all round. As soon as there was nobody looking, the victim would begin the cycle again. At about nine o'clock, a rickety, old, burgundy Salvation Army wagon would pull up at the back and the first brew of the day would be purchased. The wagon was known as the 'Sally Bash' and was staffed by the oldest man in the world. He got smaller every week. When I first got there he could only just see over the counter. After six months he had to stand on a box to serve me. His fingers were covered in warts, and when he stirred your tea, if you were really lucky, one of his spoon holding fingers might enjoy a quick dunk. It was best not to look really. He also sold an assortment of rolls. Well, more of a straight choice than an assortment, cheese or ham. I remember someone asking him once if they could have cheese 'and' ham. He looked like someone had walked across his very small grave.

Consumption of the Sally Bash brew would be spun out until about 0940, leaving you only 20 minutes to push until NAAFI break. Sometimes Pete would use this time to give me some instruction in the ways of the HF det. In Harrogate the only vehicle-mounted HF radio they'd taught us was the 321. This was a combination of TURF, SURF and radio. It took up a little corner on the breadboard in the back of the wagon and was as quiet as a mouse. The 322 was a much weightier beast. It was basically a souped-up 321, with a 250W amplifier and associated equipment. It took up the entire breadboard and generated more noise than a Chinook landing. The first lesson Pete gave me was on how to assemble it all. It looked ridiculously complicated, but Pete simplified it immediately.

"Just stack 'em all up like this." He positioned all the separate pieces of equipment in their relevant places on the breadboard.

"Bolt 'em together." Each piece of kit had a bracket on its base, to secure it to the item beneath.

"Then join 'em all up." He pointed down to a huge black ball of assorted leads. I stared, goggle-eyed from the leads to the radios, and couldn't begin to work out how they went together. Pete started laughing.

"Don't look so fucking stupid; it's a piece of piss. If it'll go on, it's the right lead. Try it."

Using his method, I selected a lead and had a look at the end. I then matched it up with a similar sized cavity on one of the radios or amps, and connected it. Incredibly it worked, and within ten minutes I'd successfully set up my first 322 det. I don't suppose it mattered that I didn't have a clue what I'd just done, or what each lead was for. Pete whacked the power on and it all made the right noises, so we were happy. When I stepped back out of the wagon and looked at the 322 in all its glory, it resembled the controls on Flash Gordon's spaceship. It looked so dated, with its big, clunky black dials and brass, right-angled connectors. Whirring noises would sporadically emerge from the radio, barely piercing the overpowering, jet engine noises of the fans on the amp.

It was state-of-the-art stuff, and no mistake. After one of Pete's impromptu radio lessons, it was time for NAAFI break. There'd be a bit of a sprint on, as the NAAFI didn't stock too many of the nice pies. The contract had been won by Ginsters. If you got to the shop early, you could enjoy a beef and onion slice or a steak and kidney pie. If you got held back slightly, your legacy was the dreaded ploughman's pasty. They were minging, and obviously in plentiful supply. Rather than sit in the NAAFI bar, quite a lot of people used to just go and eat their snack in the stores. If you did this though, you had to be on the lookout for sneak thieves. It only happened to me once.

I'd just got back in the stores, with my Ginsters and a bottle of Lucozade. I left it down so I could pop to the toilet. I couldn't have been gone for any more than 30 seconds. When I got back, I realised that I was another food-theft statistic. The Lucozade bottle was empty, with the lid screwed back on. The pie was gone. The silver tray had been placed back in the foil, with a Post-it replacing the pie. I picked up the wrapper and read the note.

"Mmmm, that was nice, cheers loser."

I had to take my hat off to the speed and class of the crime.

By the time NAAFI break was over, it was half past ten, leaving us with an hour and a half to push until lunchtime. Unless there was something specific to fix, or pretend to fix, somebody would think of a stupid job for us to do.

The most memorable was the changing of the cam-nets. Cam-nets always looked the same. A large expanse of green netting, covered randomly, in brown and green cam squares, made of nylon. They would be placed over the Land Rovers when in an exercise location, and after being propped up by wooden poles, would effectively break up the shape of the vehicle. A new OC Squadron had just taken over. He decided that squares were not naturally occurring shapes in the wild and that we should change them for triangles. I think the MOD had just spent £20,000 teaching him this on a course, and he was keen to apply his new knowledge practically. Nobody could be bothered to utter the obvious 'but triangles are equally uncommon' phrase. When you realise that a normal sized cam-net was about the size of the penalty area on a football pitch, it was no small task. We had to cut off every cam square, cut them in half, then re-attach them in a random pattern. It took us about a week. All the cam-nets were laid out across the square. Everyone chuntered for the entire duration of the work. The combined, under-the-breath muttering of over 100 men had chucked up seismographic anomalies for local geologists. When we'd done all the work, the cam-nets were inspected with great ceremony. Every one passed, apart from Dave "Crazy Legs" Crane. He was the Corps Orienteering Champion, but I've never met anyone thicker. He'd done exactly as he was supposed to do, but when he sewed his triangles back on, he thought he'd be clever and pair them up to make squares. The RSM hollered at him for ten minutes, whilst the rest of us rolled our nets up, ready to receive our next pointless tasking.

Dave's stupidity was legendary. He once took one boot to the stores to exchange. When asked where its partner was, he replied that there was nothing wrong with that one. A year after the great cam-net switch, it was decided, by another new OC Squadron, that triangles were not naturally occurring shapes in the wild and that we should revert to the squares. Maybe Dave was just ahead of his time. The only other skill I can remember him possessing was the ability to burp and say 'Archbishop of Canterbury' at the same time. The average bloke could only manage 'bollocks' or 'Bulawayo' which were far shorter and lent themselves to 'belchspeak', so Dave's skills in this department were much admired. It wasn't something he could put on a CV, but it made people laugh, which was just as important, unless you were looking for a job!

Lunch was from 12 until one. Some of the keener lads would manage to squeeze a run in instead of eating. The rest would go and have something to eat in the cookhouse, followed by a quick watch of Neighbours before getting back down on parade by five to one. That particularly timing always meant that you missed the last couple of minutes of the low quality, Aussie soap. It never seemed to make any difference when trying to keep up with the plots. The received wisdom that British squaddies are hard-headed, dangerous individuals with a penchant for casual violence, could have been completely undone by a bit of fly-on-the-wall in Bongo Battery, at ten past one. Large men would be engaged in earnest conversation, debating whether Scott was really right for Charlene or whether Madge really just needed to clear her throat to stop sounding like Marlon Brando. The afternoons were just a longer version of the morning routine. We had to find something to do from one until half past four. The Sally Bash would show up around three, to serve another round of wart poisoned brews. Now and again someone would be picked to run an errand, which was effectively an afternoon off. I was sent one day, to the Marconi factory in Southampton to return some equipment that the unit had been trialling. Joey Donaldson came with me. He'd passed P-Company by then and was now resplendent in his wings and leather banded beret. We turned up at Marconi, parked the Land Rover at the front of the building and walked in. We were both in uniform, and when the receptionist looked up, she was a bit startled. Thinking back, she probably looked like this all the time. There was more than a passing resemblance to Olive from *On the Buses*.

"Can I help you?" she squeaked.

"We're here to drop some kit off," I looked down at the delivery note, "to Ken Sharples."

"I'll see if he's in." She picked up the receiver of her desk phone, punched in four numbers and waited for a response.

"Oh, hello, Ken. It's Diane on the front desk. I have two men here with some equipment for you. Pardon? Hang on, I'll ask. Are you from the Army?"

We looked at each other quizzically, before Joey responded: "Yeah, just tell him we're from 5th Airborne."

She nodded and returned to the call.

"One of the gentlemen is called Cliff D'Airborn."

We laughed all the way back to Aldershot. I always thought that if I ever took up acting, I'd use it as my stage name.

At four-thirty each day, except for the obligatory Wednesday sports afternoon, we'd form up as a troop and be knocked off for the day. Everyone would go to the cookhouse for tea and then your evening would be your own. This riveting itinerary would go on for week after week. The big exception to this routine was during the run up to an exercise. Because of the nature of the unit, people took going on exercise quite seriously, so they'd have you preparing for one week prior to deployment. Lots of inspections, making sure everybody's archaic radios were good enough for one more roll of the dice, and that all the gear required had been packed. The wagon kit list for a two week exercise was enormous. By the time you'd crammed it all into the Land Rover and trailer, there was just enough room for a couple of humans to shoehorn their way in. We used to look like the Beverly Hillbillies when we were driving out of camp.

Most of the exercises were done on Salisbury Plain, with occasional diversions to Otterburn or Catterick (Hatterick as it was known to the Para-trained lads). Prior to leaving, we were forced at gunpoint to watch a video, which detailed the environmental dos and don'ts on Salisbury Plain Training Area (SPTA). Officers would be stood at the door of the lecture theatre with bayonets fixed to prevent us leaving. It was mind-numbing in the extreme, and consisted of a Robin Cook look-alike pointing at signs of various colours and shapes, then explaining their meanings in earnest tones. His intentions were good, but had the opposite effect to the one desired. Telling belligerent squaddies when and where they can't shit is asking for trouble. After 45 minutes listening to Cooky preaching, you could see the resolve materialising on peoples' faces, and know that the first thing they were going to do when they got into the field was to curl one down on a rare flower.

We'd usually get to our exercise location in the middle of the night. The convoy of Land Rovers were supposed to slip quietly into position. Unfortunately, the locations were always in the middle of the woods somewhere, so there would be lots of cursing, as bumpers hit trees, whilst guides frantically waved torches to try to direct the vehicles. As soon as we got into our location, we would set the detachments up. Our portion of the headquarters consisted of four vehicles, backed on to a 12 by 12 tent. The tent had two canvas socks at each end, which were fixed over the rear of the Land Rovers to provide a lightproof seal. Tables and seats would be set up in the floor space of the tent, to provide an area where we would process and distribute the messages we received over the teleprinters. Our HQ was pretty far back from the action. The only formation further back from the front line was the Brigade

Maintenance Area or BMA. The abbreviation was more commonly translated as Bloody Miles Away in reference to its proximity to the trenches. A lot of the Para-trained lads would have an altogether different experience. They would jump in from a C130 Hercules, with a Bergan strapped to their legs. For the radio lads, a Bergan full of batteries and equipment would end up weighing about the same as a Fiat Uno. Once they'd landed, and if they hadn't shattered all the bones in their legs, they would chuck the Bergans on and tab to a predesignated spot, usually six or seven miles away, then set up comms when they got there. It was what all the Pre-Para and P-Company training was about.

Back in Delta Group Headquarters, as soon as we had set all our masts and radios up, we dropped into a standard shift system of four hours on, four hours off. If you weren't on shift you were supposed to eat or sleep. Both activities were carried out in your shell scrape, which had to be dug as soon as comms had been established. Once the set up had been completed, things were quite dull. A regular flow of practice traffic would be transmitted, to demonstrate the availability of the circuits to the command structure. One of the only highlights during the 24-hour cycle would be waking the next guy up for shift. You were supposed to give him a shake ten minutes before you came off, to give him time to come round, and make his way back to the tent from his scratcher. Invariably, whoever you were waking up would be grumpy as fuck and really unhappy at the prospect of leaving his beautifully warm sleeping bag to go and sit shivering in the back of a Land Rover with a headset on, having loud Morse blasted into his tortured ears. When you woke him up with a bit of a prod from your boot, the response would come, from deep inside the bag.

"Right, I'll be there in a minute."

You'd go back to the tent, and wait for five minutes. When there was no sign of your replacement you'd have to go back out to him and get a bit more vocal.

There'd be loads of this toing and froing, so by the time you handed over to him 15 minutes of your precious sleep time would have been eaten up. Of course, when he came to wake you up four hours later, the pantomime would be repeated.

To combat this, the waking of the next man had to be rapid and violent. You'd go up to the bag and, as before, give it a prod with the toe.

"Right, I'll be there in a minute," came the familiar reply. This time, instead of leaving him, you assaulted him. You'd undo the front of his sleeping bag and shine a Maglite in his eyes. When he tried to crawl away from the light, like a vampire, you'd give him a couple of slaps across the face, hissing: "Come on, get up you lazy fucker."

Followed up with a bit more pushing, shoving and swearing, you'd soon have him angry enough to start climbing out of his bag, with murder in his eyes. At that point you could run off, back to the tent, laughing. Hopefully, by the time he got there, he'd calmed down enough to not beat you up. Once the handover was complete, you could climb into your bag, safe in the knowledge that in four hours, somebody was going to accost you in a similar fashion.

One of the other great pleasures on exercise was going for a shit. The compo rations used to bung you up nicely, but after three or four days, something the size of a wombat shell would be pressing its tip against the inside of your boxer shorts and it was time to go for a shovel recce. I favoured the chocolate éclair approach. I'd find my spot in the woods and dig three sides of a small square. I'd lift the patch of turf like a small trapdoor and make my deposit. When I was finished, I'd gently close the trapdoor before stamping it into place vigorously. Occasionally, diet permitting, this would result in some of the faeces escaping through the sides of the square, emulating the reaction to someone biting into the popular pastry. Naughty, but nice. I remember one of the lads being a bit coy about alfresco defecation. He used to detest going on exercise and would try any method to avoid having to take a shit until he got back to camp. If there was a resup run anywhere, he'd try to get on it, so that he could use the toilet at whichever camp they went to. On one exercise, he was stranded for a week and a half, between functioning toilets. He was in the next shell scrape to me and one morning, I peeped out of my sleeping bag to find him pushing out knees to the chest exercises.

"What the fuck are you doing?"

He stopped for a moment and looked at me, panting.

"I'm bursting for a shit, and this makes the turd pangs go away."

I zipped the bag back up and left him to it. Apparently it worked though. Every time he got the urge, he'd do ten knees to the chest, and the need to crap would pass. When he eventually found a toilet, he described the log that he produced as being like a 'clay model of a caveman's club'.

Every morning we'd have the usual stand-to at first light. If you were on shift you didn't have to bother, but if you were sleeping you had to get up. The Squadron were keen on this sort of stuff. No staying in your sleeping bags. They wanted you lying down, out of your bag, and in a good firing position. The RSM and the OC Squadron would tour the shell scrapes, and anyone caught sleeping, or not particularly alert, would get a rollicking. They always took the same route though, so you could spot when they were getting close. I used to lie on my back, facing into the compound with my helmet on back to front and my rifle pointing back across my shoulder. This gave the impression, in the limited light of breaking dawn, of a perfectly good defensive position. It also allowed me to stay warm in my bag, until the RSM was about three shell scrapes away. I'd then adopt a more conventional pose, and the RSM would pass by without a word.

Right from the start of an exercise, you would always be waiting for 'endex' to be called. It wouldn't matter how far away it was. Speculation would always circulate that for some unspecified reason, the exercise was going to finish early. It never did. The exercise would always finish as planned, usually on the Friday morning. There would be a quick teardown, followed by a mad rush back to camp. The role of the unit dictated that nobody would knock off until the wagons were all ready to redeploy. This meant that you only had Friday to turn the whole detachment round. All the blokes would work like Trojans to try to get finished before four o'clock. Some wanted to get home, to various parts of the country, and had mental images of traffic jams getting longer and longer. The rest of us just wanted to get a shower and get out on the beer. If a payday had occurred whilst you were out in the field, the desire to get it spent served to enhance the work frenzy. Clean all the kit, washdown and POL the wagon, get all broken kit into the techs, re-pack the trailer and sort out the cam-net. The OC would come round once all the work was complete, and inspect all the dets. If they were to his liking, he'd give an eagerly anticipated nod, and we were free to go.

During one of the turnarounds, an accident occurred, that helped me understand what Pete had been on about when he told me never to bang on a wagon when someone was doing their batteries. One of the turnaround jobs was to get the radio batteries disconnected and check the electrolyte levels. The four 12v radio batteries, each about the size of a portable telly, were connected in series and parallel and sat underneath the breadboard, with a gap of about three inches between them. The proper way to remove them was to take all the radio equipment off the breadboard and undo the four bolts that held the breadboard in place.

You could then move it out of the way and gain free access to the batteries from above. Of course, this was far too sensible for most of us. To save ourselves having to mess about with the radios, we would prefer to take our chances with the tiny gap between the bottom of the breadboard and the lugs of the batteries. It could be done, but it was akin to safe-cracking. To remove the connecting leads from the lugs, took watchmaker-like precision. You would have to lie on the floor of the wagon and crawl forward until you could get your arms in over the top of the batteries. Your head was crooked sideways to get a good look at what you were doing. Using an adjustable spanner, you would then start loosening the lug bolts. The restricted space available meant that you could only turn the adjustable a couple of centimetres before removing it and putting it back on the bolt. To add to the excitement, parts of the breadboard were made of metal. If the adjustable touched them, an excellent electrical connection was made, resulting in lots of blue sparks and burnt facial hair. It was customary when walking past a wagon, where this nerve-wracking operation was taking place, to give one of the side panels, a good whack with the flat of the palm. It was what was known in the trade as a cunt's trick. The person inside, already on tenterhooks, and with a single bead of stress induced sweat about to drip off the end of his nose, would jump, causing him to twat his head on the underside of the breadboard and arc the batteries. This is what happened to Tommy Curry. Unfortunately for him, when the battery arced, it blew up. I was in the next wagon along. The contained percussion was similar to the sound of a depth charge exploding underwater. There was a gap of about half a second before Tommy came piling out of the back of his wagon, clawing at his face, screaming.

"My eyes, my eyes." Some of the acid from one of the batteries must have got in there. He went off, blindly running round the wagon compound. He was a bastard to catch. By the time he ran into the wing mirror, of one of the other Land Rovers, there were six of us chasing after him. A couple of the lads pinned him down, to stop him doing himself any further damage. Brummy Jenkinson ran to the med-centre to get one of the butchers. Tommy was writhing and gnashing like Linda Blair in The Exorcist.

Pete Allinson shouted: "Get some water to rinse the acid away." We all ran to our wagons and got water bottles out of our webbing. People started emptying the contents of the bottles into his eyes. It started to have some affect and he began to calm down, until it was my turn. I took the lid off my bottle, and proceeded to empty a pint of super strength Screech into his red-raw peepers. He started to scream like a Japanese soldier on a suicide charge. The Screech must have had a higher PH value than the battery acid, and they were combining to try and make his face melt like a Nazi who'd just opened the Ark of the Covenant.

Fortunately for Tommy, and the rest of us, a medic quickly turned up with loads of eyewash and distilled water, and sorted him out. They said later that the acid hadn't been too bad, but the Screech could have permanently blinded him.

Unfortunately for Tommy, as far as the Squadron was concerned, the accident was his fault, and they charged him the £85 to replace the busted battery. When he went in on Orders to sign the charge sheet, he still had patches over both eyes and had to have his hand directed to the document by the RSM. He could have been signing anything.

Everybody learnt a valuable lesson from the experience and always accessed their batteries in a safe way from that moment onwards. Did they fuck. At the end of the next exercise, there were more blue sparks and acrid smoke issuing from the back of the wagons than ever before. It was like the welders' section of a school of construction.

As soon as the OC had given the Caesarean thumbs-up, everybody bomb-burst from the square as quickly as possible. There was a good reason for this. You were guaranteed that one of the senior NCOs or officers would remember a job that needed doing. The slowest Tom would get gripped and find himself working for another hour or two. The rest of us would get scrubbed up and head down town to blow our wages.

Despite the fact that I was in Aldershot for four years, my non-Para-trained status meant that some of the pubs were permanently out of bounds, and going drinking could still be a risky venture from time to time. On the whole, the 'Wild West Town' of the local newspapers was a great place to go out, get drunk and meet ladies of dubious moral fibre. A normal night out would start in McDonald's. A bit of pre-session carbohydrate was always considered the height of good planning. People complain that McDonald's has homogenised the High Street, making everything look and taste the same, no matter where you are in the world. There is obviously some truth in that, but you only had to look out the windows of the Aldershot branch, to know exactly where you were. There was always some sort of drama unfolding on the street. Usually it was a domestic dispute, but occasionally it would be something more juicy. I remember sitting in the window once with a couple of lads. We were having a laugh at a guy from 3 Para, who was having a kip in the doorway of Rumbelows. It was seven o'clock on Saturday evening, so he'd obviously had a bit of a day of it. As we were watching, a Military Police Land Rover rolled up quietly beside him. The two occupants were smiling to each other, as they climbed out of the vehicle and donned their red forage caps. We all looked at each other and Willie Edwards said: "Fucking wankers, he'll be in jail tonight."

Scouse Marriott chipped in: "Brave bastards aren't they? They'll only pick up the ones that are sleeping.

There's probably a brawl going on in the Rat Pit, but you won't catch 'em anywhere near that, the tossers."

The MPs aren't well thought of generally, but they were particularly despised in Aldershot. They seemed to spend most of their time catching people urinating in bushes or staggering home from the pub. It was dead easy for them to get a bloke bounced for the catch-all charge of 'bringing the Army into disrepute'. It was nothing to them, but for whoever had been charged, it either meant jail time or a fine, or both. If there was anything happening that required bravery to deal with, they could be relied upon to be on the other side of the county.

Sniggering, one of the monkeys approached the dozing Para whilst the other called it in on the radio. It was an easy pinch for them, an additional drunk to add to the quota. Or so they thought. God knows what he'd been dreaming about, but as soon as the MP touched him, the Para was on his feet and swinging. The first punch landed dead centre in the MP's face and sent his cap spinning across the pavement. The second was an awesome, right-hand haymaker which caused the monkey to bounce his head off the Rumbelows window and collapse to the floor.

McDonald's was double glazed, so we were watching without the benefit of sound. It added a surreal touch to the proceedings and made it all the more riveting. The whole of the clientèle and staff were enjoying the entertainment. As soon as it was apparent that monkey number one would play no further part, everyone's attention switched to the other one, who was now jabbering into his handset like a Vietnam-era, US Marine, calling in a contact. If he'd played it a bit cooler and kept quiet, the drunken Para might not have noticed him. The moment he heard him, he headed for the vehicle. The MP dropped the handset and plotted his escape. A lethal game of 'tig' began. It was like witnessing a couple of children chasing each other around a kitchen table. The MP had obviously called for reinforcements and was trying to keep as much of the Land Rover as he could between himself and his attacker. The Para was equally determined to put lumps on the monkey before his mates arrived, for having the cheek to wake him up. Various spectators in the restaurant with us were adding touches of commentary.

"Ten quid says he fills him in."

"Nah the rest of 'em will be here in a minute."

But then the monkey fell for the oldest trick in the book. As he went round the back of the wagon and out of sight for just a second, the Para switched back and ducked low. They met by the passenger side door, right in front of the burger-eating crowd. Before he had time to turn round, the MP received two jabs to the chin, and he dropped like a stone. We all shouted an impromptu "Hurrah," which accompanied his fall. The Para was eager to finish him off and moved towards him, fists clenched. He was just drawing back to deliver the next punch, when he suddenly stopped and looked up and down the road like a meercat. We couldn't hear the sirens but he obviously could. He pinpointed the direction the sound was coming from, and went off like a roadrunner in the other direction. Ten seconds later, an identical MP Land Rover, crammed with the red-hatted scoundrels flew past. I don't think they ever caught him though, and of course, nobody in McDonald's had seen a thing.

Another time, we saw two blokes from 1 Para having a bunny-hop race the length of the high street. Not especially interesting you'd think, but it was one o'clock on a Sunday afternoon, and the only clothes they had on were their socks. The good, church-going people of Aldershot were rightfully horrified by the shrivelled cocks and bad squaddie tans on display. The next time I saw the pair was the following Tuesday. They were getting marched to the cookhouse by an RP sergeant at an incredible rate of knots, with saucepan helmets on their heads and no laces in their shoes. Somebody had obviously been waiting to wave them over the finish line.

After the McDonald's, we'd usually just conduct a general tour of the pubs, drinking as much beer and avoiding as many fights as we could. The Queen's, The Trafalgar, The South Western and onto The George for last orders. The George was even stranger than some of the other pubs, in that one side was for craphats and the other was for Para-trained personnel. Nothing was ever written down to this effect, but you transgressed at your own peril. On the way back, I'd always stop for a pizza. No matter how drunk I was, or however close I was to alcohol poisoning, I could always say: "Large ham and mushroom, wi' extra mushroom." It must have been some weird culinary auto-pilot. Post-beer food was, and has remained, an important part of my life. Types of food I wouldn't touch with a barge pole when sober make me slobber with desire after a gut full of lager. I remember being back in the room one night, sinking my last piece of pizza, when Joey Donaldson came back in, sporting a bust lip and a crazy hairdo.

"You'll never guess what's fuckin' happened, Eddy?" Without waiting for me to reply, he carried on: "I've just been mugged by three blokes from 1 Para."

This was surprising. Despite there being lots of crime in Aldershot, it was all of the drunken brawl variety. Theft of property or money from the person was far more rare.

"How much did they get?"

"Fuck all, they just nicked my Kentucky."

In the true spirit of the man who has had too much to drink, Joey had bought himself a bargain bucket, with enough chips and chicken for four starving dockers. He'd been tucking into it, on his way up Gun Hill, which ran to the left of the hospital. It was a particularly dark stretch of road, but a good short cut. When he was halfway up, the three muggers had jumped out from a bush and confronted him.

"They said 'Give us your food'," Joey continued whilst applying a fat wad of toilet roll to his lower lip. "I told them to fuck off and they jumped me, the bastards. They gave me a bit of a shoeing, but once they were sure I was going to stop fighting, they just grabbed the scoff and bimbled back towards town."

"What did you do?"

"What could I do? They were all twice my size. I did what anyone else would do in the situation."

"Go on," I urged.

"I waited 'til they were about 50 metres away and shouted 'Wankers' after them."

I started laughing.

"That's it, mate. You fucking tell 'em."

He'd started to see the funny side and smiled.

"As soon as I said it, one of 'em came running back up the hill. I thought I was going to get another panelling, but he only wanted the wet wipes. They must have fell out of the bucket while they were doing me over."

When the rest of the Squadron heard about the mugging, Joey was ribbed mercilessly for two weeks by blokes walking past him doing chicken impressions. Everybody that used Gun Hill for the next month or so was careful to have eaten their takeaway before they started the ascent. Any member of 1 Para encountered on guard for a long time after was viewed suspiciously, as a potential bush-dwelling, food-grabbing bandido.

If you were lucky, you might get the chance to take something more than a pizza back to the block. Lots of the women who frequented the bars in Aldershot, were renowned badge collectors, and were attempting to achieve the proud personal goal of shagging someone from every corps or regiment in the town. This could work to your advantage. No matter how grotesque your haircut or dated your fashion sense, if your cap badge was on her ‘to do’ list, you were guaranteed some action. Alternatively, I spent entire evenings wandering up to women, ready to work my limited charms on them, only to be rebuffed at the first attempt.

“Alright there? Haven’t seen you in here before. Can I get you a drink?”

“What unit are you in?”

“Erm, 5 Airborne Sig Squadron, why?”

“Sorry love, I just need a Gunner to complete the set, then I can move on to the Navy.”

When you did strike lucky, you counted your blessings. Let’s face it; a squaddie isn’t much of a catch in the copping-off stakes. She wasn’t going to get whisked away to a bachelor pad and serenaded for the evening, before being made love to in ways she’d only seen in her dreams. The reality was that she’d be taken to a squalid room, full of empty pizza boxes and shagged badly on a single bed, whilst the guy in the next bed shouted for them to keep the fucking noise down. As an addition, you could be guaranteed that someone else would be watching silently over the partition, with his eyes set to ‘record’, doing a bit of research for his next wank.

Incredibly, some girls would actually want to stay the night. Sharing a single bed was no fun. After making a few unsuccessful attempts to get comfortable in the spoons formation, you’d generally give up and go for something more practical. Top to toeing wasn’t the most romantic way to spend a whole night in bed with a woman, but it meant you got a decent night’s sleep. This was okay for you, but your companion would have nightmares about your P-Company-ravaged feet for months.

In the morning they’d leave. To get out of camp from the Signals block meant a stroll through the entire grounds before they reached the camp exit. When you were on back gate, they’d leave sometime between eight and ten on a Saturday morning. They always looked a bit forlorn. The outfit that they'd been wearing the night before, looking like a million lira, had now spent the evening on the floor of the singles block, after being unceremoniously removed by her lover. There would be stains all over it, some identifiable, others more mysterious. This was okay if they were only walking round the corner, but travelling home on the bus, looking like one of the dancers from the Thriller video can't have been much fun.

I remember that, for a little while, some crackpot from one of the other blocks, used to get busy with an air rifle from the roof. It only happened a couple of weekends running, but he managed to gain the name 'The Saturday Morning Sniper'. He'd always get women as they headed up the path towards the cookhouse. He exclusively went for 'bum shots'. The average Aldershot lady made it almost impossible for him to miss. I was leaving the cookhouse one morning and heading back to the block with a brew. I watched two women adopt excellent Section battle drills to escape the sniper. Their movements drew a small crowd, who couldn't help but admire their speedy dashes and effective use of available cover. The fact that this was all done in high heels and miniskirts was all the more impressive.

The routine of weeks of tediously pretending to work on wagons, followed by rapid bursts of activity, prior to, during, and after an exercise continued and before I knew it a year had flown by. I'd managed to pass another Pre-Para and fail another P-Company in that time as well. There was no injury to hide behind this time. I hadn't prepared properly and just got through Pre-Para by the skin of my teeth. I had to spend an hour convincing Staff Sergeant Herbert that I wouldn't let him down in Depot Para. I did, though. I didn't even last a week. The P-Company staff rumbled me immediately and I was booted off on the Thursday. I nearly went AWOL. The idea of explaining myself to Herbert made me shake like a shitting dog. When I went up to his office, he saw me through the glass panel in the closed door. He was on the phone but stopped talking the moment he spotted me. He said a couple more words and hung up. He got up from his desk, visibly angry, and lumbered towards the door. I nearly ran for it, but he'd have only caught me.

He opened the door, and uttered slowly and quietly through gritted teeth:

"What...the...fuck...are...you...doing...back…here?"

The only thing to do was be brave and take my bollocking.

"I've been sent back, Staff."

"Why?" His voice was still quiet, but the threat was palpable.

"Everybody was running faster than me, Staff". I didn't mean to sound flippant but it just came out that way.

"Nugent, you are a fucking disgrace. If I had my way, I'd post you out today, with the word SHITBAG tattooed across your forehead in red ink."

I was no barrack-room lawyer, but I knew enough about Queen's Regs to know that this wasn't a permissible punishment.

"Staff."

He shook his head in disgust.

"Get your excuse for a body out of my sight. Report back to Staff Sergeant Jeans in your troop."

He shut the door in my face and went back to his desk. The reception I got back at the troop was a little bit kinder. I'd worked hard enough over the year to be quite well thought of, and despite still being a craphat, had made quite a few friends. I got loads of earache for coming off the course and was called various exotic names, the most splendid being a 'lazy, shit-munching wankbag'. It abated after a month or so. I'd obviously performed better than I thought, because – just over a year after I arrived – I was tipped the wink that I was going to be promoted to lance-corporal. Out of a pool of

12 siggies, there were three of us: myself, Joey and Mark Gorse – an older soldier who'd been sweating on promotion for a couple of years. We were going to be promoted the week after, but Staff Sergeant Jeans wanted to give us the news early, as long as we kept quiet about it. It was a Wednesday, so we had Squadron PT the next morning, but Joey wanted to celebrate the news. The plan was to have four or five pints and toast each other's success. Of course, it never worked out like that. We had ten pints and bought a pizza before starting the walk up Hospital Hill to the back gate. There was a building site halfway up the hill, and for reasons known only to himself, Joey wanted to eat his pizza in one of the house shells that were springing up within the compound. In my drunken state, it seemed like a splendid idea. I climbed the fence first. Joey threw the pizzas over and followed. We sat in the footings of a soon-to-be living room and ate our scoff.

"Turn the fucking telly over, Eddy," Joey shouted from his breezeblock armchair – a big piece of pepperoni flying out of his mouth in my direction, when he articulated the 'f' in fucking.

"Do it yourself, I'm checking out the drinks cabinet." I'd found a builder's standpipe and took a long swig from the tap, hanging there like a calf at its mother's teat.

We finished our food and got up. We stepped over the footings and headed back to the fence. Joey stopped and with a look of pissed concern said: "Did you set the burglar alarm?"

"You're always asking me that, 'course I did," I replied. We neared the fence, laughing at our own 'hilarious' double act.

"Hey, Eddy, fucking check that out." I looked over to Joey. He was stood by the edge of a great big hole. It was about eight feet in diameter and a similar depth. A foot, or so, of oil-stained water sloshed about in the bottom. As I peered over the edge, watching my footing,

Joey did the schoolboy classic. He shoved me in the back but then grabbed me immediately, whilst shouting: "Tell your mam I saved your life."

I shook free of him. "You daft twat."

"Give us a hand with this." He'd spotted a cement mixer that was teetering on the edge of the hole, and his intention was plain. My sense of social responsibility had disappeared with the ninth pint, so I gave him a hand and we shoved it into the hole, taking great satisfaction in watching it almost disappear beneath the water. As we turned round, my balls dropped. They'd dropped already, immediately prior to the onset of puberty, but the shock was great enough to make them retract as far as my ribs before they tumbled back into their appropriate scrotal sacs. A military police car was parked right by the fence. The lights were off and they'd obviously seen everything. They both got out of the car with undisguised glee on their faces.

"Good night out, lads?" asked the one nearest to me.

"Nice bit of criminal damage to round it off?" his mate chipped in.

Joey looked at me with the same expression he used before the PT sessions on Pre-Para but I was no use to him. We were absolutely bang to rights. Even as I contemplated a runner, another monkey wagon pulled up on the other side of the building site and all the fight went out of me.

We were put in front of the Squadron OC the next morning and warned for orders. Everyone I met for the next two days bollocked me. By the time the first MP had got out of his car, I'd realised what a dick I'd been, and it was great fun being reminded of this by all and sundry.

We actually got charged on the same day we were supposed to be promoted. Mark Gorse went in before us and came out beaming, after winning the first tape of his career. As soon as he went past us, the RSM rounded on

Joey and me. Stood there in our Number Two dress, we wilted under his verbal onslaught.

"Right, you pair of fucking halfwits listen to me. I'm fucking glad you got caught. The idea of two little fucking vandals like you, getting a promotion makes me want to commit murder. You've dragged this Squadron's reputation through the dirt, and you will fucking pay, of that you can be certain. Listen in to my word of command."

We were sprint marched into the OC's office and made to mark time for a whole minute before we were given the halt. We stood there panting and received another rifting from the OC, this time with less swearing and longer words. The sentiment was the same. Our punishment was a £150 fine each and seven days ROPs, which were to start that night. We were bounced out of his office at the same speed and sent back to the troop.

ROPs are a bastard. ROPs that start on a Friday night are a bigger bastard, and ROPs that start on a Friday night on Montgomery Lines are the biggest bastard of all. It was only seven days, but we were worked like dogs. They had us doing some of the shittiest jobs possible. We had to weed the parade square, paint bollards black, then green, then black again. We had to clean toilets with wire wool. We had to scrape off all the wax floor polish that had accumulated on the skirting boards of the guardroom, armed with only a cookhouse spoon. It was a nightmare. A normal day on ROPs involved reporting in to the guardroom in Number Two dress at 0630 hours, and getting inspected. After working all morning in the troop we would then have to report for a working dress inspection at 1200 hours. After work and tea, we had to spend from 1800 hours to 2130 hours doing all the shit jobs listed, followed by another Number Two dress inspection at 2200 hours. All the inspections were done by the duty SNCO of the day. If he was a tosser, we would get called back for repeat inspections until he was satisfied. As a deterrent though, it was marvellous. I didn't drop another disciplinary bollock for the rest of my time in Aldershot. This wasn't down to an age-related, increasing maturity, but an overwhelming desire to never have to crawl on my hands and knees across an area the size of an airport runway, pulling up dandelions.

After my punishment, I knuckled down in the troop and kept my nose extremely clean. When another nine months had passed, I got the delayed promotion and became Lance-Corporal Nugent, Royal Corps of Signals. I was now only 16 ranks away from becoming a field marshal. The first time I wrote home after getting made up, I actually put that on the bottom of the letter. Within the Squadron, my life didn't change perceptibly as a result of my new rank. I remained on RATT Delta working under Pete. The only real advantage of being a lance-corporal was that I was less likely to be dealt shitty jobs. Added to that, I suppose, was the slight increase in pay, which meant, in real terms, that I could afford an extra couple of pints of beer a day, and an additional, non-meat topping on my pizzas.

As soon as I'd been promoted, I was obliged to attend the Royal Signals Detachment Commander's Course (RSDCC) at 8 Signal Regiment in Catterick. It was a four-week ball-ache of a course. Signals units from within UKLF would send all their newly promoted men to be taught in the ways of the Corps. There was a huge cross-section of ability and intelligence on show. A lot of the lads who showed up had been in Harrogate at the same time as me. The emphasis throughout the four weeks was on leadership and military skills. Due to the role and amount of training conducted in Aldershot, lads from our unit always breezed the course. You were expected to get, at the very least, a top-five finish, and we regularly provided the top student. I came fifth on mine, which I was quite happy with.

After getting back from detties, I fell back into the troop routine. I'd now been in the Squadron a couple of years and was considered 'not a new bloke any more'. This was nowhere near the coveted title of 'old sweat', but enough to gain a bit of respect and know everyone in the Squadron. Not being Para-trained was always going to hold me back, and there was always pressure from the Training Wing to get on the next Pre-Para. They used to run about three courses a year, in January, June and September. I was keeping myself fit, but I wanted to be sure I was going to pass on my next attempt. I started training a lot harder, running distance most evenings and at weekends. This was augmented by Squadron PT. There were generally three sessions a week, Tuesday and Thursday mornings and Friday afternoons. The Friday afternoon didn't always happen if there was a lot of work on, but when we did do it, it was always a tab. It could be anything from six to ten miles. We'd get finished at about half past three and knock off for the weekend. The Tuesdays and Thursdays were a bit more unpredictable and relied entirely on the whim of the Training Wing. It could be anything from a game of volleyball in the gym to a six-mile cross-country run at breakneck speed, or sometimes a go on one of the P-Company events, usually the steeplechase or assault course. There was always a huge dilemma about going on the beer the night before Squadron PT. Everyone would be scrabbling around to find out what we'd be doing, but it was very difficult to obtain information. The Training Wing enjoyed wielding this bit of power and were keen to keep the morning's activity under wraps until the last possible moment.

Generally, people thought 'fuck it' and went on the beer anyway. Most of the lads were fit enough to cope with it and were happy to suffer from some Olympic standard shuggying as a consequence of a good night out. There was a small group who actually made a point of it. As soon as they were told that we were on a BFT on this or that day, they would make plans to get absolutely blootered on the night preceding the run. This was solely so they could say, and it was the archetypal

Aldershot mentality, “Ha, ha, seven minutes 45, and I was on the fucking lash all night.”

Occasionally, very occasionally, we’d get an easy session. We’d turn up at Maida gym at 0730 hours. If the parade was at the gym, it could be anything. A run starting in the car park, indoor assault course, circuits or battle PT; all of which were potentially knackering activities. It was too much to hope for, that we’d do something dossy, but it did happen from time to time. Medicine-ball tennis was the best laugh but resulted in similar injury figures to that of a company attack, up a well defended hill. A line of vaulting horses would be placed side to side across the middle of the gym, forming a halfway line. Scores of medicine balls would be placed on the horses. The Squadron would then split into two teams who formed up on either side of the line. The game was simple. When the PTI blew the whistle, the clock would start. The aim was for the other team to have more medicine balls on their side of the line when the whistle was blown again, usually one minute later. The approved method of despatch was, with your back to the horses, to squat down with the med ball on the floor between your legs. Using your arms and legs as pistons, you would then explode upwards, launching the bugger as far and high as physically possible. There would be 30 people on each side of the line, duplicating this manoeuvre, and it was always bedlam. As well as trying to get your own balls over, you had to dodge all the incoming from the other side. It was like a recreational version of a sustained mortar attack. A medicine ball is made of old brown leather and weighs about the same as a newly born hippo. If one landed on you from a reasonable height, it would flatten you. By the end of the game, there would always be a slack handful of people lying around on the floor groaning. The worst injury sustainable was a direct hit to the head from immediately above. If you didn’t see it coming, the medicine ball had the capability to force your head down through the gap between your shoulder blades. The people in the Med Centre would always know when a game of med-ball tennis was on. They'd have a waiting room full of people who looked like Sandy Toksvig.

I had a really good Christmas that year. It was my Dad's fiftieth birthday party, and I did lots of catching up with mates and family that I hadn't seen for a while. As soon as we got back though, we were straight back into it. There were enough exercises going on to take us all the way through to summer. Having continued to increase my strength and fitness, I'd asked to stick my name down for Pre-Para in September 1990. About a month before, I was upstairs in the troop offices, putting all the mail into the relevant pigeonholes. I overheard Staff Sergeant Jeans talking to one of the other lance-corporals, Johnny Bergsen.

"You've got no chance; I'm never going to get a replacement now."

"Honestly Staff, I wouldn't ask if it wasn't really important."

Johnny was due to be going out to Belize the following week. The Squadron manned three rear link detachments on a six-month rotational basis. It was considered a real swan, and this was the first time I'd ever heard anyone trying to get out of it. This was Johnny Bergsen, though. He was the most henpecked soldier I'd thus encountered. His wife used to turn up at the troop sometimes, and berate him for committing unspecified crimes. As well as having to listen to his wife, he'd also be able to hear the rest of the troop, behind her back, making the universal 'hock tssshhh' sound whilst brandishing imaginary whips, to indicate Johnny's put-upon status. As time drew close to their enforced half-year separation, which Johnny must have been looking forward to immensely, she'd started trying to scupper his escape. This had resulted in him having to beg his troop staffie not to send him to Belize because his wife couldn't cope without him. What he actually meant was that she wouldn't have anyone to shout at, without him.

"Right, well, if you can find someone who fancies it, fair enough, but I can't see it," said Staff Sergeant Jeans dismissively.

"Cheers, Staff."

As he left Jeans' office, I blocked his path with my grin.

"I'll fucking do it."

"What?"

"Your Belize, I'll do it." There was no chance I was going to let him past me to ask someone else. There was no need to worry; he was as chuffed as I was.

We knocked back on Staff Jeans' door and got asked in.

"What's it now, Lance-Corporal Bergsen?" he said impatiently.

"Lance-Corporal Nugent says he'll take my spot, Staff."

Jeans looked over at me and then back to Bergsen.

"That was a bit fucking quick. Did you have this set up before you came to see me?

"No, Staff. Eddy was outside doing the mail." I nodded in assent.

Jeans sat there for a few seconds before saying: "Okay, Bergsen you're off the hook. Nugent, go and see Corporal Smith. Let him know what's going on. There are six of you including him. You'll need to get your skates on. All the rest of the lads have had their jabs and been issued their troppies."

"No probs, Staff."

"Get going then, if you get sorted quickly, you can get off on a few days' leave before you have to emplane."

Fucking hell, it just got better and better. A few days' leave, followed by a six-month holiday in Central America at the taxpayers' expense. I immediately went and found Mark Smith and put him in the picture. He was unfazed by the change to the plans, and gave me a list the length of my arm, of things to do before I went on leave. I got all my injections and started taking my malaria tablets. I went to the stores and got all the clothing I'd need. The tropical combats were actually quite smart and comfortable. It was the first piece of kit I ever got out of the stores that I didn't hate the sight of. The jungle boots were quite nifty too. Well, one was. Kenny Rogers tried to fob me off with an eight and a nine but I was getting a bit long in the tooth to fall for any of those tricks.

The next day was hectic, but once I'd got all my gear MFOd and cleared from the Squadron, I was allowed to go home. We were flying out from RAF Brize Norton the following Friday, so I had a whole week off. I spent the whole time on the beer with various family and friends and managed to steer every conversation onto Belize. It was one of those countries that you'd heard of, but whose location you couldn't point to in an atlas. I became an expert in the construction of Central American maps, with ashtrays and beer-mats. By my last night, my Dad knew more about the place than me. Over a final couple of pints on the Wednesday night, he said: "I don't mind telling you, Eddy. I'm bloody envious."

"Why's that, Dad?"

"Why do you think? You're going to be having a whale of a time in the sunshine, drinking out of coconuts and what have you. We'll all be freezing our bloody bollocks off over here."

"It won't all be fun, there's plenty of work to do you know."

He burst out laughing.

"My arse, you'll be on the pop from sunup to sundown. The only work you'll be doing will be on your tan."

We both laughed, then went quiet for a couple of seconds, before he said, more seriously, "It'll be weird, not having you around at Christmas, son. Make sure you keep in touch as much as you can. Your Mum'll appreciate it."

"I will, Dad." Amidst the euphoria of getting such a plum detachment, I hadn't really thought of the impact it would have on my folks. I was 21 now, and they'd got used to me being away, but not for such a long time and it would be our first Christmas apart. I made a mental note to write at least once a week and phone whenever availability and coin permitted.

The next morning, they both came with me to the train station. We had an emotional group hug on the platform, and I got on the train. As it pulled away, I could see that they were both mouthing something to me. Mum's was easy to decipher. It could only be 'elephant juice' or 'I love you'. I presumed the latter and mimed it back to her smiling. Dad's was a little bit more obscure. It looked like he was saying "We are jolly". As the train picked up a bit of speed, he could see that I hadn't yet understood, so he started to enunciate flamboyantly, like a kid trying to impress a music teacher. The penny finally dropped.

"Wear a Johnny."

Chapter 5

Easy Belizee

When I got back into Aldershot, it was just after lunch. Our transport was leaving at 2pm, so I mooched round the troop for a little while. The lads were carrying out the particularly mind-numbing task of stock-checking their wagons, piece by piece. The wagons were laid out, for all to see. Staff Sergeant Jeans would shout out an item, and everyone would hold it up. They'd only just started, so they had at least another two hours to go. It only served to highlight the providence of our temporary escape. The six of us that were Central America-bound were conspicuous by our happy demeanour. When our transport duly pulled up at five to two, we hopped aboard like excited school kids. As we left the Squadron lines, we gave a big cheer to the assembled stocktakers. In unison, they quickly held another item aloft. Staff Sergeant Jeans checked his list but, try as he might, he couldn't find 'two-fingered salute' listed.

We were flying out of RAF Brize Norton, so the journey took a couple of hours. We amused ourselves for the entire trip, by comparing stories that we'd heard about the various pleasures on offer, in the former British Honduras. We also discussed how we were going to split up when we got there. The Squadron manned three rear link detachments, and two of us would look after each one. Sig Derek 'the Dalek' Dale and I were to take care of Holdfast Camp, located a couple of miles down the road from the main, western town of San Ignacio. Corporal Mark Smith was the highest in rank and therefore responsible for our lack of welfare. He and Sig Rich Keogh were to be located at Rideau Camp, in the south. Lance-Corporal Herbie Naysmith and his mate, Sig Kev Laithwaite, were going to Salamanca Camp, which was even further south than Rideau. We didn't know it then, but it became apparent later, that the Dalek and I got the best of the bunch.

When we got to Brize, we received the shock of our lives. In a first for the RAF, our VC10 was ready to depart at the specified time. We climbed aboard, got ourselves comfortable and waited. In the ten minutes it took for the plane to taxi into its departure slot, I had a good look round the cabin. I don't know how old the plane was, but all the livery and internal décor had an extremely 'sixties' feel to it. The 'call' button had a small picture of a pointy-breasted stewardess next to it. She looked a bit like Betty Rubble, Wilma Flintstone's strangely attractive cartoon friend. I presumed that the plane hadn't had an internal refit since it was built. It wasn't dirty, but it looked a bit ragged. It didn't bother me; I just hoped that the engines had had a bit more attention down the years. At 8pm, the plane attempted to shake itself to pieces as it thundered down the runway, then we were airborne. We were due to refuel at Dulles Airport in Washington and we landed there at 6am local time, the next morning. After a quick turnaround we were back in the sky, and we touched down at Belize Airport at three o'clock in the afternoon.

As we walked down the steps from the plane, Herbie commented: "Fucking hell, I'm sweating like Eddy on ROPs."

Although the sun wasn't shining particularly strongly, the temperature must have been in the early eighties. I was already beginning to get dinner-plate sized sweat patches under my arms. A four-tonner was waiting for us at the entrance, and once we'd got all our bags, we clambered aboard. The first stop was Airport Camp. This was the biggest British camp in Belize. I'd see a lot more of it later, but in this instance, we only got as far as the gates. Mark, Rich, Herbie and Kev jumped off the wagon and Derek and I threw their kit after them. They would all be heading south the next morning, with the mail run to Rideau and Salamanca. We said our goodbyes in the traditional squaddie manner of a smattering of swearwords accompanied by various offensive hand signals. Soldiers have always taken their goodbyes in this fashion and I've never been sure why. As the wagon pulled off, Herbie and Rich held their arms up to nose level, parallel with the ground and with fists clenched. They started shouting: "Exterminate. Exterminate."

This was Derek's cue to turn his back to them, drop his trousers and perform a full moon. To add to the already horrific view of his hairy backside, Derek pulled his cheeks as wide apart as he could, and shouted at the top of his voice: "Can ya see me tea?"

As the wagon picked up a bit of speed, we flicked our final V-signs and headed off to Holdfast Camp. The journey down the Western Highway was very pleasant. There were only the two of us now, with the whole of the back of the four-tonner to ourselves. We sat near the tailgate and took in the scenery. This was my first trip out of England and I was bowled over by the sights, sounds and smells, which assailed my senses. Within a couple of days they would all become perfectly ordinary, but for now, I was getting a real buzz from their unfamiliarity. I turned round, to say something to Derek about it, but thought better of it. He was busy, shoving the thumb and forefinger of his right hand, up his right nostril and removing nasal hairs with a theatrical yank. I turned back, and carried on enjoying the countryside. Derek was a real Squadron character. He'd only been posted in the year before, but was a very popular figure of fun. The Dalek nickname had accompanied him from the Apprentice College. He was from Doncaster, and his accent, coupled with an extremely staccato but monotone delivery, made him sound like a Yorkshire-based Doctor Who foe. I'd met a few lads since joining, who had dirty habits. Some would pick their noses, some would pick their noses and eat the proceeds and I'd met various nail-biters, scab-munchers and toe-jam flickers.

Derek did the lot. He was a proper horror and all the lads loved him for it. He had no shame whatsoever and was quite happy to wolf down a bogey whilst he was eating his tea. It was great fun on a night out with him. He took particular pleasure in disgusting complete strangers in Aldershot pubs. That aside, he was a perfectly competent tradesman, and would – I was sure – give me no problems at Holdfast.

The distance from APC to Holdfast was about 70 miles and it took a couple of hours to complete the trip. We turned into camp at about 5.30pm, just in time for tea. We were met by the two lads from 216 who we were to replace. Andy Roundtree and Jase Geaney had been in Holdfast for six months and it showed. They both had mahogany-tinged tans and wore nothing but shorts and flip flops.

"Alright lads, welcome to paradise," greeted Andy as we jumped from the truck and started pulling our bags off. We all shook hands. Andy and Jase could barely contain themselves. They'd obviously been having a good time, but their flight home was only a week away, and the Dalek and me showing up was making that date all the more real. He carried on: "Right, Eddy, Derek, this is the script. I'll show you your bedspaces and take you over to tea. It'll be getting dark in a bit, so you need to get your longs on, or the mozzies will eat you. I won't bother giving you the work briefing tonight, you look ballbagged."

He was quite right. It had been a long haul, since flying out of Brize, and I could have probably done with a good night's sleep, but Andy wasn't finished.

"So what we'll do is have a few in the NAAFI, then go down to San Ignacio."

My heart sank, as I knew it was going to be a right Saturday night sesh, and quite frankly, I just fancied a kip. But who was I to spoil the party? The lads would be going back home to their families in seven days and they were in the mood for partying. We were shown into a bright, cool and well-lit room. There were seven beds down each side, separated by lockers. A few of the beds were occupied by blokes sleeping off a big tea. Three ceiling-mounted fans lazily circulated the fart enriched air. I was given the space nearest the door, and Derek dropped his bags in the pit straight across the room from me. Andy and Jase waited for us outside, and we quickly moved off to the cookhouse, once we'd dropped our bags. The cookhouse could have been in any UK based barracks. It was no different at all. The same, sour-faced sloppies stood behind the hotplate, hoping to leap on anyone taking a liberty with the amount of food they thought they were entitled to have. The food on offer was the same as well. The Army was demonstrating its fierce resistance to any local culinary customs being assimilated, by providing us with jam roly-poly, three and a half thousand miles away from home, bless 'em.

Despite promising not to talk shop until the next morning, Andy couldn't help himself, and gave us a bit of a briefing about the camp and its inhabitants, whilst we were eating.

"It's a spot-on camp, honestly. You're the only two Signals blokes here, so you'll get left alone. You're the only people allowed in the Commcen, so if anyone's giving you a bit of gip, you can just go in and lock the door behind you. Fucking hell, Derek, give it a rest."

The Dalek had just pulled his finger out of his nose and was reaping the nasal benefits of having just driven 70 miles down a dusty road. The thing on the end of his digit looked like a green Monster Munch. For once, he thought better of it, and wiped it on the underside of the table. Andy shuddered, and continued.

"The Glosters are the duty infantry battalion. The lads are sound, but the seniors and Rodneys are dicks. Just try and keep away from them as much as you can. Aside from that, there's a battery from 29 Commando. They're a great laugh, all mad bastards. There's a troop of Engineers, nice fellas, but they tend to keep themselves to themselves and there's another troop of Blues and Royals. They're the same detail as the Glosters, watch out for anyone higher than your rank, Eddy."

I nodded, and asked: "Is that everyone?"

"More or less; there's a handful of REME lads and there's an RAF geezer who POLs the helicopters. He's a good lad actually, but he stinks of AVTUR all the time. The good thing is, most of the units have got their own little bar. They don't like lads from the bigger outfits coming in, but 'cos there's only two of you, they won't mind."

"So there's plenty to do on camp?" I asked.

"It's alright. They show shit films in the NAAFI bar every weekend. The usual thing to do is have a few beers in one of the bars and then head down town. San Ig's a good laugh. There's loads of restaurants and bars, and a couple of nightclubs. The Blue Angel's probably the best. We'll show you that one later. Any questions?"

Before I could say anything, Derek jumped in.

"Is there an hooerhouse?"

Andy smiled. "Oh yes, my friend. It's only a little bit down the road as well. It's called Caracol Farm. It's out of bounds of course, but nobody really gives a fuck, as long as you don't cause any trouble. The going rate is seven US dollars for a shag and 20 for the whole night. We'll go later if you want."

I thought Derek was going to get his money and knob out there and then, he looked so excited. His unsavoury habits meant that he didn't get much action in Aldershot. I'd never been in a brothel but was keen to expand my knowledge in this direction.

"Jesus, Davros, calm down," said Jase, laughing.

By this time, we'd finished eating and headed back to the block. Andy looked at his watch.

"Right it's half-six. Get scrubbed up, and we'll see you in the NAAFI at half-seven."

With that, they shot off back to their own room. We did as instructed, and arrived in the bar, just after Andy and Jase. There was a huge TV in the corner, blaring out CNN news. There was a table in the opposite corner, so we got sat down there. Andy remained standing.

"Right then, me in the chair. You've got a choice, beer or rum?"

I'd only drunk spirits once before and that experience had taught me to keep well clear.

"Beer please, mate," I replied.

"Fucking both," said Derek.

"I'll have a beer, Andy, cheers," chimed Jase.

"Roger, out." Andy headed off to the bar. He came back with the round and we started drinking. They showed us a great evening. I soon forgot that I was knackered and got into the swing of it. Drinking in the camp was just like being in the UK, but San Ignacio was a different story. It was a town of about ten thousand people, and they all liked having a good time. The bars were fairly ramshackle, except for one or two. We went to a little restaurant near the Red Rooster Inn, and had a brilliant meal of steak and chips, for next to nothing. It was one of the great things about Belize. You could have a night out that would cost you upwards of 80 quid in Britain, for 30 US dollars. After eating and visiting a few bars, we headed for The Blue Angel. It was a big club, with room for three or four hundred people inside. Loads of punters and street vendors were milling about outside. We headed in and were instantly assaulted by the volume of the music. A brilliant reggae tune was being played over the PA. Apparently, it was a big local hit, entitled 'I Wanna Wake up wid' Whitney Houston'. The clientèle was representative of Belizean cultural diversity. The country is a real melting pot. Mayans, Creoles, Caucasians, Hispanics and combinations of them all are dispersed throughout the cities in similar numbers. The country was originally settled by the Mayas. After the collapse of their civilisation, the vacuum was filled, formerly by the Spanish and latterly British colonial interests. Many of the colonists fell in love with the country and remained, along with the descendants of the African slaves that originally sailed with them. By the time I arrived, Belize had been officially independent from the UK for nearly ten years, and was beginning to find its feet as a destination for the discerning tourist. As the Blue Angel demonstrated, there was plenty of fun to be had in San Ignacio.

The whole place was jumping. Everyone was very friendly and you couldn't help but pick up on the rum-soaked positive vibes generated by the clubbers.

We spent a couple of hours in there. Rum and Coke was the preferred tipple everywhere. Beer was pretty expensive, but a bottle of rum and a couple of cans of Coke cost peanuts. I quickly found myself moving away from my 'strictly no spirits' policy and as a result got drunk pretty quickly, and drummed up enough Dutch courage to introduce my clumsy, fused-joint dancing into the mêlée. The other big hit of the time was 'Me Donkey Want Water'. It was a brilliant tune, done in the style peculiar to Belize, known as punta-rock. This was a type of music that had descended from Carib Indians and African slaves. It was like a combination of ska and reggae. 'Me Donkey Want Water' became the first of a trilogy of songs, which all went to top of the Belizean charts and dealt with the ongoing fortunes of the aforementioned donkey. In the second song, the donkey had obviously received water, and was now expected to pay for it. It was called 'Work de Donkey'. In the concluding part, the donkey had outlived its usefulness and was about to be traded in for a newer model. Its title 'Shoot de Donkey' left you certain that this particular animal had featured in its last punta-rock track. The other tune that they were really into at the time was the unbearable 'Sacrifice' by Elton John. They used to play it at least three times a night. As a change in tempo from punta-rock, it was akin to changing gears in a car from fifth to reverse. Every time it came on, I found myself weaving my way back to the bar, to rejoin Andy, Jase and Derek. They were occupying a corner that gave them a good view of the entire joint, and Andy waved as he saw me coming. As I neared them, he approached me, and crooking his thumb over his shoulder towards the Dalek, said: "Fuck me Eddy, you're going to have a right laugh with that dirty cunt."

"What's he done now?"

"He's not shut up about going down The Farm since we got here."

I looked over his shoulder to see Derek, demonstrating his rhythmic pelvic movement shagging technique to a disinterested Jase.

"I wouldn't fucking mind, but he could have copped off with a girl earlier on, and it wouldn't have cost him a penny."

"Who was that, then?"

"One of the Yank, Peace Corps birds. She was chatting him up. I was quite impressed. They're never normally interested in us lot."

"What happened?"

"She was mid-sentence, when the grotty fucker stuck a finger over his right nostril and blew a big oyster out of the left. It landed on her shoe."

"That's Derek."

"Lucky for him, the prozzies aren't too choosy."

We went back over to the two of them, who were just getting to the bottom of their rum bottle. It seemed like an appropriate time to leave, and Andy announced, with suitable fanfare.

"Edward, Derek, if you'd like to accompany me to a taxi, your ladies of the night await."

We jumped into a cab outside the club. It was an enormous white, 1963 Chevrolet Impala, with enough room for three people on the front seat. The driver was a powerfully built black guy, with shoulder-length dreads.

"Andy, Andy, Andy, you are a bad man," he said laughing, "Usual destination?"

"Alright, James? These are the two new guys that are replacing me and Jase. This is Eddy and that's Derek."

James looked in the rear-view mirror and smiled.

"Hello, fellas. You'll like The Farm. Mimi will look after you."

James and the two old hands started laughing conspiratorially. As we spoke, James had pulled out into the road and set off towards our destination. It was about a 20 minute drive from town. The windows were down, allowing a cool breeze to circulate through the car. James was playing a mellow, reggae tape, and we all had a belly full of booze. There was lots of laughter and good natured ribbing, and I remember it so vividly that it could have happened a couple of minutes ago. As we turned down the long drive to The Farm, Derek started tidying himself up, as if he was going on a date. James noticed and started laughing.

"Don't worry 'bout your appearance, my good man. If he had seven bucks, them girls would fuck a scarecrow."

Caught in the act, Derek stopped what he was doing and sat there nervously.

As we pulled up, three or four more taxis were disgorging military personnel in various states of disrepair. Andy squared James away with a couple of Belizean dollars and we jumped out. He gave a friendly wave and drove away immediately. I met my very first prostitute at the door. She was a meeter-and-greeter, and she was quite beautiful.

She smiled and simply said: "Welcome."

I managed to keep enough cool to say: "Thank you." And we all walked in. Behind me I could hear Derek pumping Andy for information.

"So, can we fuck any of 'em Andy. Even 'er at the door?"

"Jesus, Derek. Take it easy. We'll go in and have a drink and a game of pool first. It's only 12 o'clock. The place is open 'til the last man leaves. We'll be here until at least four."

I slowed down to let Andy take the lead, and we followed him inside. It was a decent sized place, with enough space to have 15 or 20 tables dotted around the main room. Off to the right there was a smaller area, with a bit more seating and a pool table. The lighting throughout was just right, low but not too dark. There were about 30 people sprinkled around the tables, drinking beer from the bottle or rum from a glass. The majority of the punters were soldiers but there were a handful of local lads as well. Being set back off the road, it wasn't the sort of place that got passing trade, so the working girls were easy to identify.

Andy parked his arse at an empty table near the bar and we all followed suit. One of the girls came over immediately, ostensibly to take our drinks order. She was pretty, about 23 or 24 and looked quite like Gloria Estefan. She wore a black miniskirt and red bra.

"Ola, Andy. Can I get you and your friends a drink?" She spoke a lovely, heavily Latino-accented English.

"Yeah, cheers Mariana. Beers all round?"

We performed a synchronised nod.

"Quatro cerveza por favor."

She moved off to fetch the drinks, with myself and Derek taking the opportunity to ogle her backside. When she went behind the bar, I turned back to Andy.

"I didn't know you spoke Spanish."

"Oh yeah, mate, I'm fluent. I can order beer *or* food." Three of us burst out laughing but Derek had other things on his mind.

"Was that Mariana a prozzie?"

"No, Derek," replied Jase, completely deadpan "she's the MP for Harrogate."

“Eh?”

“ ‘Course she fucking is.” He turned to Andy. “We better get him in quick, or he’s going to ruin his trousers.”

Mariana returned with the drinks.

“Hey, Mariana, the new guy’s taken a shine to you.”

She laughed as she put the bottles of beer on the table, then turned to Derek and said, smiling: “Would you like to fuck me, new guy?”

“Er, I think so, yes.”

Jase spat his first mouthful of beer out with laughter, on hearing Derek’s lame response. Mariana ignored Jase and took Derek’s right hand. She placed it on to her right breast and purred: “What about now?”

His voice moved straight from low-pitch Yorkshire to cartoon-chipmunk.

“Yes.”

“Good,” she replied. She turned to face the rest of us.

“You enjoy your drinks, while I enjoy your friend.”

Derek stood up and allowed Mariana to lead him away. Her sexual authority had given his nerve a severe denting and he looked like a naughty schoolkid getting taken to see the headmaster. They went past the pool table and disappeared through a purple curtain, into the nether regions of the bar.

Andy looked at Jase.

“How long do you reckon?”

“Five minutes tops,” he replied, before rounding on me.

“What about you then, Eddy?”

“Erm, I think I’ll have a few more beers first.”

“Not nervous, are you?” said Andy.

“Are they all as…” I searched for the word, “confident as Mariana.”

“Yep, more or less. Best thing to do is get your first one out of the way. You’ll be back all the time, then. I’ll have a word with Mimi for you.” He shouted over to a woman playing pool, “Mimi!”

I got an attack of nerves and said "Leave it, Andy," but he just chortled and replied: "You're too late, mate. She's on her way over."

I looked over to the pool table and watched her carefully stack the cue in the rack, on the adjacent wall. As she sashayed the 15 feet to our table, I made a visual inspection of her body. She was maybe three or four years older than Mariana but a little taller and even prettier. She had the same outfit on but the colours were reversed. Her shoulder length hair was jet black and straight. She was far curvier than the younger girl. You could tell that she was going to be a bit of a porker in the next couple of years, but right then she was just beautifully voluptuous. She was smoking a long cigarette, which she stubbed out in our ashtray when she got to the table. She smiled at me and sat down in Derek's recently vacated chair.

"Hello, Andrew, Jason. Who is your friend?"

"Mimi, meet Eddy." Andy was enjoying his role as master of ceremonies.

"Eddy, meet Mimi, the sexiest woman in Belize."

"Andy, you're too kind." She turned to me, "Well, Eddy, how do you like Belize?"

Conscious of Derek's unsuccessful attempts to play things cool, I tried extra hard.

"It's great. Do you live here?" Fucking rubbish. All my cred was blown at the first attempt. She ignored my embarrassment.

"I'm from Guatemala originally. I'm just here for a couple of years to make my fortune."

Jase interjected, "She's not fucking joking either. Everyone reckons that all the girls earn more than the mayor of San Ig."

"That's because we do," Mimi beamed, exposing a set of perfect white teeth, "and so we should, we work harder." We all laughed and then she brought me up short with the killer line: "If you come with me, Eddy, I can help you to like Belize even more." Without further announcement, she stood and started heading towards the curtain. After a couple of steps, she paused, turned and beckoned me to follow.

I took a big gulp of my beer and got out of my chair. Andy and Jase were enjoying the spectacle, and started shouting as I caught up with Mimi.

"Marks out of ten, give 'er one." They then fell about laughing at their comic ingenuity.

As we approached the curtain, Mariana emerged. She looked completely unflustered, and was smoking a post-coital cigarette. She headed towards the bar to take her next drink order. Derek came through a couple of seconds later and looked like he'd done a couple of laps of the steeplechase. His wild eyes locked with mine as he walked past, but all he could say was: "That were fucking great." He'd only been in the room for five minutes and this fact wasn't lost on the occupants of all the other tables. Hoots of derision, calling his manhood into question, peppered him from all directions. He seemed oblivious and sank down into his chair heavily, before taking a long pull on his beer, as Andy and Jase started debriefing him.

As I looked back round, Mimi was just disappearing through the curtain. I took a deep breath and went through. I came out in a dimly lit corridor with a few doors on each side, about ten in all. Mimi had just gone into the first room on the left and I followed suit. The room was sparsely furnished, unsurprisingly. A single bed occupied the right-hand side and a small vanity unit, the left. Subdued lighting gave the place a sultry ambience, but this was quickly stripped away by the strong smell of disinfectant – the prostitute's friend. By now, Mimi was sat on the bed, with her legs on the floor, but I was still by the door. She patted the bed next to her, with her left hand and I took my cue. I sat down stiffly, facing straightforward, with my hands on my knees, like I was posing for the front row of the Squadron photograph. I was nervous and completely at Mimi's mercy, and she knew it.

"Stand up, Eddy," she instructed. I did as I was told. In one quick movement, she moved off the bed and knelt directly in front of me. With the speed of a pickpocket, she undid my belt and jeans and quickly dropped them to my knees, closely followed by my Johnny Fartpants boxer shorts. My penis had never been so erect. A cat couldn't have scratched it. It wasn't big or small, but it was about to burst. As she moved her mouth towards it, I picked a spot on the far wall, about a foot below the ceiling, and started trying to think of something unsexy, to stave off the inevitable. I racked my brain, but all I could dredge from my memory was a drill session in Harrogate. I clenched my eyes shut and started trying to imagine a grizzled instructor, barking: "BY THE LEFT, QUICK MARCH."

I adopted the standard blow-job recipient stance of clenched fists on hips – kind of like Superman surveying Metropolis from a hill above the city. Just as I thought the drill thing might help me out, I felt an extra peculiar sensation around my genital area. I made the fatal mistake of looking down. For a second I couldn't suss it out, but then realised that Mimi had my entire wedding tackle in her mouth. My dick and both balls were being subjected to what felt like the spin cycle of a washing machine. The only way it could have been any more mind-blowing was if she had started humming "Me Donkey Want Water." That was academic anyway, as about two seconds later, with a roar of "Bloooodddddy Hell," she brought me to climax. After my eyes had stopped spinning round in my skull, I sat back down on the bed, then collapsed and lay down, panting heavily. Mimi was doing a bit of post-nosh admin and left me to it for a minute. She lit a cigarette and said: "You can leave the seven dollars on the table when you're ready."

"No problem." My trousers were still round my ankles, so I fished around and found the fee. I put the money where she'd said and started tidying myself up. Something suddenly occurred to me. I looked at my watch. Christ, I'd only been in there for about two and a half minutes. The blokes out there would make mincemeat out of me. Even Derek had the moral high ground, probably for the first time in his life.

"Er, Mimi, I couldn't ask a big favour could I?"

"What is it?"

"Do you mind if I hang around here for a few minutes?" I flicked my head back in the direction of the main room, and added: "Do you know what I mean."

She laughed quietly and said: "I could make you a cup of coffee for a dollar."

It sounded like a complete bargain. She whacked a small kettle on and when it was boiled, made the brew. She made one for herself at the same time. She asked me a few questions about England, and I made a couple of ham-fisted attempts at small talk questions, the most subtle of which was: "So what's it like, being a prostitute then?" It was all water off a duck's back to Mimi though. She must have had to endure thousands of conversations with knobbers like me, whilst maintaining a façade of rapt interest.

By the time the coffee was finished, I'd managed to spin out a more than passable 15 minutes. We went back through the curtain. As Mimi headed back to her unfinished game of pool, I made my way to my compadres. They all saw me coming, and I was given a cheer to celebrate my fraudulent longevity. It put a bit of a spring in my step, and I adopted a 'Saturday Night Fever' swagger until I got to the table. Andy started.

"Not fucking bad, Eddy. Quarter of an hour with Mimi is good going."

"Well, you know, bit drunk an' all that," I replied furtively.

"Still, mate, you did better than Johnny Two Squirts here." Derek still looked a bit wiped out, but had enough energy to tell Andy to "fuck off".

Jase contributed, conspiratorially, “I tell you what, though. The first night I went in with her she ripped me to bits. I didn’t last much longer than Derek.”

“Really?” I asked. He started laughing loudly.

“She made me a cuppa, so I didn’t have to come back out too quick.”

We all joined in the laughter, though mine was identifiably more hollow. It was now twelve-thirty and we carried on drinking and taking the piss out of each other for the next hour or so. Andy pointed out the proprietor of the bar. He was a malevolent looking middle-aged man called Dutch Pete. He wore a patch over his right eye and had a close-trimmed beard. Rumour had it, that he kept a small crocodile round the back, which he would set on any punters who had difficulty paying. Of course, it was another squaddie urban myth. Neither Andy nor Jase had seen the beast, but both knew someone vaguely who had heard it roaring one evening. Eventually, the combination of long flights, strong rum and professional sex took its toll on me and I started to hear my bed calling. Fortunately, the other three had had a good skinful and wanted to get off as well. It was about two o’clock when our taxi pulled up outside and beeped. We dragged ourselves away from a half-full beer, and made for the exit. Some of the girls were hanging around near the pool table, including Mariana and Mimi. Mariana called over to us, winking.

“See you soon, Derek, for a little bit longer next time maybe, eh?” After the laughing died down, I felt confident enough to shout goodbye to Mimi.

“See you next time, Mimi,” I called, nonchalantly.

“I can’t wait, Eddy,” she cooed, “I’ll have the kettle on.”

There was a huge roar of laughter from everyone within earshot, but especially from Andy and Jase.

“Ha ha ha, Eddy, you fucking waster,” hollered Jase, wiping tears away from his eyes, “Did she get you with the ‘spuds and knob in the gob’ trick?”

I was seeing the funny side now as well, and joined in the laughter. Jase continued: "When she did it to me, I counted my bollocks after."

We got into the cab in absolute fits, and laughed all the way to camp. James was driving us again, and every now and again I'd catch a view of him in the rear-view mirror, chuckling at our banter.

When we got back to camp, there was no drama. The guys on the gate were well used to having rummies turn up at all times of the night, so they just raised the barrier and waved our four staggering bodies through. I got back to my room, which was quiet except for the noise of the fans. I collapsed on to the bed in all my clothes and was asleep before my head hit the pillow.

Sunday being the next day, I had a lie in until about 11am, when Andy and Jase came to give us both a shout.

"Fucking hell, Eddy, you mingbag. Haven't you got any other clothes?" Andy scolded. I sat up on the end of my bed and spent a couple of seconds waiting for my hangover to kick in. Remarkably, there was nothing there. I felt fine. Pleased at this unexpected bonus, I got out of my clothes and stuck my Belize uniform on. Flip-flops, shorts and a clean T-shirt would be my off-duty clobber for the next eight months. Derek was also stirring, but seemed a bit more the worse for wear. Jase was giving it to him about the Peace Corps girl.

"You daft fucker, you were well in there, until you fucked her shoes up."

Derek had to think back to remember the incident, but then started grinning.

"Oh aye, yeah. Easy come, easy go though eh, Jase? I'd rather just keep it simple and give the prozzies me cash."

Andy directed us over to the ablutions and toilets.

"When you're done, meet us over at the HQ and we'll take you through the rear link det and do a handover of all the gear. Shouldn't take more than a couple of hours."

They shot off, and I went to the toilet block. It was in the middle of camp, adjacent to the NAAFI and was a brick construction with about 14 traps, seven on either side of a central gangway. It had a high ceiling, which meant that the acoustics generated by the occupants carried to the street outside. As I approached, I could hear various wails and grunts, followed by what sounded like an oompah band, tuning up. I got in there and eventually found a trap that was empty and wasn't swimming in the previous occupant's detritus. As I treated myself to a long, sit-down piss, I noticed how much graffiti there was on the walls. There was loads of it, and even the unfunny stuff was quite entertaining. Two line jokes and rudimentary drawings of female genitalia formed the bulk of the work. The jokes were generally at the Glosters' expense, and were done by members of the other units on camp. They were all geared towards the usual accusation about the Infantry, that they were brainless. Not true, of course, but the source of endless wind-up opportunities. A couple of the better ones that I remember were:

"Why don't the Glosters eat pickled onions?"

"Because they can't get their heads in the jar."

And:

"What do you call a section of Glosters in a tank?"

"Tinned, mixed veg."

Plus:

"Why don't the Glosters get NAAFI breaks?"

" 'Cos it takes too long to re-train them."

After I'd got ready, I waited for Derek and we both wandered over to the HQ building. The weather was absolutely beautiful, sunny and baking hot with not a sign of a cloud in the sky. Andy and Jase were both waiting for us, and began to take us through our duties. We were required to send, by HF RATT, any signals that authorised personnel gave to us. They would be transmitted back to APC, and forwarded on to their destinations from there. Andy explained that, on average, there would be two or three a day, including a sitrep which was sent at 6pm every evening. Between myself and Derek we would work day on, day off. The 'day on' sounded like about two hours' work.

I put this to Andy and he replied.

"You've got it, mate. It's a complete doddle. I've been doing a couple of hours' graft every two days for the last six months."

The 'all this and pay an' all' man swam into view. Maybe he hadn't been lying after all. Our little Commcen was about the size of a large toilet, but had air-con to keep all the radios cool. It was the coldest room on camp and, more importantly, we were the only ones allowed in there, due to the presence of cryptographic material. The radio kit was the same as RATT Delta, but not vehicle mounted.

"Where are the batteries, Andy?" I enquired.

"Thought you might ask that," he frowned, "follow me."

We all went outside and walked along the side of the building, until we were level with the outer wall. A little brick hut had been built on to the side. It was about three feet high and had a small, red, wooden door with a large padlock keeping it shut.

"They're in there, but we haven't touched them since day one. It's fucking horrible. Some wise old owl thought that it'd be a great idea to create a four-foot-by-two-foot, pitch-dark cubby hole. When we got here, we wanted to check the batteries, to see if they needed topping up. I got the door opened but shut it straight after."

"Why?" Derek and I asked, at the same time.

"It was like something out of Scooby Doo. There were loads of little yellow eyes looking at me. Fuck knows what they were. Spiders, rats and snakes, probably. I had the padlock back on two seconds later. "Fancy a look?"

I didn't, but Derek wasn't as fazed.

"Go on, get the fucker opened, you puffs."

Jase responded. "If you want it opening, do it your fucking self." He threw him the key.

Without a hint of trepidation, Derek approached the door, the key held out in front of him protectively. We all stayed behind, but close, so we could watch over his shoulder. He fiddled with the lock for a few seconds, but eventually forced it open. He undid the hasp and pulled the door ajar, allowing the outside light to pour in. It took us a couple of seconds of squinting to get a glimpse of the interior. You could see the batteries, but they were under a mass of little squirming bodies. There were a couple of snakes further back, and an enormous tarantula was sat across one of the front lugs. Jase, mouth gaping open, said: "It's like a fucking horror film."

Derek was already shutting the door, and summed up everyone's thoughts when he said: "Right then, that's battery maintenance done for the next eight months."

With the Commcen inspection complete, they then took us on a little tour of the camp. It covered about the same area as a decent sized primary school, and had all the usual barracks buildings. In addition, there was a 20 metre, outdoor swimming pool. We walked up to have a look. There were a couple of lads lounging around, sunbathing whilst listening to a Proclaimers tape. The pool looked great and I planned on spending quite a bit of time round it, but not until that fucking tape was finished.

The final stop was the NAAFI. We'd only spent half an hour in there the previous night and I hadn't really looked around. It was quite packed. Most of the table occupants were necking soft drinks and eating toasted egg banjoes.

As we sat down, Andy said: "Scoff's pretty good in 'ere. Rancid makes a mean banjo."

"Who's Rancid?" Derek enquired.

"The guy behind the counter. They all call him Rancid Flip-Flop." We looked towards the cash till, where a tall, middle-aged gentleman was scowling at one of the engineers, who was trying to pay for his lunch with a small mountain of five cent pieces. When Andy looked back, he could see that we were waiting for an explanation.

"You never see his feet, 'cos he's always behind the counter, but apparently they're honking. One of the 29 Commando lads was telling me that he saw them the other night. He was walking round the back of the NAAFI and Rancid was bottling up. He reckoned that he could smell 'em from across the road. His toenails were like extra large, tortilla chips. I don't think anyone even knows his real name. It's just Rancid, or Mr Flip-Flop 'til you get to know him."

Derek despatched himself to get a round of Sprites in, and we watched a bit of telly whilst we waited for him. A few seconds later, raised voices at the bar caused us to turn round. Derek had managed to get himself into Rancid's bad books immediately. Mr Flip-flop was verbally terrorising the Dalek in a strong Mexican accent.

"Honest, Rancid, it was a fucking twenty."

"Fuck off, you fucking soldier bastard. It was a ten, and my name is not fucking Rancid."

Despite being provided with this information, Derek continued to annoy him.

"Alright, alright, fucking calm down, Rancid. My mistake. Fuck's sake."

"I don't know you and you try to cheat me and call me Rancid. Fuck you, you bastard."

Derek was retreating with four bottles of Sprite and his change. He was trying to placate Rancid, using the novel approach, of making him more angry.

"Jesus, Rancid. It was a ten then. They all look the same to me."

"My name is not fucking Rancid." He slammed the till violently shut, and stormed into the back room to sulk. Derek bimbled over to us, put the drinks on the table, and looked at us with a hurt expression.

"Touchy bastard, in't he?"

"Yeah, Derek," replied Jase, sarcastically, "Some people, eh?"

Over the drinks, Andy carried on explaining the various workings of the camp. All in all, as suspected, it was going to be a real swan. For the purposes of discipline on camp, we would come under the authority of the Glosters. All our admin would be taken care of by 633 Signal Troop in APC, our parent unit. There was PT to do on a Tuesday and Friday morning. If we'd had a big night out beforehand, we could always play our joker, and lock ourselves in the Commcen, whilst conducting an imaginary 'crypto-check'. We quickly fell into our routine. By the time Andy and Jase hopped on the transport back to APC the following Friday, Derek and I were on top of all our duties.

On my days off, I'd either lounge around the pool all day or shoot off into San Ig. We tried to stay off the beer on the weekday nights, usually limiting ourselves to a couple of bottles in the NAAFI. We got to know a few of the lads from the other units, and generally got invited to any piss-ups, being the Billy-no-mates of the camp. The most fun was had in the 29 Commando bar. They were all, absolute head-the-balls and got drunk most nights. Despite this, they were all fit as fiddles, and any spare time they had off from drinking was spent in the pool or on the multi-gym. They had a penchant for naked bar frolics, and if you were a guest, you were expected to disrobe accordingly. Any hesitation would result in four or five of the fuckers helping you.

It was on my way back from one of their dos that I experienced the horrible trauma of the 'drunken flip-flop blow-out'. Most of the guys on camp had taken the trouble to bring decent sandals with them. I was making do with the cheapest flip-flops on sale in the Aldershot NAAFI. They only cost 45p and they weren't even worth that. They lasted me a couple of weeks. On my way back from the said do, I broke into a bit of a drunken jog down the main road past the ablutions, to get back to my scratcher that bit quicker and avoid the powerful stench wafting out of the windows. The blow-out occurred when the front portion of the sole of my right flip-flop caught on a bit of the road. The paper-thin foam suddenly curled under itself, taking my toes with it. I dragged them along the ground with my full weight pressing down for the two seconds it took me to stop. I shrieked like an eight-year-old girl. The pain was phenomenal. It felt like someone had taken an industrial sander to my toe-knuckles. Two Glosters coming out of the NAAFI had a good laugh at me, rolling round whilst holding my injured right peg. They quickly assessed the situation and nodded wisely to each other, like two aerodynamics experts, "Flip-flop blow-out," before walking off without any offer of assistance.

I hobbled back to my room and went to bed, feeling very sorry for myself. I was even sorrier the next morning. I woke up to find my sheet stuck to my foot. After minutes of fruitless probing and long deliberation with Derek, we agreed that the best course of action was for him to rip it off as quickly as he could, in the style of the magician who wants to leave all the cups and plates standing on a table. Derek could hardly wait. I pleaded with him to be gentle with me.

"Stay still, you shitbag," he shouted, before ripping the sheet away with a flourish. It hurt even more than the original blow-out. Derek was stood there, smirking insanely, holding the sheet up for my inspection.

The pain was so great, that along with the dried blood, I was expecting to see all five of my toenails stuck to the sheet as well, like a row of plectrums.

A lesson was certainly learnt, and I bought a pair of sandals from Rancid's small selection.

Of course, no swan lasts forever, and a signal that came in from 633 burst our little fun-bubble. One of the lads from the troop had been posted out at short notice, and they needed a temporary replacement. Apparently, this guy had gone nuts in the bar one night and had gone round smashing all the windows with a golf club. Although this seemed like fairly standard behaviour to the rest of the lads, the Army brass were sufficiently worried about him to have him sent back to England, to be assessed at Woolwich, the Forces' booze clinic. I found out later that he'd been a bit of a turps-nudger since before he joined. He'd had a few discipline problems at his working unit, so his troop OC thought that the perfect course of treatment would be to send him to Belize for six months. It had obviously escaped the Rodney, that the main pastimes in the country were fucking about and drinking rum. Perhaps he thought that if his charge was supplied with unlimited amounts of booze he'd get bored of it, kind of like when your Dad made you smoke a load of cigars after catching you smoking. The over exposure treatment had backfired, resulting in the soldier being bundled out of the country unceremoniously, and his troop OC failing his Open University Psychology degree. Derek would have to look after Holdfast on his own for a short time, whilst I stood in at APC. With everything being relative, Derek believed himself to be the victim of a huge miscarriage of justice. His working week had been increased from seven to 14 hours and he was outraged. He complained bitterly that he was never going to find the time to squeeze in the extra work, and whinged like fuck, until the moment I got on the transport to take me back down the highway to Belize City.

The duty clutch was a talkative kind of guy and he gave me a blow by blow, quite literally, account of his activities in The Farm. He was just in the middle of telling me about how the rooms that he had been in had had dirt floors and that jungle toads would hop around in them and put him off his stroke, when a sign for 'Mile 33' came into view and we pulled over.

Mile 33 was the home of JB's, which was a roadside café in the middle of nowhere along the Western Highway. It was quite nice inside with an open bar/eating area and the walls were adorned with plaques from almost every unit that had served in Belize. To top it all off, they did a great cheeseburger, which, along with chips covered in the local 'Melinda's hot pepper sauce', really hit the spot. Wash this lot down with a freezing cold stim and you would be more than ready for the final half of the journey back to APC.

JB's also did some good T-shirts and most guys bought one when they got the chance. So whilst I was paying for my scran, I purchased a famous JB's T-shirt that had about 20 lines of text plastered over the back, the contents of which basically referred to the owner of the shirt being a seasoned traveller and soldier who had seen goats fuck in the market place, but had never seen anything like JB's.

We got back into the wheels and set off again, but as soon as the engine started, so did the next sordid tale of the driver's rectal integrity-disrupting antics.

I must have put too much of the local fire sauce on my food because I started sweating even more than normal. But, by the time we started to hit the outskirts of Belize City (or just BC as it was known), my perspiration had gone down to the steady drip that is the norm' in The Tropics.

We flashed through the ramshackle, galvanised metal suburbs of BC and soon we were approaching what looked like a large roundabout with an open centre that you could drive straight across. There were no road markings, let alone any signposts. The traffic that was negotiating the roundabout had no discipline and it really was every man for himself. I looked at the driver and said: "Fucking hell, this all looks a bit disorganised, I bet it takes ages to get across doesn't it?" At which point he turned to me wild-eyed and screamed: "Fuck that shit! This here's Kamikaze Junction, baby!" He then looked ahead, floored the accelerator and closed his eyes. Just as we crossed the point of no return, he called out the horn noise from *The Dukes of Hazzard's* 'General Lee' and did a huge rebel yell: "Dada da da dada dada da da da da, YEEEEEEEEEEEEEHHHHHHHHHHHAAAAAAAAAA!"

We rocketed across the junction and I pulled my feet up onto the seat, whilst holding onto anything that I could get my hands on, all the time saying "Jesus-fucking-H-fucking-Christ", over and over. We made it to the other side and the strangest thing was that all the other drivers, even the ones that had to swerve or brake, didn't even bat an eyelid and just carried on as if it was the norm.

The driver eventually opened his eyes and turned to me with a big cheesy grin and said: "Not bad eh?"

I just called him a fucking knobber and we laughed a nervous laugh.

We arrived at Airport Camp without further incident and once through the gates we turned left and drove for about 400 metres then parked next to a swimming pool and a bar called 'The Blackbird Club'. The pool was surrounded by sunburnt and tattooed blokes in dodgy swimming trunks.

I said my farewell to the mad driver and he gave me directions to the 633 offices, which were only across the way, then he did a three-point turn to head back the way we had come. Finally, in one last valiant effort to cement his reputation as a crazed maniac, he sped off as fast as he could and gave a thumbs-up out of his window. He only got about 100 metres up the road when a warrant officer pounced out from behind a bush and waved his pace stick at the speeding vehicle. The driver hauled on the anchors and even as the blue tyre smoke was billowing out from the locked wheels, I could hear the warrant officer start to scream abuse at him.

Still smiling to myself, I picked up my baggage and headed to the troop office.

The OC wasn't around, so the troop staff sergeant gave me the welcome speech and the mandatory laying down of the law.

The staffie was very old and spoke with a gravelled northern voice. "Right, Corporal Nugent, I'm Staff Stone. It's nice and relaxed here, but PT is Tuesdays and Thursdays at 0500 hours so don't get too pissed the night before. Also try to stay on top of your Malaria tablets. Your weekends should be free most of the time, but again try to stay out of the shit." He went on for sometime covering the admin side of troop life, then finished off his speech with: "Finally, don't forget that some blokes bring their wives over here for R and R. So, when you do go down to the pool, just remember, the last thing they want to see is some fucker climbing out of the water, in his ten-year-old Speedos, and his Black Forest gateaux spilling out all over the fucking place. Do you get my drift?"

"Sensible swimwear, Staff?"

"Egg-fucking-zactly!"

With his points made, Staff Stone summoned in the troop clerk who showed me to my block which, it turned out, was only a stone's throw from the offices themselves and was also next to the Commcen.

The troop took up three blocks, each building had four two-man bunks and two eight-man rooms. Each pit space was separated by lockers or strung up blankets. The blocks were joined together by a covered concrete walkway that offered protection from the elements during the monsoon season, although the corrugated iron roofs made rain sound like a machine gun and kept you awake. In between the blocks was a communal ablutions that also had an additional room for the cleaners to do the dhobi. The laundry actually entailed the age old method of thrashing clothing off an immovable object until the cloth became so ravaged that the stain disappeared. I know of one officer who had threatened to give a cleaner the sack if they didn't put his shirts inside a Tom's, before braying it off the rocks to reduce the amount of damage caused to his clothes during the process. I had also heard rumours that if you left 20 bucks on your bedside locker and pretended to be asleep, then the cleaners would nosh you off. However, one look at the toothless monster that was doing the cleaning, soon dispelled any such thoughts from my diseased mind. Still, I would always be wary of crossing the cleaners, because I had heard about one of the guys that had complained about the washer woman not removing a stain from the leg of his jeans. Her reaction had been to take the garment away for a few minutes, and then return with the dirty leg removed. So the bloke who had complained was left with a pair of jeans with one and a half legs, which he then had to convert to a pair of shorts.

The clerk showed me to my pit space, and when I'd put my kit in my locker, he told me that he had to take me to the radio sergeant. So I followed him again, but this time we went from the blocks – which I now noticed bordered a cricket pitch – and onto the main drag through camp. Our walk took us past the NAAFI and the cookhouse and the clerk pointed the buildings out to me as we approached them. Just at the point when the clerk identified the kitchens, a huge rat obligingly hopped out from a doorway and disappeared into the swill bins. It was the largest rat I had ever seen and its size was so noteworthy that I mentioned it to the clerk.

"Fuck me; did you see the size of that hairy fucker?"

"What, that rat?"

"Well, it was either a rat or an Irish wolfhound."

"Yeah, that's Bubonic Trev. He's kind of a permanent fixture around the kitchens."

I made a mental note to stay on Trev's good side.

Our walk took us over a small bridge and past a line of five, half-moon Nissen huts, on the left. The centre hut was the Sunspot Club which was the bar for 633, and was to be my spiritual home for the next few months –

well, that and Raoul's Rose garden. Once we had passed the huts, we took a dirt road off to right that led into a swamp, but it also went up to the transmitter site and the radio stores. The transmitter site consisted of a huge antenna field, and a building containing powerful radios that carried all of the high level traffic to the rest of the world. Attached to this building were the radio stores, where we found the sergeant to whom I had to report. The clerk introduced us and left.

The sergeant was called Jim Dale and he was a very relaxed individual. He told me that over the forthcoming months, he would try to rotate me between working in the camp radio room, helping him in the stores and doing the occasional stint up at the Cooma Cairn REBRO.

I was to start the first leg of this programme the next day in the force HQ radio room, but in the meantime Jim squared me away with the low-down on APC life. He gave me a once-over in the stores and, from what I could gather, working in there involved doing fuck all other than bumming around all day, drinking stims, eating sausage sandwiches and watching pornographic videos with the blokes who maintained the transmitters.

After an hour or so of lounging around, I picked up my bedding and unpacked my kit into my new pit space. Then, I headed to the cookhouse and joined the queue for scoff. I kept a watchful eye open for Bubonic Trev, lest he sneak up on me with evil intent on his rodent mind.

By the time I got back to the block, the guys who worked the day shift in the Commcen had knocked off and the accommodation was buzzing with blokes squaring their shit away for a night on the lash. I said 'hello' to some of my new room-mates, then got a shower.

Two of the guys, Tony Jenkins and Paul Whittaker, were decent enough blokes and waited for me, so as to make sure that I got down to the Sunspot alright.

When we arrived at the bar, we were already sweating, as the heat of the day had not fully died down. Somewhere in the distance a swingfog was blaring away, gassing all the horrible beasties that bite you to death in the night. The conversation on the walk down had just been about Holdfast, and how long I had been in theatre. The usual stuff really.

Opening the door to the Sunspot was like walking into the engine room of the Titanic – when she was afloat – because the heat and the noise were like a solid wall that instantaneously overwhelmed the senses. There must have been about 30 blokes packed into the small space. The bar itself was at the far end of the hut, and on the left was a group of about eight chaps, crammed around the dart-board and playing Mickey Mouse. There were a couple of circular ceiling fans slowly turning, but having negligible effect, other than to circulate the stifling air.

I followed Tony and Paul up to the bar and I ordered three cans of Charlie. Carlsberg was the preferred brew in Belize, and when that ran out we would drink Miller, and worst case scenario, if even the Miller went dry, we would be forced to consume Schlitz – which sounds like 'shits' for a good reason. There was, however, one beer worse than Schlitz, that only the die-hard drinkers would go near, and that was Belikin or Bellyache as it was known. It was fucking gipping stuff and was brewed from the local swamp water in which Bubonic Trev and his pals would regularly waz.

Halfway along the hut was a door leading outside to an atap (a kind of palm frond lean-to) where there were even more blokes drinking. The atap was cooler and less confined than the bar, but the mozzies and sandflies that frequented it were hell-bent on eating you alive. Every so often, one of people drinking outside would slap themselves and shout: "You fucking bastard!" Then examine the splash of blood left by the dead insect.

Despite the trauma of the blood suckers, we decided to drink in the atap. We were standing next to the palm frond wall, and over on the other side of the floor was a throne made from sandbags. I asked Paul as to what it was used for, and he replied: “Gazomes, mate.”

“What’s a gazome then?”

“It’s just a piss up for when someone goes home. Every Friday night before people fly out on the Wednesday, we have a gazome. Basically they just sit on the throne wearing a ceremonial sombrero, and we tell stories about all the knobbish things they’ve done since they arrived. After each story we lob cans at the poor fucker in the chair. If he’s been a real dick, then the odd full one goes in for good measure. It’s a good crack, Eddy, and we also have some other weekly awards, but you’ll see those later, mate.”

As the night progressed, we got steadily drunker and drunker. I think you get pissed quicker in the tropics, because you sweat a lot and are therefore dehydrated, not to mention very thirsty and prone to drinking more. Also you have less blood to dilute the booze because all the shitbag mosquitoes have drained you dry.

At half past ten that night, Paul was in the middle of an extremely animated anecdote that had us in stitches. I can’t remember the exact details, but it was describing a game called ‘Slap Cock Treacle Belly’, the rudimentary rules of which involved lying on your back naked, smearing jam on your stomach, then getting wood and forcing your panhandle down away from your body. You then stay in this position, and when a fly lands on the jam, you let your erection go, and it comes flying up at Mach 3 to slap on your belly. If you’ve got it right, then the impact from the inbound woody will kill the fly and that constitutes one point. Whoever kills the most flies by this method, wins. The punch line was about one of the participants accidentally releasing his erection attack on to some strange jungle wasp, and being bedded down for a week with a poisoned knob. As Paul delivered the final line, Tony leant against the atap wall, with his arm outstretched, and disappeared as if sucked into a time portal. What had happened was – because the wall was only made from overlaid palm leaves – when Tony put his weight against them, they parted to let him by and once he had fallen through, the leaves closed up behind him, thus giving the appearance of him vanishing. A minute or so later, Tony came back into the bar, but this time he reeked of shit and was covered in some ghastly green slime. On enquiring as to his current state of disrepair, he told us that on the other side of the wall was a monsoon drain that he had landed in, hence him being smeared in cack. Tony was a good sport about the whole thing, and he stayed on the piss for the rest of the night without going for a shower. Although we did encourage him not to leave, because it kept the flies away from the rest of us.

I hate waking up with a hangover in a hot environment, as the heat makes my mouth taste even worse than normal and only serves to magnify my suffering. Still, I got up, had a shower, shimfed like a bitch for five minutes about the insect bites that had befallen me in the night, then headed off to the Force HQ radio room.

My first shift in the radio room was done alongside another lance-jack called Nick 'Kate' Bush. Kate was a PTI, but on this tour he just did normal trade work, like the rest of the guys. I got on with Kate really well and he told me that although 'Kate' was the most common name that people called him, he was also subjected to being named after every conceivable expression for the female reproductive organs – all being derived from 'Bush', obviously.

Although I was familiar with all of the kit that was used in the radio room, I did the first shift with Kate, just to learn the in-house procedures that were adopted in the HQ, for the processing and documentation of official signals/messages etc. Kate also briefed me up on the workings within the HQ, and told me that most of my dealings would solely be done with the duty officer who was known as the watchkeeper. There would only be one watchkeeper working at any one time, and the duty was spread between four officers from various units. Three of the four watchkeepers were very quiet, nondescript people, who would only venture into the dingy backwaters of the radio room when work necessitated it. The last one, however, was a total rocket polisher. He was called Captain Peterson-Smythe and he was a Royal Artillery officer, on detachment for four months from Germany. He didn't earn the title of Knob because he fucked us around, in fact – discipline wise – he was no worse than any of the other watchkeepers. No, he scored such high marks on the 'twatometer' because every time he got bored, he would just come into the radio room and start meddling with things beyond his knowledge, or just talk out of his arse and distract the guy on shift from doing his work.

I remember one evening during a particularly savage tropical storm, when the radio networks were in a shit state, and I was trying to engineer in the links for the daily sitreps. Just in the middle of everything going tits-up, Peterson-Smythe strolled in, put his hands on his hips, and said:

"Ah, Nugent. Do you know what I miss about Germany the most?"

I responded in a flustered manner amidst flashing red lights and wailing alarms: "No, Sir. What would that be then?"

"Nightclubs, Nugent. NIGHTCLUBS! I am a superlative dancer you know!" To emphasise his point, the watchkeeper then broke into one of the worst displays of dancing I have ever seen. He clapped his hands together, stuck his arse out, then started doing a very bad version of the twist, interspersed with erratic hand gestures and more clapping. All the time, he had a big happy smile on his face, and occasionally he would close his eyes, whilst imagining he was back in some boxhead disco. Suddenly, he went from this devil-may-care persona, into a bolt-upright, serious stance and then embarked on an incredibly bad routine of robotics dancing. To cap it all, when he had finished, he flicked his hair back, exhaled deeply, then let out an unnecessarily loud “Woooooooo!” And shook off his limbs in a ‘post-workout warm-down’ fashion. The only way he could have bettered it was to have attempted a half-hearted karate kick, and put his back out in the process.

I don’t know what he was dancing to, but the only musical accompaniment for his entire routine was the chugging of the teleprinter, the warning beeps from the radios and my swearing at the poor communications conditions. Oh yeah, there was the occasional crash of thunder as well. It didn’t stop there though, he was obviously still bored, so he sat down in a chair next to me and looked around for something to do. At the time, I was standing over the teleprinter, watching what looked like the first successful message of the night come through. Then, driven by the mundane curiosity of a bored ape, and at the most inopportune moment possible, the watchkeeper leant across and said: “Oh, what does this do?” And unplugged the printer’s power cable. To my horror, the three-quarters complete message that I had just spent the last hour trying to get in, just stopped printing out, and went dead. I jerked upright, then in a fit of rage, smashed both fists down onto the printer and roared: “WHAT THE FUCK! YOU FUCKING CUNT!” at the machine.

I looked around and Peterson-Smythe was gazing up at me like a scared rabbit, stunned by my insane outburst. In his hand was the printer lead and he stuttered: “Er, I think this may have come loose.”

I took the lead from his hand, plugged it back into the printer, then got onto the engineering network and said, in a voice leaden with anger: “Hello, Hotel Three Zero.

Hello Hotel Three Zero. This is Zero. Retransmit your last on the other means. I say again, re-transmit your last on the other means. Over."

When the reply came, it was obvious that the bloke on the other end was pissed-off, and thought that I had fucked up in some way. He said: "Roger that, Zero. Sending now. Out." But what he actually meant was: "YOU FUCKING WANKER!"

Whilst this was going on, the watchkeeper was staring up at the ceiling as if nothing had happened. However, once the printer leapt back into life, and the message starting coming through again, he too became more animated. As I was racing between each bit of kit to make sure that they were still 'all green', Peterson-Smythe piped up with renewed enthusiasm: "Did I tell you about my car, Nugent?" I didn't reply as all my attention was on the incoming message. Still, he carried on regardless.

"Ah yes, she's a real beauty, I can tell you. Peugeot 205, GTI, 1.9!" Then, whilst still sitting down, he started making engine noises, and re-enacting driving motions, complete with steering wheel, gear stick and foot pedals. He looked like an escaped mental patient, although – I have to give him his dues – the noises were perfectly in time with the motions. For example:

"Brrrrrrrrrrrrrrrrrrmmmmmmmmmmmmmmmmmm," gear change, "brrm brrm brrrrrrrrrrrrrrrrrrrm." I noted the double-clutch in there, and he even made screeching tyre noises when he turned the invisible steering wheel. This went on for about three minutes, and it was quite painful to behold. Eventually, he was snapped out of his driving experience, when the final message came through in its entirety, and I handed it to him and said with a sigh.

"There you go, Sir. These are the patrol sitreps for the last 24 hours."

By the grace of God he didn't unwind the window to receive them, as that would have finished me off.

Instead, he just cleared his throat, stood up, and in his best business-like voice said: ”Oh, ah yes. Well done, Nugent. Carry on.”

With that, he disappeared back into his office, no doubt to fall asleep. After all, high speed driving is hard work.

The only time Peterson-Smythe ever properly gripped me was when I was, in fact, completely innocent. I remember it well, as I had just taken over shift from Kate. As soon as Kate left, Peterson-Smythe came striding into the radio room in his best attempt at an intimidating manner. Before I could say anything, he said, in an angry tone, “Ah, Nugent, why have you been boiling your handkerchief in my kettle?”

My brow furrowed in confusion and I thought to myself “Fucking hell, he’s finally gone mad.” But all I said was: “I’m sorry, Sir. I don’t know what you mean; I haven’t even got a handkerchief.”

“Well, when I commented to Lance-Corporal Bush about the water in my tea tasting off, he reliably informed me that YOU have been boiling your handkerchief in my kettle!”

I thought “Kate, you fucking bastard!” Because I knew that when the watchkeeper was asleep, Kate used to boil eggs in the kettle to make himself a snack on night shift, and here he was blaming it on me, the fucker! Still, I could see the funny side and I didn’t want to get Kate in any shit, so I just said that there must have been some kind of misunderstanding. So Peterson-Smythe just made some comment about ‘Don’t let it happen again’. And left me in peace for a change.

Come the first Friday in APC, I had a double of first experiences. There was my first gazome attendance in the Sunspot, and my first night out in BC.

The night started off as per normal with drinks in the troop bar. Then the troop OC called out above the noise: “Right, gents. We’ll get straight into it. Let’s have our first nomination for ‘Chopper of the Week’.”

This award went to the person who had done the biggest fuck-up during the week. Various people put forward a candidate with a reason for the nomination. The winner would then be decided by the crowd, and whoever got the most votes would win. The award took the form of a broom handle with 'I am a Chopper' written on it, and on the end of the piece of wood was a cardboard cut-out, that was shaped and painted to look like an axe head. Finally, a piece of string was attached to the shaft, in a manner that acted as a sling, and thus enabled it to be worn across the back. So, to all intents and purposes, it looked like a big axe. The main humiliation, however, was that the newly crowned Chopper had to wear his prize for the rest of the night.

The other award was the 'Brown Bottle'. This was decided in exactly the same manner as the Chopper award, although it went to the person who had done the best act of drunken aggression the previous week. The prize for this was a four-foot-high, inflatable bottle of Newcastle Brown Ale, or Dog.

That night, the Chopper award went to one of the Commcen wallahs who had fucked up in work. That award was quite uneventful, but the Brown Bottle was a different matter indeed.

The winner of that night's Brown Bottle was a driver called 'Scouse' Richards. Scouse had got pissed the Saturday night before, and pretty much offered out all the blokes in the bar, at the same time.

This in itself was funny, but when his name was called out as the winner of the Brown Bottle, the already inebriated Scouse became massively indignant, then lurched forward and shouted: "You what! Yous' can all fuck off, yous' cunts! I don't get gobby when I'm pissed! And if you've got a problem with it, you can fuckin' step outside for a chat! Alright?"

He then bounced off a few walls, and staggered out of the hut whilst shouting abuse at invisible objects and shaking his fist at everything in general. All of this was to the raucous laughter of everyone else in the Sunspot.

I didn't know whose gazome it was, but nevertheless, I joined in the canning of the poor chap, along with everyone else. It all passed off just as the guys had explained it would, on my arrival. All, that is, except for the fact that the bloke leaving had to drink a yard of ale. This was one point of which Paul had neglected to inform me. The stories about the chap who was leaving all had a common theme; he had either been a drunken idiot or a deranged sex pest. The one story that stuck in my mind was that he had got pissed in San Ig, then staggered around town looking for a place to lay his head. He eventually broke into the bedding store of one of the few hotels, and on finding a stash of sheets and pillows, he immediately fell into a deep sleep. The chirping of the birds woke him up early, well, that and the vile stench from his grand slam, that had ruined the week's worth of bedding on which he'd slept. I don't know from where he had got a pen and paper, but he left a note inscribed with just one word, 'Sorry', on the pile of soiled linen. Then he did a runner.

After the gazome, we all stayed in the bar for a few more hours, and the sloppies did their normal Friday night thing of bringing down some chilli con carne and rice. Finally, there was a mass exodus into town. We went out through the guardroom, and next to the booking out sheet was a big tray of Johnnies. Everyone grabbed a slack handful, in the vain hope that they might actually get some sex for free later on. But if that didn't happen, then the condoms could always be put in storage for a rainy day, and that special treat of a 'posh wank'. We waited outside camp for the next Batty's bus, and as we stood there, Scouse Richards dropped a load of coins and rubbers onto the deck. When Scouse bent down to pick up his belongings, Kate nudged me with his elbow, whilst pointing at Scouse's arse, then shook his head and said: “Look at the state of that catcher’s mitt. He ain’t gonna make it.”

Scouse heard this, then turned to everyone and challenged us all to a fight, thereby ensuring his nomination for the following week’s Brown Bottle.

The Batty’s bus eventually rolled up, and we all piled on board. The bus was called ‘Batty’s’ solely because that was the name of the company that ran them, and it had nothing to do with homosexuality. Batty’s buses did more than just shuttle runs to and fro between APC and BC, they also did trips up to Chetumal in Mexico, and guys from the troop would regularly cross the border for a weekend on the razz.

The rickety bus clattered over an old bridge and chugged past a single-storey building that had its front illuminated. The picture on the house front was of a peacock and a peahen ‘having it off’. Kate pointed to it, then said to me in an exaggerated Mexican accent: “That’s Raoul’s hombre. Numero uno fuck shop; we’ll have us a nightcap in there later on, dude!”

The lights of Raoul’s faded into the distance and after about 15 minutes, we were pulling up in the centre of Belize City. The bus stopped near a cast-iron swingbridge, and about ten blokes from the troop took it upon themselves to inform me that it was the bridge used in the film ‘The Dogs of War’. Then, to make their point, some of them started running down the road making machine gun noises, whilst the others got into an argument about who played the best nutter, Christopher Walken, or Robert De Niro. Eventually Tony Jenkins tried to draw me into the discussion, on to his side of course.

“What do you reckon, Eddy? It’s gotta be Bob hasn’t it, eh?” He then pulled out an imaginary pistol as fast as he could and tried to look all mad, whilst badly reciting ‘Taxi Driver’.

“Are you talking to me? Well there ain’t nobody else here!” He looked over his shoulder and then back to his invisible assailant. "Are you fucking talking to me? Yeah, I got you, you shit heel!"

Tony had stopped to do his little number, and he looked like a right mentalist, stood there in the middle of the street by himself, re-enacting the scene. By the time he snapped back into the reality, we were halfway down the street. So he ran after us to catch up, and shouted: "Oi, wait for me, you fucking jack bastards!"

When Tony drew level, Kate had already put across the 'Walken case'.

"Listen, Eddy. It's got to be Chris, because let's face it, he is actually mad in real life!"

Both Kate and Tony then asked in unison for my decision, as if it would bury the subject forever. So I scratched my chin in a thoughtful manner for a bit, and then gave my decision on who was the greatest ever big screen psycho.

"Well, gents, after much deliberation, I can say that, without a shadow of a doubt, the ultimate nutter is" …theatrical pause… "Big Ken Williams."

"Who the fuck's Big Ken Williams?" asked Tony.

"You know, Kenneth Williams! That crazy cat off the Carry On films."

They called me a cunt, and I received a few dead arms for my troubles.

By the time the pain had subsided, we were walking up some steps to a bar, the real name of which I still don't know to this day. But because it was the first port of call when in town, and also it was situated on the first floor, it was always known as either 'the Upstairs NAAFI' or 'the Upstairs Gadaffi'.

It was a nice enough place, which served cold beer and played punta-rock; one of the Donkey trilogy songs was playing, and Kate got the beers in. We filtered out of the bar area and onto a balcony that overlooked the street. Underneath us was the typical street life of Belize City; there were food vendors, the occasional shoeshine boys and a constant stream of worse-for-wear soldiers.

We stayed in the Upstairs NAAFI for several beers, then made our way to the Hard Rock Café. A few months later, the Upstairs NAAFI had to put chicken wire over the balcony. This was due to a spate of soldiers getting drunk and ending up going head-first over the railings, and into the street.

I don't think the Hard Rock was a bona fide member of the bar chain, but who cares; it certainly was the best bar in BC. It had a good sized bar and dance floor, not to mention a roof garden that was ideal for cooling off whilst waiting for your raging panhandle to subside, after a sweaty arse-grinding dance with a local lass. When on the dance floor, it was like a bigger, modern version of the Blue Angel. The night became a mixed memory of flashing lights, punta-rock and Appleton's 151 proof death rum.

Kate found me at about two in the morning. I was wobbed-out in a chair, my clothes soaking in Belikin and sweat. It took him over five minutes to get me compos mentis enough to move, but once awake my mind turned to food. We staggered down the stairs and out into the street. The air was still warm and wet, so it offered no respite from the heat of the club.

We were heading back up to the swingbridge to pick up a taxi, when a mouth-watering smell of food, cooked over an open fire, hit my nostrils. I followed the aroma, running on culinary auto-pilot, and soon I was standing in front of a big, brightly dressed Afro-Caribbean woman. At her feet was a large open fire and suspended over it were two large, steaming pots. She greeted me with a big smile – the kind that you can't do anything about, other than to respond to in kind, and I said: "Hello, what are in the pots?"

She pointed at the first and said "Rice and pea," then pointing to the next one, she continued "an' chicken."

It smelt and sounded like the answer to my prayers, and to entice me further, she lifted the lids to the pots for me to inspect her wares. The rice and peas looked lovely, pure fluffy white rice, shot through with sweet, bright green peas. This was getting better and better, and I was just starting to fish out a fistful of crumpled Belizean dollars from my pocket to buy some food, when I looked into the last pot. At first I couldn't make out any details of its contents, due to the steam that was billowing out. But when the clouds cleared, I could see a strange bubbling grey fluid. It didn't look like there was any chicken in there, but then a piece of meat broke the surface. The piece of meat in question was actually a whole chicken, complete with head, feet, half its feathers and a neck like Deirdre Barlow. The sight of the half-cooked fowl instantly turned me off the idea of food and I told the woman that I wouldn't bother with any food tonight, but thanks anyway. I felt like a twat for this, but there was no way I could bring myself to eat the stuff that I had just seen. After all, it wasn't as if I was starving. Kate had been standing on the sidelines during all these goings on, and he was laughing. In the taxi, he informed me that he had done exactly the same thing before, which assuaged my guilt a bit.

I was tied up in my thoughts, when the taxi pulled to a halt. I got out, paid the driver, Kate got out of the other door, and I turned to the guardroom to head back to my scratcher. But in front of me was not the entrance to camp, but the floodlit mural wall of Raoul's Rose Garden. So, this was it – the famous Raoul's.

There was an old Rasta standing by the door; he had a big white beard and wore only a pair of jeans. Kate gave him a dollar, and suggested I did the same. I did as Kate said, and as we were entering, he explained to me that Raoul's was out of bounds at the time, due to the new MO refusing to check the working girls, on moral grounds. So, by paying the old guy on the door, we were ensuring that he would come in and warn us at the first sign of the monkeys.

On entering Raoul's, I was treated to a blast of 'Me Donkey Want Water'.

Standing there in the doorway, I could see that the place was broken up into two parts. It was split down the middle by a four-foot-high wall that ran almost from the main door and went down the full length of the room, to another door in the back wall. This back door led to the rooms where the girls plied their trade, and was the only place where the monkeys were not allowed.

The left portion of the place had a few steps going up to a raised bar area. This part of the building was better lit than the rest, and there was an L-shaped bar where we would do our drinking. There was a long row of tables up against the central partition, and they went all the way to the back door, but between the last table and door was another low wall. The right-hand half of the room was on the same level as the entrance and was predominantly used as a dance floor, but it too had a line of tables and chairs that were lined up along the parting wall. Access to the back rooms could only be made from this right-hand side of the building. So if you were drinking in the bar on the left, when the monkeys raided, you would have to try to run round to the dance floor, to gain access to the relative safety of the back rooms. Unfortunately this would mean going past the entrance and into the evil clutches of the law. And that is why 'The Grand National' was born. The National was so named due to its similarity to the famous race, in that it involved running over many table jumps, to escape getting booked. It was run on an irregular basis, in fact it was done purely on the whim of whenever the monkeys had nothing better to do, and decided to grip a few lads for having some fun.

I was lucky enough to enter my first Grand National that night. I was drinking with Kate and Tony at the bar, and talking to a few girls, when the old Rasta poked his head into the room and shouted: "RMP, RMP, RMP!"

Suddenly, everyone did a bomb-burst. It was like lifting a rock to expose the insects beneath and watching them scatter for cover. All the guys that were on the right-hand/dance floor side, were in the back rooms before the monkeys could even de-bus from their Rover. But us dudes that were pissing it up in the bar on the left were shit out of luck. One of the blokes, who I didn't know, tried to get past the entrance, but a couple of monkeys piled in through the door and tackled him before he could reach safety. The rest of us just took to our heels, and had it away over the tables, heading for the sanctuary of the back. There was a horde of us, running three-abreast and charging over the table jumps. A few blokes went down, and there was even a faller at the first, but we didn't look back to check on their fate.

I remember my heart pounding and I was giggling insanely, it was like being a kid and getting chased by an irate homeowner, during a game of knock-door-run. Kate and Tony were the same, and we spurred each other on, focusing on the far door. A couple of monkeys were running along the dance floor to our right, trying to intercept us at the finishing post. Seeing them in my peripheral vision just drove me on even harder, and I was like a top-fuel dragster running on Appleton's Methanol. As we approached the final hurdle of the end wall, I pulled ahead of Kate, and leapt the obstacle in a single bound. Then I was through the door, and holding it open for the herd of laughing, sweating drunkards who piled in after me. Once all the runners were through, I slammed the door, just as a monkey started hammering on it like a nutter. Kate came back, pressed his mouth against the door and half shouted/half laughed: "FUCK OFF, YOU MONKEY SHIT DICK BASTARDS!"

I should imagine the coppers must have been going ape-shit on the other side of the door, but I was too busy laughing to notice. I turned to Kate and he said: "Fucking hell, Eddy, I thought I was going to be a faller at Becher's Brook, back there!"

"What's Becher's Brook?"

"The last wall, mate! It can be a killer, but you were over the fucker like Spring-Heeled Jack."

"Aye, well I could see the bastards coming around on the dance floor, and I thought we were bang to rights!"

My conversation with Kate was interrupted by a hand touching my shoulder, and I turned around to come face to face with a huge pair of tits. The woman standing in front of me was enormous; she was over six feet tall, heavily set and had breasts of biblical proportions. Her skin was extremely dark, and she spoke with a deep husky voice: "Hey, new bwoy!"

"Er, hello." I ventured in a pathetic tone, then – feeling slightly intimidated – I shook her hand as if greeting another man.

She looked down quizzically at my hand, then up to my face, and burst out laughing. It was a gravelly but hearty laugh, and I couldn't help but laugh myself. Kate heard this, and turned to see what was happening. When he saw the big woman, he said: "Hey, alright there, Flo. How are you doing?"

Flo turned to Kate.

"Ha, Ha, Katie me bwoy! What ya doin' 'ere? Are ya wantin' some fun?"

"You know what, Flo. I think I do!" grinned Kate.

She turned to me and grabbed my packet in her large hand.

"An' what about ya likkle friend?" she chuckled.

Kate then added: "What do you reckon, Eddy, two's up old boy?"

This was a strange situation for me, I had never done anything like a spit roast, but I suppose it would be something to tell the grandkids. So I agreed.

Flo led Kate and me into her room and, if I am to be totally honest, I was shitting myself. Just before we crossed the threshold, Flo turned to us, and on seeing the look on my face, she said: "Now don't you be worryin' me likkle Eddy. I is gone give you me special 'wax treatment'."

Then that was it; we were in there for about an hour, and Flo took Kate and me to the cleaners. I think she used the term 'wax treatment', because she employed all manner of strange oils and sticky substances to aid the proceedings. However, I personally think it was more aptly named, because when she finished me off, I swear the fucking wax shot out of my ears!

When we left, I was walking like a 95-year-old with Parkinson's disease. Don't get me wrong, I'm not belittling the condition, but it is the only way to describe the state that I was in. It was a good job the monkeys weren't waiting for us, because there is no way that I could have managed another Grand National.

Kate helped me into the taxi, and we made for camp.

It must have been about five in the morning when I eventually got into my scratcher. The walk from the guardroom to the block had been a nightmare. We had made the mistake of taking the drunken shortcut directly across the cricket pitch, instead of following the road and paths to our destination. The results of doing this were to disturb every sleeping mosquito and biting, buzzy thing within a 400-metre radius. Even though I was munched to death, I still flaked out within seconds, as my exhaustion and the drink took a heavy toll.

I woke up at lunchtime on the Saturday, and made tracks for the Sunspot, stopping off for a stim on the way. Most of the blokes were in there, including Kate and he was talking to a Geordie guy, who was visibly drunk and being very loud. As I approached, Kate saw my bedraggled state, and said: "Fucking hell, Eddy. Look at the state of you. I was just telling Geordie here about last night."

"Oh don't, mate," I whinged, "I tell you what, it was like being in a wrestling match. I'm aching like fuck this morning. That Flo really did a number on us."

Geordie burst out laughing. "Fookan' hell, Kate, ye never telt us ye went wi' Orinoco Flo last neet!"

When he said Orinoco Flo, it actually came out as 'Ori-nur-kur Fleur'.

Kate interjected: "Don't listen to him, Eddy. He's only spouting off, because every time he goes into Raoul's, he wakes up in the morning, and finds out that the girls have rolled him onto the floor, and tied the sheet around him like a giant nappy because he's a bed lagger."

Geordie defended his honour: "Haway and shite, ye bastad!"

Kate continued: "Don't get shirty with me, just because your scratcher smells of sugar puffs!" He then turned to me and said: "I've got to tell you, Eddy. When Geordie came over here, he brought across a lightweight civvie doss-bag liner. It was this bright blue thing, and he forgot to give it a wash before he used it. Anyway, every night that he got lashed, he ended up wazzing the bed. Not too bad you might think, but whenever this happened, the colour in the bag ran, and he would end up with big blue streaks all over him. Honestly, mate, he looked like some mad Celtic warrior in his war paint."

A few years later, I went to see 'Braveheart' at the flicks, and I couldn't help but think of William Wallace as a medieval splashdown expert.

The bar only had Schlitz left, but I was in dire need of some hair of the dog, so I fired the first few down as fast as I could manage, just to get myself 'back in the zone'. The 'zone' in question being the place where all the burbling drunks hang out. So within a short time I was in the swing of things again. That afternoon, one of telemechs – the guys who fixed the phones – called Dusty Miller, entertained the bar with his amazing 'stop the ceiling fans with his head' trick. It was quite a thing to behold. Dusty would crouch on a table beneath a ceiling fan that was spinning at full speed. He would then stand up and his bonce would gradually go up into the fan and eventually stop the blades. It took about three or four good smacks before it worked, and each time the fan struck his skull, a dull thud would echo around the bar. But, nevertheless, he pulled it out of the bag, and the spinning blades eventually came to a halt against his head. Then Dusty would stand there victorious, his arms aloft, his head in the fan and the electric motor whirring away as it fought against the obstacle that was preventing its progress.

After a few games of Mickey Mouse at the dartboard, we retired outside to the atap, and were instantly overcome by a vile smell. The ghastly aroma was coming from the chilli that the sloppies had brought down the night before, for the gazome. As a general rule, the food containers were returned to the cookhouse the same night as they were delivered to the bar. So obviously, the duty slop-jockey from Friday night had neglected his duties and not picked them up. The importance of the container collection was now manifestly obvious by the unholy stench seeping out from the insect infested chilli. We reacted to the whiff, as would anybody else, by swearing a lot and accusing each other of farting. When Dusty came outside, he was still on an adulation driven high from the fan stunt, so on detecting the rancid food, he headed for it without a second's delay. Then he delved his hand into the seething goo and took a big bite. He turned to us smiling and his face was smeared in the vile substance. He looked like a child that had just licked the cake bowl clean, but the difference was, that he had various grubs and other small animals dropping out of his mouth. Some of us retched at the sight and we all declared him to be 'a very bad man'.

After that first weekend, I was into the swing of things pretty quickly, although the early PT was a bit unpleasant, and it was made doubly so when conducted in a haze of rum fumes from the night before. PT would either take the form of circuit training on the cricket pitch, or a run outside of camp. Like anything, these options had their pros and cons. The downside to circuit training was the previously mentioned mozzie problem. But the worst aspect of going for a run was negotiating the Sweet Water canal stench on the return leg to camp. The Sweet Water ran under the road that led into and out of camp, so it had to be crossed when leaving and coming back on a run. The early hour at which PT was conducted meant that when running out, the Sweet Water was dormant and had not yet started to smell. However, by the time we were coming back, the sun had started to gather some of its savage heat and was warming the canal until it was radiating its terrible gases. Running through a cloud that reeks of rotting eggs is bad enough, but combined with the fact that it was at the end of the session when we were all ballbagged, it caused a mass choking and vomming session. It was most unpleasant.

I spent the next month and a half in the Force HQ radio room, and once into the routine, life passed by very quickly. At one point, Kate managed to source a buckshee mini-grill, so the hum drum of sending messages and reading copies of *Club* and *Men Only* was now broken up by making a sausage sarnie. I had to make a really conscious effort not to become a complete porker, because knocking up a sandwich was a good way to kill time during the quiet hours. On night shift, I was often faced with the dilemma of: 'Shall I have another butty, or my fifth thrap of the evening instead?'

If the shift pattern meant that I had a free weekend, then I would sometimes go out to Caye Caulker with some of the other blokes. With Belize having the second largest barrier reef in the world, this meant that it also had many of these sandy Cayes, and they really were like the idyllic islands from the Bounty adverts.

To get out to the Cayes, we would get the bus into BC, then hop onto a water taxi, which in turn took us out to our destination. The boat journey took about half an hour and the waters over which the powerful speedboats travelled, were very shallow.

Caye Caulker was split into two islands. One was an unpopulated mangrove swamp, and the other was a sandy piece of land, where all the tourists went, and where the inhabitants lived. The two islands were separated by a narrow channel of water, which was only about 20 yards across. This channel was where most people congregated. However, the narrow width of the water created a very strong current and, more often than not, a sunburnt British soldier, under the influence of rum punch, was seen being swept out to sea. They would always make it back to the shore though, and over the last 20 metres of the return swim, they were so bedraggled they took on the appearance of a wire-haired Jack Russell, frantically paddling to the bank of a canal.

When the day was coming to an end, we would all pile on board the water taxis, which – in turn – would speed us back to BC. On the few occasions that I visited Caulker, all of the return journeys were delayed, and always by one bloke or another diving off the boats as they were going at full lick. It looked very spectacular, but it meant that the boat would have to turn round and pick the diver up. Almost all of the guys who did the stunt said that it was a really bad idea, and that bruised ribs, and a 40 mph sea water enema, were by no means the best way to end the day.

As Jim Dale had said before, after a month or so I moved from the radio room to the stores up at the transmitter site; it was the ultimate doss! In fact, if anything, it was too quiet. In the month and a half that I was in the stores, I painted one set of shelves, issued one backpack radio to the infantry lads, drank 200 stims, ate 90 sausage sandwiches and watched 60 pornographic videos. Also, to relieve the boredom, I had on average, about one stone fight a week with the technicians.

When we weren't watching art, we would either listen to BFBS, or watch Belize TV. BFBS had normal Forces radio piped in, but sometimes they would have in-theatre Forces personnel doing the radio shows. It wasn't a bad idea, but every now and then one of resident infantry lads would get a slot and wreak havoc.

An example that springs to mind was when one of the Harrier sites had an incredibly vicious parrot called Moriarty, who had a penchant for biting visitors. This problem eventually reached boiling point, when the infantry DJ put it to public vote over the airwaves, as to what should happen to Moriarty. He crossed the line, when he suggested on air that the parrot should be passed through a spinning Harrier turbine, and that whatever came out of the exhausts should be shoved up the Garrison Sergeant-Major's arse. The one constant on BFBS at that time was that every Wednesday, as soon as the VC10 touched down, the radio would start to play 'Welcome to the Jungle' by Guns 'n' Roses.

Belize TV was just as entertaining. When they ran out of adverts and programmes, the screen would take on the appearance of Teletext, then 'The Death March' would start playing. To finish things off, the obituaries would scroll up the screen. Belize TV's trump card was a presenter called Steve Lovell. Steve was a nice guy, but he constantly looked confused, and this always gave an entertaining air to his shows. He normally did the news, and if he wasn't reading the headlines, he would be out and about doing features. There was one particular article by Steve that stuck out from the rest. He was on the streets of Belmopan covering a story about some recent floods. He was knocking on doors in the affected area and getting the opinions of the residents. He knocked on one door, then after about five minutes, a middle-aged Rasta came to the door, and just stood there in a pair of ragged denim jeans. Steve immediately jumped into action.

"So tell me, what 'appened 'ere?"

The Rasta gestured to the road. "Well, me woke up dis mornin' and dair was water in de street."

"So what did you do?"

The Rasta looked at Steve as if he was stupid, then sucked his teeth and replied: "Me went back to bed."

I was still supposed to be in the stores when Christmas came around, but Jim had pretty much closed shop for two weeks beforehand, so, realistically speaking, I had been on the lash continuously over that period.

I didn't eat anything on Christmas Day, and did nothing but drink and take part in a volley ball match that was conducted in torrential rain. The volley ball pitch bore many similarities to the fields of Glastonbury, and we were covered in mud from head to toe, although the rain was coming down so hard, that it didn't take to long to get clean again.

Soon we heard that there had been some kind of accident; it reportedly involved the bloke who caught all the beasties on camp that found their way into people's rooms and boots. The rumours were soon confirmed, by an appeal being sent out over BFBS, for all sober people of blood group O to report to the Med Centre. After a bit of sniffing around and rumour mongering, the truth came out. The snake catcher had always kept a live fer-de-lance, caged, in his office. The reason for this was so that anybody could go along and get an idea of what they looked like, in case of a wild encounter in the future. On that Christmas Day, the snake bloke had come bouncing into his office after a skin full of Bellyache, then on seeing the snake he suddenly felt all friendly towards it. So in a momentary lapse of thought, he lifted the lid to the glass cage and mumbled: "Here you go, mate. Get that down ya. I tell ya what, you're alright you are!" Then to finalise his new friendship, he poured beer over the snake's head. I guess the snake didn't like Belikin, because it bit the guy several times and he had to be cas-evac'd to Miami. The call for blood over the radio had been to try to get some fresh claret into him, before the flight across the Gulf of Mexico.

Between Christmas and New Year, the troop staffie gripped me in the bar, and informed me that I would be going back to Holdfast, because they had finally been able to get a replacement for the maniac whose departure from theatre had brought me to APC. So, it came to pass that in the death throes of 1990, I found myself Holdfast-bound again on the Western Highway.

It was just after lunchtime when I got back in through the gates. Derek was waiting for me, and brought me up to speed on news and events round the camp. It didn't take more than a couple of minutes, because nothing had been going on – just the relentless drudgery of swimming, drinking, volleyball, sunbathing, drinking and more swimming. It being New Year's Eve, the camp was in a buzzing mood, with everyone neglecting their minuscule workloads completely. After ditching my bags, we quickly joined the party, which had started in the NAAFI. The only real decision we had to make was which bar to be in at midnight, to ring in the New Year. We plumped for the Artillery Bar. 29 Commando had completed their tour in November and had been replaced by another battery of equally deranged bomb-slingers. They had decided to celebrate the British New Year at 6pm and then work their way across the time zones until midnight. It was very weird. In the five minutes preceding each hour, everyone in the bar would whip themselves up into a frenzy, before commencing the ten second countdown with religious fervour. As the hours went by and we rang in the New Year for our friends in Iceland, South Georgia and Newfoundland, the enthusiasm was undiminished and each rendition of Auld Lang Syne grew louder than the last. Most of us were quite plastered by 11 o'clock, and some blokes actually got quite tearful whilst toasting the Puerto Ricans. I survived up until the Belizean New Year, but had to be carried to bed and missed the Mexican toast at 1am. Derek told me the next morning in the NAAFI, that after celebrating the arrival of 1991 with the Pitcairn Islanders at 3am, a big brawl started when nobody could agree whether Hawaii was next. As with all squaddie brawls, extreme drunkenness ensured that no real damage was done before it dissolved into a hug-fest of sobbing idiots.

On January the second, I got another surprise when I was asked to take out one of the jungle patrols. The Glosters lance-corporal who was supposed to be the patrol leader, had an eye infection and was confined to camp. I quite fancied it, so agreed immediately. The patrol would consist of myself and three privates from the Glosters. In addition, two NCOs from the BDF would accompany us, to assist in translation and to offer local knowledge.

We were all waiting by the helipad at 7am the next morning. We were then taken, by Puma, to a predesignated grid reference and dropped off. Our job was, over the next seven days, to make our way to another agreed location, whilst patrolling in the unlikely hope that we would encounter and apprehend drug-smugglers from Guatemala. The secondary purpose of the patrol was to talk to people in the villages as we went along, to gather any useful information about smuggling activity in the area. Our seven-day stint was incredibly interesting and enjoyable. As expected, we never came across any drug-smugglers. Each night we would harbour up near one of the villages and go to sleep. The next day, we'd visit the village, and, with the aid of the BDF guys, speak to the Primero and Secundo of the settlement, who were the mayor and his sidekick. They were polite to a fault, and extremely affable. We had a big medkit with us. It was supposed to be for our use only, but we ignored that instruction and dished it out to whoever needed it. None of us were medics, but cleaning up parang cuts and dishing out antiseptic was straightforward enough. We would usually swap a bit of food with the local women. They made tasty, floury tortillas which we could get for a couple of our tins. Of course, the kids in the villages found us interesting and always hung around whenever we stopped to talk to someone. We were happy to let them relieve us of most of our sweets and chocolate. After we finished in the village, we would patrol for the day, with me leading. My map reading was adequate, so we didn't get lost. One of the BDF guys, Miguel, knew the area like the back of his hand anyway, so there wouldn't have been much drama if we had gone the wrong way. Santos, the other guy, was a proper bullshitter though. He had himself down as a bit of a Crocodile Dundee and thought we were gullible enough to go for it. I was quite interested in the local surroundings and he quickly latched on to this. Any time I asked a question about an animal or a tree, he'd embark on a lengthy explanation, whilst Miguel could be heard chuckling in the background. On the fourth day, we were moving along a small footpath. Just before it emerged into a cutting, Santos – who was in front of me – stopped and dropped to one knee. I moved towards him and squatted alongside him.

"Why have you stopped?" I asked, puzzled.

"Listen, can you hear?" I strained my ears in the direction he'd indicated. After a couple of seconds I picked out what sounded like an electric razor being used.

"What is it?" I enquired, genuinely interested. He contemplated his answer for a few seconds, before nodding in agreement with himself.

"Hummingbirds."

I'd never seen one before, so I told him to proceed, with me closely following. As we got into the cutting, I looked to my left, towards the source of the noise. Instead of a little family of hummingbirds, there was a fucking great bees' nest. It was the size of a fridge freezer and there was lots of activity around it. Without hesitation, I did a quick 180 and legged it back about 50 metres, with the rest of the patrol following bemusedly.

When I stopped and confirmed that we weren't about to be stung to death, I confronted Santos angrily.

"You fucking dickhead, you said they were hummingbirds not bees."

Unconcerned, he simply replied in a wistful, man-of-the-wilderness tone.

"There were hummingbirds there too." He may have been right, but I didn't bother my arse to ask him anything else for the rest of the week.

On the seventh morning we made our RV point with four or five hours to spare. We gave away the rest of the rations to some more kids and waited for the pick up. It showed up bang on time, and flew us back to camp. After getting scrubbed up, we handed in our radio and other bits and bobs. I got an anticipated bollocking for giving away all the medical supplies, but it was worth it.

Derek was really pleased to have me around again. His backbreaking workload would now be halved, almost into non-existence. It would enable him to shoehorn even more leisure time into his packed schedule. It didn't last long though. After a week of the day-on-day-off routine, we got a phone call from 633. One of the lads on the Cooma Cairn rebroadcast station had to go home on compassionate grounds. His father was gravely ill and he was to be flown back immediately. One of us would need to replace him for a few weeks. 633 had decided that it would be me, as Derek was a signalman, and the departing lad was a lance-jack. Predictably, Derek was gutted at the reversion to the old arrangement. It made sense though. Cooma Cairn was a hilltop site. It was resupped with some essentials by helicopter, but once a week two of the Cairn-dwellers would descend the hill and stock up on supplies at Holdfast. They would pick me up then, and drop off similarly, when the compassionate case returned.

They showed up the next morning at 9am. They went to the NAAFI to stock up on beer, fags and any newspapers that were lying around. After they were done, they came and gave me a shout, and helped me carry my kit to their wheels. The REBRO resup wagon was ravaged. It was covered in mud and all kinds of shit. The bloke driving was called Knocker Door, and he was the power guy who maintained the generators up on the mountain. Knocker looked like an aid worker, because he had such long hair and sidies. I suppose that was one of the benefits of being stuck up on top of a hill in the middle of the jungle. There was no one around to give you any shit.

Once we had loaded the Rover up with all the rations and my kit, we were off. We hadn't travelled for long, when we turned off the highway and up a red, clay, dirt road. The road was pot-holed to shit and gone, and on several occasions I hit my head on the vehicle's roof, because we were bounced around so much. It was a very steep drive, through some amazing thick jungle, and every so often we were treated to a stunning wildlife display. Once, during my stay on the mountain, a wild jaguar ran out in front of the Rover. It was a truly majestic animal, but I still shat myself and locked the doors.

As the drive continued, I took in the incredible surroundings. Apart from the track, the mountain was entirely covered in dense foliage. It was so different from everything I had seen so far, with the exception of the patrol. Throughout all of this, Knocker gave me the low-down on life on the mountain, and it seemed very relaxed indeed. He told me that there would be three radio guys, myself included, who took it in turns to monitor the radios. His sole domain was ensuring that we all had power. Finally there would be three guys from a sneaky unit called JSSU. They were up there to earwig on the Guats, but we paid them no bide in the work stakes. We would all take it in turn cooking, and the freezers were stocked with plenty of comestibles. Eventually, we crested a final hill, and the compound was in front of us. There was an old watchtower, two half-moon tin accommodation huts, and two concrete blockwork buildings – one for JSSU, and one for us. There was also a generator shed that housed the big machinery that Knocker looked after. All of this was surrounded in barbed wire, with just a gap in the fence for the vehicle to get through. To get into the perimeter, we drove across an open square of ground, which it transpired was the helipad. Bordering the pad, and next to the jungle itself, was a three walled, wriggly tin, hole-in-the-ground toilet, with no door. So if you wanted to shit in the night, you would have to walk out to the undergrowth and brave the wildlife.

Once inside the compound, I noticed the masts for the radio links. Also there were two long, deep trenches that were used for burning all of the camp rubbish. The concrete generator sheds had ramps leading up to them, and at the base of these were about a dozen 44-gallon diesel drums. These would have to be humped up the ramp to keep the generators topped up.

When Knocker stopped the wagon, I heard the barking of several dogs. Two short-haired mongrels ran up to me. One was a black docile thing, who I later found out was called Ego. He was a young male, and he constantly had his knob out. It was a vile habit, because his tackle looked like an angry red turkey-baster. The other was a fat ginger beast called Fergie, who had an obsession with sniffing my plums. Trailing behind these two was the most useless, savaged hound in Belize. He was called Pronto, and by all accounts, had been on the REBRO for about 18 years. He had really been through the mill in the name of entertaining bored soldiers, and there were rumours that he had even caught a dose off one of the lads! He had a bad limp and no bark to speak of; also there was almost no depth to the muscle on top of his head, so his protruding skull made him look like he had a horn. Once he got close to me, Pronto sniffed the air and began growling in a savage manner. Knocker shouted for him to fuck off, and Pronto obliged.

The view from the REBRO was breathtaking, I could see right down into the mist clogged, jungle valleys of the Mayan mountains. I met the other two Signals blokes that I would be working with. The person in charge of the place was John Moore and the Tom was called Aidy Holmes.

Aidy cooked that night, and he knocked up a chilli, which was quite decent. After food, John briefed me up, for what it was worth. It was a very simple existence. If you weren't listening to the radios, which were remoted into the TV room, then you could pretty much do anything you wanted. Every so often the rubbish had to be burned, the guy on shift had to check the generators and refuel them at night and each bloke cooked once a week. That was it. The only other thing was that if there was no rain for a while, then we would drive down to a creek, situated in one of the valleys, and fill a trailer bowser with water.

All of this was fine, but the problem with having an easy life, is that you get bored very easily. And the problem with bored soldiers is that they start to do stupid things. Mix this with beer, and they start to do very stupid things.

It started off with trying to dhobi the dogs. Ego and Fergie took it in their stride, but the chronically senile Pronto went berserk and chased us for about five minutes, until he was tired, and had to lie down. Then, once the dogs were sorted out, we were still strapped for entertainment, so when Aidy went to the toilet on the other side of the helipad, we grabbed a handful of rocks each and stoned the shithouse until our arms got tired. It certainly kept us entertained, although – judging by Aidy's swearing – he was not amused. The bog stoning was called off a few weeks later, when we tried it drunk. Aidy was the target again, but unfortunately – instead of staying in the shelter of the trap until we got bored – he tried to make a break for it, only to be rewarded with a good sized stone in the napper.

I had been up on the REBRO for about a week when Rick, one of the JSSU guys, decided to take the dogs for a walk. He took them up to a place called Baldy Beacon, which was another hill top about a kilometre from camp. It was sometimes used for live-firing exercises, but because it was a Sunday, there was no danger of anything happening. When Rick returned, he was minus Pronto, and on questioning him as to the dog's whereabouts, he told us that whilst walking up Baldy, Pronto had sat down and refused to go any further. So, understanding that Pronto was old, Rick turned around to head back to the compound. However, Pronto would not budge, not even to return home. Rick said that he had tried to coax Pronto onto his feet, but the cantankerous old git had just tried to bite him. Apparently, this refusal to move was something that Pronto had done before, but he had always come limping back the next morning. So Rick left him there to get some rest, and returned with the other dogs.

The next day, we were awoken by engine noises and the sounds of equipment being unloaded, coming from just across the valley. By the time I had got my lazy arse out of bed to see what the noise was, I saw about four 105mm artillery pieces being set up and prepared for firing. The Dropshorts were scampering over the guns and making their final adjustments. Then I thought: "Wait a second, isn't Pronto up by the impact area?"

Too late. The first gun bucked, let out a cloud of smoke and, about a second later, the thunderous firing report hit me with a 'BOOM'. Almost instantly, the other guns did the same, and then the area where Pronto was last seen was turned over by four shells of high explosive. On seeing this, the only thing I could say was: "Fucking hell!"

Pronto wasn't seen again, which was a shame, although I didn't miss being chased by the old bastard whenever he had one of his mental attacks. Still he was never found, so instead of being marked down as dead, he was considered as missing in action, along with Chuck Norris' career.

Pronto's replacement was a young puppy called Rowdy, and when he came on board, we constructed a miniature assault course and gym to get the little fella into shape. I don't think the dog understood what 'Come on you lazy bastard, you'd better start sparking and get over that shagging wall!' meant. But he certainly gave it his best shot, and by the time I left he was a mean little fucker!

My time up Cooma was to be limited, because I was going on R and R in mid-February. But nevertheless, it was by no means devoid of entertainment.

After a particularly long drinking session to lament the passing of Pronto, we decided to burn the rubbish that was now starting to fill one of the gash-trenches. Boredom is not the only thing that does not mix well with soldiers and drink. Neither does petrol.

In our drunken state, we had no comprehension of how much petrol we were pouring over the rubbish pit, but it must have exceeded 40 litres. We used a further 20 litres to trail away from the trench, and thus use as a remote lighting device. However the majority of the 20 litres was dumped around where we were standing, which – we presumed – was a safe distance from the supposed main fire.

John then pulled out a box of matches, and shouted: "TO PRONTO!" He lit the entire box in a 'genie' and tossed them onto the fuel soaked ground. There was a terrible blast of heat and light that engulfed John, and then shot across the earth and erupted in the trench in the form of a fireball. This in turn, sent rubbish flying high into the sky. Almost immediately, John came running out of the flames, trailing fiery foot prints, it was like a scene from an eco-friendly version of *Back To The Future*. We were just about to run after him to smother the flames, when a flying piece of an old pedal bin, that had been blown out of the rubbish pit, descended to earth and hit him on the head. He went down like a sack of shit, and we got the flames out in time.

A short while later, I was on a resup run back to APC, so I went into the hospital to visit John. He was in a large ward that was kitted out for 12 patients, but there was only him and one other bloke in there. The other guy was in a right state. He had a broken jaw, and was missing his left arm.

John's pit space was barren other than a card from the troop. The 'get well' wishes were composed of witty and compassionate comments like:

"Fuck off you wanker! Love Jonah."

"You malingering cunt. Kate."

"If you die can I have your mozzie net? Best wishes, Tony."

I sat down with John for a bit and he told me he was alright. He had second degree burns to his lower legs and had suffered a mild concussion from the bin impact. To lighten the tone, and also to take his mind off things, I pointed to the other patient who was now sleeping, and said: "Still, mate, it could be worse; look at that poor sod. What the fuck happened to him?"

"Yeah, that's Tommy. He's in the Glosters." replied John.

"What happened to him then?" I enquired.

"He lost his arm in a car crash."

"Fucking hell, that's a rough deal. He's smashed his jaw up pretty badly as well, eh?"

"Yeah," said John, "but he didn't do that in the crash."

"What happened there then?" I asked.

"Well, the other day, Tommy was up and about in the ward and we were talking about all the normal shit, you know, shagging, footy and all that. Then he sat down at that table." John gestured to a square, white table with four chairs positioned around it, and continued. "He started to tell me about how he could still feel itches in his missing hand, when he went to lean on his elbow. Of course, the fucking thing wasn't there to support him, so he just fell forward and cracked his napper on the edge of the table. Honestly Eddie, he's the unluckiest bloke I ever met. If he fell into a barrel of tits, he'd come out sucking his thumb."

We both had a laugh, and no doubt Tommy would have joined in as well, had he been awake, that is, and his jaw not wired together!

Another reason for the run to APC was to pick up a replacement for John. The person in question was a bloke who was new in theatre, and on tour from 2 Div at York. Nick Bruce was – like John – a full screw and he would be the big cheese up on the mountain. He had only just landed in country and was, therefore, very wary about going out into the 'J'. I could imagine his dismay, when even as 'Welcome to the Jungle' was fading into the air, he was loading his kit onto the battered Cooma Rover, and heading into the unknown.

For the majority of the drive, Nick was asking non-stop questions about the animals that he might encounter whilst up on the REBRO.

"Are there spiders? I fuckin, hope not! I hate spiders, me! What about scorpions? They're even worse. If there's one thing I fuckin' hate, it's fuckin' scorpions. They're a right bunch of cunts, I tell ya!"

Nick was a bit of a sporting type, and when he unpacked his kit in the half-moon tin hut, he also pulled out a cricket bat. He told us that he had played for the Corps, but because the rest of us were either shit at cricket, or just too drunk to play it properly, we ended up playing 'French Cricket' instead. It was a great laugh, and a truly carefree time. The sun was hot, the beer was cold and the six of us just played cricket on the mountain top helicopter clearing, with the jungle valleys forming a spectacular backdrop. Every now and then, one of the dogs would run off with the ball in its gob, and we would end up chasing the bastard for half an hour. The wagging of the dog's tail made it obvious that it thought the whole thing was a big joke. It obviously didn't understand the bad language and threats coming from the participants of the cricket match. It was normally Fergie who would steal the ball, because Ego was too stupid to perpetrate such a crime. Instead, he would just happily sit on the sidelines, airing his lipstick as per usual.

Nick was a good full screw to have on the mountain, because he would act as a shit umbrella, and stop most of the stupid ideas filtering down from the APC hierarchy to us lads. He was also the father of an immeasurable number of children. Of all the blokes I had met in the Army, he was the most fertile. The duty rumour was that he only had to wash his underpants at the same time as his old lady's knickers, and she would get up the stick.

The first week up Cooma was a great time for Nick; he was having all the fun imaginable with the sun bathing, the drinking and the cricket competitions. But it came to an abrupt end on the morning of his ninth day, when he woke up to his ultimate nightmare. He was roused from his sleep by a strange scratching sensation. Nick had been sleeping on his back, and when he woke up, there was a large, black jungle scorpion walking slowly across his chest. His sudden movement caused the scorpion to stop in its tracks, then ready itself by raising its claws and tilting its sting forward. Even though Nick knew that jungle scorpions aren't very poisonous, he was still shitting himself. The scorpion was locked onto Nick and was not moving for anything. Eventually Nick decided that he had to do something about the situation. He thought that if he were to shout for help, then the animal may sting him, so after a while of deep deliberation, he came to the conclusion that the best way to deal with the beast was to flick it off his chest as hard as possible. The theory being that if struck hard enough, the scorpion would only have time for one sting. The reality, however, was a completely different matter. The scorpion had lightening reflexes, and as soon as it felt the wind from Nick's approaching hand, it started stinging him for all it was worth. By the time Nick had removed the scorpion from his chest, it had jabbed him five times.

We heard Nick bellow from outside the block, and this was followed by what sounded like a GPMG opening up in sustained fire mode. Our instant reaction was to run to the accommodation hut and see what the noise was all about. When we opened the door, all we could see was Nick standing there breathless, in the raw, and his chest was bright red. He was beating his bed with the cricket bat in a manner that was so frenzied that it really did sound like a machine gun going off. The bat took on the appearance of a rotating blur, like Billy Whizz's feet when he's running. The focus of the savage braying was the remains of the scorpion, which was now about two feet wide, after being flattened out like a piece of filo pastry. Eventually Nick stopped his savage attack, and administered the coup de grace, which took the form off him taking the bat in both hands, then swinging it over and behind his head. Finally when his back was so arched that the tip of the bat was just touching the floor behind him, Nick brought it swinging up, back over his head and crashing down onto the remnants of the scorpion. When the bat impacted, both of Nick's feet were off the deck, and I felt a shock wave ripple through the air.

Nick's injuries were actually quite light, especially compared to those that he had given the scorpion. The stings were comparable to a slightly more painful bee attack, but Nick was also suffering from minor shock, due to the mental aspects of the encounter with his nemesis. After getting a few brews down his neck, Nick started to feel better, and merely had surface burning in his chest, so it was decided that an emergency death race down to medics in Holdfast was not necessary.

Eventually, after a month or so, the time came for me to go on R and R, and the night before I left, we had a little piss-up. We had purchased a ruck-load of ale on the last ration run, so there was no danger of running dry. Things were going swimmingly, and once we had polished off the better part of three slabs of Miller, Knocker disappeared for a few minutes, and headed off down to the generator shed. On returning, he was carrying a demijohn of a strange milky fluid. Nick let out an enormous burp that echoed down the valleys, and said: "What the fuck have you got there, Knocker? It looks like spunk! Have you been saving up all your wanks or something?"

"Nah, fuck off, man. This is me home brew. I've had the fucker bubbling away for ages now, and I've been waiting for the right time to try the bastard out."

"What's in it?" asked Aidy.

"Everything, mate. There's potatoes ('cos that's how you make moonshine), sugar, rice (as in saki and all that), compo fruit salad (for flavour), and the magic ingredient – a bottle of Appleton's 151, just to get it started like."

He held up the demijohn, and it was fucking minging! He had obviously been storing it amongst the diesel drums, because it reeked of fuel, and it had all sorts of unidentifiable traces of animal faeces around its base.

"Get some fucking glasses then, gents, and let's give this little beauty a try!" called Knocker, with a lot more enthusiasm than the rest of us felt. Still, Aidy went inside and returned with four glasses, a coffee mug and a soup ladle, as many of the other drinking vessels were dirty. Because I was leaving, I got the ladle, and also the dubious honour of the first taste of 'Knocker's Stevie Wonder Firewater', so called because of its potential to induce blindness.

It was fucking vile. However it was also incredibly potent, and after only a few sips, I could feel its toxins surging through my veins and giving me an uncomfortable hot flush. The other lads followed, and all took a drink themselves. There was a mass choking fit, a few screwed up faces, and the odd comment of "Fuck!" being blown out through gritted teeth.

After a short while, the firewater had taken suitable hold on all of us, to an extent where we could no longer taste it. At the end of the night, there were bodies strewn everywhere, and the odd fire was still burning away in the background. The place looked like a post-airstrike, Vietnamese village.

The next day, I crawled on board the wagon for my lift to Holdfast, where I would turn my stuff around, and get my cheeks down to APC as soon as possible, for my R and R flight to New Orleans. I was in rags for the entire journey and the side of the Rover was treated to a liberal coating of vomit, on more than one occasion.

I was running a bit late, so I had a negligible amount of time at Holdfast to sort myself out. So I said a quick "Hello and goodbye," to the Dalek, before commencing another trip down the highway.

I was going on R and R with Kate, and we met at the airport. We started drinking early, and we soon struck up a conversation with a group of Wyoming Air National Guard blokes, who were preparing to depart Belize in their C-130 Hercules. One of them asked Kate: "Hey man, so where are you dudes goin' to then?"

Kate downed his drink, then leant to one side, screwed up his face and farted the fart of a man who's been drinking beer for a few hours. Then he said: "New Orleans, mate."

The American aircrewman looked a bit unsettled, but carried on: "Say, do you guys know that it's Mardi Gras this time of year?"

"No, mate," I replied, "so what's that then?"

The American got very excited. "Shee-it! It's only the biggest pardy in the fuckin' world man!"

"Oh right," said Kate in a nonchalant manner, "so I take it there's a lot of drinking to be done then?"

"Brother," the American paused dramatically, "you'd better prepare your fuckin' liver, my man!"

Before we could get anymore information from the Americans, our flight was called forward for departure. The airline was called TACA. I don't know what that stood for, but amongst the blokes, it was always known as 'Take A Chance Airways'.

The aircraft was a little bit rickety, but no worse than the Crab Airlines VC-10 on which we'd come into theatre. The flight took about an hour and half, and soon we were descending into New Orleans International. I didn't get a chance to sleep – not because of the short duration of the flight, but because I was getting up to take a slash every five minutes, due to the ale.

On arriving in New Orleans, the first thing I found out was that it should actually be referred to as 'Nawlins'. We were treated to the famous Southern hospitality almost immediately. Everybody I met was all smiles and chirpy attitude.

A portly, gruff, old taxi driver called Zeke dropped us off at our hotel. It had been an amusing journey, as Zeke had showed us how he dealt with 'no good for nothin' freeloaders', by brandishing a Smith and Wesson snub-nose .38. So it was with some relief that we booked into our hotel, The Economy Motor Lodge. It was a clean enough place, but it looked like the sort of joint that a politician would take his hookers, and where you could pay for the room by the hour. Because we were a couple of skinflints, Kate and I had booked a twin room to share. After all, it would only be a place to crash-out in between bouts of drinking. The hotel was about a five minute walk from The French Quarter, so it was only a brief matter of time before we were staggering from one bar to the next, down the infamous Bourbon Street. Our holiday soon fell into a routine. We would start drinking at about midday, finish at eight in the morning, fall asleep and wake up three hours later with a raging hangover, that could only be calmed by the intake of more drink. We ate at wherever was closest to hand, come the onset of the munchies, and we tried as many of the bars as possible.

New Orleans was a great city, with a non-stop buzzing atmosphere, that was always permeated by raucous jazz, or haunting blues. And come the Mardi Gras, it increased tenfold. Every now and then, we would watch one of the huge parades, which was good for catching the plastic bead necklaces that were thrown from the floats. I initially thought that this was a waste of time, but I soon learnt that these beads were the currency of the Mardi Gras. Once the evenings were in full flow, the well-oiled women of New Orleans would willingly expose their breasts for just one cheap necklace that had cost me nothing. Even though I had become used to the attentions of the girls from The Farm, I was still amazed by this sight. I suppose it was the thought of a normal girl on a night out, being willing to get naked in front of me, for no real financial incentive. After the first time I was treated to this colonial udder-fest, I was left gawping, motionless, as if struck down by the gaze of Medusa. I stayed in this position long after the flasher had walked out of sight. Sometimes, groups of 100 or more inebriated people would gather around the balconies of the bars and start chanting "Show your tits," and normally a few women would oblige, much to the approval of the crowd. The nudity thing was not only confined to women though. Every now and then, a drunken bloke would stagger past in the raw, completely unaware of everyone laughing at him.

One night, I was drinking on the wrought-iron balcony of a bar called 'The Cat's Miaow'. I was regaling a ridiculously attractive college girl from Texas, with anecdotes of jungle hardships and the taking down of drug cartels. My stories were interrupted by a shout from below, and on looking down, I was met with the sight of a fat, staggering lad, who looked about 19. He was wearing baggy shorts, basketball boots, and a football top, and had his baseball cap on back-to-front.

He was pointing to the girl next to me, and shouting: "WOOOOOOOOOOOOO HEY PRETTY MOMMA, SHOW ME THEM TITTIES BABY, HOOOOO-WEEE, DAMN THEY LOOK REAL FINE!"

I think he was expecting people to join in with him, but everyone in the street just gave him a wide berth. Instead of doing as the guy wanted, the girl just shouted down to him: "Show me yours first!"

Without further ado, he placed his beer on the ground, lifted his shirt over his head and began licking his nipples. As if that wasn't stomach-churning enough, he then dropped his shorts and underpants, and started thrusting his hips back and forth, until his knob and plums started to slap against his gut whilst on the up-thrust, and against his arse/chin-rest on the back stroke. Soon he had forgotten about the girl's tits, and was completely engrossed in his sex dance. He speeded his rhythm up, until the air was filled with 'slap, slap, slap, slap'. He also clenched his eyes tight, then bit his bottom lip, and held both hands aloft with his fingers in the front-row-of-a-Megadeath-concert style. I had to give the guy his dues, he was really going for it – so much so that he didn't notice the big police cruiser pull up behind him. He was snapped out of his trance, when one of the cops gave him a minor nightsticking, and bundled him into the back of the cruiser. My final memory of the fat guy was his white arse disappearing into the car, closely followed by his pleading voice, calling out: "Hey, man, it wasn't me!"

Although Mardi Gras is known for being a hell-fire piss up, I actually felt like I was on a break from the booze. Especially when compared to the relentless onslaught of Appleton's 151 and Knocker's ocular degenerating death juice, that made up the normal heavy drinking schedule of everyday life in Belize.

Mardi Gras finished the day before Kate and I flew back to Belize, so we spent the final day taking in The French Quarter properly. We checked out the odd voodoo shop, and bought a few 'When I' T-shirts. When we booked out from the hotel, we had to spend a bit more money on damages to the room, after Kate had charged at an imaginary assailant, during a gin-fuelled bout of psychosis, and put a huge dent in the wall.

We landed at Belize International just before midday, and got the transport back to APC, where I said cheers to Kate. Then I loitered at the guardroom, until the fortnightly Cooma resup run stopped off, then I jumped on board and slept all the way back to Holdfast.

I got back in at teatime and found Derek in the cookhouse. He was at a table on his own, which was no doubt down to his subhuman table manners. You know your eating behaviour is at rock bottom when even squaddies won't sit with you. I wasn't hungry so I didn't bother examining the hotplate and made my way straight over to him.

"Alright, mate. How's it going?" I shouted when I was five feet from the table. He was pleased to see me and grinned broadly, displaying the half-chewed mouthful of bread he'd been eating. I grimaced and sat down, steeling myself for the trial of watching the Dalek eat his tea, without food of my own to distract me. Swallowing a sausage in a manner strangely reminiscent of a pelican, he still found it possible to ask me: "Did you have a good time then?"

"Yeah, it was a top laugh, mate. I'm glad to get back here to give my internal organs a rest." Derek would be going on his R and R in two days and it would mean me being permanently on duty. The enforced lack of boozing didn't seem like too much of a drawback as I'd been going hard at it, pretty much since we landed. My fitness had taken a real beating in the last couple of months, and it was gnawing at the back of my mind that we'd be back in Aldershot in a month and a half, running round the training area with Staff Herbert and his training-wing corporals.

"Where are you going anyway?"

"Just up to San Pedro, mate. I'm a bit too skint for America."

I was a bit gobsmacked. I'd been living quite lavishly and had still managed to box away just upwards of £1,600 in the six months. I hadn't seen too much of Derek since the back-end of September, but I had a good idea what he'd been blowing his cash on.

"Have you been spending it all down The Farm?"

"Too fucking right, mate. I've been with every single one of 'em now." The girls down there must have been ticking off the days until Derek flew home.

On his day of departure, I waved him off on the transport, by indicating in sign language, that – in my opinion – he was a wanker. He responded by throwing an apple at me, which narrowly missed. I spent those two weeks trying to get myself into some sort of shape. I didn't touch a drop of booze and got out training most afternoons. Not drinking had a bit of a novelty value, but mainly served to highlight what a dull place an Army camp is without its reassuring presence. A couple of days before Derek got back, I was talking to one of the Glosters recce platoon in the NAAFI. I'd noticed a bit of activity on the grassed area near the front of the camp and wondered what was going on.

"The CSE show's comin' on Saturday, mate." Words which would strike fear into the soul of anyone with an ounce of taste.

The Combined Services Entertainment shows were noble enterprises. The poor bastards toured every little nook and cranny of the world, where more than three British soldiers could be found, and confined to camp. They would then try their hardest to entertain them. They came unstuck in the quality of their delivery. They were uniformly terrible. In the entertainment industry food chain, they were about 15 links lower than a nul-point entrant in the Eurovision Song Contest. I don't know from where they actually recruited, but the casting sessions must have been supervised by people who were locked inside sensory deprivation tanks. I'd seen a few before and they always followed the same rigid format. A middle-aged, slightly rotund comedian would serve as our compere for the evening. He would tell a few bad jokes, which had previously received telegrams from the Queen. Then he would introduce the 'entertainment'. It generally comprised of a singer, a dance troupe and a novelty act, such as a magician. The singer would be someone that you vaguely remembered seeing on *Opportunity Knocks* in the seventies. They always looked like they'd spent the interim years propping up a bar in their home town, telling anybody they could corner, how they were 'one point away from beating Keith Harris'. The dancers were always an affront to their trade name. A group of six, looking like rugby players, would clump around the stage, fully clothed, trying to communicate an eroticism that they were physically incapable of generating. The dances were of the Pan's People school of literal interpretation. To the tune of 'MacArthur Park', they would treat us to a nursery school adaptation. Every time they reached the line 'Someone left the cake out in the rain', they would wriggle their fingers in front of their faces earnestly to illustrate the downpour. The magician was always shit, but then magicians usually are. Throughout the evening, our host would reappear intermittently, insisting that we give thunderous applause to the no-hoper who had just moped off stage. The entire performance was usually conducted in opposition to deafening heckling, which was generally funnier than the fare that the CSE were dishing up. If it sounds ungrateful to lambast these honest troubadours, it's because I was ungrateful. The idea that somebody could go to all the trouble to produce such a feeble spectacle, never mind fly it halfway round the world to punish innocent soldiers, always left me shaking my head in disbelief. I wasn't expecting anything different in Belize, and said as much to the Glosters' lad.

Derek got back on the morning prior to the show. We spent the day by the pool, with Derek filling me in on what he'd got up to. Apparently he'd not had that much of a good time. He'd spent the previous six months with sex on tap, at seven bucks a throw and had had to go cold turkey in San Pedro. It was quite an upmarket holiday resort, and Derek's 'rough diamond' charm had been lost on the affluent American tourists. It was a beautiful island, also know as Ambergris Caye. It was said that the Madonna song 'La Isla Bonita' was based on a visit that she'd made there. Of course, the tourist boards of every island from the Falklands to the Shetlands had probably made the same claim, so it was a difficult one to prove. He was telling me about one of the bars, called the Tackle Box. The owner was an actor, whose finest moment was a five-second part in *Die Hard*, where he played a terrorist who gets shot to death by Bruce Willis. Despite the diminutive size of the role, the interior of the bar was plastered with framed stills from the film, and of him and Bruce 'hanging out' during shooting. Round the back of the bar was a tennis-court sized sea pool where the owner kept his own aquarium. There were a few green turtles and a couple of small sharks. Most people chose to gaze at them from the comfort of the bar, but enough squaddies had decided on a riskier venture, for the owner to have placed a sign up above the back door. It read:

SHARKS AND TURTLES ARE DANGEROUS ANIMALS

BRITISH SOLDIERS WILL PLEASE REFRAIN FROM JUMPING IN THE SHARK POOL

Derek, like most of the other lads, had their picture taken next to the sign. Its very existence was considered a great testament to the idiotic bravery of the tanked-up Tommy.

I told him about the CSE show and his reaction was predictable.

“Awww, fucking hell, I thought we’d be out of their range.”

“No chance, mate. You’ll never guess who they’ve got singing?”

“Give us a clue?”

“It’s not worth the bother, you’ll never get it.” I was beginning to smirk and Derek persisted.

“Go on, you fucker, give us a clue.”

“It’s a band.”

“Mud?”

“No.”

“Brotherhood of Man?”

“No.”

“Racey?”

“Not even close. They’re from the same neck of the woods as the resident Infantry Battalion.” That stumped him, but he had one more go at it.

“The Barron Knights.”

I waited for him to give up and then dropped the bombshell. “It’s The Wurzels.” I was giggling as I told him and he flatly refused to believe me. “Honestly, mate. I couldn’t believe it myself.” He spent the rest of the day calling me a wind-up merchant, despite everyone he asked telling him the same thing.

The show kicked off at 7.30pm and Derek was still insisting that even the CSE organisers couldn’t dish up The Wurzels. As was usual with CSE shows, you weren’t allowed to vote with your feet and were obliged to attend. Failure to turn up would result in extras or a charge. It was the Army’s way of being benevolent to us: ‘You *will* enjoy yourselves, or you’re in the shit.’

The stage had been fashioned from two, flat-bed four-tonners, backed up to each other. All the officers and seniors were sat in chairs near the front, as befitted their rank and taste. The rest of us formed a huge semicircle to the rear of the seating, and waited with unbated breath for the treat in store. Incredibly, a few of the older Glosters lads were getting excited about The Wurzels and were trying to get find good vantage points.

The show went exactly as predicted. As soon as the PA whined into life, our compere, Diamond Billy Haversham, sprang onto stage pretending that he'd been pushed. He was in his mid-fifties and dressed in a red shirt and tie with black trousers. A pearly king's blazer completed the outfit. His hair was long but thinning and had been combed and hairsprayed to within an inch of its life, à la Peter Stringfellow. He wheeled through five or six jokes in a broad Leeds accent. They were all as old as the hills, and each time he reached a punch line, it was shouted out by a handful of blokes behind me. He didn't seem to notice or care and ploughed on regardless.

"Now, fellas," wink, wink, "a great treat for you all you randy lads. They're the girls you've all been waiting for. All the way from Burnley, please welcome The Foxy Six."

We all cheered half-heartedly, as the aforementioned growlers lumbered on to stage and went through a five minute aerobics routine. They interpreted, in the medium of ropey dancing, the ska classic 'My Boy Lollipop'. At each occurrence of the word 'lollipop' they would lick an imaginary ice-lolly suggestively. It was as sexy as watching your gran eat an ice-cream. Maybe it worked on sex-starved squaddies in the Outer Hebrides, but the lads in Holdfast had done nothing but drink and shag prostitutes and needed a higher level of sexual titillation. The person showing most interest in the performance was the REME mechanic, who was concerned about the hammering that the four-tonner suspensions were getting. Mercifully, ska tunes are quite short, and the girls were off after four minutes, giving Diamond Billy his cue to stumble/walk back out. He wiped some comedy sweat from his brow.

"Whoooh, bloody hell, thanks girls. I don't know about you lads but I'm feeling a bit hot under the collar."

"Lose some weight then, you fat cunt." A huge peal of laughter followed the anonymous voice. Diamond Billy did two more jokes, even managing to reach the punch line of the second. This wasn't due to its originality. It was so bad, that it had failed to register on the comedy radar of the joke-spoiling crowd at the back. He then moved on to his introduction for the next act.

"Is anyone in the mood for some magic?" he implored.

"Aye, disappear, you fucking bloater." The same, now slightly less anonymous voice retorted. Once more, amidst roars of laughter, Billy ignored his tormentor and got on.

"Here he is, boys. Fresh from a sell-out residency in Great Yarmouth, bring your hands together for Mysterio Pendragon." Billy scuttled off the stage and the lights were turned down. A few seconds later, from behind the curtain, came a disembodied voice. It was Billy, trying to put on an American accent. He was attempting to sound like the guy who does the cinema trailers, but was failing miserably.

"Be amazed, be amused, be convinced," he exhorted. In the absence of a smoke machine, one of the backstage crew set off a couple of dry fire extinguishers and Mysterio bounded on to the stage to the tune of Pinball Wizard, dressed in top hat and tails. He went through his entire repertoire without eliciting a single 'Ooh' or 'Aah' from the crowd. As multi-coloured handkerchiefs emerged from his sleeves and a woman in the front row was tossed a bunch of plastic flowers that had appeared from nowhere, people checked their watches and waited for him to finish. When the song was over, he hadn't quite got to the end of the act, so we spent a couple of minutes watching him do sleight of hand tricks in silence. Surprisingly, the hecklers left him alone. On the completion of his last trick, pulling a live chicken out of his top hat, he took a bow and walked off stage to weak applause, with the chicken under his arm. Billy came back on, feigning astonishment and reverting to his original voice.

"Bloody hell, that was cracking, eh fellas? Let's have another big hand for Mysterio."

A couple of people at the back had started chanting disinterestedly.

"We want The Wurzels, we want The Wurzels." We all joined in for something to do. Billy didn't detect the sarcasm and tried to calm us all down.

"They'll be on in a minute, don't worry." He tried another joke but was drowned out by the Wurzel chant. Eventually, with a quick look back stage, he announced, grinning.

"Gentlemen, for your delight, I bring you, the chart topping Wurzels."

As they took the stage, I was more interested in Derek's reaction. He was just standing open mouthed, slowly shaking his head. It *was* The Wurzels. Not a tribute band, or a new line up, but the original members. They'd put on a bit of weight since their days on *Top of the Pops* but wore the same bumpkin-chic outfits they'd had on 15 years before. They took their places and the lead singer starting talking to us in his exaggerated Yokelese.

"Evening, lads. How're you all doing?" Without waiting for an answer they launched into their set, kicking off with that old favourite 'I've Got a Brand New Combine Harvester'. Some of the lads were joining in with the familiar tune. Derek turned to me, smiling.

"I can't fucking believe it, Eddy. They're so shit, I quite like them."

I knew exactly what he meant. They played for 40 minutes, repeating the combine harvester song twice, by popular request. They performed with unbridled enthusiasm and against all the odds, won the crowd over. All of them had incredibly sunburned faces. I mentioned this to Derek and he replied: “That’s not fucking sunburn, that’s what drinking ‘dead-cat cider’ for 30 years does to you.”

Their cider-burnt faces sweated as they approached the end of their set. For the last tune, they played ‘Blackbird, I’ll ‘ave ‘ee’. By this time, everyone was up and joining in. They finished to rapturous applause and even had to sign a couple of autographs as they exited the stage. Diamond Billy was pleased as punch, but as soon as he walked on, the atmosphere that the Wurzels had managed to generate, disappeared. It was time to wrap up the show, but Billy had one more surprise left for us. He walked round the stage, mike in hand, as a vaguely familiar melody drifted eerily, from an organ behind the curtain.

“It’s been a great night, lads,” he said, and with a superhuman resolve he ignored an almost unanimous roar of “Oh no it fucking hasn’t”. He continued. “The girls were a real treat and Mysterio blew our minds. But what about them Wurzels? They really had the place jumping, didn’t they?” To our eternal shame, he was right about the last point.

“Just before I say goodnight, I’d like to finish with a little song, that’s close to my heart.”

There was an enormous groan from the crowd, followed by Derek shouting in my ear: “You’d have a job getting anything close to that fat bastard’s heart.”

Billy continued, undeterred. “Take it away, Jimmy.” The organist started playing the introduction to the song, and the 200-strong crowd listened keenly, dreading the evil that was about to be visited on us by Diamond Billy. It didn’t take long to suss out that it was ‘True’, by Spandau Ballet. Nobody could tear their eyes away from our compere, as he proceeded to murder Gary Kemp’s ballad in the coldest of blood. He managed to sing it without losing any of his accent and sounded like he had a greenie lodged in his throat throughout. His finest touch was to try to make the song more specific to his audience by chucking in a couple of spoken ad libs, between lines. The most memorable were during one of the verses: "I've bought a ticket to the wor-hur-hurld (*just like you fellas*!) But now I've come back again (*On leave*!)"

He finished the song on his knees, totally lost in the genius of his performance. Everyone waited to the end, just to see if he could top such an appalling cover version, but Billy was done. He took a couple of tearful bows, and left the stage. That meant the gates were open and we could piss-off down town. Everywhere you looked that night, in the Blue Angel, you could see squaddies doing spontaneous impressions of Billy's final scene. I suppose, in their own way, the CSE shows were a great spectacle, but for completely unintentional reasons.

We were now at the start of March, and Derek and I only had another month to push at Holdfast. For the last few weeks, we made attempts to train, but always derailed ourselves in San Ignacio during the evenings. Well aware that time was running short, we really went for it at the weekends. Derek had as much financially assisted sex as his bank account could stand, knowing he'd be back on a strict masturbation diet quite soon. I asked him about the imminent sex drought, but he was philosophical. Making a vigorous wanking gesture with his right hand, he said: "Sex is alright, mate, but there's nowt like the real thing." On the penultimate night at The Farm, Mimi made the Dalek an offer he couldn't refuse. She offered to 'trombone' him. He had no idea what this entailed, but didn't want to appear naïve, so agreed immediately. He was sat back at the table within three minutes, with a faraway look in his eye. I had to know.

"So, what the fuck's a trombone then?"

It was a full ten seconds before he replied.

"I'll tell you what, Eddy; I don't know what to think. I shouldn't have liked it, but I blew my beans in five seconds flat."

"What did she do?"

"She made me stand there with me trolleys round me ankles. Then she knelt behind us and gave us a reacharound hand shandy." I was a bit puzzled.

"What's that got to do with a trombone?"

"While she was pulling the head off it, she gave me hoop a licking as well."

Fucking hell, she deserved a Victoria Cross, never mind seven bucks. Maybe she was as rich as the Mayor of San Ignacio, but he'd never have to experience the horror of a close encounter with Derek the Dalek's ricker. A couple of weeks before we left, I rang home to let them know about my leave dates. I'd done as Dad had instructed and kept in touch throughout the tour. Phone calls cost an absolute arm and a leg, so it was mainly via blueys, but I'd managed to call them around Christmas and a couple of times since. As was usual in the Nugent household, Dad answered the phone in his familiar brusque tone.

"Hello."

"Dad."

"Alright, son. How's it going?"

"Great. How's everything at your end."

"Champion, son. Are you back soon?"

"That's what I'm ringing about. I'm coming straight home from Brize Norton. I've got three weeks' leave. I'll be getting home on the third of April."

"Great stuff, it'll be nice to have you back, son. I hope you're behaving yourself out there. Are you keeping it in your trousers?"

" 'Course I am. Listen, Dad, I can't stay on long, it's nearly six dollars a minute on the phone." It occurred to me that Mimi charged a similar price for her tromboning services.

“Alright, just have a quick word with your Mam. I’ll see you soon. Stay safe.”

I heard the muffled scratching of the receiver changing hands before Mum’s voice crossed the Atlantic.

“Hiya, son. Are you having a good time?”

“Brilliant, Mum. I was just telling Dad, I’ve got three weeks off and I’ll be home on April the third. How are you?”

“Oh you know, same as ever. We’ve missed having you around, son. Your Gran’s really excited about you coming home.”

“I’m looking forward to seeing you all. I’ve got you all presents.”

“You don’t have to bother with all that. Just bring yourself back safe.”

“I will. Look, I’ll have to go, Mum, someone else is waiting for the phone, and it costs a bomb.”

“Ok, son. See you soon.”

“Bye.”

Like always, I had a real pang of homesickness after hearing my parents’ voices. There was no doubt that I’d had the absolute time of my life in Belize, but I was looking forward to getting home. One week before we emplaned, our replacements arrived. Lance-Corporal John Turner and Signalman Eric Burridge, showed up – as we had – on the back of a four-tonner. I hadn’t realised just how tanned and healthy-looking Derek and I had got. Eric and John looked like they’d been painted with Tippex. Our handover to them was a carbon copy of our takeover from Andy and Jase. We took great pleasure in introducing them to Mimi. At Derek’s insistence, they both applied to join her brass band. I signed over the det to John and we conducted the biennial opening of the battery shack ceremony. Suitably horrified by its writhing occupants, it was closed without any attempt to check voltage or electrolyte levels.

For our last night, we had a drink in each bar on camp, to say goodbye to all the other units, then proceeded down town. We had loads of accumulated Belizean shrapnel and blew the lot. I bought lots of drinks for lots of people in The Blue Angel. The Donkey trilogy was at completion now, and I enjoyed some dirty dancing with one of the local girls to 'Shoot de Donkey'. Inevitably, we finished up at The Farm. In the spirit of camaraderie, Derek wanted us both to go in with Mimi. Mimi was up for it, but the thought of having to look at Derek in action, made me feel unwell and I excused myself. I ended up playing topless pool with one of the other girls. Her breasts were quite pendulous and every time she bent over the table to take a shot, they settled on the green baize like a couple of big, brown, beanbags, either side of the cue. When we left, we said goodbye to all the girls, who went through the motions of pretending they were arsed about us leaving. In the taxi on the way back to camp, Derek got all misty-eyed about the pleasures that would be denied him, now that he'd said his last farewell to Mimi. To snap him out of it, I said: "Listen, Derek. I don't know how to say this, but I think she might be seeing someone else."

He replied, jokingly: "I fucking knew it. Why didn't you tell me sooner?"

"I didn't want to hurt your feelings. I thought you'd find out on your own, you know, with her being a prostitute and all that."

He shook his head in mock solemnity.

"They always let you down, eh?"

We burst into laughter as we swung through the camp gates for the last time.

We got all our gear together first thing in the morning and hopped on the mail-run transport. As soon as we got into APC we searched around for the rest of the group. They were in one of the NAAFI ataps, surrounded by rucksacks and sombreros and drinking stims. We had a lengthy debriefing session whilst we waited for the nod to get on the transport to the airport. It emerged from the conversation that Derek and I had had the best time. There wasn't as much to do at Salamanca or Rideau, and boredom had been a big feature. Everyone had completed the eight months, relatively unscathed, though a little bit more out of shape than when they'd arrived.

As the plane took off, I had mixed feelings. I was glad to be getting back, but I wondered if I'd ever pull another jolly like this again.

After another hefty couple of flights, we touched down in Brize at 9am the following morning. It was grim as fuck. It was chucking it down and I'd made the classic British holidaymaker mistake of not wearing enough clothes. My teeth were rattling like castanets whilst we cleared customs, and I had to dig a fleece out of my Bergan, that had been redundant in Belize. As soon as we got out of the terminal, everybody legged it in different directions, amidst a flurry of 'See-yas' and 'Fuck-offs'. Derek's dad was there to pick him up, and greeted him fondly, with a big bear-hug. I was getting a train from Oxford and he offered me a lift, which I accepted gladly. It took half an hour and I tried to hold my breath the whole way. I could see where Derek had picked up his dirty habits. His dad resembled a healthy tramp. I was sat in the back seat directly behind him and could see his BO. It was coming off him in those cartoon wavy lines, and catching at the back of my throat. His shoulders and back were covered in dandruff, making him look like he'd just climbed out of a snowdrift. Not wanting to give offence, I opened my window stealthily, bit by bit until my head was hanging out of it, like the family dog. I gulped the fresh air, greedily, until we got into Oxford station. Derek helped me with the bags then climbed back into the front passenger seat of the car. As the car pulled off, he wound down his window, and shouted, so that everyone on the concourse could hear.

"Now, Eddy, don't you be going with any more of those prosty-ma-tutes, you dirty dog." Caught without a retort, I just pretended I couldn't hear him, and headed into the station, pausing to shrug my shoulders at an old dear, who was glaring at me and tutting loudly. I rang Dad when I changed at Crewe, and he was at Manchester to meet me, on platform 11. I didn't realise just how pleased I was to see him, until I actually clapped eyes on him. He had a huge smile on his face as he stepped forward and hugged me.

"It's bloody great to see you, son." Atypically, he spoke softly and emotionally. He broke off after a couple of seconds and looked me up and down.

"You look really well, son. You've got the best tan in Manchester."

"Where's Mum?"

"At home, making you some lunch."

"Nice one." We walked out of the station and into the car park. The sun was out now, but it was still cold. I had to have the heater on in the car on the way home. My reunion with Mum was a bit more tearful, but we were soon laughing. She wanted to know all about Belize, so I gave her the strictly edited highlights, dwelling on the flora and fauna, but skirting over any mention of trombones, or Orinoco Flo. This set the pattern for the entire three weeks. I was flush with money, so set about blowing it as quickly as I could. I went out almost every night. Following strict Army guidelines, my Central American adventure story grew more elaborate with each telling. By the end of my leave, I'd turned an uneventful jungle patrol into a cross between 'Deliverance' and 'Predator', and all of the girls at The Farm were retired Miss Worlds. My mates lapped it up anyway and encouraged my flights of fancy. Ironically, the only story they refused to believe, The Wurzels gig, was completely true. In my last week, I started to dread having to turn up back in Aldershot. I was well aware that my fitness was extremely lacking. I got out running in the afternoons but was quite far from my peak when the time came to go back. I showed up on a Wednesday night and started to sort my bedspace out. Coming back to an Army camp after a big chunk of leave, is always depressing. I suppose it's the realisation that you're currently at the furthest point possible from your next leave. I was sat on the end of my bed with my chin in my hands when Joey Donaldson came in.

"Heyyy, alright, Eddy. How's it going?"

"Fucking great, mate. It's good to be back."

"Bit down in the dumps are you? I know how to cheer you up. We're doing the Horseshoe for PT tomorrow. Ha ha ha."

"Aww fuck, you're joking aren't you?" I knew he wasn't though. If there's one thing that squaddies like more than giving good news to each other, it's giving each other bad news. Whenever someone was in the shit, there was always a stampede to be the first bloke to tell them. The Horseshoe was a six-mile cross-country run that went all round the training area, taking in most of the big hills. It was a Pre-Para staple and they used it to gauge what state the candidates were in. I averaged around the 40 minute mark on it, but had gone round in 36 on my second Pre-Para. I couldn't see myself breaking my personal record for a while. I always slept badly on my first night back and that night was no exception. I was tossing and turning all night, and I had nightmares that combined all my recent experiences with what was to come. It was awful. Staff Sergeant Herbert, dressed as a prostitute, was chasing me round the training area, holding a trombone. I couldn't get away because I was only wearing flip-flops. Thankfully, I woke up before he caught me. When I got down to Maida gym, the Squadron was assembled. Eighty or ninety blokes stood there, half-asleep, in tracksuit bottoms and maroon T-shirts. Almost all of them had both hands plunged down the front of their Ron Hills, cupping their ballbags to keep warm. The only animated person there was Herbert. He'd decided that the run was best personal effort, not squadded. He set us all off, with the warning that no one should take longer than 42 minutes. I was absolutely chinstrapped from the moment I set off. I suffered like fuck all the way round. Out of all the Belize crowd, only Mark Smith put in a decent time. The rest of us went round like slugs, with Frankson running alongside us, giving us a hard time.

"Not been training eh, lads? Don't fucking worry, we'll knock you back into shape." I sweated rum and sausage sandwiches and felt like I was going to die. I got round in 45 minutes, with Derek spewing his way in a minute after me. We got a bollocking off Herbert, but I was too knackered to listen to him. I shuggied my way back to the block and got ready for work.

The troop hadn't changed a bit and I dropped into the routine immediately. Just before NAAFI break, Pete Allinson got hold of me and said: "Eddy, Staff Jeans wants to see you."

"What about?"

"He didn't say. He probably wants to give you a medal, for working so hard in Belize."

"I deserve one as well, just for having to watch the Dalek eating." Pete winced and replied.

"Ooh, I know what you mean. He was at my last unit. Nobody would sit near him in the cookhouse 'cos he used to spray his food everywhere. They used to call him the Cookie Monster. Anyway, mate, you'd better get up there, or you'll miss NAAFI break."

"Good point." I legged it up the stairs and came to a halt outside the partly-ajar door. I gave it a quick tap and Staff Jeans shouted: "Come in, Corporal Nugent."

I moved inside and stood near the door.

"You wanted me, Staff."

"Yeah, we've had your new posting details in from Manning and Records."

"Oh, right." I hadn't really thought about it, but my four years would be up in August. I'd filled in a dreamsheet whilst I was in Belize, but I was expecting to hang round Aldershot for a couple of years more. If I was Para-trained I could apply to extend, but that wasn't going to happen now. The next Pre-Para was in September and I'd be gone by then.

"Want to know where you're going?" he enquired, picking up a single sheet of paper from his desk.

"Is it somewhere nice, Staff?"

"Fucking lovely, son. You're going to Sunny 7."

"What date?"

He looked down at the paper.

"You're due to start on Monday 15th July, but you'll get a couple of weeks embarkation leave before then. By my reckoning, that means you've got a month to sort all your shit out before you leave. I was going to get you to sign for a det, but there's not much point now. It's a shame you didn't get yourself through P-Company, you could have done another five years here."

"Yes, Staff."

"Not to worry. You can always stick your name down again." He checked his watch.

"You'd better fuck off, or you'll get no NAAFI break."

"Cheers, Staff."

That was that then. I had conflicting feelings about my time in Aldershot. On the one hand, I knew that I'd find things a bit easier at another unit, particularly on the PT side. On the other, it rankled that I hadn't had what it took to pass P-Company and got to do all the parachuting etc. I didn't really think I'd be coming back. Once I'd been sucked into the BAOR vortex, I probably wouldn't get spat out again, until I was married to a huge German woman and had grey hair. I didn't get much work done in the last month. I MFOd all my gear to be sent on to the 7 Signal Regiment base in Herford. I had the boxes in my room for a couple of weeks, which was a bit of a mistake. Just like a skip, outside someone's house, every time I left the boxes alone for a few minutes, I'd come back to find them with some more rubbish in them. I was pulling out McDonald's bags and half-eaten apples every night. I got them filled up and nailed the lids on a few days before I left.

My last day at 216 was a Monday. In a hastily assembled presentation in the troop stores, Staff Jeans gave me a copy of the recently commissioned Airborne Signals painting, with the comment, that it was the closest that I would get to actually parachuting. Although I was grateful to receive it, my first thought was that it was fucking massive, and I was going to have to carry it all the way home.

I made a short speech, which was constantly interrupted by industrial-strength heckling. After the abuse had finished, everyone wished me well, and I was given a lift to the station, in one of the spare Rovers. As expected, the train journey home was a bastard. I had to change at Waterloo and get my arse across to Euston, carrying two rucksacks and the painting. Furthermore, the painting's dimensions were just big enough so that I couldn't carry it under one arm. I managed to annoy almost everyone in London, as I stumbled around the tube stations, before finally emerging at Euston. By this time, I was trying to carry it between the thumb and forefinger of my left hand. This method only worked for five seconds at a time, before my hand cramped up and I had to rest. By the time I got to the train, I was ready to leave the fucker on the platform, but I eventually got it on board and sat down, sweating. I gonked for most of the journey, waking up for the last time as the train pulled into Stockport.

Dad, as ever, was waiting for me, and took one of the rucksacks off me when I got to him.

"What the fuck have you got there?"

"A painting. It's me leaving present."

"It's big enough innit? I thought it was half a bloody door."

When we got home, I gave it pride of place in my Dad's shed where it has remained ever since. I enjoyed the unexpected leave. Mum had started to reconcile herself to the fact that – as time went on – I was going to become a less frequent visitor. My Gran, typically for her age group, was completely un-PC about the Germans. She'd worked in the heavily bombed Trafford Park area during the war, and had lost quite a few friends from the enemy shelling.

I had my tea at her house a couple of days before I left, and she gave me a pep talk.

"Watch out for 'em, Eddy. They're bloody sly buggers."

"Who, Gran?"

"The Jerries; who do you think? They'd bloody bomb you as soon as look at you." I chuckled into my dinner but she was quick to scold me.

"It's not funny, Eddy. My friend Ivy married a German and he was horrible. Always bloody shouting he was, about this, that or the other."

Like grandmothers the world over, mine made no sense at all when talking about current affairs, and tended to just spout out a stream of consciousness until it was time for another cup of tea.

"The war finished 46 years ago, Gran. Things have changed."

"Have they buggery. Look at *Auf Wiedersehen Pet*. That bloke in charge of the building site was horrible to them Geordie lads."

Fair point, I thought. When I left, she gave me a big hug and kiss at the door, and ruffled my hair, as she'd done since I could remember.

"Bye then, Gran. I'll be back in a couple of months."

"You look after yourself, Eddy love and don't trust a bloody one of 'em."

My flight to Germany was leaving from Luton and I had to get up early to get my train down there. Dad was getting ready for work at the same time. We were heading in opposite directions so I ordered a cab. Mum came down, rubbing sleep from her eyes as the taxi pulled up. We all hugged, and separated. Dad went to work, Mum went to bed and I went to Germany.